MURDER IN THE GARDEN OF GETHSEMANE

ANDY SHAW

MURDER IN THE GARDEN OF GETHSEMANE

Chapter 1

THE DREARY NOVEMBER day promised little. The winter sky was obscured by a thick blanket of featureless grey clouds. Under this overcast sky stood Tudor O'Connell, shortish, fat-bellied and scrawny legged; his son Hugo, tall, fair-haired, and smiling; and six others, three men and three women. The group stood in the shadow of a large Georgian Grange. This was an arts and crafts property. Its many windows were Crittall, its Japanese-style roof tiles ocean blue, and its trim burnished orange.

"Welcome to the TreeHouse, once home to my parents Gethsemane and Emlyn and now home to me and my family," Tudor O'Connell said. "It's a miserable day, but at least it's dry."

He motioned to the house behind him. "I grew up in this house and am privileged to still live in it. I have made it my life's work to keep Gethsemane's memory alive. We are honoured by your interest in her, and we welcome the chance to work with you all. We're still on course to open the grounds next year. Who knows? Maybe one day we'll open the TreeHouse itself. Today's aim is to learn how we can help each other in this venture. We'll start with a tour of the grounds. About halfway through the day, we'll have some lunch and bounce ideas off each other. Hopefully, Hugo and I can answer any questions you have."

Some of the group were studying the wooden carving of a tree which hung from an ornate wrought-iron support.

"Isn't it magnificent?" Tudor asked. "It's the house sign. Emlyn carved it himself as a housewarming present for Gethsemane." The group murmured in appreciation. "It has enormous sentimental value. Please take a look."

Five of the six visitors gathered around. The sixth, an older man in a thick coat and scarf who looked as though he had spondylitis, declined to even glance at it. A camera was produced.

"Just one thing," Hugo said, his hands raised. "No photographs at this stage, please. We are still a work-in-progress. Thank you. You're all welcome to return free of charge and snap away when we eventually open."

The camera was put away.

"We all share a love of the arts and crafts movement, and we all want to make a living from it. Agreed?" Tudor said. The group agreed. "Let's get going, then."

Tudor led the group around the side of the house to a small garden. At this time of year, nothing but some evergreen shrubbery grew. A path crossed the garden and stopped at a wall. A cast-iron gate, currently open, led to a flagstone courtyard behind the house. The gate was tall, and its railings were topped with gold spikes. Tudor led the way. Hugo waited until the last of the party was through the gate before allowing it to gently swing closed behind him.

The courtyard was enclosed by three buildings: The Tree-House, a cottage facing it, and a long building with a glass roof labelled as the Orangery. The Orangery joined up with the cottage to form an impenetrable right angle. The cottage windows were shuttered. On the other side of the cottage, about two-and-a-half car lengths apart from it, sat a fourth building, about the same dimensions as the Orangery. Terracotta pots filled with plants stood around it.

Tudor, with his back to the cottage, stretched his hand towards this building and addressed the group. "Gethsemane's studio," he said proudly. "It's totally preserved and remains as it did in my mother's day. The objects ordinarily on display are her own, including some of her art materials. Unfortunately, it now needs some TLC and everything is currently in storage to allow for redecoration. Work is starting shortly on that, and on converting the cottage behind me into a café with outside seating and a gift shop. I hope some of you end up selling your products there."

Tudor lowered one arm and raised the other to motion to his left. "The grounds are accessible only through the Orangery," he said, leading the group towards it.

Although the Orangery was windowless, its glass roof ensured there was plenty of light inside, even in winter. Its walls were lime-washed in eggshell blue. It didn't contain a single piece of furniture.

"It's a nice space," Tudor said. "And as the only way into the grounds, it's a brilliant place for selling. In fact, just the right setting for a plant shop." His comments were primarily aimed at Alf and Ren Hoffbrand, a couple who cultivated and sold rare orchids.

"We rarely say no to a captive audience," Ren replied.

The group assembled on the lawn just outside the Orangery. Tudor faced them. The boundary wall was to the group's right. On their left was the side of the cottage, its only window closed and shuttered. Then came a solid yew hedge behind which lay the cottage garden. The grounds were behind another, taller, yew hedge, at a right angle to this hedge. Tudor motioned to his left to some unidentified object concealed under tarpaulin, perched on a wooden pole. "You're probably wondering what that is?" he asked. He didn't wait for a reply. "My partner is a talented sculptress. This is her latest piece, which she's kindly donated to the TreeHouse. The mayor's official unveiling is in a week. Until then, what's under the tarpaulin must remain a closely guarded secret."

Hugo shuffled in embarrassment. The group were clearly uninterested. They were there to sell their products, not be sold someone else's.

"You're all cordially invited to the unveiling," Tudor said.

Hugo's awkwardness increased when he overheard one of the group members whisper to his wife, "If it's anything like the ones on the webpage, we'll be doing something else that day."

"Tell them about the grounds, Dad," Hugo said.

"I was about to," Tudor said testily. "The entire grounds come to over five acres and are divided into separate gardens which we call garden rooms. The tour will formally commence at the Events Room. It's a bit of a walk, I'm afraid."

Hugo wasn't sure why his dad now wanted to start the tour at the Events Room at the other end of the grounds. The space was available for hire and considered a highlight. Hugo thought they'd agreed to leave it till last, but with his dad already disappearing through an archway, the tour group in his wake, he shrugged and went after them.

The archway led into the Herb Room. This was boxed in by a yew hedge and split in two by a pathway. Herbs grew in rows from the path to the edge. Their scent filled the air. Tudor was setting a quick pace. "There's plenty of time to look around afterwards," he said over his shoulder to a woman who'd stopped to smell the rosemary. Hugo realised someone was missing. He turned and saw a plump, middle-aged woman hurrying to catch up. She was grateful he'd waited.

"Shoelace came undone," she said.

"There's no hurry," he said, wishing someone had told his father that. Tudor was already two-thirds of the way through the garden room and wasn't slowing down. Hugo and the guest reached the others as Tudor led the party through another archway and into the Rose Room.

The Rose Room, too, was surrounded by the boxed yew hedging, which was intact save for the archways at each end. Pathways dissected more flowerbeds. What must have been beautiful in the summertime was a sorrowful place in winter with rose plants cut back to their roots, leaving no more than shrubs and brown soil. Hugo had a look around and noticed the well-wrapped-up gentleman had fallen behind at the rear. He joined him and walked alongside.

"Can I ask about your interest in the TreeHouse?" Hugo asked in an attempt to make conversation.

"Arts teacher. Want to take groups around."

"I hope you can," Hugo said. He remembered taking the booking but couldn't for the life of him remember the name. "Could you remind me of your name?" he said. "I'm terrible."

"The name's Nick Pilsworth. Dr Nick Pilsworth," he said without a glance in Hugo's direction.

As that was clearly going to be it, Hugo abandoned the small talk and started to whistle to fill the void. Nick Pilsworth suddenly stopped.

"Are you all right, Dr Pilsworth?" Hugo asked.

Without warning Nick Pilsworth took hold of Hugo's arm and said, "Going back, not feeling right."

"Do you need me to call someone?"

Nick Pilsworth shook his head.

"What's going on?" Tudor demanded from the far end of the Rose Room, his question directed over the heads of everyone else.

"Gentleman doesn't feel well," Hugo said. With every eye on

him, Nick Pilsworth turned his back on them and started walking away.

"You can't go with him, I need you here," Tudor said.

"He won't be able to get through the gate without the key code," Hugo said.

Tudor's next comment was directed to the back of Nick Pilsworth's head. "Just knock on the back door. My wife will let you out."

"Hope you feel better soon, Dr Pilsworth," Hugo called after him, but he had already stepped into the Rose Room and disappeared. Hugo couldn't see him on the path, leaving him to wonder if Nick Pilsworth was throwing up in a corner.

"Hugo, we have to get on," his dad called out, striding away.

In the Winter Room, foraging birds took flight in a mass of flapping wings upon the arrival of humans and congregated on the room's hedged walls. The group gave a collective murmur of appreciation. Espaliers of holly, juniper and rowan trees, their branches heavy with winter berries and haws, fanned the length of the garden room. Tudor had slowed down slightly but was still crossing the room at a good pace as the group tried to take in the space, looking from side to side as they crossed it.

"Dad, you need to slow down a bit," Hugo called out. "We're not on a boot march."

Tudor slowed to a standstill but after a few minutes his impatience got the better of him and he turned to lead the way out.

This time, the hedge archway didn't lead straight into an adjoining garden room but to a path sandwiched between the Winter Room and another hedge running parallel to it. Into this was cut a double archway where Tudor took himself as the group packed tightly together on the path. In one direction, the path came to an abrupt halt at a bench abutting the boundary wall with a trellis and a pruned-down bougainvillea. In the other direction, the path ran up to another yew hedge and disappeared around a corner.

"Behind me is the Events Room," Tudor explained. The double archway enabled the group to look past Tudor and onto the space. It was quite large. The lawns were about thirty by forty metres in size, broken up only by a bed of ornamental wispy feather grasses. Beyond that came a fishing pond, trimmed on each side by lawn and spanned by a wooden bridge. Behind the pond came more lawn and, just before the rear wall, an old gnarled beech tree. An overlooked Halloween ghost hung from a branch. Tall yew hedging made one side, the long boundary wall the other. A closed wooden gate, in the shape of a domed door, stood about a third of the way along the wall.

"Unfortunately, something rather unexpected has come up and I'm going to have to leave you in the hands of my capable son, Hugo," Tudor said. That his father was going to abandon him on this, their first tour, came as news to Hugo. He leaned back slightly on his heels. His father beckoned him over. He politely made his way through the group, who remained where they were, to join his father just inside the archway where his father whispered, "Something's come up, shouldn't be too long. Make sure they don't come in till I'm gone."

Hugo knew why his dad didn't want the group following him inside. The gate was operated by a keypad. Tudor wasn't a tall man. If the group were in the Events Room as he keyed in the code, it could be seen. Tudor turned to the group. "I'll be back as soon as I can and will certainly join you all for lunch."

Hugo returned to the group, still huddled together on the path, and cracked a joke, "I'd better rename this Faulty Tours." The group had the decency to laugh along. Hugo glanced over to his father. He was unwrapping a stick of chewing gum. Other than that, he hadn't moved. He wasn't taking any chances. "Let's continue. This way, please."

Hugo used his arms to politely herd the group along the path until they'd moved around the corner where they found themselves in a semi-circular alcove created from trained hedges. A stone seat sat in part of the hedge. Hugo felt his phone vibrate in his pocket. Was it...? He sensed the waiting group were growing impatient and pointed to yet another hedge archway. "That takes you into the Topiary Room. Please go through. I'll join you in a minute or so. I believe a couple of you are wedding planners." Nico and Zyline Angeles identified themselves. "If you'd like a better look at the Events Room, you'll find another way in at the far end of the Topiary Room. It takes you to the other side of the pond. You'll get a better sense of its size from there." Hugo knew abandoning the group to return a call wasn't very professional but with his dad out of the way he had to seize the opportunity. He might not get another chance that day. It might be... Anyway, these people weren't paying guests.

The group didn't look impressed at being left for a second time, but they shuffled through the archway and into the Topiary Room as bid. Once they were out of sight, Hugo parked himself on the stone seat and pulled out his phone. He didn't recognise the number but this didn't stop him from returning the call.

Hawthorn Garden Maintenance arrived at the TreeHouse with Harry Thorne at the wheel of their white van and his son Will following in their digger. Will parked the digger next to the van and joined his father at the front door. When the front door wasn't answered, Harry rang the bell again. Still the door wasn't answered.

"Wherever has she got to?" Harry said. He rang the bell a little longer. This did the trick. From somewhere inside the house came a cross, "I heard you! I'm coming!" and the sound of a toilet flushing. Father and son exchanged a silent look. Following some angry stomping across the hall, the front door was flung open by Bettina O'Connell.

"Sorry to have hurried you, Mrs O'Connell," Harry Thorne said. "Worried you might not have heard."

"It's a big house in case you haven't noticed," she snapped.

Harry Thorne had been in the business a long time. Testy customers came with the job. "It's the cottage garden you need scrubbed up, yes?" Harry said.

Bettina O'Connell visibly mellowed. "Apologies," she said. "I'm going through a difficult time."

Listening to his customer's life story was something else Harry was long used to. "Shall we go and have a look?" he asked.

"Tudor's showing a group around. We'd better go the other way." She led father and son across the front of the house to a double gate made from wrought iron railings cut into a wall. Harry helped Bettina open both sides to accommodate the digger. The paving at the front continued around this side of the house up to the studio and, after more paving, to a double garage on its left. The paving stopped at the edge of the flagstone courtyard. The three crossed it, moving in the direction of the cottage. Before stepping into the gap between the cottage and the studio, Will looked to his right across the empty courtyard up at the glass roof of the Orangery.

They gathered in the private garden behind the cottage. "We're turning the cottage into a café so the garden needs scrubbing up for seating," Bettina said.

Although bordered on two sides by the yew hedging, the side where they currently stood was open. "What about the hedging?" Harry asked.

"Leave that," Bettina said. "We want to funnel them into the grounds through the Orangery. Just the shrubs and paving."

She suddenly clutched her stomach. "Uh-oh got to go." She ran off in the direction of the house.

Young Will couldn't help but break into a grin, but his dad merely stepped into the cottage garden. Will followed him. Harry walked across the garden to an established shrub which he gave a kick. Will joined him as Harry squatted and tugged at the shrub's roots. "It's old and deep, like your dad," he said. "Shame to scrub it up, but can't be helped. Needs must."

"Reckon we can get it all done in a morning?" Will asked.

"Why? You got somewhere else to be?"

Will frowned. Could he hear the digger? He ran back across the garden, stopping just outside it where he swore and gave a strangled, "Dad!"

Harry Thorne jumped up and ran over to his son. Bettina O'Connell was up on the digger and heading straight towards them. "You left the key in?" he yelled at his son.

"I...I..." Will stammered.

They ran towards her. She looked to be steering a path between the studio and cottage.

"Mrs O'Connell, get off that immediately, it's not a toy," Harry yelled. Bettina O'Connell completely ignored him. The digger was going at full speed. Young Will bravely stood in her way and stretched his arms out, only for Bettina to suddenly change direction to avoid a terracotta pot, swerve around him, and drive straight at the cottage where she collided with a corner. She screamed and was thrown off the seat up into the air. She managed to hang on and landed back in the seat.

Will ran towards her but was forced to jump out of the way as she reversed, spun the digger around, and headed for the cottage again, yelling, "Yee Haw!"

A second collision caused a window to break.

"Call the police. Go into the road if you need a signal," Harry screamed at his son. Will hesitated before running off in the direction of the road. Bettina was driving too fast and erratically to allow Harry to safely manhandle her from the wheel. He could do nothing else but yell at her to stop. "Mrs O'Connell, get off now." As she positioned herself to accelerate towards the cottage again, a young woman emerged from behind the studio and ran towards them, waving her arms around.

"You crazy bitch," she yelled at Bettina.

The digger stalled. Harry grabbed Bettina's arm. "Get your hand off me, Thorne," she ordered.

"I don't know what your game is, Bettina, but that digger is my property."

Bettina remained where she was, forcing the young woman to yell up at her again, "You crazy bitch! You crazy, crazy bitch! I could have been inside. You could have killed me."

"Oh, give it a rest, Ivy," Bettina said. "You were at the skip."

"You should be locked up. You're crazy," Ivy cried.

Behind them a woman yelled, "Stop it, the pair of you."

Harry Thorne spun around and saw Valerie Simpson hurrying towards them. For her part, Val couldn't believe her eyes. Ivy telling Bettina she was mad was normal. But why was Bettina bright red? Had she been drinking? What was she doing on a digger? And what had happened to the cottage?

"I told you she was crazy," Ivy said to Val and Harry. "You all defended her. Crazy!" Ivy made a circular motion of her head to indicate that Bettina was insane.

Will reappeared, running over to the group. "The police are on their way."

Val looked at Harry Thorne. He was furious. "Get that woman off my digger," he hissed.

"Bettina," Val said, reaching out to her. "It's all right."

"All right?" shrieked Ivy.

"Ivy, please," Val said, raising a hand in Ivy's direction to try and calm the situation down.

Val didn't need to coax Bettina down. She climbed down quite readily. "Well, that was fun," she said.

From somewhere in the grounds came the sound of a man running and yelling. They turned to see a man none of them recognised emerge from the Orangery, phone in hand. "Call an ambulance. Tudor's had a heart attack," he yelled from its doorway. He waved his phone in the air. "I can't get a signal."

Once again Will Thorne ran off in the direction of the road, this time with Nico Angeles hard on his heels.

Chapter 2

IN THE MORESEA Residential Care Home, Detective Inspector Guido Black was shown into a resident's room by a stout middle-aged man. The resident was hard of hearing, forcing his carer to raise his voice. "This is Guido Black, Dudley," the carer said loudly.

"Who?" Dudley cupped a hand to his ear.

"Guido Black. You've been expecting him," the carer said. Turning to Black, he added, "Give us a shout when you're done. It's a bit of a warren." He stepped outside, closing the door behind him, leaving the two men alone in Dudley Dennington's room.

Dudley Dennington sat bolt upright in a recliner, covered in a blue blanket, an oxygen mask feeding him oxygen from a nearby tank. A wheelchair was folded up in the corner. Until he was forced to give up his trade through age and ill-health, Dudley's occupation had been petty criminal. Now in his late seventies, a lifetime of heavy smoking had left him in a poor state of health. "Got any smokes?" he asked Black. His destroyed lungs rattled as he spoke.

"We'll set the alarm off."

"Not if you get on a chair and take the batteries out of that thing, son," Dudley said, his eyes flickering briefly in the direction of the smoke alarm on the ceiling.

Dudley's chair was the only comfortable looking one in the room. Guests had to make do with plastic stacking chairs. Black stood on one and, with some difficulty, removed the smoke alarm's battery. Once back on the ground, he cracked open a window before reaching into his pocket for cigarettes and a lighter. He'd met enough criminals in his career to know what to bring with him. As Dudley lit a cigarette, Black positioned the chair to face him.

Dudley inhaled and said, "You want to talk about Storey?"

"I do, yes."

"Ain't heard his name for a long time. Poor bastard." The Storey they spoke of was Davy Storey, the last man in England to hang for the crime of murder. "What you want to know?"

"I'm told you don't think he was guilty," Black said.

"Who said I don't?"

"Judy McDermott for one."

"Who's Judy McDermott when she's at home?"

"Well, she's done okay for herself," Black replied. "She's a Super now. When you knew her, she was what they called back then a WPC. WPC Judy Kelly. Your paths crossed early on in your careers. She remembers you telling her Davy Storey couldn't've murdered Warren Fairchild."

"That's what she said I said, is it?" He inhaled, triggering a coughing fit. When this subsided, he inhaled again and said, "Why do you care? You a journalist?"

"No, I'm a Detective Inspector in the Vale of Tye police."

"They reopening the case?"

"Not yet."

"So, what brings you here, digging around?" Dudley asked.

"Davy Storey was my granddad on my mum's side."

Dudley considered the reply. "Where are my manners?

Would you like a drink? Only got squash to offer you, son, but I can ring for coffee."

"I'm fine, thank you," Black said.

"Well, who says *I* am? Got anything stronger than this rubbish?" he swirled the jug of squash in the air. Black opened his jacket and produced a small bottle of whiskey which Dudley Dennington snatched greedily.

"Why did you tell Judy my grandad couldn't've done it?"

"Maybe I done it for the attention?" Dudley said. This was probably the highlight of his week, Black realised, and he was going to milk it. "You wired?" Dudley asked.

"No," Black said.

"Take your jacket off, son."

Black did, hanging it over the back of the chair. This satisfied Dudley. "I know he didn't do it 'cause of when he called me."

"When my granddad called you?"

"No – Fairchild. Called me from a call box wanting me to fence some stuff for him. Sounded shaken up. We set it up, but next I heard he was dead and your grandad had been arrested getting off the London train for his murder."

"He and his accomplice drove to Fairchild's place in a stolen car, which they later abandoned, to catch the train back to London," Black said. "No one disputes that. What's in contention is..."

"...Whether they killed Fairchild before they left or someone done it afterwards," Dudley Dennington said. "Well, that's the thing. I think your grandad was telling the truth. You see, Fairchild called me the same afternoon he died. Can't have been much before he was done in. He called at four. Know what makes me so sure of the time? Me missus' cuckoo clock went off, on the hour, like clockwork. Couldn't hear meself think with the racket that thing made. Had to wait for it to cuckoo four bleedin' times. Fairchild had to say it all over as I 'adn't heard a word first time round. Now, your grandad was arrested stepping off the three o'clock. I checked the timetable. That train takes two hours. Trains can be late but never that early. There's nowhere else they can have got on, but the station their car was found at. Whatever your grandad's accomplice said, neither of 'em could've done it, 'cos they was both on the train when Fairchild was done in."

Black studied him. "Why didn't you say something at the time? Why let him hang?"

"Me missus had just had a baby. Whoever killed Fairchild was still walking around. Now I ain't been much of a husband or a dad — spent most of me time inside, least I could do was not get myself murdered. Or them."

"If it comes to it — will you make a statement?"

"A lot of water has gone under the bridge since then. I'm an old man. Ain't got long." He inhaled, his smoke-damaged lungs rattling again. "Yeah, I will. Time I did one good thing."

Black got to his feet and extended a hand. Dudley waved it away.

"Thank you, Dudley. Must've taken a lot to talk to a police officer."

"Thanks. Don't get my six-year-old grand-kiddy the nice pink bike with a bell and a basket she wants for Christmas from her grand-pops."

"I'll see what I can do," Black said. "It might not come from me. Don't want things being misconstrued."

With Dudley's granddaughter's address written on a piece of paper, Black crossed to the door. He hesitated. When he'd started on his quest, he'd known it would take a long time to clear his grandad's name. Maybe, along the way, he'd establish who really did kill Fairchild that day? But at that moment his concerns were more practical. Dudley's statement wouldn't be anything like enough to get the Appeal Court to reopen the case, let alone exonerate his grandfather. Dudley was a career criminal and inveterate liar; but his words were another chink in the case against his grandad. Dudley wasn't a well man. Black needed something he could produce in court if needs be, when that day finally came.

"Can I send a colleague to take a more formal, signed statement from you?" he asked.

"Worried I'm going to peg it?" Dudley asked.

"In truth, I am a bit," Black replied.

Dudley chuckled. "Whenever you want, son. I ain't going nowhere."

As Black stepped out of the room, Dudley said after him. "Never thought they'd do it. Never thought he'd drop. Thought the Home Secretary would send a telegram. Never thought he'd drop."

Chapter 3

THE EARPLUGS DETECTIVE Sergeant Eden Hudson had rammed in her ears were proving only partially successful at blocking out the children shrieking from the pool. It was the Halloween swimming gala. Eden, sitting amongst the other parents who had given up their Saturday, was watching her daughter in the pool below furiously attempt to race a girl two years older.

The smell of chlorine filled her nostrils. As the girls cut through the water, swimming away from her, Eden could just imagine the look of determination on Dora's face. At the end of the previous lane Dora, beaten to the post, had looked up to the spectator stand crestfallen. Eden had given her two thumbs up and she'd perked up, immediately starting off after her nearest competitor. Eden checked her watch. It had taken ages to get started due to the number of girls who'd insisted on donning sparkling mermaid outfits for the event. What that had to do with Halloween, she couldn't imagine. The mermaid collective had been carried from the changing room for a poolside photo-graph, one had been hauled out after falling in, fibre tail attached, and the lot then carried back to the changing room to de-tail. It had taken forever. If Eden had her way, they'd have all been disqualified before they'd started. The other girl may have been beating Dora, but at least her bathing costume had a pumpkin face on it. Her mum had bought it for the occasion. Eden's finances didn't stretch to that, forcing her to spend the previous evening sewing silver bats on to Dora's pink swimming costume. She was quite proud of the end result, even though some now floated in the water.

Dora had turned in the lane and was now heading for home, the broomstick Eden had glued on to her bathing cap cutting in and out of the water. She wasn't going to win, she was too behind, but she was going to be a determined second. Eden couldn't have been prouder. She jumped to her feet to cheer her daughter on. A dad next to her said something, but she couldn't hear him with the yelling of parents, the splashing of children, and the earplugs. He gave her a dig in the ribs. She took her earplugs out, expecting him to say – *She get that from you?*

"You might want to answer your phone. It hasn't stopped ringing. Must be important," he said.

She pulled her phone out. Over the previous ten minutes, she'd had three missed calls, with two messages left. The station had called twice (and messaged), Detective Inspector Guido Black once, but hadn't left a message. What on earth has happened, she wondered. The race had finished. Dora came second. Eden waved and blew her some kisses. She put the phone to her ear to listen to her messages, but the callers were no match for screaming children, enthusiastic parents, splashing and whistles. It was hopeless. She left Dora to the class photographer and edged along the seats, apologising to the other spectators as she went. Once she reached the steps, she ran up them and into the foyer to listen to her messages.

Black wanted her to call him back. She did, only to get his answerphone. She called her colleague, Detective Philip Philpot, always known as Pilot.

"Yeah, bad news," Pilot said. "Weekend's cancelled. Cat A."

Damn. What was she meant to do now? She'd promised to take Dora to the cinema and for a pizza after swimming. She pictured her daughter's disappointment and closed her eyes.

"You've got to go into the station, haven't you?"

Eden spun around and found Sheryl Teal, mum to Jos, a boy at school with Dora. Sheryl wasn't one of Eden's favourite people at that moment. Jos, along with other school friends, was going to the cinema after swimming, but Dora hadn't been invited. Sheryl claimed there wasn't room for any more children, but Dora had been upset. The cinema and pizza trip were to make up for it.

Sheryl moved uncomfortably close and whispered, "Can I crib a favour?" You must be joking, Eden thought. "If Alex asks, say I've been here all the time. Tell him I arrived with you."

Eden looked blank. She didn't want to get involved in a domestic between Sheryl and her partner, Alex Doherty – not to mention Dora's exclusion. "Why would I want to do that, Sheryl?" she asked.

Sheryl looked somewhat taken aback at Eden's tone, then said, "What say Dora comes with us to the cinema?" So, there was enough room, thought Eden. "We're getting Peri-Peri chicken afterwards."

Eden didn't like Sheryl, but her suggestion would get her out of a bind and make Dora feel included. "Okay," she said, "but make out that her not being invited first time round was an oversight."

"Will do," Sheryl said. "Long as you make out I've been here longer than I have."

Eden had no idea how long Sheryl had or had not been at the swimming pool, nor did she care. Dora charged over, her hair still damp, Jos with her. They were laughing.

"Dora's coming with us to the cinema, Jos," Sheryl said.

"And for Peri-Peri chicken afterwards," Eden added.

"Brilliant," the lad replied, sounding genuinely pleased. Eden always thought him a lot nicer than his mum.

"I told you it was just a mistake. You were invited all the while," she said to Dora. "Jos's mum will drop you back afterwards."

Sheryl hesitated and with a smile that didn't quite reach her eyes said, "No probs."

Eden kissed her daughter goodbye. "See you later, love."

Chapter 4

IN THE CAR, Eden read the text just in from the station:

Sixty-three-year-old male found stabbed to death in the grounds of his property.

The text went on to give the name and address of the victim. Good heavens, Eden thought. She frequently drove past the TreeHouse and had promised to take Dora once it opened its grounds to the public in the summer. They had matching Gethsemane print aprons, not that she got much chance to bake, now that she was on the murder squad. She called to say she'd be there within the hour.

She saw the property before she reached it. She turned a corner and there it was. A house perched on a hill, its white walls, blue roof and orange trimmings defying the overcast day. She drove on and reached the police cordon. After showing her badge, she was allowed through, passing search teams with sticks and dogs scouring for clues. She parked out front in a space reserved for her. She put on her PPE while a young police officer informed her, "The Detective Inspector's already here, Ma'am, along with the pathologist. I'll take you to the scene."

They walked through the garden rooms in silence, keeping

strictly to the footpaths, now covered with protective plastic. A friendly police dog ran up to give them both a sniff in turn. Having eliminated them from her enquiries, she returned to the search.

From the footpath, Eden peered through the double archway into the Events Room. She saw a police photographer capturing the scene and police officers scouring the area, some on their hands and knees, some poking sticks into the hedges. She saw a diver emerging from the pond and a body tent. This began at the long boundary wall and extended over the grass. Eden used the stepping plates provided to cross to it. There, she pulled open the tent flap and stepped inside. Her boss, Detective Inspector Guido Black, and the Pathologist, Matthew Pritchard, stood on either side of the body of a man, lying on his back by a wooden gate. She glanced at Matt Prichard. He'd recently asked if he could take her out one evening. She realised seeing him again made her happy but felt a bit shy in his presence. Well, now she knew how she felt.

It was Matt Pritchard who brought her up to speed. "You're looking at the body of sixty-three-year-old Tudor O'Connell. Tudor was found face down by a group of people, who upon seeing him prostrate on the ground, ran towards him from different directions. Believing he'd had a heart attack, they promptly turned him on his back to attempt resuscitation. When they saw blood underneath him, they decided he'd suffered an accident and turned him on his side to look for the wound, before turning him back again."

"Basically, the entire scene's contaminated," Black said.

"It's a double stabbing," Matt said. "Here are the incision points." Another officer gently turned the deceased onto his side, allowing Matt to indicate two small incision points, one just below each shoulder blade, puncturing the heavy coat worn by the deceased. "Looks like he died immediately. Here's the interesting bit — both entry points look to be evenly spaced from the central spine and, at a guess, look to have been made between the eighth and ninth ribs. I'd say they were made simultaneously." The body was returned to its original position.

"The killer had a knife in both hands?" Eden said.

"Wounds are a bit too symmetrical for that. I'd say one weapon, two blades. Something like a pitchfork. He also has a micro injury to his finger."

"A defensive injury?" Black asked.

"Possibly. It's fresh." Matt pointed to a pair of glasses, still lying with the frame on the grass and the lenses vertical. "These were found next to him. Probably came off in the attack."

"Do we know if he wore them to see or just to read?" Black asked.

Eden deftly stepped onto a stepping plate and squatted down by them. She removed her notepad and made a few small pencil crosses on a page. This she held against a lens. Her letters were magnified.

"They're readers, Sir," she said as Matt placed them carefully into a police evidence bag. "He probably needed them for the keypad. If the killer escaped through the gate, he or she would've had to input the code."

"Yes," Black agreed. "It would have to have been input by someone. The security company can tell us how many times it was entered."

"Do we have a time of death?" Eden asked.

"Do we," Black said. It was a statement, not a question. He held the tent flap open and they stepped outside. "He was killed in the time it took half a dozen people gathered there..." he pointed towards the double archway, "...to walk the length of that hedge," he drew his hand along the length of the hedge, "to there," he pointed across the pond to another archway. "The witnesses all agree the space was empty when he entered."

"Good heavens," Eden said, looking around. "Good heavens," she repeated. "What an audacious crime."

The front room of the TreeHouse was pleasantly bright and large enough to fit both a six-piece suite around a walnut coffee table and a grand piano adorned with family photographs taken in happy times. Its ceiling was panelled.

Bettina O'Connell sat between a female police officer and a clergyman. Behind her was an Art Deco walnut cabinet crammed with crockery. She dabbed her eyes. She wore a dark-blue, patterned silk designer dress. Her bobbed hair, showing no hint of grey, was tousled and her make-up smudged. As Black and Eden entered, the police officer discreetly got up and moved to another part of the room.

The clergyman rose and extended an arm. "I'm Father Dermot Hanrahan. I'm Bettina's religious advisor and friend."

Black and Eden walked over to him to shake hands. Bettina remained sitting. Father Hanrahan resumed his seat next to her and took her hand in his as Black and Eden took seats opposite. Black opened his leather-backed notepad.

"We're sorry to find ourselves here in such tragic circumstances, Mrs O'Connell," he said. "I understand you and your husband had recently separated, although you continued to live in close proximity."

"I live here, they live in the cottage."

"Can you tell me about this morning, Mrs O'Connell?" Black said.

"Which bit, dear? The bit where I ran amok with a digger or the bit where they told me my husband was dead?" she replied coolly. The façade cracked almost immediately. "I can't face your questions just yet. Can't I be left alone with my children to grieve?"

"Please, Detective Inspector," Father Hanrahan said. "Is there anything which can't wait?"

Black and Eden got to their feet. "We'll need to speak to you at some stage, Father."

"Any time, Detective Inspector. Any time. I live in the priest house next to the church."

They spoke next to Hugo O'Connell who waited in an adjacent room. This room was less formal than the previous one. The furniture showed use, books and games crowded shelves and there was even a TV in the corner.

"We've read your preliminary statement, Mr O'Connell," Black said.

"Call me Hugo, please."

"Hugo, we'll need a more detailed look at the chain of events, but for now could you please tell me why you separated from the tour party?"

Hugo fidgeted. "My husband and I have separated. I haven't been able to get hold of him. Don't even know if he's in the country. I had a missed call and thought it might be him. I might not have had another opportunity that day to call. I didn't think the group would mind much. I just needed a bit of privacy. If I'd known this was going to happen, I'd've stayed with them."

"Were you on the phone the whole time?" Eden said.

"I didn't move. Just sat there waiting for someone to pick up."

"Did they?" Eden asked.

"Sadly not."

"Hugo," Eden said, "in your initial statement you said your dad asked you to ensure the group didn't follow him inside, as he didn't want them seeing the code for the gate. But as there isn't a security panel on the outside wall, why did your dad care whether they saw it or not?"

"The code doubles up as the code for the burglar alarm," Hugo explained. "Although Dad strenuously denied it, I know he also used it as one of his pin numbers."

"Hugo," Black said, "when you realised your father had been attacked, why didn't you open the gate and look outside? The attacker might still have been in the field."

Hugo looked anguished. "I would've, only I couldn't remember the code. I couldn't! My mind went blank... Alf Hoffbrand ended up giving his wife a leg up and she looked over the wall. But whoever attacked Dad had legged it." He slumped forward and thumped his forehead. "If only I'd remembered the code. We might have seen him. I know it now."

"You told my colleagues a man broke away from the tour," Eden said.

He looked up. "Dr Nick Pilsworth. He was taken ill. He's an art teacher who wants to bring sketching parties around."

"How did he book the tour?" Eden asked.

"Online. They all did. We're advertising for businesses to work with us. We've had a lot of interest. Today was the first of many tours..." He stared at the ceiling blinking back tears. Eden moved beside him. "I can't believe this is happening," he said.

"Hugo, do you wish to talk later?" Black asked

Hugo shook his head. "I want to get this done while it's still clear in my mind."

"Did anything stick out about Dr Nick Pilsworth?" Black asked.

"He was much older than I'd expect for someone who was still working. Didn't look very well. Hardly said a word. We hadn't gone far when he announced he was going back. I offered to go with him, but he wouldn't have it."

"How did he propose getting through the locked gate?" Black said. "Had it been left open?"

"No. It was closed. We told him to knock on the back door and Mum would let him out."

"Did she?" Eden asked.

"I assume so. I haven't asked," Hugo said.

"You didn't see where he went after he left the party?" Eden said.

Hugo shook his head. "Not after he left the Winter Room, no. I'd have expected to see him still on the path but I couldn't. I suspect he was being sick, poor man. Oh!" His hand went to his mouth. "Oh my God! He's the killer, isn't he? He seemed so nice."

"Can you think of anybody who wanted your dad dead?" Eden said.

"A lot of people disliked him," Hugo said. "But I can't think of anyone who'd want to murder him. It's horrid."

Black and Eden returned to the formal front room to speak again with Bettina. She'd been joined by Hugo's sister, Lilah O'Connell.

"Bettina," Black said. "Did a man knock at the back door asking to be let out of the property?"

She looked blank. "No, no one."

"Did you happen to see anyone leave the property? One of the tour group, say?"

She shook her head. "No, I didn't."

As Lilah was there, Black and Eden questioned her. "Your real name, Ms O'Connell, is Ophelia, but the family know you as Lilah, yes?" Eden asked.

"I go by Lilah," she replied. Although older than her brother Hugo by eighteen months, the siblings could have been twins. They took after their mother. Both were quite tall and slim, pale, blue-eyed, with strawberry-blonde hair and high cheekbones. The dissimilarity was in their dress sense. Hugo was like his mother. Although now in a police jumpsuit, he had been immaculately presented — his jacket, shirt and trousers laundered and colourful; whereas Lilah wore an army flak jacket over a pair of ripped jeans and Doc Martens. She also wore her hair much longer than her brother, with the lower half coloured blue. Another dissimilarity was in their personalities. Hugo was diffident. Lilah was calm and detached. Eden thought her slightly supercilious.

"I'm very sorry for your loss, Lilah," Black said. "Can you tell me where you were when your father was attacked, please?"

"I was up by the old sessile oak tree. About fifteen minutes from here. We actually own the field. We're thinking of opening it up for Glamping. Maybe putting up a tree house. People'll pay good money for back-to-nature holidays. I went to sketch out some ideas, but ended up sketching acorns. They looked so pretty caught in the winter sun." She picked up the sketchbook lying by her feet and opened it to show Eden her charcoal sketch. The sketch was signed by Lilah and dated. Eden took a couple of photographs and returned the sketchpad. It wasn't what she'd call an alibi.

"One of our officers came across you just outside the Tree-House," Black said.

"Once I realised where the sirens were coming from, I came straight back."

"Do you live at the TreeHouse, Lilah?" Eden asked.

"I live in the village. A short walk."

"Can anybody confirm your story?" Black said.

"It's not a story."

"Well, it's certainly not an alibi unless someone can confirm they saw you there at that time."

"I didn't see anyone," she said, "so I'd say not."

. . .

29

Val Simpson was close in age to Bettina O'Connell, but unlike Bettina she didn't wear any make-up, her long hair was streaked with grey, and her clothes second-hand and functional. After introducing themselves, Black said, "Mrs Simpson, I understand you were employed by the O'Connells?"

"It's Val. And, yes. I've worked for them for years. I help out every way. I looked after the kids when they were young. To start with, I worked for Tudor and Bettina, but nowadays the Trust employs me. The idea is for me to manage the gift shop when that's up and running. I've just signed a new contract."

"Val, I understand you arrived for work to discover Mrs O'Connell attempting to drive a digger into the cottage to the rear of the TreeHouse?"

Val Simpson rolled her eyes and raised and lowered her hand. "I couldn't believe my eyes. Don't know what Bettina was thinking of. I know she's angry but..."

"Can you tell me where you were before then?" Black said.

"I walked here from my cottage in the village, stopping off at the orchard. I was going to do baked apples for their lunch. I'd used all mine up making toffee apples for Halloween, and Annie in the village had sold out. We have an orchard full of eaters and bakers, even this time of year. I filled a bag to bursting, then came here."

"Can anybody confirm this?" Eden asked.

Val nodded. "Oh, yes. I got talking to a dog walker. Didn't recognise him. Not local. City type. Looking for property, I reckon. Barbour jacket, flat cap, friendly dog. Young. Quite good-looking. Man and dog. He said it could be warmer, I said least it was dry. The usual. We said goodbye and he went off. Took the footpath between the fields, if I remember."

"Where are the apples?" Eden said.

"Haven't a clue," Valerie said. "When I saw what Bettina was about, I dropped them. Probably still on the drive in my string bag."

"How did you learn about Tudor?" Eden asked.

"From Hugo and the tour party. One of them came running out of the Orangery, yelling to call an ambulance. Tudor had suffered a heart attack. I learned later his name was Nico. The lad Will – the gardener's son — made the call and Nico went with him, while Ivy, Bettina and me made for the Events Room. We never got there. We ran into Hugo and the others coming the other way. They were in such a state. Hugo collapsed to his knees, sobbing that Tudor was dead. When she heard, Ivy started screaming. She and Bettina had to be stopped from going to the body."

"Who stopped them?" Black said.

"Me and some from the group. They suspected foul play. I knew that meant keeping the scene untouched. For evidence. We all made our way back. Ivy ended up in the cottage, Nico with her. Bettina couldn't face sitting with the tour group and went into the front room with Hugo. The rest of us waited in the study. Except for Will and Harry. They stayed outside for the police and to keep an eye out."

"Val," Eden said, "can you think of anybody who would want to do this to Tudor O'Connell?"

"A lot of people wouldn't have minded smacking him in the teeth, his family included, but actually kill him? No – I can't think of anybody who would want to kill him, nor what they'd gain by it, if I'm honest. I'm wondering if an argument got out of hand."

"Thank you very much, Val." Black said.

They next made their way over to the cottage to speak to Tudor O'Connell's partner, Ivy Lee. She was sitting in the cottage's small front room on a wooden foldable chair. The cottage was almost bare, its furniture either already in storage or smashed up in the skip behind the garage. Even the carpets had been removed, leaving rough, unvarnished boards in their place. Ivy had yanked her feet up and was hugging her legs. Her eyes were bright red. The young officer waiting with her took himself to the other side of the room as Black and Eden entered.

Ivy looked up at them. "He was the love of my life. How can he be dead? What am I going to do without him? What is my little girl going to do without her daddy?"

"My sincerest condolences on your loss, Ms Lee," Black said. He and Eden took a seat.

"Thank you. Incidentally, I've taken Tudor's name, I'm Ivy Lee-O'Connell, but please call me Ivy. I'd prefer it."

"Ivy, I am sorry to have to ask you this at such a terrible moment, but I need to know your movements this morning," Black said.

"You can't believe I did it? What reason would I have to kill him? His death leaves me homeless and heartbroken."

"We're sorry you find yourself in this position, Ivy, but I'm afraid we do need to know where you were when Tudor was attacked," Eden said.

She flinched. "I took the last bits and bobs to the skip."

"How long did this take you?" Eden asked.

"To make it easier on myself I carried everything from here to the garage, then to the skip. About three round trips in all — no, four. I decided to get rid of a rug at the last minute. I piled everything up behind the garage. Then, after finally clearing this place, I took it all to the skip."

"Why keep the skip behind the garage?" Black asked. "Why not right outside your house?"

"Tudor didn't want stuff like that spoiling the look of the place when we had groups visiting — and it wasn't far. I had my ear-pods in. I was wearing gardening gloves, you know, to protect my hands. I was listening to music and chucking the stuff in when I thought I heard a crash. I had to take my gloves off to take the ear-pods out, and all I could hear was this crashing and banging. And shouting. I ran over to see what was going on and there she was. Oh my God, I thought. She's trying to knock the cottage down." She raised her hand. "You know what? I don't care anymore. I want to forget all about it. I have lost the love of my life. If only I'd been with him — this wouldn't have happened."

"Ivy, Tudor was last seen making his way to the gate at the Events Room. He claimed something had come up and left the tour in the hands of Hugo. Do you know why?" Eden asked.

"It's the quickest way."

"To?"

"To get to the windmill. Once out of the gate, it's a few fields in a straight line."

"Why did Mr O'Connell want to go to the windmill when he'd arranged to show a group of potential business partners around?" Eden asked.

"We got a letter this morning. Pushed under the door," Ivy said. "Tudor took it with him. Have you not found it?"

"The body will be searched at the morgue," Black said.

His words caused Ivy to breakdown. Eden rushed to her side. "We're sorry to upset you, Ivy."

"The words are so final," Ivy said.

"What was in the letter that made him change his plans?" Black said.

"For the last two years or so, someone has been sending me strange items. I don't want to talk about that. It's unimportant now. Val will tell you all you need to know. The letter said to finally discover who was behind everything, Tudor must be at the windmill at quarter to eleven. I told Tudor to ignore it, it was a prankster. He wasn't sure. Said it could be our only chance to find out one way or the other. If it was a joke, it was on him. I said I'd go, he had a tour to conduct, but he wouldn't hear of it. Said Hugo was quite capable of taking charge for a couple of hours. I wanted him to take a knife, but he refused. Said I was being melodramatic and how would he explain a knife if he was searched by the police. Oh, my God!" She covered her mouth with her hand. "You don't think he was lured there?"

To Eden and Black it sounded a distinct possibility. "Did Tudor need reading glasses?" Eden said.

"Did he?" she said. "He couldn't read anything without them."

"Tudor had a small cut on one finger," Eden said.

Ivy looked blank. "He cut himself jumping when Degas burst a balloon. Why?"

"It may have been a defensive wound," Eden said. "Ivy, can you think why anyone would want to do this?"

"I can't. Not to kill him. I can't."

"It's all so silly," Val Simpson said when asked by Black about the items sent to Ivy. "It all began when Ivy received a theatre programme for a regional performance of *Hamlet* in the post. Just the programme. No letter, nothing. The meaning was obvious. You're aware that Lilah's real name is Ophelia?" They nodded. "'Magine saddling a kid with a name like that? Mind you, the little one's got it even worse. They called her Degas Gethsemane Tiger Peony because she was conceived under *The Dance Class* in a tiger-yellow room with Peony growing outside. I ask you. Too much information. I'm getting sidetracked."

Val went on: "Bettina found out she was pregnant with Ophelia the morning after she and Tudor had seen *Hamlet* performed live, which is why their first-born is named Ophelia. Although Bettina vehemently denied everything, the programme was basically Bettina's way of reminding Ivy that she and Tudor were once deliriously happy new parents. Sometime after that, I can't really say how long exactly, a Brotherhood of Man album sleeve appeared, pinned to the cottage door with the album inside snapped in two." She mimed the snapping of an album in half. "I should explain that Tudor asked Bettina out after seeing her perform in a Brotherhood of Man tribute band. She was the one who ripped her skirt off — she was always glamorous, Bettina.

"This time, Tudor and Ivy played it cool. They threw the album out and pretended it never happened. No one said anything, apart from Bettina, who said it was nothing to do with her. No one believed her that time either. But we did all think that having got it out of her system, and made her point, that would be that. And it was. For a while. Then, would you believe it, Ivy and Tudor came home and found a DVD of *The Tudors* on their doorstep."

"*The Tudors*?" Eden said. "The TV series?"

Val raised her hands. "I know, weird. Dunno if the name was a coincidence or not. Ivy found it funny. She insisted on calling Tudor, Henry VIII and Bettina, Catherine of Aragon. *That makes me Anne Boleyn,* she'd say. *Please don't cut my head off!* Ivy chucked them, but I found out the DVDs were the Catherine Howard episodes — the ones where she was unfaithful to Henry."

"How do you know that, Val?" Eden said.

"I went through the bins. The DVDs were a childish attempt to malign Ivy. Stir things up. Make Tudor doubt her. He thought it puerile. So did I, tell you the truth. Ivy wouldn't be so stupid as to rock that boat. Too much to lose. Again, Bettina denied having anything to do with it and again no one believed her. Things died down again, but just after Tudor told Bettina she had to stop digging her heels in and move out, Ivy couldn't get her car to start. She ended up calling out the garage. They found a scrap of denim deliberately wrapped around the carburettor. Once again, Bettina swore it had nothing to do with her, but this time Tudor told her he'd go to the police if anything like that happened again. That seemed to work. Everything calmed down, until, oh wait a minute," she raised her hand, "I've missed the pile of shredded ivy scattered over the doorstep. Can't remember if that happened before the DVD incident or after. I cleared it up and we all pretended the wind had blown the leaves there, even though it was all bits of ivy. But no one could put what happened to the lapwing down to nature. That was the nastiest yet."

She took a breath, then continued, "Ivy came across a little injured lapwing when out pushing Degas in her pram. There's a lot around here. The poor little thing had broken its wing. Ivy took her home and made a box for her. Somehow or other she survived. Tudor made a little run for her, and Ivy and the little one fed her bird seed. She was thriving. Then one morning Ivy went to feed her and found her dead and wrapped in barbed wire. As I understand it, the police were informed."

"Can we wind back a bit?" Black said. "Tudor told Bettina she had to stop digging her heels in?"

"They'd split up. Her staying on in the big house, as I call it — the TreeHouse – was only ever meant to be temporary. Tudor and Ivy always intended to move in. Tudor told Bettina that now the cottage was being converted, she'd have to go. Tudor told her she'd had a good run for her money, but she was furious and very hurt. It was her idea to open up the grounds, and now everything was going to be taken away from her is the way she saw it. I thought she'd finally come round to things. But she can't have, can she?"

"How would you sum up Tudor's personality?" Black said.

"In childhood, Catholics learn about *The Fruit of the Holy Spirit*. Charity, kindness, peace, that kind of thing. Tudor held such traits in other people in high esteem but, truth be known, he never bothered much with them himself."

. . .

Black and Eden had a quick word with Harry Thorne. "I've done work for the O'Connells over the years. Now Will's old enough, he's joined the family business. They have a few regular gardeners what go in a few times a week over the summer, less in winter. But we're the heavy squad. If a tree needs lobbing, or one of the lawns reseeding, they get us in. Bettina booked us herself — to scrub up a garden, she said. We didn't really need a digger for what she needed doing. She was like a woman possessed, that's for sure. I get she's got problems and I'm sorry for her, but my equipment is damaged, and I have a business to run."

"How was Bettina able to start the digger?" Eden asked. "Didn't you or your son have the fob on you?"

"Fobs are too easy to hack," he replied. "Can't tell you how much agricultural machinery goes walkabouts as a result. Where possible, I use vehicles with keys. Way harder to nick. The old-fashioned ways are the best — 'cept when your son leaves the key in the ignition."

"Can you describe what happened?" Eden said.

"Quite a lot happened. Some of it at the same time. We couldn't get her down from the digger. I sent my boy to call the police. Ivy came running over screaming and yelling. Val Simpson turned up and tried to calm everything down. Just as I think things can't get any worse, this man's running towards us yelling Tudor's had a heart attack. Will and him run into the road to call an ambulance. Why no one thought to use the landline inside the house, I can't think. Blind panic, I suppose. Val, Bettina and Ivy run off to Tudor. I stayed put. I wasn't leaving my digger. Will and Nico were the first back, then the others from the Orangery. Ivy ran straight past me into the cottage, screaming her head off. Hugo was yelling Tudor was dead. Everyone was talking at once; the women were crying. We could hear Ivy being sick. It was chaos. No one really knew what to do. Eventually, Nico followed Ivy inside and everyone else ended up in the house — 'cept for Will, who stayed at the front, and me. I stayed in the courtyard to keep an eye on things. No one could've got past me or Will without us seeing."

"You didn't see anyone leave the cottage, studio, garage or the house until the emergency services arrived?" Eden asked.

"Didn't," he said. "Ambulance came first. Then you lot."

Finally, Black spoke briefly to the five remaining members of the original tour group. He asked them to confirm their names and the purpose of their visit that day: Alf and Ren Hoffbrand were specialist florists; Caroline May owned a gift-shop; Nico and Zyline Angeles were wedding planners. Each member of the tour party claimed to know only those they had arrived with. Each swore they hadn't met Tudor O'Connell, nor visited the TreeHouse before that day. Each provided details of their business, the journey they had taken to the TreeHouse, and what happened after they'd parted from Hugo O'Connell. Each confirmed they were intending to go straight home, once allowed to do so. Every single version of the events of the day given, supported every other version.

At the end of a long day, the team went home.

Chapter 5

BLACK CALLED a team meeting first thing next morning. As team heads, Eden and Pilot were there, as well as Judy McDermott, the Detective Superintendent overseeing the case.

Topping the incident board, next to his name and age, hung photographs of the deceased — one of him still alive, the other of his corpse. Below him came the names and photographs of those at the TreeHouse on the morning of the murder. On a second incident board were photographs of the murder scene and an Ordnance Survey map of the area with the position of the TreeHouse highlighted.

"Tudor O'Connell was sixty-three years of age when he was murdered in the grounds of his own property," Black said. "He was stabbed to death. He suffered two stab wounds to the back, penetrating both lungs, probably made at the same time. He is survived by three children." He pointed to the corresponding photographs as he spoke: "Hugo, twenty-two; Ophelia, always known as Lilah, twenty-three; and Degas who is eighteen months old. Hugo and Lilah are his children by his wife, fifty-two-year-old Bettina. Tudor and Bettina are in the process of divorcing. Degas is his daughter by his partner, twenty-eight-year-old Ivy Lee-O'Connell. This is the extent of the family, as far as I'm aware.

"Tudor O'Connell was the son of the late Gethsemane O'Connell. For those not in the know, Gethsemane is famed for her *Tree of Life* pictures and prints. The family trust licenses the sale of Gethsemane merchandise. The TreeHouse is the family home. Gethsemane's studio is there. The family are opening the studio and the grounds to the public next year, and Tudor and Hugo were showing a group around when he was attacked. These are the people..." he drew the room's attention to a row of faces along the bottom of the incident board, below each of which had been written a name and an occupation:

Alf and Ren Hoffbrand: specialist florists

Caroline May: gift-shop owner

Zyline and Nico Angeles: wedding planners

"Nick Pilsworth": art teacher

"I'll come to why there's no photograph of Nick Pilsworth and why his name is in inverted commas at the end. Each of the six make a living from the Arts and Crafts industry. As I understand it, the ultimate purpose of the day was cross-selling."

Black held up an apron. Its design was a tree, concealed within which was a woman in a long flowing dress; the tree's branches, her long, plaited hair, blowing in the wind. "This was kindly provided by Detective Sergeant Hudson and gives us an idea of the Gethsemane merchandise. Exactly how much income the brand generates annually, and by how much that is likely to increase with opening the grounds, are important lines of enquiry, as is who, if anyone, benefits from Tudor's death. Pilot – what has your team learned so far?"

Pilot read from the report in front of him. "Gethsemane O'Connell's fame and influence had somewhat diminished over the years since her death, but with renewed interest in the works of inspirational women and the Art and Crafts movement in general, Gethsemane is being rediscovered. Gethsemane O'Connell may not be a fully-fledged goddess of the Arts and Crafts movement along the lines of Frida Kahlo, but she's fast becoming a demi-goddess with her once-forgotten home and studio, her shrine."

On the screen on the wall, Black opened an aerial photograph of the TreeHouse and its grounds, using the curser to point out the various locations as he spoke. "Tudor, Hugo and the rest of the tour party began at the front of the house and moved to the rear of the property via a side gate, which we know was left open to let them through, then closed and locked behind them. You'll notice a courtyard behind the house. This is flanked by this cottage here and this long building they call the Orangery. There is no access between the two. The building to the other side of the cottage, which, as you can see, has about the same dimensions as the Orangery, was the artist's studio. Along from that is a flat-roofed double garage. The group entered the Orangery. The Orangery doesn't have any windows and is lit from its high glass roof. It has two doors — one opening out onto the courtyard, the other onto a small patch of lawn, screened off from the grounds and the cottage by yew hedges. The only way into the grounds from the house side is through this archway." He pointed to the archway which led to the Herb Room.

"The cottage has a front and back door, and a normal number of windows, which all have wooden shutters. Each window was found closed and locked from the inside, with the shutters also closed and secured with a bar across. The window-lock keys were all in a pot on the window sill, along with the key to the back door, which was also locked from the inside. The shutter door to the garage was closed and locked. It has no windows. There is only one door in and out of the studio. This leads onto the courtyard. This door was left unlocked as the studio formed part of the tour. The studio has a number of windows, all closed and locked. Whilst there are some cubbyholes inside the studio, it's difficult to see how anyone could have got in or out without being seen. There are three ways in and out of the main house: the back door, which was locked; French windows at the side into the study, also locked; and the front door. This was opened by Bettina and is on a Yale lock. All the windows were closed and locked, but not shuttered as Bettina was inside."

He paused for those taking notes to catch up. "The grounds total approximately five acres and are broken down into smaller themed gardens, known as rooms. Each garden room is divided from the next by a yew hedge with access afforded through archways. Having been there, I can tell you that no one can see through or over those hedges, all of which are pretty dense. There isn't any obvious way through any of them, other than the archways. The group took the most direct route to the Events Room."

Black moved the cursor through the Herb Room, the Rose Room and the Winter Room. "The group had reached the end of the Rose Room when Nick Pilsworth turned back, citing ill-health. We have no idea what happened to him, or how he got out, as the gate he'd entered through was locked, and he couldn't have used the other gate without being seen. Significantly, each of the gardens they went through led only onto the next one, and they are all flanked by an impenetrable border." He highlighted the Events Room. "The murder took place here. This is a large space, consisting of a lawn with a fishing pond at one end. The family intend hiring it out for weddings and other events, hence its name."

He took a breath. "The Events Room can be accessed in three ways. This double archway, which faces the entrance to the Winter Room," he pointed at it, "and this single archway on the far side of the pond, which leads to and from the Topiary Room; and a wooden gate in the wall, which affords access onto neighbouring farmland. The gate can only be opened from the inside and by an electronic keypad. For security reasons, there isn't a keyboard on the outside wall, nor a handle."

He paused again for a second, then continued. "A footpath straddles the Winter and Events Rooms. The path starts at the boundary wall, where there is a seat and some trellis, creating a possible exit for our killer, and continues in the other direction where it turns the corner into a boxed alcove. The group of six ended up here after Tudor unexpectedly directed his son to take over the tour, claiming urgent business elsewhere. We believe this urgent business was a chance to learn the name of the person responsible for sending a series of strange items to Tudor's partner, Ivy, over a period of time. Tudor didn't want any of the visitors to see him entering the gate code and insisted Hugo take them to the Topiary Room. Tudor was last seen alive inside the Events Room. Everyone who saw him there is adamant that no one else was in the space. Tudor got no further than the gate.

"I will be returning to the scene as soon as I can without getting in the way, but at the moment I can't see how anyone could've been lurking in the corners nearest to Tudor without either him or Hugo noticing. Nor does it seem likely that anyone was hiding or followed the group along the same route they took that morning. There aren't any large trees to hide behind. The plants are all cut back and next to nothing is growing. After seeing the rest of the party into the Topiary Room, Hugo remained in the little alcove, allegedly to make a call. In the Topiary Room, everyone moved at different speeds. The Hoffbrands, with their interest in plants, made their way over to the leylandii colonnade. Caroline May, the seller of curiosities, spent time admiring the topiary. The Angeles, believing their customers might enjoy the space, took some photographs. They moved through the room the fastest. They'd stopped to admire a garden ornament just outside the Events Room when they heard a crash coming from the direction of the house. Caro May also heard a crash but couldn't work out where it came from. The Angeles, first into the Events Room, saw Tudor on the ground. Zyline ran over to the body while Nico ran back into the Topiary Room, calling out to the others for help. Unable to get a signal, he ran back through the Topiary Room, colliding with Hugo on his way in. Everyone agreed Zyline Angeles was the first to reach the body, followed quickly by Alf and Ren Hoffbrand and Caro May. Hugo ran along the path with Nico to enter the murder scene from the direction of the double archway. Meanwhile, Nico Angeles was still unable to get a phone signal — a common problem in remote country properties — so he continued onto the courtyard.

"In the Events Room, Tudor is surrounded by people coming from all directions. He has been turned on his back, his side and his back again. At least two people have attempted to resuscitate him, and an attempt is made to scale the wall. I can't tell you how much evidence was inadvertently destroyed by all of this."

Black waited a few moments for the information so far to be digested by his team, then continued. "So, what have we got? Tudor O'Connell reached the gate to the outside but didn't go through it. He had his reading glasses in his hand. He was murdered in broad daylight, with people a hedge away. We've found footprints running across the field away from the gate, but none approaching. Despite these footprints being some-what trampled under hoof by the sheep in the field, at this stage it certainly looks as though the killer escaped through the gate.

"Others at the TreeHouse on the morning of the murder were father and son, Harry and Will Thorne, there to work on the cottage garden and Bettina O'Connell and Ivy Lee-O'Connell, who became involved in a fracas, and Valerie Simpson, who has worked for the O'Connells for a very long time. On hearing from Nico that Tudor had suffered a heart attack, the ladies apparently set off to the Events Room. They didn't get there. They met Hugo and the rest of the tour group on their way back — ironically, so as not to destroy any evidence at the scene. At the main house everyone dispersed to various locations. From that moment, and until we arrived, none of the suspects were ever alone. There are a couple of locations which will need checking out — an old oak tree alone in the field which the daughter, Lilah O'Connell, claims to have been sketching when her dad was attacked; and the abandoned windmill Tudor was trying to reach. We're still waiting for the search teams to finish, and on door-to-door to complete their enquiries. Cars, clothes, shoes and the usual samples are still with forensics."

"My team is on phone and computer records," Pilot said, "including the number Hugo called. We're also requesting records of all drones flying over the area that morning, and we've asked Google for their satellite images."

"My team is checking out the visitors and the family," Eden said. "The Thornes were the only gardeners there that day. The regular gardeners were working elsewhere. In winter, that's quite normal for them."

"The individual of most interest remains Dr Nick Pilsworth," Black said. "If he isn't who he claimed to be, I want to know who the hell Nick Pilsworth really is and where he is."

"Any news of the murder weapon, Guido?" Judy McDermott asked.

"The search for that is still ongoing," Black replied. "Matt Pritchard is carrying out the post-mortem later this afternoon, which I'll attend. Eden, I'd like you to visit the tree, the windmill, and the apple orchard. We need to know where they are relative to the murder scene. Has anybody got anything else before I take a stroll to the village?"

"Only that we found Val's missing bag of apples wrapped around the tyre of a squad car, Sir," Eden said. "We believe the driver ran over it."

Chapter 6

AFTER ARRIVING IN THE VILLAGE, Black wandered over to his colleagues who were making door-to-door enquiries. "Anything?" he asked.

"Not yet, Sir. Everybody knew him, but no one's got an answer as to what happened."

"CCTV?" Black said.

"Only at the village store."

Father Dermot Hanrahan was waiting for Black by the front gate of the Priest house — an unassuming, bow-windowed Victorian building adjacent to the church. Upon seeing Black he hurried towards him, extending a hand. "Such a tragedy we have to meet again in such sad circumstances. Do please come inside, please." He ushered Black along the path and inside. "Let's go through to the parlour, let's do."

The parlour room was at the back of the house. Black got the impression it was mostly used for visitors. A rug covered a carpet. Soft furnishings, covered by throws and cushions indented by use, circled a small coffee table. A floor lamp loomed over an armchair. In one corner, a Chinese vase displayed dried hydrangeas. In an adjacent corner stood a grandfather clock, its chimes removed, the time in this room told by a mantel clock next to an aspidistra atop a sideboard pushed against the wall. Lace curtains hung snug at the windows; cords held back heavier velvet curtains. There were the usual pictures on the wall.

Father Hanrahan said, "Please let me get you a tea or a coffee."

Black declined.

"Now, are you quite sure, Detective Inspector?"

"Quite sure, Father, thank you."

"Not even a glass of water, now?"

"No, thank you, Father."

"Well, let us get off our feet, then."

The two men sat down, and Black said, "I'd like you to tell me everything you can about the O'Connells."

"I'm more than happy to assist," the Father said. "Bettina too. She begged me to help you in every way I can. Let's see, now – I've been the family priest for more years than I care to remember. I arrived around the same time as Bettina. We were young together; her a young bride, me a young priest overseeing a congregation. We were both novices with a lot to learn." He laughed.

"Were Tudor and Bettina members of the congregation?"

Father Hanrahan hesitated. "Throughout most of their married life, yes, but Tudor's attendance had waned recently. I remain sure he would have returned to our church, had this terrible thing not happened, as Bettina has. For she too has grappled with her faith." He gesticulated as he spoke. "There was a time not so long ago when she failed to attend mass or confession, but her faith proved too strong, and once again Bettina is a popular member of our church. Her faith is now stronger than ever, I'm very happy to say. I'm certain Tudor would have rediscovered his faith also, given time."

"What about Tudor's partner, Ivy Lee-O'Connell? Does she attend your church?"

The priest shook his head. "Ivy is very scornful of religion. She didn't even want the little girl baptised, but Tudor insisted. They argued terribly about it. Happily, Tudor won that argument. What will happen regarding the child's religious education, now that he has been taken from us, I dread to think."

"Is Ivy the reason Tudor stopped coming to church?"

"I am sure he had his reasons. He was a busy man." Father Hanrahan hesitated. "His faith hadn't left him. He insisted on Degas's baptism, for heaven's sake. He kept God in his heart, of that I am certain. To speak candidly, Tudor was like most men, Detective Inspector. He wanted a quiet life, and if that meant not going to church to appease his partner, then so be it."

"Please tell me more about your church. From where is your congregation derived? The village alone doesn't seem big enough."

"I have quite a large catchment area. Takes in villages and towns. We have a Polish mass once a week. Why do you ask?"

"Well, I'm wondering if Tudor O'Connell might have had a falling out with another church goer."

Father Hanrahan shook his head. "I would have known if he had. I'd have been asked to intervene. Whoever did this terrible, terrible thing certainly isn't a member of my congregation."

"Do you know of anything that might help me with my enquiries? Anything you saw or heard, even in passing — which, looking back, might be important? An argument, for example?"

"Tudor didn't reveal anything to me that could in any way aid your enquiries or have led to his murder."

"What is your opinion of Ms Ivy Lee-O'Connell?"

"I wish she'd let God into her life."

"And Bettina O'Connell?"

"Bettina is a God-fearing, devout woman. She isn't capable of an evil thought, let alone action. What happened with the digger was completely out of character, Detective Inspector. On top of all those horrible accusations Ivy made about her, she'd received the Decree Nisi. Her marriage was over, and she was going to have to move out of her home. Everything overwhelmed her, and she snapped. She is distraught, absolutely distraught, by her behaviour. I know her well enough to know that."

"By accusations, are you referring to the strange objects Ivy received, Father?" Black said.

"She claims to have received," was the priest's reply. "As well as accusing Bettina of that, Ivy also accused her of stealing her earrings. Bettina O'Connell would never steal anything. Theft is a sin."

"You don't believe Bettina sent Ivy the theatre programme and all the other stuff?"

"Good God, no," the priest said. "Not for a minute. Bettina wouldn't stoop to that level. She was mortified anybody could think she would kill a child's pet. In an odd way, though, it helped her rediscover God. She told me it showed her the fate that befalls those who fall by the wayside."

"If not Bettina, then who do you think was responsible?" Black asked.

"If you're asking me do I believe Ivy capable of sending those objects to herself to besmirch poor Bettina's character and make herself out the victim, then all I can say is that she wouldn't be the first. As if she hasn't hurt Bettina enough."

"How did you learn of Mr O'Connell's death?" Black asked.

"I found a distraught message from Bettina on my answerphone. I hadn't realised she'd called. I'd been in the shower. Hadn't heard the phone. I drove straight there and stayed with her after you left. She's truly devastated. She loves Tudor, she always will. The shenanigans at the cottage only add to her shame and guilt. For some women, the last few years would be too much to bear; but Bettina is a strong woman. Her faith will see her through."

Eden began at the field where the centuries-old oak tree grew. The field was surrounded by a barbed wire fence and accessed by a wooden farm gate displaying a *PRIVATE KEEP OUT* sign. She looked across the field. It gradually rose into a hillock with the tall, ancient tree at its pinnacle, dominating everything around. The gate was padlocked, forcing Eden to climb it before trudging across the field, damp and soft underfoot from overnight rain. As she approached the tree, the fallen leaves and brown acorns littering its feet crunched beneath her boots. She stopped to look up at the imposing tree. At eye level a huge bur protruded, and further up the gnarled trunk a branch grew downwards, almost to the ground. From then on it was straight up to an enormous canopy. Eden tipped her head further back to peer up. The day was as grim as the one before, silhouetting the tree's leaved branches against the cloudy sky. She took out her phone to look at Lilah's sketch. It was unspectacular — lobbed leaves grew from a branch, a bunch of acorns in their cups hung from a long stalk. She wondered how Lilah, even with her young eyes, could have sketched in such detail from such a distance.

She moved closer to the downwards-growing branch and saw a cluster of acorns and a sprig of oak leaves growing from it. Your sketch doesn't prove you were here, Lilah, Eden said to herself, but neither does it disprove your story. She walked around the tree and stopped on the side away from the road. Its old trunk was wide. Too wide for her arms to envelop. She couldn't see the road and couldn't be seen from it, nor by anyone else in the field unless chanced upon. Eden stepped out. From this distance, she could just make out part of the

TreeHouse's pale blue rooftop, but nothing else. She circled the field. None of the barbed wire fence surrounding it appeared to have been cut or trampled down. If Lilah had been in this field that morning, she'd used the gate.

Eden returned to the TreeHouse along the route Lilah claimed to have taken. This took her across a field, over a stile, under a tree canopy and across another field to a country lane and past the church. It took her fourteen minutes to reach the TreeHouse, whereas Lilah had appeared eighteen minutes after the first emergency vehicle had arrived at the scene. Lilah was young and used to trudging around the countryside, but she hadn't set off at the first siren. Had she really prevaricated for four minutes? Possibly. Eden made her way to the rear of the property.

With the field the killer escaped across still being searched for clues, Eden began at its other end by the metal farm gate which separated it from the next field along. Once over it, and a few steps to her left, she'd be in a thicket of trees. In its midst was a piece of hardstanding surrounded by enough trees to conceal a two-wheeled escape vehicle. The thicket also abutted the road.

Still by the metal gate, Eden turned and, leaning on it, looked towards the TreeHouse. The field she looked over was surrounded by both hedgerow and an electric fence (to keep in the sheep). A water trough was upside down, the yellow grass underneath exposed to the light for the first time in years. Teammates sifted through haystacks piled up in a corrugated iron windbreak. A pathway, made over the years by heavy use, ran diagonally across the field from the farm gate she leant upon to the dark blue wooden TreeHouse gate, prominent against the property's red brick wall. Where the flock were now, which the murderer had swerved between, Eden knew not. The farmer had rounded up his flock and taken them away, worsening the destruction of evidence. She turned her back on the TreeHouse and set out over the next field.

However carefully Eden tried to avoid stepping on the rows of winter field beans poking through the soil, she felt stalks and leaves squelching into the mud under her feet. She got, though, why Tudor O'Connell had chosen this route — it was direct, even though it meant climbing over yet another stile to finally reach the windmill. The locals, she decided, either had very good knees or very bad knees.

The windmill stood a solitary sentinel over the surrounding countryside. It had seen better days. Its wooden cap and sails were long gone; the door and windows in its cylindrical walls firmly boarded up. Eden and the windmill shared the muddy cowpat-strewn field with a herd of cows.

"How's it going, girls?" she asked. The cows viewed her suspiciously. "Anything I should know?"

A few mooed.

Taking care to avoid cowpats, she circled the mill. It was partially visible from the TreeHouse, but not the other way around. When she'd returned to its boarded-up door, she reached out and laid her hand on the old, cold stone walls. Now, here is where a killer would strike, she thought, looking up at it — not in a garden full of people.

She ended her tour in the apple orchard where she discovered pear trees alongside apple, heavy with a late harvest. Fallen fruit lay on the grass under the trees. Wild blackberry brambles climbed the wall surrounding the trees.

"Help yourself," a voice behind her said.

Eden spun around and saw Lilah framed in the open gate. "Take as much you want. It'll only rot otherwise." Lilah casually moved off in the direction of the village. Eden wasn't far behind her, only in the opposite direction, towards the TreeHouse.

.   .   .

Annie and Ted Threadneedle owned the village store. A sign on its door proclaimed the store closed until further notice. Black understood they lived above the store and tried the door. It was locked. He knocked but nobody came. When he heard a noise inside, he hammered loudly, yelling, "Police."

A window above him opened and a woman peered out, her face concealed in shadow. Guido Black held up his badge.

"I've already spoken to you lot, I've nothing else to say. I've already given you the CCTV."

"Am I speaking to Mrs Annie Threadneedle?" Black asked.

"You are."

"My name is Guido Black. I'm the Detective Inspector in charge of the case. Can we have a chat?"

"I want to see that close up," she said of the badge. "I'm not getting tricked into speaking to journalists."

"Don't blame you," Black replied.

The window closed, and he heard her come downstairs. A short while later, a very suspicious Annie Threadneedle put her head around a partially opened front door. He held the badge out to her. She put her face to it. Reassured, she let Black inside. They remained in the shop, surrounded by stacked shelves and gently humming chill cabinets.

"I understand you and your husband own this store," Black said.

"That's right." She was still quite suspicious.

"Is your husband also around?" he asked.

"Ted's dad died last week. He's had to go up there to sort things out. His mum's senile. She'll need to go into a home. He'll be gone awhile. I'm holding the fort."

"Were you behind the counter on the morning of Tudor O'Connell's murder?"

"I spend eighty percent of my time behind the counter, love."

"Did you notice anything unusual on the morning of the murder?"

"Not in the shop itself. But there was this man hanging around outside. Funny looking. He got off the bus right outside," she tilted her head in the direction of the bus stop outside the door. "He got off the number 34a. It's a request stop. Right furtive he was. Looking around him all the time, like someone was going to jump him."

"Could I have a description?"

"A man. Bent over, but probably tall in his youth. To be honest, he looked a bit like an ageing werewolf. Thick white beard. Well wrapped up."

Annie's description was very similar to Hugo O'Connell's description of Nick Pilsworth. "Did he come into the shop for anything?" Black said.

Annie shook her head. "No. But he should be on the CCTV we have of the door."

"At some stage, I'll need you to come into the station to provide an e-fit. In the meantime, can I ask how well you know the O'Connell family?"

"Quite well. Although she's technically not family, Val Simpson's the one I see the most. She lives in the village and doesn't drive. I see her most days, coming and going."

"Did you see her pass on the day of the murder?" Black asked.

"I did, yes. Gave me a wave. Lilah comes in most days, too. Even known her to buy her breakfast here, and be back the same evening for something for her dinner. Didn't see her on the day of the murder though. Hugo buys ciggies and his sugary drinks here. Bettina pops in once in a blue moon. Didn't see either of them that day either."

"Was Tudor O'Connell a regular?"

"Tudor next to never shopped here."

"What about Ivy Lee-O'Connell?" Black said.

"She comes in. Likes her scratch cards, that one."

"Do you ever have anything to do with them socially?"

"Val, yes. Not the others."

"Is Bettina, Hugo or Lilah ever seen in the company of Ivy?" Black asked.

She started laughing. "You must be joking, love."

"How did Hugo and his dad get on?"

"Tudor was always running the boy down. Finding fault. Hugo's not the type to stand up for himself, poor kid. Danced to his dad's tune. Drove Denys mad. Got worse when he and Denys got engaged. Tudor went all preachy. Came out with a load of rubbish about marriage being a sacred bond between a man and a woman — only to go and dump poor Bettina not that long afterwards. Denys called him out for being a hypocrite. Had a big fight. He wasn't welcome at the TreeHouse after that, although he and Hugo still came around. To see Bettina."

"How did Tudor get on with his daughter, Lilah?" Black asked.

"Until Ivy came along, she was his blue-eyed girl. To my mind, Lilah's nose was put out of joint by that. Felt she was squeezed out. She told her father he was being ridiculous over Ivy. He didn't care to hear that, as you can imagine."

"Sounds like you didn't care much for Tudor O'Connell," Black said.

"He wasn't my favourite person, no, but I'm sorry he died the way he did. No one deserves that."

"How does Val Simpson fit into the family dynamics?"

"She's been there for years. Nothing's too much trouble. Her and Bettina are as thick as thieves, they go way back; but it's not up to Bettina any more. I understood Ivy didn't want Val running the café, wanted to get someone in with a bit more glamour, but now I'm hearing she signed a new contract. She's a grafter and the customers like her, but with a question mark over her loyalty, can't see her lasting long. Same goes for Bettina. She's been told she can stay on as manager, but how long's that going to last?"

"Please don't be offended when I ask this," Black said, "but how do you feel about the TreeHouse potentially opening to the public next year? Will it affect your business?"

"Certainly hope so," Annie said. "Can't wait for it to open. Should bring in people from all over. It'll be brilliant for the area. We're going to go more upmarket. Artisan sausage rolls, home-made honey. Ted used the word vegan the other day for the first time in his life. We've put in to open a café ourselves, with a B&B upstairs. I only hope to God this business hasn't put the kibosh on the whole thing."

"Thank you for your time, Mrs Threadneedle," Black said.

"Do you know about the magazine interview Tudor and Ivy gave, Detective Inspector?" she asked. When he hesitated, she added, "Stay put a mo."

She left him in the store to go upstairs. He heard footsteps overhead, the sound of a drawer opening, then Annie returning downstairs. She clutched a glossy magazine entitled *Spirit!* Tudor O'Connell and Ivy graced the cover, she holding baby Degas. The headline read:

Tudor O'Connell and partner Ivy Lee, at home with new baby, Degas.

And the subhead:

They call me Poison Ivy, but our love is true.

"Do they call her Poison Ivy?" he asked.

"Well, if the shoe fits."

"Can I hold onto this?"

"Be my guest."

Black checked his watch. It was time for the autopsy.

Chapter 7

LILAH O'CONNELL WAS at the garden centre at opening time. She'd picked a drizzly weekday to visit, hoping the weather would deter other visitors. She'd chosen the garden centre with care. Nowhere so close she'd run the risk of bumping into someone she knew, but neither could she risk visiting a garden centre so far from home that she'd arouse the suspicions of the police she knew would be watching her.

She remained outdoors, raising her hood against the rain, and made for *Pots, Planters and Troughs.* She steered her trolley through Wooden, Contemporary, Wheeled, and many other types of planters before navigating her way through almost as many varieties of garden troughs. Finally, she reached *Pots.* A faux lead pot with lattice sides caught her eye. Rectangular and waist-high, it was just what she was looking for. To make sure, she took out her tape measure. The pot's width at its narrowest point was wide enough for her needs. Pot on board trolley, she set off for *Decorative Stone.* The price of a small bag of stones came as a surprise. Needs must, she thought, lugging a sack of the cheapest pebbles she could find onto the trolley. From a table of garden ornaments, she helped herself to a little hand-painted robin and a bag of white marbles. She wondered how long it would take the police to dig through pebble after pebble in a futile search for the weapon or other evidence. She chuckled and headed off to buy some plants.

When she reached the raised platforms displaying their rows of plants, Lilah realised she didn't know the first thing about pot plants. She pounced on a young assistant busily arranging a display. "I'm looking for some shallow-rooted perennials," she said. He looked like a schoolboy and she half expected him to call over a more senior member of staff.

"For the front or back garden?" he asked.

She thought for a few minutes. "Back garden's nicer and sunnier."

"In that case, what about a nice mixture of irises and pinks?" He motioned towards a table on which stood rows of pots of delicate, rich purple flowers. She selected six pots.

"Good choice," he said. "They'll develop into lovely large clumps over time. You'll wonder how you lived without them." His eyes fell on the sack of pebbles on the trolley. "But they'll need compost."

"They'll be okay," she said casually over her shoulder, pushing the trolley towards the exit.

On her way to the cashpoint, at the far side of the gift shop, a stylishly patterned pair of Crocs caught her eye; she added them to her shop.

"These are pretty," the cashier said.

"I lost my other pair," she replied. She paid with cash.

The angle of the approach, together with the height of the winter sun, made it appear as though the building ahead — a hangar of dark glass and steel — floated on the pond it over-looked. Black parked as close as possible to the regional specialist centre for post-mortems. On his way to its door, he passed a group of smokers braving the cold. How glad he was at having long since given up.

Professor Matthew Pritchard, the Forensic Pathologist who'd attended the murder scene, waited with a couple of members of his team to begin the post-mortem on Tudor O'Connell. The deceased currently lay face-down on the pathology table. When Black had taken his place, Matt Prichard began. He dictated as he carried out the post-mortem:

"Tudor O'Connell, sixty-three years of age and 1.63 metres tall — about five foot four; weighing 82.55 kilogrammes — about thirteen stone. Initial MRI scan, and the deceased's medical records, reveal visceral fat around the internal organs; an enlarged precancerous prostate; a benign kidney tumour; an enlarged heart and borderline diabetes type 2." He made a note of the mole on Tudor's foot, another on his left arm, and the small but deep wound on his middle left finger. He highlighted the fatal stab wounds. "Shape of the wounds atypical. Entrance to both wounds shrunk. Two single, rear penetrating traumas made by a sharp object, almost identical in position, on either side of the central spine. One is two centimetres from the spine, the other four centimetres. Posterior scapular point of entry in both wounds between the right eighth intercostal space; stabbing object or objects removed."

Matt then proceeded to open him up. He removed and reported on the condition of each internal organ, dropping them into kidney dishes as he worked. "Stabbing injuries penetrating seventeen point seven centimetres deep. Injury traumas inconsistent in diameter, likely due to the twisting of the weapon while still in place. Wounds consistent with injuries made by a dagger or stiletto knife. Intercostal blood vessels wounded, causing bleeding and visceral pleura, quickly resulting in tension pneumothorax, prohibiting air outflow."

Matt stepped aside as his assistant closed up the wound. The body was turned on its back. After noting an appendectomy scar, Matt used a torch to peer into the deceased's mouth. "There's something lodged in his throat," he said.

His assistant picked up a pair of stainless-steel splinter forceps and removed an object from the throat, showing it to Matt before dropping it into a kidney dish.

"A lump of chewing gum removed from the throat," Matt dictated as his assistant opened the cavity wall. "Unsealed opening in the chest leading to open pneumothorax, impeding normal ventilation. Penetrating injury causing trauma to both lungs and accumulation of large volume of blood into chest. The deceased died of acute respiratory distress, double pneumothorax and haemorrhagic shock resulting in cardiac arrest and rapid death. His last meal was toast for breakfast. No evidence of undissolved medication in the stomach. We're still waiting on toxicology."

Black summarised his understanding of the post-mortem. "Basically, two wounds made by a long, sharp instrument, which perforated the lungs causing both lungs to collapse and rapid blood loss into the abdomen, and cardiac arrest?"

Matt agreed, adding, "The attacker struck from behind. There's no evidence that the deceased attempted to get out of the way or shield himself from the attack. We haven't any defensive wounds. It's safe to say he never saw it coming."

"He didn't cry out or scream after the attack?" Black asked.

"He couldn't," Matt said. "His lungs had collapsed, his heart had arrested and he had a piece of chewing gum lodged in his throat." He held up the kidney dish. "He was dead before he hit the ground."

· · ·

Black rang Ivy. "Ivy, Tudor had a lump of chewing gum lodged in his throat. Did he habitually chew gum?" Black asked.

After a choke, she said, "Always."

Chapter 8

THE NEXT DAY saw a return to the TreeHouse. Black was first to arrive. He wandered over to the double gate to the left of the property. Through the railings he saw the studio side on and some of the garage. He crossed to the property's other side. Through that gate he saw the right angle made by the Orangery and cottage but little more. He returned to the car to await Judy McDermott and Eden Hudson. He killed time by reading an email from the Chief Constable. Its subject matter was *Movember*:

Colleagues,

None of us needs reminding that the Movember foundation is the world's leading charity for men's health, working to reduce the number of men dying prematurely by 25 percent. Last year a number of us tashed up and together managed to raise over £1,000 for Movember. This year I'd like us to do a bit better by entering as a force. Gentlemen, I invite you to choose your moustache. On the advice of my wife that it's more flattering for the mature male, you'll soon see me adorned by what is known as the standard moustache. But don't let me cramp your style, gents. Ladies, you can do your bit with your own mocktaches. There's a prize for Best Moustache/Funniest Mocktache.

Despite some criticisms, last year's decision to add a Public Donations Page to the web page proved popular and will be repeated this year. May the best Tache win!

A tap on the window alerted Black to Judy and Eden's arrival. He stepped out of the car and they all made their way to the grounds. Talk turned to the Chief's email.

"To quote Hercule Poirot himself, *In England, the cult of the moustache is lamentably neglected.*" Black mimicked the Hercule Poirot walk as he spoke.

Eden wanted to know what the Chief meant by...*despite some criticisms.*

"A particularly charming post that comes to mind is – *That why no one came round when my Nan was burgled? Too busy gramming the shit out of your bum fluff were yous?*" Judy said.

They began at the cottage. The corner hit by the digger was missing a chunk of stone and a window was cracked but intact. While the Orangery and the studio were vertical in relation to the house, the cottage was horizontal. They glanced inside the empty property. Downstairs was a narrow hall entrance, reception room to the right with another room to the left. The kitchen was to the rear as was a tiny cloakroom. Upstairs were three bedrooms, a box room and a small bathroom. Once their window shutters were open, the back rooms looked across the grounds. A door from the kitchen led into the cottage's small garden. This contained ornamental shrubs, small trees and pots of winter plants on a hard patio, boxed in on two sides by dense yew hedges.

From the cottage they went to the studio. Although of similar dimensions to the Orangery that it faced across the courtyard, the building which had served as Gethsemane's studio differed from the Orangery in a number of ways. Its roof was not made of glass. It had only one door. It was lit by long windows which reached almost from floor to ceiling. Its floors were stonewashed. Two long wooden tables, pushed next to each other, took up the centre; elsewhere, shelves and cupboards filled every available space. A varnished and painted manger hung on one wall.

Black opened the door to a cupboard and found more shelves. "Arts and crafters like their shelves," he said.

"Equipment," Judy and Eden replied.

The garage was being emptied of detritus by their colleagues and they left it to cross to its other side. Here, between garage and boundary wall, sat the skip where officers — one at each end — struggled to remove a rolled-up rug.

"Once we get it empty, we'll hoist it up, see if anything's underneath," one said. A skip loader waited on the other side of the wall.

Black, Judy and Eden peered inside. They saw quite a lot of cardboard; an upturned comfy chair, one arm hanging off; a bathroom wall cabinet, doors shattered; broken kitchen cabinets, including a cracked Formica top; an old electric heater; and an old food mixer, which Eden thought was probably older than she was.

Inside the Orangery more colleagues dusted for prints. The three stopped to look around the long room. It had no windows to escape through, nor any furniture, not even shelves to hide in or behind. They left the officers to do their job and congregated on the small lawn outside. The tarpaulin concealing Ivy's sculpture had been removed, revealing an icosahedron. A uniformed officer named Fishergate, with his sleeves rolled-up (and his jacket neatly folded on the lawn), was precariously balanced half-way up a stepladder, attempting to dismantle the sculpture by variously hitting, pulling and twisting it in places. When nothing moved, Fishergate decided to step off the ladder and took hold of a bar with both hands. He swung it briefly before dropping it to the ground. "Yeah, it's definitely all one piece," he reported. "Smelted together."

Black looked up. The top of the sculpture had been left wide open in the shape of a regular pentagon. "You're slim, see if you can squeeze in and out," he said to Fishergate.

The officer stepped back onto the ladder, took hold of the sculpture and scrambled to its pinnacle where he lowered himself inside, quickly reappearing.

"Someone could've been hiding there," Black said. "Okay, it would mean crawling under the tarpaulin to get in, but that wouldn't be impossible."

"There weren't any footprints at the base, but they could've had a stepping plate," Fishergate informed them, jumping down from the top of the icosahedron.

Black moved to position himself just inside the hedge archway. "Could the killer have been inside the sculpture when the group were out here, then climbed out and followed them? Doesn't seem credible that the killer could've been on the group's heels the whole time without being seen?" he asked. "One lady stopped to tie her shoelaces. They all turned around when Nick Pilsworth peeled off. How would they not have seen him or her?"

"There is a way, Sir," Fishergate said. "If you could follow me into the grounds."

Black stepped aside to let the officer through the archway, before he, Judy and Eden followed him. Just inside the Herb Room Fishergate took a side-step and disappeared inside the hedge. He was back almost as quickly as he was gone. Black walked up to him. A diagonal slant cut into the hedge, invisible to anyone who didn't know it was there, gave access to the next garden room. They all piled through it into a long, narrow, featureless strip of grass. Black checked the map of the grounds provided by the family. This was the Buttercup Meadow Room, shown on the map as a blaze of summer yellow. It stretched the length of the Herb, Rose and Winter Rooms and ended in another tall hedge and another archway.

"That takes you through to the Topiary Room, which in turn takes you to within a spit of the beech tree," Fishergate said.

"Would the killer have had time to get there before the group?" Judy asked.

"Once out of the sculpture, they had a straight run. A fit person can move pretty quick when running flat out, Ma'am," was Fishergate's reply.

Black, Judy and Eden returned to the Herb Room and continued onto the Events Room along the route taken by the party on the day of the murder. They spent a few minutes at the bench and trellis by the wall. If the killer had entered or left this way, there was no sign of it. No footprints nor fingerprints had been found on the seat, the trellis, the wall or the ground around. Neither the trellis, nor the plant, was damaged. No bits of fabric had been ripped and left behind in the escape, nor strands of hair. Nothing to suggest a human being had clambered across it in a hurry.

They moved along the path and around the corner to the stone seat in the hedge alcove where Hugo had remained after separating himself from the tour group. Black took a seat and had a look around. Greenery encircled him. Its curves extended further than the seat and severely limited the range of his view.

"It's not obvious from here there's a path around the corner," he said.

While Judy remained standing a few feet from Black, Eden took herself back around the corner to stand halfway along the path with the entrances to the Winter Room and the Events Room behind her. "All I can see straight ahead is hedge," she said. "I can't see the way into the Topiary garden from here, nor either of you."

She rejoined them. Black said, "I'm on the phone. I'm surrounded by hedge three metres tall and sixty centimetres wide. I can't hear what's going on behind me any more than I can see." He got to his feet and took a few steps to look along the pathway. "The tour party are in the Topiary Room. What's there to stop Hugo running straight back the way he's come, killing his dad, and running back here?"

"Time?" Judy said.

"Well, let's see. I'm going to start running. Please time me."

He waited for Eden to move behind him and open the stopwatch on her phone. "Go!" she shouted. He jumped to his feet and sprinted around the corner and along the path, almost skidding as he hurtled through the archway into the Events Room. Eden was right behind him. Judy, the eldest, arrived last. Eden reached the archway just as Black reached the gate. He slapped it a couple of times and spun around. Eden and Judy, realising he was racing towards them, leapt out of the way. He ran past them and out of the archway where he turned to his right. Eden just managed to keep up. He stopped when he reached the stone chair, and Eden paused the stopwatch. "Under two minutes, Sir," she said. "One hundred and eight seconds to be precise."

"You haven't allowed much time for the murder, Guido," Judy said.

"I haven't," Black admitted. "But there's time in hand. And let's not forget, Hugo is younger than me."

"It would explain why his dad waited," Eden said. "But how did he get his dad's attention? Wouldn't one of the group have heard if he'd shouted 'Dad'?"

"Not necessarily," Black said. "The group aren't that close to events — they're chatting amongst themselves, engrossed in their surroundings. The hedges are noise flatteners."

"If it was him, where's the weapon?" Judy asked.

"In one of these hedges?" he suggested.

"It's a hell of a risk," Judy said.

"The profile of an opportunistic killer is very similar to and overlaps the profile of a risk taker," Eden reminded them. "Although, whether Hugo matches either profile, I'm not so sure."

"He had time and opportunity," Black said, "and by retracing his steps after his dad's body was found, he would have obliterated his own footsteps."

They moved to the double archway leading into the Events Room. Black paused to allow Judy and Eden to position themselves just inside, then walked into the space, turning as though to address people looking in. "No way was anyone lying in wait in the corners," he said. "They'd've stood out like a sore thumb. And Hugo was in here with him for bit. On to timings."

Eden started the stopwatch and he calmly walked over to the gate, walking slightly slower than his normal speed. There he stopped.

"Less than forty-seconds, Sir," Eden said.

"We know Tudor waited for the group to move off, so let's say fifty seconds, at most sixty, from the entrance to the gate," Black said.

Black removed his own specs and dropped them into the pocket of his jacket. With the stopwatch timing him again, he put them back on and pretended to input the code in the security panel. The gate clicked. "Fifteen seconds tops," Eden said.

"It wouldn't've taken him long to get through that gate once it opened. It couldn't have taken him more than a few minutes from setting off to the gate to it slamming closed behind him, max. He reached it, yet didn't go through it. He didn't budge from this space." Black looked around. "The killer could not have taken the same route through the grounds as Tudor and the tour party. If Hugo is our killer, he could have entered the same way as Tudor – but no one else could. If Hugo isn't our killer, our killer either came through this gate," he laid his hand on the wooden gate, "or emerged from the other side of the pond, most likely from behind the tree."

"I'll be the killer," Judy said. "It's my third favourite role play."

Black opened the gate for her, allowing it to close completely once she was through it. They now knew the code had only been inputted once. Black entered it, the gate unlocked, and Black gave it a push, forcing Judy to step backwards to avoid being hit.

"If our killer came through the gate, he or she either started from there," she pointed to the side facing the open gate, "or now has a black eye. Okay, the gate's open. Did the killer just barge in or did Tudor step to one side?"

"Let's try both," Black said. Although he could have easily prevented her getting any further, he let Judy push past him into the Events Room. He had to take a couple of steps backwards to do so. "I'm not in the same place I started – I'm facing away from the gate, which has closed. Why do I then turn my back on you?"

"To prevent the gate from closing?" Eden suggested.

"I'd have thought I would've been more interested in the person who's just burst through it, but let's try it."

He re-opened the gate, moved back, then lunged forward to stop it swinging closed. "If I'm stabbed in the back in this position, I'm falling half-in/half-out of the gate."

"You've also run out of time," Eden said. "The Angeles have just appeared, wondering what's going on."

"Let's have another go. This time I'll invite you in," Black said.

Judy resumed her position outside the gate, with Eden back

on the stopwatch. The gate swung open. "Hello, what are you doing here?" Black said.

"Easier than going around," Judy said.

Black stepped back, and Judy stepped inside. "Hello, goodbye," Black said, moving quickly to prevent the gate from closing. One hand on the gate, he turned around. "If I'm holding the gate open to allow you in, I am facing you and you're not going to stab me in the back. If I let you step through the gate, then turn my back on you, again I'm landing more in than out, and..."

"... you'll be wedged in the gate, forcing me to clamber over you or be trapped inside," Judy said.

"With no time to escape before the Angeles appear," Eden added.

"If I'm here to kill you, which I must be as I'm armed, and I'm on the other side of this gate, why would I step through it? Why not hide up and wait until you're outside with me?" Judy said.

"The killer didn't come through the gate. That just leaves the tree," Black said. "I'll be the killer this time."

He strode to the pond and crossed the bridge to conceal himself behind the large beech tree where he was completely invisible. Eden waited for him to reappear before starting her stopwatch. He made his way along the narrow strip of lawn edging the pond and strolled across the lawn in the direction of the gate. He did this neither hurriedly nor unhurriedly, but at his normal pace. He reached them, and Eden said, "Just over a minute, Sir. Maybe an extra twenty or thirty seconds if they took the bridge."

"Must have had an exchange of words at least," Judy said.

"Not to mention the time it took to kill Tudor, open the gate and escape," Eden added. She stopped the watch and showed the time recording.

"The killer sure escaped by the skin of their teeth," Judy said.

"The killer can't just have emerged from behind that tree without Tudor noticing. It's not possible. Yet Tudor neither tried to escape, nor called for help. In fact, he seems to have calmly waited for his killer to join him before turning his back. Why? Was his killer pointing a gun at him? Why then was he stabbed?" Black asked.

"No silencer? Too much noise?" Eden suggested.

"A credible scenario, but why kill him here?" Black said. "Why not lead him away to somewhere more remote, like the windmill? Even the field outside?"

"Who would just stand there as someone approached from all the way over there with a gun in one hand and a pitchfork in the other?" Judy said. "With all those people nearby? No one."

"He waited because whoever it was, they didn't pose any threat," Eden said.

Chapter 9

FROM THE TREEHOUSE, Black drove to his first appointment of the day, a meeting with the O'Connell's family solicitor, Robert Standley.

"Detective Inspector," a voice rang out from the intercom. "Do please come up. I'll meet you at the top of the stairs. It's four flights, I'm afraid, and there isn't a lift."

The stairs were narrow and flanked by woodchipped walls with banisters embedded in the walls. The exertion left Black slightly out of breath and vowing to take the stairs more often. He climbed the last flight and there stood Robert Standley, dressed in green tweed, waiting on the small landing outside a door announcing *Robert Standley and Co.*

"You get used to them after a while," Standley said. Black would've put Standley at past retirement age. Through the door was an open-plan room shared by two people, one typing, the other on the phone. There was a small waiting area to the side. A door at the end of this room took them into Standley's spacious office. A desk and the usual office furniture took up one side, some comfortable chairs surrounding a wooden table the other. This is where the men sat.

"Can you tell me a little about the Gethsemane Trust?" Black said.

"Allow me to begin by telling you a little about myself and my involvement with the Trust," Robert Standley replied. "For many years, I was part of a partnership which was privileged to act for Emlyn and Gethsemane. I sort of inherited Tudor from them. When the partnership split, Tudor asked me to continue to represent the O'Connell family Trust. I agreed and now work exclusively for the Trust, in that I have no other clients. As you can see, I am well past retirement age, but as long as this works," he playfully slapped his head, "and this works," he slapped his heart, "I'll keep turning up for work."

One of Standley's colleagues brought a tray of coffee and shortbread biscuits through and placed it on the table.

"Have one, Detective Inspector," Robert Standley said, pouring Black a cup. "I know you're not meant to when on duty, but I won't tell. I can recommend the biscuits. My wife makes them. Milk and sugar?"

Black helped himself to a piece of shortbread and said, "Just milk, please."

The solicitor continued, "Gethsemane was a prodigiously talented young artist who had the good fortune to marry Emlyn O'Connell. Emlyn was already Dad to Mungo, and Tudor came along quite quickly. It seems to have been a love match as well as a business match. Emlyn combined a nose for talent with very good business sense. He was the brains behind the Gethsemane brand. Tragically, an aneurysm took Gethsemane from us when Tudor was still a teenager. Emlyn sensibly set up the Gethsemane Trust to protect his son's interests. He continued to promote her all his life, as Tudor O'Connell – and, I have to say, Bettina, have done since. Her reputation continues to grow. Her resurgence in recent years is behind the family's decision to open up the TreeHouse grounds and studio to the public."

"I'm trying to dig down to how the money's organised," Black said.

"In the first instance, all income and capital belong to the Trust and are held by the trustees on behalf of the beneficiaries. The beneficiaries begin to draw an income from the Trust at eighteen, and at twenty-one receive a lump sum. There were sufficient funds in the Trust for Hugo and Lilah to be privately educated, as Degas will be if her mother wishes it."

"Who are the beneficiaries of the Trust?"

"Until his death, Tudor O'Connell was a beneficiary, as are his three children and all remote issue."

"Do any of them stand to gain financially from Tudor O'Connell's death?" Black inquired.

"None of them benefits directly from the death of their father, but indirectly they do in that a proportion of the Trust income is divided between the beneficiaries, with the rest reinvested. Tudor's death therefore frees up a certain percentage of the income. Whether that is sufficient motive for patricide is your call, not mine," Robert Standley said, adding, "It goes without saying that the 'no one can benefit from a crime' rule applies to Trust funds as to everything else."

"If Tudor and Ivy kept producing children, those children would cut into the current children's inheritance?"

"They would, yes, but without wanting to sound like the defence, the Trust is in good shape and set to get better with the public opening and expansion of the product range. Interest in arts and crafts is exploding. The kids aren't going to be short of a penny or two. There's life in the old girl yet."

"Who are the trustees?"

"Bettina was a trustee but recently resigned with umbrage."

"Umbrage?" Black asked.

"She wanted to stay on but with the divorce it wasn't practical. The trustees are now myself and a partner in the accountancy firm the Trust retains. Tudor O'Connell was a trustee and will need to be replaced. At the moment it seems likely his son Hugo will take his place as he is more involved with the Trust than his sister, but that's a decision still to be reached."

"Did you also act for Tudor O'Connell in his personal capacity?" Black asked.

"Ordinarily I did," Robert Standley said, "but when he separated from Bettina, I advised him to instruct a divorce lawyer as I felt my involvement might be a conflict of interest. He took my advice. Terms have been agreed. The Trust is to purchase a small bungalow fairly close by for Bettina's use during her lifetime. She's to stay on as manager for at least a year. The Trust has agreed to provide her with a small income for life. In recognition of her contribution over the years."

"Does any of that change with his death?"

"It won't."

"What about Ivy?" Black asked.

"As things stand, Ivy is currently not provided for," Robert Standley said. "Tudor's income was derived from the Trust, and the TreeHouse is owned by it. Tudor intimated that he and Ivy were to marry once the divorce was through. He gave Bettina more than he had to, just to get the divorce over with as quickly and painlessly as possible. That said, Bettina, Hugo and Lilah have indicated their agreement to my idea of granting Ivy a small allowance from the Trust until Degas turns eighteen."

"Is there anything else you can think might help the case?" Black asked.

"Not presently."

Chapter 10

AT HER STATION DESK, Eden logged on to the TreeHouse website. Stretched across the top of the homepage was a photograph of the TreeHouse taken in hazy sunlight, shimmering against a clear blue sky. Below the photograph came the text:

The TreeHouse was once home to Emlyn and Gethsemane O'-Connell. Gethsemane is generally considered one of the most inspirational female artists of the twentieth century. It was in her studio that she created her most famous pieces of art, including the Tree of Life, *immortalised as the Gethsemane Print.*

Below that came one of the many versions of the *Tree of Life* created by Gethsemane. In this version, fruit and foliage shaped from jewels hung from the branches of an exquisitely hand-painted tree against a backdrop of tiny dots — blue for the sky, green and yellow for the meadow. *Look carefully, can you see the mythical beast concealed?* the caption invited. Eden narrowed her eyes and saw a serpent within the tree, coiled up the trunk: its many tails, the tree's roots; its many heads, the tree's branches. *Gethsemane's style was partly post-modern expressionist, part Anglo-Saxon, part uniquely her,* announced the caption.

A link took her to pictures of various settings in the

grounds. All taken in the summer. The text invited visitors *to walk through the garden rooms designed by Gethsemane and Emlyn,* described as a *delight to gardeners and garden lovers alike,* promising themed garden rooms, open views, frequent seats, a café and a gift shop. Above an image of her studio, described as *perfectly preserved to retain her character,* Gethsemane O'Connell's family proclaimed its delight at its forthcoming opening to the public. They promised more details shortly. The webpage didn't mention Tudor O'Connell's untimely death. There was a link to Gethsemane's artwork and another link to the merchandise pages. The first of the items for sale, Eden noticed, wasn't connected to Gethsemane O'Connell, but was one of Ivy's weird sculptures.

We're delighted to offer you the chance to own an original piece of artwork by talented sculptress Ivy Lee-O'Connell. POA.

A photograph of Ivy was followed by:

"I love to work with icosahedrons. I never know what direction I'll be taken in. For me, the nonconformity in size and shape of an icosahedron represents our journey through life."

Ivy Lee-O'Connell.

Yes, but is it art? Eden thought. She Googled *Sculptress Ivy Lee-O'Connell.* The webpage portrayed Ivy as a serious and successful artist in her own right, but every mention Eden found of Ivy was made in conjunction with the O'Connells or the TreeHouse. She returned to the webpage. Eden wasn't inspired to buy an icosahedron sculpture. She didn't have the space and POA was shorthand for ludicrously expensive.

She began scrolling through the other merchandise for sale, making a note to purchase a pretty wastepaper bin in the Gethsemane Print for Dora's Christmas stocking. The merchandise ended in gardening gifts. After trowels, tree-face decorations, gloves, and seed tins adorned with the Gethsemane Print, a collection of cast-iron garden stakes caught her attention. She leant forward, concentrating not on the innocuous garden decorations topped variously with a bulrush, a sunflower, or a poppy seed head, but on their two-pronged base — a pair of lethal sharp spikes.

Eden reached for the phone. "I think I may have identified the murder weapon."

Chapter 11

THE NEXT MORNING saw Eden called back to the TreeHouse. She was first to arrive and made her way to the study to await Black, stopping outside the door to admire its stained-glass fanlight in the image of a tree.

Inside the room only the larger items of furniture remained: sturdy leather wing chairs, a leather-topped oak desk, and a dismantled antique globe.

"Give us a hand, will you?" a voice called across the room as she gazed around.

She crossed to the French windows where her colleague was in the process of reassembling a piece of furniture, taken apart in the ongoing investigation. Although it was still early, the two officers in the study were coming to the end of long shift. "Put your paw on there, would you?" he asked, pointing to a cut-glass headrest.

"What on earth is it?" she asked.

"Apparently, it's what's known as an Indian mirrored loveseat," her colleague answered. Eden noticed the beginnings of a moustache on his upper lip. She gripped hold of the headrest and held it steady as her colleague screwed it back into place to complete the piece of furniture.

The loveseat was the size of a two-seater sofa. It stood on four cut-glass legs, its back, seat, armrests and headrest made from intricately decorated cut glass. Back, seat and armrests were upholstered in blue velvet. The ornate headrest was finished off with a pair of carved finials. "Imagine having to keep that smudge free," Eden said.

"Over here, when you're ready," the second police officer in the room requested.

She crossed to the other side of the room to help hold a picture steady as its frame was re-secured to its backboard. She saw a numbered list, made in immaculate handwriting, varnished to the picture's backboard:

1. Cat (first floor)

2. Swan wings (sails)

"Are they dodos?" she asked of three birds in descending size, apparently flying.

"How should I know?" her colleague replied.

"I thought they were flightless," Eden muttered, noticing that one of them was also pregnant.

It took the two of them to rehang the large picture on the wall — a three-dimensional artwork titled *Arc of Life*. Eden stepped back to take a better look. It was the Arc at sea. The artwork was 3-D in places. Her eyes took in a golden dragonfly hovering above a fat dog sleeping on deck, a cat peering out of a porthole on the first floor, a sweet little monkey climbing the rigging, an ox walking the plank, a giraffe with a bird's nest ruff keeping watch, and a dragon, tail tied to the mask, fluttering in the wind. The list on the rear, she realised, was an index of the lifeforms featured in the picture alongside their location. She took a photo of it, both from the front and at an angle to better capture its three-dimensional aspects. She'd have it turned into a print for Dora.

"How much do you think it's worth?" Eden asked.

"It's not genuine," her search-team colleague informed her.

"They're all replicas. The originals are worth a packet. What's made from glass and semiprecious stones in the ones in the house are made from precious stones in the originals. The house would get done over if they kept them here."

"Do you have a cat?" Eden asked, staring at the cat in the painting who appeared to be staring back. She moved to one side then the other. The cat's eyes definitely followed her.

Her colleague briefly made eye contact. "Two," she said.

"Are they always there in the morning? Our cat didn't come in last night. She's always in the utility room when I come down. But she wasn't there this morning. And her food hadn't been touched. Is that normal?"

"I never let mine out. Too much traffic round my way."

"I don't know what I'm going to tell my kid if something's happened to her."

Black walked into the room, nodded at Eden, and said, "What've you got for us?"

The first officer Eden had assisted strolled to the desk and picked something up from it: a small jewellery box, lid down. The officer opened it, revealing a set of pearl button-ball earrings nestled inside.

"What am I looking at? Black asked.

"Pair of freshwater cultured pearl earrings on solid silver studs inside a lined box, Sir," the officer said.

"Where were they found?"

"Recovered from inside the globe. The globe was intact and didn't look from appearances to have been tampered with." The antique globe he spoke of stood in the corner. Its lower half, now an empty shell, remained on its steel axis, prised apart from its upper half which was on the floor in its own evidence bag. "We've carried out a thorough search of the study, Sir, but apart from these earrings, we haven't found a thing. Odd place to leave a pair of earrings, inside a globe."

In an interview room, Black and Eden re-interviewed Bettina O'Connell. Bettina was accompanied by her solicitor, Robert Standley, who, although not a criminal lawyer, had agreed as her family solicitor to sit in on the interview. Standley was dressed for the part of the country solicitor in corduroy trousers, a checked shirt, tie, and a tweed jacket with leather elbow patches.

"Just so you are aware, Bettina," Black said, "this interview is being recorded by the black box in the corner with the flashing red light you can see. The interview is also being filmed." He pointed to a domed camera on the ceiling.

"There was a slight delay in your answering the door to Harry and Will Thorne. Why was that, Mrs O'Connell?" Eden asked.

"If you must know, I was on the bog, dear. I've got piles. My GP will confirm."

Next to her, Robert Standley looked embarrassed.

"According to your own statement, you feigned illness to return to the front of the house, having decided on impulse to hijack Thorne's digger to drive at the cottage," Black said.

Before Bettina could speak, Robert Standley leant forward. "Bettina is extremely upset and remorseful for her actions. Despite any appearances to the contrary, she didn't plan any of it. Quite the opposite. The idea behind employing the Thornes was to demonstrate her willingness to be part of the new venture. Everything which happened did so spontaneously and without premeditation. Bettina saw the keys in the ignition and the idea came from nowhere. To repeat, Bettina is extremely sorry for her actions."

Eden studied her. She was smartly turned out in matching

slacks and a jumper. On the morning in question, she'd been dressed in a designer silk dress along with the gold necklace and the crucifix she still wore. On her feet she'd worn court shoes. Was that really attire chosen by a woman hellbent on demolition?

"I snapped," Bettina said. "The sight of the Thornes brought it all home. I was being forced out of my home by that marriage breaker."

"I'm not concerned with that part of the morning, Mrs O'-Connell. I'm concerned with the murder of your husband," Black said. "We merely need to establish the sequence of events."

"Well, I couldn't have done it, could I?" Bettina said. "I was bulldozing his love-nest when he was..." She looked away. "The last thing I said to him was to ask him how he could live with himself. God help me."

Black put the earring case in front of Bettina. After referencing them for the record, he opened the case to reveal the pearl earrings and said, "Do you recognise these, Bettina?"

She leant forward to study them and scratched one with her thumb nail. "They're not mine. They're cultured. I don't do cultured pearls."

"We believe these are the earrings Ivy accused you of stealing after your son's wedding," Eden said. "They were found inside the antique globe in your late husband's study."

"She had them the whole time?" Bettina said. "And she had the audacity to accuse me of being a thief. Me!" She slapped herself on the chest a few times in indignation. "I don't know what her problem is. Hasn't she hurt me enough?"

"We don't actually know if they were deliberately hidden or by whom," Eden said.

"They could scarcely be accidentally hidden inside a globe, I would suggest," Robert Standley said.

Bettina's eyes narrowed. "She put them there to make out

I'm some kind of bunny-boiler! I bet she's behind all that other stuff she's been harping on about getting."

"Are you referring to the anonymous and sometimes unpleasant items Ms Ivy Lee-O'Connell has received over the past two years or so?" Black said.

"I am."

"And you know nothing about that?" Eden asked.

"Not a thing. None of that had anything to do with me, I can assure you of that," Bettina said. "And may I point out that her name is Ivy Lee. I was still Tudor O'Connell's wife when he died, and I am his widow — not her."

"What's your opinion about the items sent to Ivy, Bettina? Was the whole thing some kind of campaign waged against her or some weird practical joke?" Eden asked.

"Bettina has already told you she knows nothing about that," Robert Standley said. "Nor can I see the relevance to the matter in hand."

"Bettina, I want to show you another piece of evidence," Black said. After citing the reference number, he directed Bettina to turn to a letter in the folder in front of her. "This is a copy of a letter found on Tudor O'Connell on the morning of his death."

Eden read the letter out loud: *If you want to know who's been sending those presents to your lovely lady meet me at the windmill...*

"He broke off from the tour party to go to the windmill?" Bettina asked.

"It would appear so," Eden said.

"It would've been nice to have been told that," Bettina said. "I am his widow."

"I apologise, Bettina, if we've caused you any distress. It's certainly not our intention," Black said. "Have you seen this letter before?"

"Of course, I haven't. I wish people would listen to me. I don't know anything about that. Wouldn't surprise me if Tudor wasn't behind the whole thing. Smear my name and make him and her into victims."

"Who else knew about the items Ivy received?" Eden said.

"Everyone. The whole bloody village. No doubt they all believe sad Bettina's behind it. Hell hath no fury." She started to cry. "I'm sorry. It's becoming too much for me." Bettina dabbed her eyes. "Just because my husband stopped loving me, doesn't mean I stopped loving him."

Robert Standley spoke. "Detective Inspector, my client has denied involvement with the campaign and told you she knows nothing about the letter. Bettina couldn't have killed Tudor. She was nowhere near where the attack took place."

The interview over, Eden gave Bettina details of a counselling service for the victims of crime. "It's entirely confidential and free," she said.

Next to be re-interviewed was Ivy Lee-O'Connell. The interview took place in an adjacent interview room. "Tudor wasn't found with a phone on him. Was that normal for him?" Black asked.

Ivy sighed. "He only had an old phone Bettina gave him. He never used it. It lived in the drawer."

Black produced the pearl earrings. "Are these the same earrings you wore to Hugo O'Connell's wedding reception, which you later accused Mrs Bettina O'Connell of stealing?"

Ivy buried her face in her hands. "I knew this would happen." She peered up childishly, through open fingers. "Okay, okay — they're mine."

"They were found inside the globe in Tudor's study," Eden said. Ivy looked down, then up guiltily. "Are we to take it that you put them in the globe, Ivy?"

Ivy nodded. "For the record, Ms Ivy Lee-O'Connell has

nodded. Did you put the earrings in the globe before or after you accused Mrs O'Connell of stealing them, Ivy?" Eden asked.

"I'll level with you," Ivy said. "At the reception, I spilt wine on my dress and went to wash it out. In doing so, I very nearly lost an earring down the sink. I decided to take them off and put them in my jacket pocket for safe keeping. I left the jacket on my chair. When I got to my hotel room at the end of the evening, I discovered they weren't where I'd put them. I was so sure Bettina had taken them to spite me. I said so to Tudor. He told me I was being ridiculous. We had a big fight. I threatened to call the police if he didn't say something to her, and I made him call her room. I could hear her shouting down the phone. When we got home the next day, the atmosphere was terrible. Worse than ever. I was so sure she'd taken them. Eventually, I took the dress and jacket to the dry cleaners. They rang me up to say they'd found some pearl earrings in an inside pocket. I'd forgotten the jacket had an inside pocket." She looked down and up again, giggling childishly. "They were there the whole time. Exactly where I'd put them. I remember putting them there."

"What we don't understand is how they ended up in the globe in the study?" Eden persisted.

"I wasn't big enough to own my mistake," she said, sheepishly, "but I didn't want to give up the earrings either. They were my grandmother's. It was easier to hide them where no one would find them and say nothing. I'm not proud of it. I realise now how my accusations caused her to start sending me such hateful material."

"You still believe Mrs O'Connell was responsible for that?" Eden asked.

"Who else? You saw for yourself what she's capable of."

"If you were so certain it was Bettina behind things, why then did Tudor decide to go to the windmill when he received the letter? He could've been walking into anything. Why didn't he just ignore it?" Eden asked.

"It didn't seem dangerous. It was mid-morning. A public place. If I'd known this was going to happen, I'd have wrapped myself around his legs to stop him from going." She wiped her eyes.

"Even so," Eden said, "with a tour group to show around, I really can't see why he went, particularly when you were certain Bettina was behind everything anyway."

"We needed proof it was her. Something to confront her with to make her stop. She killed my little bird. The little lapwing I rescued. That was just cruel. She's deranged, I really believe it. When she did that, Tudor promised me he'd report her to the police, but when I rang them for a follow-up, they didn't know anything about it. He hadn't kept his word. That's the worst thing. I was still angry with him for breaking his promise to me and lying. That's why he decided to go to the windmill. He felt guilty for lying to me. That's your reason, Detective Sergeant. Guilt."

"Do you have any idea who sent that letter, Ivy?" Eden asked.

"Val Simpson. It had to be. She knows Bettina best of all."

"Why do you think Val suddenly decided to speak up, if she knew all the time?" Eden said.

"Val is a good person and a good friend to Bettina, but I think the bird was a step too far. She decided to stop things from getting worse. That is all in the past now. I genuinely didn't understand why Bettina couldn't move on. Now I do. She lost him, but she still loved him. She was furious. I've lost him," she touched her heart. "I'm furious. That's why Tudor chose to ignore her games. That's why he didn't go to the police. He understood what I didn't. He got it."

"Can I ask where Degas is?" Eden said.

"She's with my mum, visiting family. I thought it would be

easier with her out of the way, what with the renovation works and the tours." She buried her head in her hands. "How am I going to tell my little girl she's lost her daddy when I can't accept it myself? How?"

From across the desk, Eden unfolded a map of the grounds. Hugo pointed and said, "I was here, on the phone, when I heard a crash coming from the direction of the house which I now know was Mum playing at being Niki Lauda. Now what? I thought. I decided to get the group as far away as possible. I'd just stood up when I heard yelling from across the hedge. I ran inside and collided with Nico. He said Dad had had a heart attack. I didn't really take it in. Nico had to push me along the path." He looked down. "When I saw Dad lying there, all I could think was – *Not again. I can't believe it's happening again.*"

Black and Eden glanced at each other.

"Can you tell us what you mean by that, Hugo?" Eden asked.

Hugo raised his hands defensively. His voice rose an octave. "I don't want to talk about it. I can't. I can't. Ask Lilah or my mum." He looked pleadingly at them.

"Would you like a break, Hugo?" Black said.

Hugo shook his head. "I want to help. But I can't talk about that."

"Okay. I want to talk more about the man calling himself Nick Pilsworth," Black said.

"I've been thinking about that. He could've doubled back on himself. There's a hole in the hedge here." On the map, Hugo indicated the cut-through in the Herb Room hedge.

"How would he have known about that?" Black asked.

"I can't say. Saw it when he passed? Already knew about it somehow?"

On her phone, Eden called up an e-fit of Nick Pilsworth

that Hugo had helped to create. The man in the picture was heavily lined, white-haired and bearded. When she'd first seen it, Eden had said: *He really does look like an ageing werewolf.*

"How confident are you that this accurately resembles the man who arrived at the TreeHouse on the morning of your Father's death, calling himself Nick Pilsworth?" she said.

Hugo studied the photo. "Pretty much, I'd say. He was well wrapped up; scarf, bobble hat, thick, thick glasses. Had a bit of a hump." Hugo touched his upper back. "When I first saw him, I wondered if he had some degenerative bone disease."

"You claimed to have been on the phone trying to contact Denys the whole time. Didn't it strike you as suspicious when no one picked up after you pressed redial?" Black said.

"In hindsight. But at the time I wanted it to be Denys so much I wasn't thinking straight." He leaned forward and pinched his nose with his fingertips. When he looked up, tears were streaming down his face. "My dad's dead and the one person I need more than anyone in the world won't talk to me."

"Are you sure you wouldn't like a break, Hugo?" Eden said.

"I want to help. It's all I can do for him now."

"Could you describe your relationship with your late father, please?" Black asked. He didn't want to ask the question, but he had to.

Hugo hesitated. "I wasn't the son he'd hoped for. He made that clear enough. But I didn't kill him. I couldn't. I wouldn't."

They didn't have any further questions. Eden gave Hugo details of the bereavement counselling services that she'd given to Bettina and Ivy. "Do please take advantage," she said. He pocketed the business card and mumbled his thanks.

In another room, they spoke to Lilah O'Connell. "Your sketch book merely proves you can sketch, Lilah. I'm afraid it doesn't prove where you were when your father was killed," Eden said.

"Can't help that. It's where I was, sketching away," she replied, coolly. "I even got a nettle sting." She showed the team her still-swollen hand.

"How would you describe your relationship with your father?" Black asked.

"I'd like to think we were close — you know, the dad/daughter thing. It hasn't sunk in yet, him dying like he did. I keep asking myself, what would Dad's take be on this?"

"How did your father's new relationship impact his relationship with you?" Eden said.

"No one can ever displace a daughter from her dad's affection, can they?" Lilah said.

"How is your relationship with Ms Ivy Lee-O'Connell?" Eden said.

"Not much to say. We'll never be besties, but we're cordial."

"She displaced your mum," Eden said.

"I'm not a little girl. My parents' marriage didn't make it. It happens."

"You visited a garden centre a day or so ago," Black said.

"I did."

"Why that particular one, Lilah? There are closer garden centres," Black said.

"I couldn't face all the *Oh my God! How are things?* comments I'd get if I met someone I knew."

"Some might find it unusual to go bulb shopping a few days after a parent is murdered," Black said.

"I needed to do something to take my mind off things. Seemed like a good idea. It'll be spring soon. If I was guilty of patricide, which I'm not, I wouldn't be so stupid as to bury the murder weapon in a planter in my back garden. I noticed you came back for a second look and had a dig around, managing to damage some of my new plants, by the way."

"Just one more question if we may, Lilah," Black said. "Your brother said that when he saw your father on the ground, he couldn't believe it was happening again, but was unable to tell us what he meant."

"He was talking about Uncle Mungo. It was all very unfortunate. Hugo and Denys had just come back from their honeymoon and Mungo took Hugo out drinking. Denys didn't want to go." Lilah rolled her eyes. "They got blind drunk, ended up at Mungo's flat. Hugo woke up to find Mungo dead. He'd passed out and choked on his own vomit." She paused. "Hugo almost had a breakdown. Everyone told him it wasn't his fault – Denys, Mum, me. Even Dad. But he completely blamed himself. Still does. He was sure he'd turned Mungo on his side. Maybe he did, and Mungo rolled back over? Who knows? They were both pie-eyed. Hugo'll take the guilt of it to his grave. That's Hugo for you." She looked quite upset. "The wedding was the last time I saw Mungo. I'd gone outside for a smoke and when I got back, he'd left for London. I never got the chance to say my goodbyes. Why does that keep happening?"

Their last interview was with Val Simpson. "Why did you choose to pick apples on the same morning you needed to cook them, Val?" Black asked.

"Annie had sold out at the shop, what with Halloween," Val Simpson replied. "I pass the orchard on the way in. There's always more than enough, even at this time of year."

"Can I ask if there was any ill-feeling between you and Tudor O'Connell?" Black said.

"None whatsoever. Why would there be?"

"What do you think of his leaving Bettina for Ivy?" Eden asked.

"None of my business."

"You must have a view?" Eden asked.

"There's no bigger fool, springs to mind. Still doesn't make it my business," Val said.

"Must have been difficult at times, though," Eden said.

"Now and then one or the other would say, *Can't you get him/her to see sense?* I always refused to be drawn in. No way was I going to be piggy in the middle."

"How do you get along with Ivy Lee-O'Connell?" Eden asked.

"She leaves me alone, lets me get on with stuff."

"We've been informed there was some tension and she wasn't happy with the idea of you running the café," Eden said.

Val Simpson snorted, "Maybe she was, and maybe she wasn't, but in the end, they had no choice. No one put it to me in so many words, but Tudor needed me to stay to stop Bettina and Ivy killing each other. I agreed. My husband was a good deal older than me and left me quite well off. I have another house I rent out and enough capital to be comfortable. I'll be retiring in a few years, but until then I need something to do. Things changed with Ivy's arrival. She has some strange ideas. But the young do, don't they? If there was a choice between working for Ivy and Tudor or finding a new job for the next few years, I'd pick Ivy and Tudor. Better the devil you know."

Black showed Val a copy of the letter that was sent to Tudor: *If you want to know who's been sending those presents to your lovely lady meet me at the windmill...*

"Did you send this letter?" Black asked.

Val looked genuinely surprised. "Never seen it before."

"It's been suggested you sent the letter to stop things getting any worse."

"I'm not stupid enough to get mixed up in that business."

"Who do you believe sent Ivy the strange items, Val?" Black said.

"I genuinely don't know. I don't want it to be Bettina. I've known her for a long time. She's adamant it's nothing to do with her. Told me she was really hurt that anyone could think that of her. Father Hanrahan swears she's innocent and she tells him everything. What happened to that poor little bird was sickening. I can't believe her capable of such spite, but when I saw her at the wheel of that digger thing, she was a woman possessed. She's on antidepressants and sleeping tablets. I'm wondering if she's hitting the bottle after dark on top of all the drugs. She might not even remember what she's done. Oh, I don't know. Everything's got so out of hand, and now Tudor's dead."

Chapter 12

"THE DIMENSIONS of the spikes fit the size and distance of the wounds," Matt said, clutching a seventy centimetre metal garden stake. He was at one end of a sports pavilion. Eden, Pilot and Black were at the other. In between them a dead pig, obtained that day from an abattoir, hung from the ceiling. Eden hadn't slept well the night before. The cat still hadn't returned. She'd even got up in the early hours to check if she was back, but no sign. She must look a complete wreck, she thought. Was her hair doing that thing it did when she was tired? She felt herself instinctively trying to flatten it down.

Oh, pull yourself together and focus, woman, she told herself, crossing her hands in her lap. Matt seemed oblivious to this. He held the stake just below its daffodil flower head, tapped the daffodil and said, "This would act a bit like a pommel on a sword and help with the grip."

He handed the stake to a young man next to him. "The pig's back is at the same height as the victim's when he was attacked." Matt stepped to one side. "Whenever you're ready, son."

His assistant took a step back and, holding the garden stalk as though it were a javelin, thrust it into the dead pig's back with one clean strike. Eden's mouth fell wide open and Pilot swore. The young man let go. The stake remained in place. The three moved closer to have a look.

"No wonder the poor bugger was dead before he hit the floor," Black said, lifting his glasses to peer at the stake poking out of the animal's back. "Could a woman do that?"

"Feasibly, depending on the woman. You've seen the strength it takes, though. Why do you think I let him do it?" Matt replied. "The element of surprise would help."

"What about blood splatter?" Pilot asked, walking around the pig.

"Add the distance between the assailant and the victim to the heavy coat worn by the victim, and it's possible the assailant got away with very little," Matt said.

"Realistically, could the killer have hurled the stake over the wall to an accomplice?" Black asked, thinking out loud.

"Not without leaving evidence," Matt said, "like drops of blood, or perhaps a hole in the ground."

"Or in a sheep," Pilot said.

"The murder weapon is still somewhere in the grounds waiting to be found, or the killer left with it," Black said.

Eden and Pilot climbed the station stairs together; her to keep fit, him to shift a few pounds. Their steps matched.

"I'm picturing an audacious killer running at full pelt across a sheep-filled field, holding a garden stake dripping with blood. Then what happened?" Eden said. "The killer can't have got very far like that, can they? If he or she escaped on a motorbike, as seems likely, what did they do with the stake? They can't have been holding it the whole way."

"I'm picturing two saddlebags, one on each wheel," Pilot said. "No one would notice a thing."

"It's looking more and more premeditated," Eden said.

Pilot stopped to catch his breath, while she suppressed a yawn.

"Cat still not back?" he said.

"If she's not back by tonight, I'm putting up posters."

"When I was a kid, we lost a cat."

"Please tell me you found it."

"Oh, yeah," he said. "Most of it. A fox got its head."

Chapter 13

BLACK GATHERED THE TEAM TOGETHER. "The deceased suffered two similar stab wounds, through both sides of the ribcage, by a pair of sharp, pointed narrow blades. The injury punctured and collapsed both lungs and resulted in massive internal bleeding, cardiac and respiratory arrest. The victim died almost instantaneously." He held aloft a garden stake. "We now believe the murder weapon was one of these. These garden stakes are found throughout the property and are also sold on the webpage and in many garden centres. I'm now going to play a reconstruction."

In silence, the team watched the dead pig being stabbed with a garden stake.

"The choice of murder weapon resulted in minimal blood splatter, although blood splatter is still a possible route to conviction," Black said. "Particles of microscopic plastic coating have been recovered from the murder scene, the adjoining field, and from the deceased's clothing. These microscopic particles match the coating sprayed on the TreeHouse garden stakes. These particles are likely to appear on the attacker's clothing. This opens another window to conviction. The post-mortem has revealed that the health of our sixty-three-year-old victim was perfectly normal for a man of his age and physical condition, and he had no apparent medical condition likely to cause his imminent death. On his current regime he could have lived for the next twenty years. We have the blood results back. His blood contained traces of medication for sleeping and he'd had a couple of glasses of wine the night before."

An aerial photograph of the Events Room was projected on to the overhead screen. Black, standing to one side of the screen, used a pointer to take the team back through the events of the morning. "I have now returned to the scene with Detective Sergeant Hudson and Detective Superintendent McDermott. We've established that the killer can't have followed the party through the three garden rooms to enter the space through the double archway. The position of the body rules out the killer having entered the murder scene through the gate. In one scenario, the son – Hugo – had just enough time to double back on himself, kill his father, and get back. But it's very tight. If Hugo was our killer, we'd expect to find more evidence of the crime on him than we have. There is also the question of how he disposed of the still-undiscovered murder weapon. We can't rule out an accomplice.

"In another scenario the killer was already in place, either hiding behind the beech tree or possibly in the archway between the Events Room and the Topiary Room when Tudor entered. The tree affords better cover. Here the killer is invisible to the group of people all the way down to here," he pointed to the pathway between the gardens. "We don't know how long our killer was in place." He moved the cursor to the Herb Room. "We found a concealed tunnel cut into the hedge here. This takes us to the other side of the Herb Room. From there it's straight ahead to the Topiary Room, and from there to the beech tree. This opens the possibility that Nick Pilsworth used this route to reach the tree after separating from the group.

"However, another possibility has opened up." A photograph of Ivy's sculpture appeared. "This sculpture was under a tarpaulin on the day of the murder. We've established that, although the space is a bit cramped, someone could have been concealed inside it. I racked my brains to come up with a reason why. Then I got it. Tudor could have taken more than one route that morning. By hiding inside the sculpture, the killer would gain the advantage by discovering the route to be taken, allowing our killer to head Tudor off. Once out of the sculpture, a man or woman, running at full tilt, could have beaten the group to the Events Room."

He gave the team a bit of time to digest this information. "Let's move to the murder itself. Our killer may be invisible when behind the tree, but the moment our killer steps out from the hiding place they become instantly visible. We know Tudor reached the gate. He'd taken out his reading glasses to tap in the key code, suggesting this was the moment he saw his killer. Yet he didn't try and escape, nor raise the alarm, even as the killer drew nearer and nearer. This, despite the number of people close enough to hear him yell for help. Instead, he waited for his killer to join him. He was not killed face on, he had turned his back on his killer – I suggest to key in the code and lead the way out of the gate. This strongly suggests killer and victim knew each other. This raises as many questions as it answers. The gate code was inputted once only, I suggest by Tudor, who was then stabbed and pushed out of the way as he fell, allowing the killer to escape through the still-open gate and for the gate to then close.

"We've timed every scenario. There isn't time for our killer to have escaped any other way but through the gate and across the field. As it was, the killer had an extremely narrow window of opportunity. That the field was the escape route is supported by the discovery of footprints running across the field from the gate, but not to it. Despite the damage caused by the sheep then in the field, we've established that these footprints were made by a pair of outdoor gardening shoes. We've found further supporting evidence in the field in the form of traces of the victim's blood and the same microscopic particles of coating found at the scene."

He allowed those taking notes to catch up. "So much for evidence, on to the suspects. The family dynamics are certainly interesting. We have Bettina still living on top of her soon-to-be ex-husband and his new girlfriend, the openly critical daughter, the undermined son, his husband, a disaffected staff member and a side-lined priest, of all things."

"On the subject of the son-in-law, Sir," Pilot piped up, "Denys Koval is expected back in the UK later today."

Black nodded acknowledgement of that, then said, "Eden, what more do we know about Tudor and Ivy?"

"They met on a dating site, he while still married to Bettina, she while single," Eden said. "The relationship moved quite quickly, and Degas came along eighteen months ago. There's nothing to suggest they were having problems. No one's mentioned arguments in the lead up to his death. Given the animosity between the main players, I think we'd have been told if there was. Neither are on any dating sites that we can find, nor have we found evidence that either was involved with anyone else."

"What do we know about the group of visitors?" Black asked.

"With the exception of Nick Pilsworth, they all check out," Eden said. "We haven't unearthed any surprising connections. Nick Pilsworth was either a very clever alias or a lucky coincidence. There is a Dr Nick Pilsworth, who does teach art at an art college, but he wasn't at the TreeHouse that day. That Dr Pilsworth was a bit groggy when I called to ask him about his movements on the day of the murder, as it was still the early hours of the morning in South America, where he's been for the last two months."

"Pilot, what more do we know about the call Hugo says he made?" Black said.

"He did receive a call from a withheld number about the time he says," Pilot said. "This call wasn't answered, but the number was redialled a few minutes later. It's a scam. Anyone who dials it ends up being passed through a series of premium-rate numbers, which are never answered, racking up a huge bill as they go."

"Worth it for an alibi," Eden said.

"Do we know if Hugo was speaking during the call?" Black said.

"We're still looking into that, Sir."

"The daughter Lilah has a pencil sketch she's trying to pass off as her alibi, and Val Simpson, a bag of smashed apples," Black continued. "The latter makes an unlikely killer with no immediate motive that I can see, but we can't rule out anyone at this stage. Both Val Simpson and Lilah O'Connell had time to get from the murder scene to the house in the time frame. The wife, Bettina, was with Will and Harry Thorne when the crime was committed. For girlfriend Ivy to have got from the murder scene to where she appeared would have meant her running around the outside of the property and shinnying over a wall. Our young, six-foot colleague only managed this by securing a foothold and physically hauling himself up and dropping himself over. Even then, it took him some time and he was left covered in debris and with a cut to his hand. A female officer, about the same build as Ivy, needed a leg up and still found it very difficult to scale the wall, and she ended up covered in a considerable amount of debris. With a ladder, she made it onto the wall with ease, but then had to either drop the whole way down, or edge around the side of the skip. This also left the ladder behind. Ivy is young, yes, but diminutive. I can't see how she could have climbed that wall without assistance or a ladder.

That means an accomplice would have had to dispose not only of the ladder but also the murder weapon.

"We've added Ivy's height to the height of the wall. She would've been visible across the roof of the single-storey studio whilst on top of the wall, but only just. It's possible she shinnied over the wall unseen, with the fracas going on, but it was a hell of a risk to take. It would just have taken Harry, Will Thorne, or Bettina to have seen or heard her.

"Significantly, even with the ladder, our officer arrived at the cottage later than we know Ivy did, and after Val Simpson, not before. Nor have we found any traces of brick dust on her hands or the soles of her feet.

"This seems a good time to talk forensics. The preliminary results are back on the clothes, shoes, skin and hair samples taken that morning, and the vehicles impounded. There is some cross-contamination found on those in close proximity to the body, but no traces of anything directly linking them to the crime, nor blood splatter, or the micro-particles. The murder weapon still hasn't been recovered, nor any discarded clothing. The fingertip search continues. We're still trying to locate the dog walker Val Simpson claims to have chatted with at the apple orchard. Most importantly, Nick Pilsworth remains unaccounted for. Who is he and where is he? If he isn't our killer, he certainly has some explaining to do."

Chapter 14

AT HER STATION DESK, Eden rang the head gardener. When asked how many garden stakes were in the grounds, she said, "Heaven only knows. The big equipment we keep in the pavilion. Everything should go in there when not being used but doesn't always. As to how many garden stakes there should be, I couldn't say. Never taken an inventory. We'll have lost some over the years. Things wear out, go walkabouts."

"Could any have found their way into the Events Room?" Eden asked.

"Easily. We move stuff about all the time. Have to, to get on."

Eden then turned her attention to a list of those connected with the TreeHouse in some way or other. She was surprised to see a name she recognised.

"That you, Eden? The kids had a fight?" Sheryl Teal said upon answering Eden's call.

"Sheryl, I need to know where you were the morning Tudor O'Connell was killed?" Eden said.

A pause followed. "Why?"

"For one, you worked for him."

"Only now and then. When they needed help."

"For two, that was the day we were at the pool, the same day you asked me to say you'd been there all morning when you can't have been." At the other end of the line, Eden heard a door opening, then another.

"Okay," Sheryl said, "I've gone outside so we can talk. Christ it's cold."

"Where were you, Sheryl?"

"Why does it matter? If I'd done O'Connell in, I'm hardly likely to ask you for an alibi, am I?"

"Sheryl, I'm going to ask one more time."

"Enjoying this, aren't you?" Sheryl was trying to whisper.

"No, not really."

"This stays between us, okay?" Sheryl said.

"I'm only interested in finding Tudor O'Connell's killer," Eden said.

"Well, it weren't me, love. Why would I kill O'Connell? I hardly knew the man."

Eden could feel herself growing angry. Sheryl must have sensed this, as she said, "If you must know, I was following Alex." Alex Doherty was Sheryl's partner and dad to Jos. "He's mucking me around. Always disappearing off some-where or on that phone of his. He denies anything's going on, but don't they always? He claimed he couldn't take Jos swim-ming 'cause he had a doctor's appointment. I didn't believe him and followed him to the surgery — where it so turns out, he did have an appointment. I drove off, then started panicking that he'd seen me. I needed another mum to support my story if he challenged me. Didn't want him getting the moral high ground. Couldn't do any better than have Detective Sergeant Eden Hudson swear I was at the pool all morning, could I?"

"Could I have the name of the doctor's practice, please?"

Sheryl snorted and gave the address.

"Thank you, Sheryl," Eden said. "I'm sorry to have troubled you."

"It's been a pleasure, love," Sheryl said in a tone dripping with sarcasm.

She'd just typed up an attendance note of her call with Sheryl when a call summoned Eden to Black's office. Pilot and Black were studying a deleted text exchange recovered from the deceased's phone:

Get out of my grill O'Connell

I'm not in your grill house and never will be if I ever find out where it is

Don't you play the innocent I'm warning you You've got all you're getting

Eden read the texts through a few times. "Tudor O'Connell was a blackmailer?"

"The texts don't prove O'Connell was a blackmailer, only that someone thought he was," Black reminded them.

"Yeah, the phantom texter might be one of those nutters who sell their garden furniture to their neighbour, forget, spot their garden swing next door then ring us up accusing their neighbour of theft," Pilot said.

"Still motive for murder," Eden said, adding, "the blackmail thing, not the garden furniture thing."

"Oh, I don't know," Pilot said.

"Any chance of tracing these texts?" Black asked.

"We'll do our best, but if the sender used a burner, we'll likely draw a blank," Pilot replied.

"Could Mr *Keep Out of My Grill* and Dr Nick Pilsworth be one and the same, you reckon?" Eden speculated.

.   .   .

Rather than summon them to the station, Black and Eden questioned those closest to Tudor by videoconference.

"Hugo, we have reason to believe your late father may have been blackmailing someone," Eden said.

"Dad?" Hugo said. "Why would Dad do something like that? Not sure I want to believe it."

Lilah was even more unhelpful. "Dad?" she laughed.

Val Simpson just said, "Whatever next? Some people just can't have too much."

Bettina O'Connell's response was, "Whatever he was up to, he was hardly likely to let me in on it. Ask Ivy, she knew his secrets."

When Ivy didn't answer her phone, enquiries were made at the hotel where she was staying because of the ongoing police investigation at the TreeHouse. Pilot asked Reception for information as to her whereabouts. *She ordered a taxi to take her to a TV studio*, was the reply.

A plain-clothed officer met Hugo's husband, Denys Koval, at Heathrow airport and transported him to the station where Pilot waited to interview him.

Denys was the same age as Hugo, similarly tall and slim. The tartan cap on his head suggested a quirkier dress sense. Pilot advised him that the interview would be recorded and asked him again if he wanted a lawyer to attend.

"No," he said in a Ukrainian accent. "I have no need for a lawyer. I have done nothing wrong. I am a substitute coach and was coaching football when Hugo's dad died. In the Ukraine. When can I speak to my husband, please?"

"As soon as you've answered my questions, Mr Koval," Pilot said.

"Please call me Denys."

"How would you describe the late Tudor O'Connell, Denys?"

Denys pondered the question. "The Russians have a suitable saying." He said something in Russian, then in English. "It translates as: *you could sharpen an axe on the top of his head.* Tudor O'Connell was a very stubborn person."

"How would you describe Tudor and Hugo's relationship?"

"His dad said hurtful things to him. Critical. Hugo always turn the other cheek. Take yourself into your hands, Hugo, I tell him, but he never did and nothing changed. As we say in the Ukraine – you cannot make a crow into a raven."

"Did you ever say anything to Tudor about his treatment of Hugo?"

"You don't go to another monastery with your own rules. Anyway – what would have been the point? He would not change. No matter how hard you try, a bull will never give milk."

"Was Tudor's bullying partly to blame for the collapse of your marriage?" Pilot asked.

Denys fixed him with a cool look. "Hugo did not murder his father. You want to know how I am so certain?" He moved closer. "I spoke to Hugo yesterday. He said his dad was dead. He was crying. He said, *'Now I'll never know if he even loved me'.*"

Denys leaned back in his seat. "I will not lie. When I heard Tudor was dead, a big stone fell from my heart. Yes. But I now believe Tudor brought us closer together. I left to think things over. Being away from Hugo made me miserable. Made me realise I still love Hugo. I said to my mum, am I making a mistake to go back and give it another go? A dream is sweeter than honey. She reminded me that if you like to sled, you have to drag the sled."

Pilot wondered if all Ukrainians spoke in proverbs or if it was just Denys and his family. "What are your views on the rest of the O'Connell family?" he asked.

Denys gave a snort. "There's a small choice in rotten apples."

"New information has come to light, Denys, which suggests your late father-in-law may have been blackmailing someone," Pilot said.

Denys took stock of the situation. After a while he said, "If he was, it would not be for the money, I can tell you that much."

"In which case, what would his motive have been, Denys, do you think?"

"To show where the crayfish is wintering."

"That's not an expression I'm familiar with, Denys," Pilot said.

"It means to teach someone a lesson. Is that why he was murdered?"

"It's a line of enquiry."

"He who licks knives will soon cut his tongue."

Chapter 15

Eden turned into a busy, traffic-clogged street. Black was in the passenger seat. Eden paused outside a building at the street's end. Grey italics etched into a panel designated it: *What's on Studios*. The studio seemed out of place. Its neighbours offered second-hand furniture, vaping, fast food and mobile phones; while the studio's tinted glass panel depicted live bands, stage performances, model shoots and interviews.

"What's she up to?" Black asked as the car behind beeped.

They parked and walked to the entrance where Black pulled the heavy glass door and held it open for Eden. He followed her in. The door closed behind him, taking with it the noise, pollution and shabbiness of the street and replacing it with the calmness, modernity and subdued lighting of the studio. On one side of the room a few people waited, mostly staring at phones or into space. On the other side, a receptionist sat at a half-round, glass-topped aluminium desk. Eden went over to her to show her badge and explain their business. The receptionist checked the recording studio's itinerary for the day. Ivy was in Studio 4 with Janie Dowd from *Spirit*.

"The magazine?" Eden asked.

"They have their own TV channel as well," the receptionist

explained. She picked up her phone to summon a nervous-looking youngster to escort them to the studio.

The youngster led them through some doors and along some corridors to Studio 4. A message on the whiteboard to one side of the door announced the studio had been hired for half a day by *Spirit*.

"Recording is just about to get started," the youngster said. "We can stop it, or you can stand at the back and watch, but I'd need to ask you to be quiet."

"We'll do that," Black said to the young man. He nodded and pushed open a door allowing them to enter.

The studio was about nine metres square and was overlooked by its own glass-fronted production gallery. This currently held one person. There was a podium in front of a green background, one camera operator and a sound recordist holding a boom. Ivy was perched on one stool and Janie Dowd on the other. A make-up artist attended to some final touches. When done, she moved away, and the interview began.

"Ivy, let me start by sharing our shock and sadness at the events," Janie said. "Everyone at *Spirit* is stunned, literally stunned." Janie touched her heart with one hand and gave Ivy's hand a squeeze with the other.

"Thank you, Janie, it means so much to hear you say that," Ivy said.

"How are you bearing up, Ivy?"

"My love for Tudor will last to the end of our days. When you came to our lovely home, Janie," Ivy motioned to the green screen behind her, "little could I imagine how cruelly he'd be taken away from me. Your team took such lovely photographs of us all, I thank you." She dabbed her eyes.

Janie gave Ivy's hand another little squeeze. "I can't imagine how you're managing to hold it all together, Ivy," she said.

"I have to, Janie, for my daughter's sake. For my little girl. It's what her daddy would have wanted."

"Please share with the viewers why you felt it so important to come here today, Ivy."

"Your audience knows that I am a very spiritual person," was the reply. "I want to ask your viewers to join with me and pray for harmony, to put the world right again."

"Not that the person responsible for taking Tudor from you be found?"

"I want the person held to account, but that isn't my job. My job is to raise my daughter and I don't want my little girl to have a vengeful, angry mother."

"Can I ask whether you and the O'Connell family speak regularly?"

Ivy didn't hesitate in answering. "We have put our differences behind us. Degas is Hugo and Lilah's little sister, after all. I want them to have a relationship with each other."

"You are a remarkable person, Ivy. Are you able to think of the future yet?"

"It's too soon, Janie," she said, "too soon."

"You're managing to produce your art despite everything you've been through," Janie said.

"It's my way of losing myself, Janie. Tudor would want my exhibition to go ahead. He was so supportive. And it will. At the end of year. I'm going to send all the proceeds to my mum. I can't expect her to look after Degas for nothing. Degas can't come home, not with all this going on. Mum and I have to make excuses to her why she can't come home. Why she can't speak to her daddy. How I'm going to tell her..."

Janie allowed Ivy to recover, then said, "Is there anything else you'd like to say to people, Ivy?"

"I'd like to thank everyone for their kindness. People have been so kind, so kind. I'd also like to ask anybody who was in the vicinity that morning to rack their brains. The killer escaped across a field of sheep into the woods. Did anyone come home with muddy boots, twigs in their hair, bits of wool? Has anyone found some abandoned clothing or a bloodstained garden stake?"

"A bloodstained garden stake?" Janie said. "Lord in heaven. Is that how he was killed?" Janie looked genuinely shocked.

"The police think so. The killer may have thrown it away. It could be in undergrowth. The police need to speak to a man with a white beard who was there that morning. He said his name was Nick Pilsworth, but it wasn't. Whoever you are, why have you not come forward? Come forward now, make yourself known."

"If you know anything, anything at all, please do go to the police," Janie said to the camera. She turned back to Ivy. "Thank you for coming here today, Ivy. You've shown remarkable bravery."

"I wanted to, Janie. It means a lot that you asked me."

With the *Spirit* interview over, Black and Eden took Ivy into an empty studio.

"I knew you wouldn't be angry, Detective Inspector," Ivy said.

"About what, Ivy?" Black said.

"My speaking to *Spirit*. It's my way of helping the investigation. How is that getting on? Is there any news?"

"We're making progress," he said. He showed Ivy the text messages recovered from Tudor's phone.

She read through them a couple of times. "Tudor showed me these. He didn't understand a word of it. Didn't even know that 'get out of my grill' means 'leave me alone.' The poor love. I told him to ignore it. It was a stupid troll or a scammer. Do you know what I now believe?" she continued. "It's a hate campaign. The strange presents, these texts, and now his murder. I can't see why anyone would hate us so much, but they do." A look flashed across her face. "It might help if you did your job and found out who killed Tudor."

Black and Eden ignored her outburst. It was understandable in the circumstances. Black said, "Ivy, can we take a look at those odd items you received?"

"I didn't keep them," she said. "Why would I? I chucked the theatre programme and the stupid album out. I gave the DVDs to a charity shop, the garage mended the car, and the poor bird I buried under the marigolds. None of it seemed important at the time. It still doesn't."

Chapter 16

EDEN HAD JUST GOT home when her phone rang. She was surprised to see Sheryl's number displayed. They hadn't been good friends before their last curt conversation. Wonder what she wants, she thought, answering the call. "Hi Sheryl."

"Yeah, I've been thinking," Sheryl said. And hello to you, too, thought Eden. Yes, I'm well, thank you for asking. "You'll be looking into Alex's movements on the morning of the murder, won't you?"

"Why would we be doing that, Sheryl?" Eden asked.

"Well, you asked where I was."

"There was a connection between you and the deceased, and you'd asked me for an alibi."

"Well, there happens to be a connection between Alex and the deceased, for your information," Sheryl said.

This, Eden didn't know. "How so?"

"Alex does a bit of handy-manning at the TreeHouse. As and when. Bit of painting and decorating. Bit of repair work. That kind of thing. That's how I got my job."

Eden was more accustomed to being fed false alibis by the girlfriends of useless boyfriends than the other way around. Nonetheless, she was grateful for the information and said so, only Sheryl hadn't finished. "See, I've been thinking," she said. "I saw him cycle into the doctor's car park and get off his bike, but I didn't hang around in case he saw me. Dunno how long he was there for. Might've just picked up a prescription then gone off somewhere else."

Eden said nothing and just let her continue. "I ain't suggesting he did Tudor in or anything, but you should know he bid for the renovation work and was as pissed as hell he didn't get it."

When Eden didn't reply, she said, "So you'll look into it then?"

"Thank you for the information, Sheryl. Any little bit helps."

"Will you let me know what you find out?" Sheryl said. "Like if he was just in and out then went off somewhere else?"

Ah, so now we get to it, Eden thought. "Just so we don't misunderstand each other, that's not something I can do," she said.

"You don't understand," Sheryl said. "All I'm asking is you keep me in the picture. He's been acting suspicious for months. If he was round some other girl's place that's nothing to do with the case, is it — and you could tell me."

"If you're asking me to provide you with your boyfriend's movements then you can think again, Sheryl."

"Well, don't tell me where he went then, just how long he was at the surgery. I'm after reassurance is all."

"I can't help you there, Sheryl, I'm sorry."

"You wouldn't even know he worked at the TreeHouse if I hadn't just told you," Sheryl snapped.

"And I'm very grateful for the information, thank you," Eden said, ending the call.

. . .

Eden shared her home with three other people: her daughter, Dora; her step-dad, Eric; and his mother, Dottie. Dottie had just arrived with a cup of tea, which she put down beside Eden. In response to the interested look on Dottie's face, Eden said, "Paranoid girlfriend."

"Oh, to be young enough to be a paranoid girlfriend," Dottie said, wistfully.

"I might get out there again," Eden said as nonchalantly as she could manage.

Dottie broke into a grin and sat down next to her. "Anyone I should know about?"

Eden still had casework to be getting on with. "I'll tell all another time," she said, wearily. "Has the cat turned up?"

Black was also at home. He was at his desk in his study on the second floor, eating his evening meal from a bowl whilst looking through some casework. He looked out of his study window at the church spire in the near distance. The spire was lit. Something on it caught his eye. A diminutive grey-brown shape with dark streaking, high up. He looked around. Where were his binoculars? He called out to his girlfriend, but she'd already left for an evening out. He searched his desk for a magnifying glass, finding it in a drawer. Taking it and his phone to the window, he put the magnifying glass over the phone camera and took a shot. The phone flashed. He zoomed in and took some more. Not as good as using binoculars, of course, but it helped a bit.

When he looked at the photograph, he found the magnification was so slight he couldn't identify the bird. He took out a small shaving mirror and, after standing it up, he reflected the photograph in it. The further he moved back, the clearer the image became. It was then he realised that the grey-brown shape was a little merlin — female. He hadn't seen her before.

She wasn't a local. Migratory maybe — wintering in warmer climes, or blown off course? As he watched her from the window again, the little bird hung in the breeze. With the magnifying glass once again pressed against the phone, he took a few snaps of the bird caught in the moonlight. Eventually, he discarded the phone and simply watched her, entranced, as she hovered then dived after some prey, pursuing it relentlessly until she was out of sight.

Chapter 17

THE NEXT MORNING began with Alex Doherty being escorted to the station. Eden and Alex knew each other from the school run. The two were close in age, as were their children. They spoke in an interview room.

"How can I help?" he said.

"I understand you handyman at the TreeHouse, now and then?" Eden said.

"Do bits and bobs for them, as and when."

"What was your relationship with Tudor O'Connell?"

"I saw Bettina more than him. She was in charge of the practical side of things. He was more into the marketing side. Both were okay to work for. Paid up when asked. Didn't look over my shoulder the whole time, unlike Ivy. Preferred it when she wasn't around."

"How well do you know the family?"

"Not particularly well. I'm just a handyman," he said. "Thought it a bit of a weird set up. Bettina still in the main house, digging her heels in; him and Ivy a stone's throw away, rubbing her nose in it. Always found Lilah a bit spoilt. Hugo could've done with standing up to his dad a bit more. Denys is a laugh, though. All those sayings of his." He mimicked Denys's Ukrainian accent: *"Dogs don't know how to swim until the water reaches their eyes.* He swears they're legit, but I reckon he makes them up."

"You must know the layout of the grounds pretty well, Alex?" Eden said.

"I've been there enough times to know my way around, yeah."

"Do you know the code for the gate to the field?"

"I do, yes."

"Was there any ill-feeling between yourself and Tudor O'Connell?"

"Not that I'm aware of," he said. "Someone been spreading rumours, have they?"

"Only that you bid and failed to get the renovation work on the cottage. Did that upset you?" she asked.

He snorted with laughter. "If I murdered everyone who turned me down for a job, love, the serial killer channel would be making documentaries about me. I didn't want the work. I only bid 'cos Sheryl made me. For God's sake, Eden. You know me better than that. You can't think me capable of something like that."

"Where were you on the morning of Tudor O'Connell's death?"

"I had a doctor's appointment. My surgery is the St. Edmunds Medical Practice. Dr Marie Pilcher. You have my permission to ask her."

"How did you travel to the surgery? In your van?"

"I cycled. It's quicker with the traffic. I went home afterwards to pick up the van for my next job. Creosoting a fence."

"Do you have any idea why anyone would want to kill Tudor, Alex?" Eden said.

"I haven't a clue."

. . .

Interview over, Eden hurried to the morning team meeting. D.S. Judy McDermott also attended.

Black spoke first. "Those who knew Tudor O'Connell don't see him as a blackmailer. Nonetheless, it's enough that someone apparently thought he was. In another development, we now have some images of Nick Pilsworth captured on the bus he caught that morning. An unusual method of transport for someone planning a murder." He called up an image of an older, slightly hunched gentleman boarding the bus. After paying in cash, he shunted down to the back of the bus, head down, constantly adjusting the cap he wore by pulling it down to shade his face. He got off the bus outside Annie Threadneedle's shop in the village high street. Although he clearly arrived by bus, there's no evidence of him leaving the area the same way, increasing our suspicions that he is somehow involved."

Black turned to Eden at the back of the room. "Did the interview with Alex Doherty harvest anything of interest?"

She shook her head. "Just someone trying to land him in trouble. I've finally had a chance to look over the magazine interview with Tudor and Ivy." She held her face rigid to stifle a yawn. She'd spent half the night comforting her distressed daughter over the missing cat and the other half worrying about its fate. To make matters worse, it still hadn't returned when she left that morning. She drank some black coffee and held up a copy of the magazine provided by corner shop owner, Annie Threadneedle. "*Spirit* can best be described as a glossy, celebrity lifestyle magazine," she said. The magazine appeared on screen. On its cover, Tudor, Ivy and Degas were sandwiched between the headline: *Tudor O'Connell and partner Ivy Lee, at home with new baby, Degas* — and the sub-head: *They call me Poison Ivy, but our love is true.*

"There's nothing like a family rift to sell copy," Judy McDermott said.

"Although Tudor and Ivy lived in the cottage, the featured photographs were all taken in the TreeHouse," Eden explained, calling up some photographs used in the article.

Black recognised the room in the first photograph. He'd spoken to Bettina in it. He noticed that all but three of the family pictures had been removed from the piano. Two featured Tudor — one with his two eldest children and the other with Ivy and Degas. The third picture was a framed photograph of Gethsemane herself.

"I haven't found a photograph which doesn't feature merchandise for sale on their webpage," Eden said. A photograph of the couple appeared, sitting in the dining room at a table long enough to seat six at each side and another two at each end. "The pattern on the tablecloth is Gethsemane's *Tree of Life*. Please also note the *Tree of Life* gilded mirror, the *Tree of Life* wall-hanging, and the *Tree of Life* lampshade." She read the featured quote: "*The whole house pays homage to the genius that was my mother, and yet remains a much-loved family home, says Tudor.*" She called up another photo of the couple, this time standing on either side of a Pistachio coloured Aga stove, each holding a mug, pattern to camera. "Yes, you've guessed it, the mugs are available on the webpage. It never stops." She moved to a series of photographs taken in the study: Tudor sat at his desk, phone to ear with Ivy standing supportively behind him, hand resting on his shoulder. The *Ark of Life* was just visible on the wall to their side. In another, the couple were sitting beside each other on the Indian mirror love-seat, Ivy's arm around Degas, her other hand holding Tudor's. Eden read out the attributed quotes: "*My father and mother watched the sunset from this seat most evenings, says Tudor. And now Tudor and I do the same, says Ivy.*"

"Oh, pass the sick-bag," Judy McDermott said. "They make out they met at her launch party, not the online dating site we know they really met on, Eden, but hey, they're not the first couple to romance up their first meeting. She makes a big deal about how much it hurts to be called a gold-digger when's she's just a girl who fell in love. The interview ends with Ivy telling the world what an honour it is for her and Tudor to be featured in *Spirit*, a magazine they so admire and respect."

"When you've finished with that sick-bag, I'll have it," someone called out.

"Apart from the occasional background photo, is there any mention of his first family?" Black asked.

"Hugo and Lilah get a brief mention at the end. Bettina not at all. She's totally cut out," Eden said, slicing through the air with her hand.

"That must've hurt," Judy said.

"The theatre programme was sent to Ivy shortly after that interview," Eden said.

"Find out how it went down at that time, will you?" Black said.

Eden visited Val Simpson in her home. When she produced the magazine, Val burst out laughing. Eden said, "I take it you've seen this before?"

"Oh God, yes. Tudor asked if he came out well in it. I lied and said yes. To me, he came across as a show-off: 'Look at our wonderful lives!' That interview was Ivy and Tudor. They lived their own lifestyle statement."

"Did Bettina find it so funny, Val?" Eden asked.

"She was far from happy. All ranting and crying. Said it was like she didn't even exist. Felt she was being squeezed out, and I could sort of see where she was coming from. Bettina was every bit the Lady of the Manor. Loved the part."

"Did she call Ivy 'Poison Ivy' behind her back?"

"Not always behind her back, but who of us isn't guilty of a bit of name-calling now and then?"

. . .

Bettina rolled her eyes when showed the interview. "Not that thing again!"

"How did the article make you feel at the time, Mrs O'Connell?" Eden asked.

"At the time, it made my blood boil. They took over my house. Nearly twenty-five years of marriage and suddenly I didn't exist. My kids hardly got a mention. But everything has a purpose. The article made me realise that Father Dermot Hanrahan was right. Only through forgiveness could I move forward. In a funny way, that interview was the best thing to happen to me. I let God back into my life and my faith has kept me going."

"The Poison Ivy thing was a poor joke," Hugo said. "A silly play on words. Ivy's not bad. She's quite funny when you get to know her. She really stepped up for our wedding. She gave Denys and me jade carvings of our Chinese birth animals. Dad probably wouldn't even have come without Ivy's influence. She loved the video of our wedding. Kept it for ages." He held up the magazine. "Mum took this too seriously. I said so at the time. It was just marketing. We enjoyed a spike in sales when it came out, which hasn't gone down."

"Hugo's right. You're making too much of the family rift, Detective Sergeant," Lilah said. "It was no such thing. I don't dislike Ivy. In many ways, I respect her. No one had heard of her before she met Dad. Now she's a successful sculptress." She made air apostrophes with her hands as she said the word successful. "Okay, maybe, she isn't as successful as she makes out, but she sells way more than she did. As a feminist, I can only admire a woman who uses her assets to make something of herself. And as for Mum and Dad, virtually all my friends have divorced parents and honestly, everybody's happier a few years down the road."

Interviews over, Eden reported to Black. "So now they're the Waltons?" he said.

Chapter 18

EDEN'S MORNING began at the inquest into Tudor O'Connell's death. She was dressed in her uniform. She got to her feet to provide Tudor O'Connell's full name, date of birth, date of death and place of death, and to request the inquest be adjourned to await the conclusion of the police investigation. It was and the body committed to the morgue indefinitely.

Inquest over, Eden drove to St. Edmund's Church for Tudor O'Connell's memorial service. She met Black outside. They entered to the sound of organ music. This was the first time either had been inside. The church was filling up.

Black saw Father Hanrahan and went over to speak with him. The priest was in conversation, giving Black the opportunity to have a look around. The church was relatively modern, having been built during the last century. A simple wooden cross hung from each of an arcade of pillars lining the nave. Carved Stations of the Cross hung on the walls; votive candles or religious figurines filled alcoves, and, on a noticeboard, folded intentions waited to be read at the next mass. Highly polished birch-wood chairs had replaced the dark pews of old.

The round ceremonial table and the altar behind it were shaped from polished bur-oak, although, and in stark contrast, the pulpit, half way up a stone pillar and accessed by stairs, was carved from traditional dark wood and was heavily ornate. Black's eyes went from it to the lectern beside which Father Hanrahan stood. It was an attractive piece, also shaped from polished bur-oak. Three separate inlaid panels rose from an octagonal stand to meet and merge into a semi-circular armrest and reading platform. The lectern appeared too tall for the priest. Black was wondering why such a new piece of furniture wasn't adjustable when he realised that Father Hanrahan was addressing him. The two men shook hands.

"Such a pity this is all the family are allowed. Let's pray the body is released for burial soon," Dermot Hanrahan said. "Do excuse me, the family have arrived."

Black made his way along the side to join Eden in the back row. Val Simpson, Black noticed, sat two rows from the front next to Annie Threadneedle. Robert Standley sat a row back from them. He nodded at each as he passed. Once in his seat, he picked up the Order of Service and cast his eyes over the front cover. Above the words: *The family of Tudor O'Connell welcomes you to a celebration of his life*, Tudor O'Connell smiled and waved with the TreeHouse behind him.

He opened it:
Father Hanrahan reads the introduction.
Bettina O'Connell reads Ecclesiastes Three.
The congregation sings Abide with Me.
Hugo O'Connell pays a family tribute to Tudor.
The congregation sings Now the Green Blade Riseth.
Lilah O'Connell reads a letter from Gethsemane O'Connell.
The congregation leaves...

. . .

127

The organ struck up, and the family started to make their way solemnly through the central aisle. In a previously unseen sign of solidarity, Bettina and Ivy walked side-by-side, Hugo, Denys and Lilah behind them. This lasted until they reached the front row where Bettina and Ivy took seats at each end. Hugo, Denys and Lilah sat between them. Once the family and congregation were seated, Father Hanrahan clambered up onto the lectern. Black was right. The stand was too high for him. As a result, the armrest and slanted reading platform stopped slightly above his waist. This gave him a rather ungainly appearance and forced him to read his sermon from an uncomfortable position. If it fazed him, he didn't show it.

"Welcome, friends, to this most sad and unnecessary occasion," he began. "We're here to remember and pay tribute to Tudor O'Connell. There is much good to be said of Tudor. He was a man of divinity and passion. A man who worked ceaselessly to keep the memory of his mother alive. A man who, with his wife Bettina beside him, raised a family..." he paused. "This is not the occasion to remind all present that marriage is a holy sacrament not to be set aside. We are here to remember and give praise, not judge those who fail. Jesus expected us to fail. He warned us so himself. As we gather here to remember the son of Gethsemane, let us remind ourselves of this lesson given to the disciples in the garden of Gethsemane. '*The spirit is willing,*' Jesus told mankind, '*but the body is weak...*'"

His sermon on the perils of falling for temptation was interrupted by the sight and sound of Ivy noisily getting to her feet and crossing to the aisle to walk out. She stopped briefly to glower at Father Hanrahan. Hugo jumped to his feet, as did Eden. She indicated that she would follow Ivy and Hugo sat down. Whispered comments and the sound of Ivy's heels clicking over the stone floor filled the church.

"It's time for the reading, I think, Dermot," Bettina said, crossing to the pulpit to climb its steps.

"To everything there is a season and a time to every purpose under the Heavens," Bettina read.

Ivy pulled open the heavy interior door, pausing to shoot a second filthy look in the direction of Dermot Hanrahan. Eden was still making her way along the back row as Ivy slipped into the porch. *"A time to be born and a time to die; a time to plant and a time to pluck up that which is planted,"* Bettina continued.

The wooden outside door was heavy and, once through it, Eden was cold without her coat. She looked around. Ivy was by the church gate, gazing away in the distance. Eden went over to her. At the sound of gravel crunching under foot, Ivy spun around.

"What was that?" she said. "He's turned Tudor's memorial service into the sermon from the Mount." Ivy looked devastated. Her arms cradled her body. "If Bettina and I can put aside our differences for one day, why can't he? He's meant to be a man of God." Ivy turned her back on the church. "He hates me. Always has done." Her hands clutched at the church gate. "Today is so hard for me. I miss Tudor so much."

Eden rubbed Ivy's arm in support. "Give yourself a few minutes and come back inside, Ivy. You'll regret it if you don't."

Ivy turned, "Rather than dispense platitudes, do your job and find whoever murdered my partner." On those words, she stomped towards the church. Eden watched her push open the door and go back inside. After giving herself a few moments, she too went back, wondering how it would look if a murder detective crowned a suspect.

Eden retook her place next to Black and picked up on the second verse of *Abide with Me*.

At the end of the hymn, Hugo climbed the pulpit steps. He glanced at Denys who touched his eye and then his heart. Hugo cleared his throat. "Burying a loved one is a heart-breaking rite of passage for all of us, but to lose a loved one to murder-" he stopped and shook his head. "Dad wasn't always the easiest man, but we are all here because we loved him. Dad was only sixty-three when he died. That's nothing. He was the son of Emlyn and Gethsemane O'Connell. One of the greatest achievements of Dad's life was to ensure that Gethsemane's talent wasn't forgotten. Dad met Mum almost twenty-five years to the day. My sister, Ophelia — always known affectionately as Lilah — and I came along in quick succession. Mum and Dad ensured we had a happy childhood. They enjoyed many happy years together. Sadly, it didn't work out and Mum and Dad separated. Now Ivy is part of our family. Ivy made Dad happy and for that I thank her, and for Degas Gethsemane Tiger Peony. A lovely name for a lovely little girl. It's not possible for her to be here today, but when Degas is old enough, Dad, we will share this day with her. Dad, I am so sorry you will never see her grow up, but I promise you, we will take good care of her and she'll be okay."

From the lectern, where he'd remained throughout, Farther Hanrahan said, "Let us all get to our feet to sing *Now the Green Blade Riseth.*"

The organ played, and the congregation rose to sing:
"Now the green blade riseth
from the buried grain,
wheat that in the dark earth,
many days has lain."

Black and Eden slipped out as the congregation moved into the second verse. They'd just reached the church gate when they heard a familiar voice call out, "Detective Inspector." Black looked over his shoulder and saw Robert Standley hurrying towards him, clutching a yellow document wallet. Black and Eden waited for him. "May I have a word, Detective Inspector?"

"Of course, Sir," Black said.

They led him to the graveyard behind the church. There they were alone.

"I couldn't say anything about this when you visited my office," Robert Standley explained. "I was waiting on permission from my regulator. Even deceased clients are entitled to confidentiality. The regulator has, given the circumstances, granted permission for me to share this with you, as have the family."

Black and Eden waited, wondering what they were about to hear. "Tudor vigorously enforced all copyright in his late mother's designs. He had recently instructed me to take legal action against a married couple, Brian and Tam Tully, for breach of copyright. I've printed off my electronic file." He handed Black the document wallet. "Everything you'll need is in there, but please call if you have any questions. I'm sure the case against Mr and Mrs Tully is unconnected with recent, terrible events, but it's important you know everything."

Chapter 19

BRIAN AND TAM TULLY lived in the next county. The couple were in their early fifties and ran a small cottage industry from their large thatched cottage. The cottage was one of a dozen similar in a remote hamlet. Despite their show of surprise at finding two police officers at the door, the couple calmly took Eden and Black into their main room and bid them take a seat.

The room took up the length of the cottage and looked over both front and back gardens. The room's beams were exposed, its floors wooden and covered by rugs. A wood burner glowed in an inglenook fireplace. Was that Gethsemane Print wallpaper? Eden wondered. Tam Tully was slim, bespectacled with short, grey hair. Brian Tully was fat and balding. Eden's first thought, when they came to the door, was that neither looked anything like the description they had of Nick Pilsworth. Tam Tully was too short and slight and Brian too large.

Black began the interview. "Mr and Mrs Tully, we believe you are acquainted with Mr Tudor O'Connell."

"We know the name," Brian said.

"You might not be aware but Tudor O'Connell was murdered some days ago," Black continued.

The couple showed no emotion. "We were aware," Brian Tully said. "Can't say I'm too bothered."

"Brian!" Tam Tully said. "My husband isn't as callous as he sounds. We're both desperately sorry for the family, but that man has made the last year a living hell for us."

"Are you referring to the breach of copyright case Mr O'Connell launched against you?" Black said.

"He wanted to put us out of business," Tam replied.

"And will his death change that, do you know?" Eden asked.

"Just what are you insinuating?" Brian Tully said. "We didn't kill Tudor O'Connell. I can assure you of that."

Tam reached over and touched his arm to calm him down. "Brian, the officer is just doing her job. His death doesn't change a thing," she said to Eden and Black. "He didn't have a leg to stand on. We did our own legal research. I knew we had a good case. We can't afford lawyers, but eventually we paid for one hour of legal advice to be sure we were on the right track. The lawyer confirmed that there is no copyright in an idea."

"He didn't have a case," Brian said. "My Tam's designs have more dissimilarities with Gethsemane O'Connell's than similarities."

"I'm a creative. I've been designing since I was at art school. I am a big fan of Gethsemane O'Connell. I saw you notice the wallpaper. Gethsemane was an inspirational woman, but my designs are my own. If Tudor O'Connell was able to ban every artist who drew inspiration from nature, simply because one of his relation's did, he'd have to injunct half the Arts and Crafts Movement. Probably more."

"He was just trying to scare us," Brian said. "Tudor O'Connell was a schoolyard bully."

"He wanted to make an example of us," Tam Tully said. "But he underestimated the Tullys. We've worked so hard to get where we are. We've built our business from scratch. We're proud of it."

"We understand you, Mr Tully, attended a mediation meeting in London with Mr O'Connell and his lawyers?" Black said.

"The court said our case was suitable for mediation and we agreed," Tam Tully said. "Brian went, not me."

"Tam was upset enough as it was. I didn't want her further upset. We sat in this room. Me on my tod, him with his lawyer. I put across our case, which Tam has articulated perfectly. Tudor's lawyer came out with a load of legal spiel. The mediator said she would take the matter on consideration and revert. We haven't heard anything since."

"I'm going to give you the time and date when Tudor O'Connell was killed, and I'll need you to tell me where you both were," Eden said.

"We know the date, we were both here for most of the day," Tam Tully said.

"We've a trade fair coming up and have a hell of a lot to do," Brian said. "Tam was working on some last-minute details, and I was downloading them on the computer. I expect you'll want to take that with you? It's no problem, I always back everything up."

"That day we only popped out to fill up the car and visit the delicatessen in town. We had people coming for supper that evening and needed some nibbles," Tam Tully said. "Oh, and we dropped some mugs off at a gift shop I sell through."

"They needed more of Tam's *Gunpowder, Treason and Plot* mugs. They'd sold out," Brian said proudly.

"Where do you do your designing?" Eden asked.

"In our studio, at the rear the garden," Tam said.

"Can we have a look around it, Mrs Tully?" Eden said.

Black and Eden were taken along a path comprising two rows of stepping stones, through a garden of vegetables and flowers, to the door of a single-storey, reclaimed bowls pavilion. Tam opened its doors to reveal a modern studio. Along one side, art materials littered a bench. At the bench's end, a small Artists Notepad was propped up on a writing stand, a blue flower pencilled there. The same blue flower, only now a watercolour, was on display on a canvas on an easel in the centre of the studio. A second bench took up the length of the opposite wall. On it were three screens and an Apple Macintosh. Two office chairs sat underneath. The wall furthest from the door was stacked with books on designing above a row of material display samples. An antique medicine cabinet stood against the remaining wall.

"May I?" Eden asked.

"Be our guest," Tam replied.

Eden pulled open the first of the little drawers. It contained numerous drawer knobs of different designs and material. The drawer below that contained rhinestones, the one next to it brooches — big, small, antique, modern — the one above, tassels, and to its left, nothing but buttons. Eden couldn't begin to guess how many. Every drawer she opened held a collection of small objects.

"We hang on to anything for ideas," Brian said.

Eden couldn't resist opening one more drawer. It was divided in two — one half for clown noses, the other half for false eyes.

"I want to get something off my chest." The suddenness with which Tam Tully said this — and her tone — made everyone jump, even her husband. She tried to control her voice, but it jarred with nerves. "I'm glad Tudor O'Connell's dead. Not because of the copyright case. That was going nowhere. I'm glad because as a Gethsemane O'Connell devotee, my dream has been to visit her studio. I was ecstatic when I heard the family were opening it. I've waited for so long to see it with my own eyes. But then he started that ridiculous case against us. How could I ever have gone with him there? But now he's dead, I can, and I shall." She smoothed down her jumper.

"Let me show you this," Brian said, turning the screen towards them. On it was a range of dining room products decorated with the same blue flower design seen on the sketchpad and canvas. "We have customers who commission Tam to design for their products. My job," he explained, "is to see how the image looks on the product. Tam's the creative, I'm the practical one. This is what we were working on the day O'Connell was killed." He pointed to the server. "Every change I made, and the time, will be on recorded on there."

"I think we've taken up enough of your time, Mr and Mrs Tully," Black said. "Thank you for your assistance."

Tam led the way out, followed by Black. From the studio door, Eden took one last glance around. Mugs for a local crafts studio, some crockery, a range of bespoke doorknobs. This was very much a small cottage business. "I hope you don't mind me saying this," she began, "but the operation you have here doesn't strike me as much of a threat to the Gethsemane O'-Connell brand. Why was Tudor O'Connell so determined to pursue a case against you? You can't be the only people incorporating the natural world into your designs?"

The Tullys exchanged eye contact.

"Is there something you're not telling us?" Eden asked. Black returned to peer over her shoulder.

Tam and Brian folded their arms in a twin movement. "If you must know," Tam said, "I was at art school with Tudor. We started the same day. He badgered me to go out for a drink with him. Eventually I did. We went out once more after that, from memory, to the cinema. I finished it there. I didn't like him. He was arrogant. His very words were: '*I can't believe you're dumping me*' with the emphasis on the words *you're* and *me*. We barely spoke after that. That's your reason. He never forgave me for dumping him and causing him to lose face with his friends."

"It sounds far-fetched, we know," Brian said, "but since this started, I've been convinced he came across some of our work, looked us up online, saw Tam and realised it was the same Tam who'd dumped him all those years ago. Not many lasses with the name Tam, let alone who went to the same art school. She's not changed much neither."

"He went after us out of spite," Tam said. "Hell hath no fury."

The couple escorted the officers to the front of the property.

"Before I forget, please give my and Brian's sympathies to the family," Tam said.

"My sympathy to them for being related to him," Brian said.

Black and Eden drove to the shops given as an alibi by the Tullys. They called first into the delicatessen and afterwards at the gift shop. The owners both confirmed the Tullys' story. The owner of the gift shop mentioned the mugs had sold out the next day. The owner of the deli added that she'd seen Brian waiting outside in the car while Tam shopped.

Chapter 20

St. Edmund's Medical Practice practised from a large, detached, formerly residential property. All of its windows were protected by blinds. The property fronted the main road and was accessed from there. There was limited parking at the front for the staff and a car park at the back for patients. The only exit was from the back of the property and led to a residential street to the side of the practice. In the car park, Black peered over the wall which surrounded it. He saw an estate agent's premises on the other side of an alleyway between some residential properties. The wall was easily scalable. "I can't see any security cameras, Sir, or warnings of them," Eden said, looking around.

They went inside where they were shown straight into Marie Pilcher's upstairs consulting room. She greeted them at the door and took them inside. The detectives knew Marie Pilcher was in her early forties and had moved to the area about ten years earlier, following the breakdown of her marriage. She had one son who lived with his father. She'd been informed of the nature of the visit before hand, allowing her to obtain Alex Doherty's permission to answer their questions. His basic details (date of birth, height and gender) were already displayed on her screen.

"Alex Doherty is registered with the practice and he did have an appointment here with me on the morning of Tudor O'Connell's death," she said.

"How long was he here for?" Eden said.

Marie Pilcher glanced at her screen and called up her morning appointments for that day. "He had only the one appointment. We give each patient about ten minutes, meaning he was with me for between five and ten minutes. I saw another patient immediately afterwards."

"Can you confirm that Bettina O'Connell is also one of your patients?" Black said.

"I can," Marie said. "I've known Bettina and Tudor for years."

"Bettina claims piles delayed her coming to the door on the day her husband was killed," Black said. "Could there be some truth in that?"

"Bettina does have piles. She's had them for years, which can make mornings very difficult for her, as you will understand if you are ever unfortunate enough to develop them."

"We understand Bettina is on medication for stress," Eden said.

Dr Pilcher hesitated before answering. "She's going through a difficult patch. I prescribed her sleeping tablets and antidepressants."

"If combined with alcohol, could the drugs cause her to act erratically and even have blackouts?" Eden asked.

"Possibly."

"I'd like to show you the post-mortem on Tudor O'Connell," Black said.

"That won't be necessary. As his GP, I've already been provided with it. I can't add much. He didn't have any medical conditions which aren't mentioned on the post-mortem that I'm aware of. His medication had successfully lowered both his blood pressure and cholesterol levels. There is one thing I noticed, though. His bloods showed he'd taken a sleeping tablet the night before. They weren't prescribed by me. He might have been taking Bettina's."

"Thank you, Dr Pilcher," Black said, getting to his feet alongside Eden. "One more thing. We couldn't see any cameras."

"There aren't any," she said. "Patient confidentiality rules that out. If people park when they shouldn't, we wait for them to return to their car and have words."

"Thank you again, Dr Pilcher," Black said.

When back at the station, Eden rang Ivy. "Traces of sleeping tablets were found in Tudor's blood, but they weren't prescribed by his doctor."

"They're too strict about prescribing sleeping tablets," Ivy said. "Tudor couldn't sleep. He worried the renovation would overrun. I helped myself to some of Bettina's when she wasn't looking and gave them to him."

"I got hold of the mediator in the Tully/Tudor O'Connell case," Pilot told Black who was standing, arms crossed by Pilot's desk. "She's going to rule for the Tullys. She accepts their contention that they drew their inspiration, not from the Gethsemane Print, but from the natural world, which, as she put it, isn't copyrighted. As a mediator her decision isn't binding and it could still end up in court. I relayed the mediator's decision to Robert Standley, and this is what he had to say."

Pilot replayed the conversation and Robert Standley's words filled the room: "As Tudor's lawyer and his friend, I'd have told him straight. He had to abandon the case. He'd lost mediation, which basically means he didn't have a cat in hell's chance of winning the case if it went to court. He'd end up saddling the Trust with his and the Tully's legal costs. As a trustee I couldn't allow it and I doubted the other trustees would either. It wasn't his decision alone, remember."

Pilot's voice could be heard asking, "How would he have reacted?"

"It was the nature of the beast to chance his arm, but he was no fool. He wouldn't have risked losing a fortune. He wasn't the type. He'd have thrown in the towel. He wouldn't have been happy about it, but he would have done it."

"That's all very well," Black said, "but Brian and Tam didn't know this. What matters is whether they believed they might have lost. They claim to have been confident of victory, but what else would they say in the circumstances? Alibis notwithstanding, we need to eliminate the possibility that Nick Pilsworth was Brian Tully."

"I'll arrange an ID parade, Sir," Pilot said.

Chapter 21

BRIAN TULLY WAS LARGE-BUILT, balding, potbellied and bespectacled, making the job of finding five similar-looking men to join him in the identity parade a taxing one, solved by Pilot driving to a local factory for paid volunteers. The ID parade took place over the course of a morning. All those who had seen Nick Pilsworth at the TreeHouse on the morning of the O'Connell murder were picked up from their homes and driven to the station.

Brian Tully took his place in the line-up. He was the calmest of the lot, having been given a tranquilliser ten minutes before the parade began. At five-minute intervals, and from behind a concealed mirror, each witness walked along the parade of men. Local shopkeeper Annie Threadneedle went first, Hugo O'Connell last. By the end of the parade, Brian hadn't been identified as Nick Pilsworth by anyone, nor as someone seen in or around the TreeHouse in the days leading up to the murder.

ID parade over, Eden returned to her desk. A large parcel had been delivered. It had arrived just in time. After partially opening it to ensure it was what she was expecting, she furtively took it with her to an empty office. She returned to her desk a short time later, wearing a full-length red and gold Mandarin tunic with black braid buttons under a floor-length red cape, accessorised with a gold belt and a stiff red and gold collar. She wore her hair squeezed into a scull-cap. A moustache, as long as the two-pronged beard growing from the middle of her chin, now sprouted from her upper lip, giving her four even-length tendrils resting at collar-bone level.

When he saw her, Pilot folded his arms and looked her up and down. He paused between every sentence. "Matt like you to dress up like that? Not judging. Am a little."

She ignored him. She sat at her desk, tunic and cape splaying around her, and started to apply make-up. Thus far her time alone with Matt Prichard amounted to a shared croissant over coffee in the police cafeteria. She could only hope her current appearance was not one which appealed to him. Arched kohl eyebrows at the ready, she dropped her eyeliner on the desk and said, "Ming the Merciless, Conqueror of the Universe and future winner of the *Movember*'s *Mocktache* competition at the ready."

"Not so fast, Ming," a voice said. Everyone turned in the direction of the voice. Judy McDermott, dressed as Dick Dastardly, had entered the room, complete with striped hat, red gloves and a small terrier. She too was there for the morning's *Movember Mocktache* photo shoot.

Eden walked towards her. The terrier, faced with the approach of the most evil creature in the universe, tried to bury himself in his mistress's arms. "What the hell happened, Muttley?" Eden asked, giving the little terrier's face a cuddle. "Someone put you in too high a wash?"

Pilot took his camera from the drawer. "Good job you two went for different outfits," he said, his eyes darting back and forth between them. "There's nothing more socially awkward than two ladies turning up dressed as Ming the Merciless." He motioned to his studio — a strip of blue material he'd hung on the wall next to the door of Black's office door. "Shall we cross to Pilot's photo booth?" he asked. "If Mung the Mirthless doesn't object, I'll start with Dastardly McDermott and mini Muttley." He placed two chairs in front of the material. "One for you and one for him, Ma'am."

Judy McDermott took one chair and placed the little terrier on the one next to her. The dog stayed still while she straightened out her lilac coat. He even looked into the camera with a cock of the head when instructed to do so by Pilot. "Any chance of a chuckle from you, Muttley?" he asked. At this the terrier started to scratch. "I'll photoshop a chuckle in later," Pilot said.

His camera was clicking away when the door to Black's office opened and the man himself appeared. He glanced at Judy McDermott and said, "Judy."

"Guido," she replied.

He turned his gaze to Eden and said, "Detective Sergeant."

"Sir," she replied.

He disappeared back into his office and closed the door, immediately reopening it to let out the little dog.

Pilot was still photographing Eden the Merciless One when a call from reception announced the unexpected arrival of Lilah O'Connell at the front desk. "Show her into an interview room," Eden said. "Tell her I'll be ten minutes. Two to take off the outfit, eight more for the make-up."

"Best I just say ten," her colleague mumbled.

Lilah was staring at her phone, her canvas messenger bag in front of her on the table, when Black and Eden entered. They chose to remain standing.

"How can we help you, Lilah?" Eden asked, conscious of the red mark across her upper lip, left from a painfully removed moustache.

Without a word, Lilah reached into the bag and pulled out an A4 envelope which she pushed across the desk to them. Black and Eden studied the envelope. Lilah's address was stencilled across it in green. The post office had added a red *Insufficient Postage* sticker to it. Black put on latex gloves to carefully remove the single-sheet letter it contained. The unpunctuated letter was composed of words and letters cut from a newspaper and glued into place:

I saw you *thieving couldn't stop* yourself could *you* £500 Now Leave at the Ru*d* bou

"When did you receive this, Lilah?" Eden asked.

"Depends what you mean by when. I got home yesterday to find one of these on my doormat." She delved into her bag for the red Post Office card announcing there was an insufficiently stamped letter awaiting her collection at her local post office. She handed the card to Eden. "I went to get it this morning, but technically it was delivered yesterday. Ordinarily, I'd've chucked the card in the bin, but with everything that's happened..."

"Do you have any idea who might have sent it?" Black asked.

"None whatsoever."

"Lilah, everything you say will be treated in the strictest confidence," Eden said.

"I haven't done anything to be blackmailed for," Lilah said. "No one saw me stealing anything. It's probably some gang on a fishing expedition. Pull some names from the electoral register, send them all a blackmail letter, see who pays up."

"Have you ever received a letter like this before, Lilah?" Black asked.

"I never have."

"Do you know where this Rudbou is?" Eden asked of the specified drop-off point.

Lilah grinned and swept her hand through her long hair, now coloured pink and green. "I guess they meant the round-about, but a few letters fell off. I've always been pretty good at anagrams. Apologies for stepping on your toes, but I asked the lady at the Post Office when this was posted. She said anything insufficiently stamped takes an age to work through the system. Could've been weeks ago."

"Odd coincidence, the dad being accused of blackmail, then the daughter being targeted," Black said when back in his office with Eden and Pilot.

"Apart from the texts, we've found nothing on Tudor O'Connell's phone, computer, bank accounts or in his spending, fingering him as a blackmailer," Pilot said, "so unless he was giving away large sums of cash to the homeless in the streets..."

"Strange, the letter was formed from cut-out words but the address stencilled," Black said.

"Blackmailer could've run out of letters?" Pilot said. "Or time?"

"We've checked with every force," Eden said. "None has a current blackmail investigation running."

"Ivy's suggestion that the texter was some troll seemed credible at the time, but Lilah's letter suggests a blackmail campaign of some kind," Black said. "And, as I've said before, whether Tudor O'Connell was the blackmailer is less important than whether somebody thought he was."

"Whoever sent him the text knew him sufficiently well to have his mobile number," Pilot added.

"Was it someone he knew so well he'd wait for them if they unexpectedly emerged from behind a tree in the Events Room?" Eden asked.

Chapter 22

THE NEXT DAY for Eden began with a visit to the garage which had repaired Ivy's vandalised car. She found the owner dressed in oily navy dungarees in the garage workshop, looking up at an overhead car, supported on a metal jack. He remembered the incident.

"Someone had only gone and wrapped the waistband from a pair of Levi's around the carburettor," he said. "Vandalism, pure and simple. No way was that going to start. Had to tow it here."

"Do you still have the material?" Eden asked.

"Chucked it, along with the carburettor. Though the lad here," he nodded to a youngster with his face in a car engine parked in a bay, "unpicked the label for his mum to sew on to a pair of five-quid jeans which he then gave to his girlfriend." The young lad peered up from the open bonnet, blushing and laughing shyly. "What way is that to conduct a relationship, I ask you?"

Eden turned to the lad. "Does your girlfriend still have the jeans?"

The coloured drained from his face.

"What you trying to do to the lad?" the garage owner said.

"If it's evidence you're after, ruining his sex life won't help. He had the good sense to scrub the label clean with detergent first."

"And put it in the microwave," the boy said.

"Did your girlfriend like her present?" she asked.

He blushed again and nodded. "Only now she wants a matching jacket."

Eden had reached the garage forecourt when her phone started to ring. She didn't recognise the number. She stopped between two cars to take the call.

"I got your cat," a husky male voice said at the other end.

She hadn't expected to get a response to the posters she'd put up and was so surprised by the call that she heard herself ask, "Is she all right?"

"You want me to put her on the line?" the caller sneered.

"Where is she? I'll come and collect her."

"A thousand quid."

Eden nearly fell over. "You must be joking?"

"Okay, okay. £100 then."

"I'll have you know, Sir, that kidnapping an animal for ransom is a criminal offence."

"You want her back or what?"

"Where and when?" she said.

He gave an address and the line went dead. Why hadn't she told him to turn the phone on the cat to prove she was still alive, she asked herself, as she climbed into her car.

Can you go to this address and see if they have Boopy? I promised them £100 if it's her. PS: best ask to see her first! she texted her stepdad, Eric.

Text sent, she started the engine, only for her phone to start ringing again. This time it was the station. "You're wanted at these coordinates," an officer told her, providing her with a map reference and suggesting she take her wellies.

The map reference took Eden to a field. She parked at its edge, up on the bank, and swung her legs out of the door to put on her boots. She caught sight of the search team on the horizon and wondered if they had found the weapon as she set off in their direction.

Of the fat orange pumpkins which had grown in the field up to only a few days earlier, now only a few remained, and they were mostly decaying. Overnight rain made the field squelchy and muddy and traversing it difficult. Eden's boots kept sinking in the mud and more than once she got stuck. She'd just used both hands to pull herself free when she saw a pair of cat's eyes staring out at her from a nest of nettles at the side of the field. She changed direction to cross over to have a better look. It might be Betty Boop. Her sudden change of direction caused a ginger cat to flee across the field and Eden to step on a rotten pumpkin, lose her balance, trip over a long vine crossing the field and land face first in the mud.

With difficulty, she got back on her feet. "For heaven's sake," she said, rubbing her muddy gloves on her muddy trousers. She used her cleanish sleeve to try and wipe the mud from her face. She was still flapping her arms around when she saw Fishergate striding towards her, smiling. She waited for him to reach her and accepted his offer of a gloved hand. As he helped her to traverse the remainder of the field, she asked, "What have you got? The weapon?"

"Not the weapon, Ma'am," he said.

The search team were congregated by a thicket of vegetation which separated the field from the one behind it. By their feet lay wooden pallets, sheets of hardboard, planks of wood, a beige Formica kitchen top, and a pile of foliage.

Fishergate explained all. "We've widened the search for the weapon. We'd started clearing away brambles from the side of that tree and found that lot underneath made into a little lean-to, with a Formica floor." He pointed to the pallets and other bits. "The pallets made the outside walls, the hardboard the inside, and the Formica was on top of the planks of wood on the ground. It was quite snug inside."

"Was there a kettle and a packet of *Digestives* in there?" she joked.

Fishergate shook his head. "Something even better," he said. He lifted the pallet up and showed her slats running in one direction; then, after tilting it, slats running in the opposite direction. Eden moved closer. A pallet inside a pallet, she thought. She was beginning to get excited. "Whoever threw it up went to the trouble of removing a set of slats to make themselves a little hidey-hole," Fishergate said, directing her to a small gap at the end of the larger of the two pallets. A hidey-hole inside a camouflaged lean-to on the edge of a field — whatever next? Eden asked herself. "Was anything inside the hidey-hole?" she wanted to know.

"Yeah, that," Fishergate said. A member of the search team raised the buff-coloured case he'd been holding which Eden had assumed belonged to the team. The case was almost the same colour as the pallets it was hidden inside. Fishergate opened the case.

"Hello, hello, hello," Eden said, taking a peek inside. "What have we got here, then?"

Eden held a sheet of newspaper aloft. Light streamed through the spaces left by the words and letters cut from it. She was in the incident room, addressing the team.

"This is one of many sheets of newspaper and magazines recovered from the briefcase found inside the lean-to," she said. "The pages were neatly folded up to fit inside the case where we also found a stencil, blank sheets of paper, glue and some pens. The lean-to had floorboards and a Formica worktop for a desk. It was large enough for one person and seems to have been used as an office. Team – we've found Blackmail Central."

Black spoke next. "The discovery puts to bed any doubts as to whether or not there is a blackmailer. We'll get everything over to forensics, see if we can get some prints or a strand of hair, then the brains at Intel can have a look."

At the end of the day, Eden paid a visit to Black in his office. "Are we chasing our own tails on this one, Sir?" she asked.

"Possibly," he replied, "but I'm confident we've spoken with the killer."

Chapter 23

AT HOME there was a knock on the front door. Eden answered. A deliveryman stood there with a parcel. Its shape gave it away. It was the pretty wastepaper bin she'd ordered for Dora. Thankfully she was upstairs getting ready for school. Eden signed for it before stealthily climbing the stairs to hide the present. This reminded her that she'd forgotten to send off for the print of the *Arc of Life*, which in turn reminded her that she'd forgotten to take a photograph of the painting's full index. She logged onto the TreeHouse webpage and went to the link dedicated to Gethsemane's artwork. *Arc of Life* was the first piece featured. After the work came a description including the index:

1. Cat (first floor)

2. Swan wings (sails)

3. Pregnant dog (deck)

The three flying dodos came in at number 57.

She saved the description and the index to send to the printers along with the photographs of the piece she'd taken. She was wondering if she had time to do this before she left, when she heard a car pull up. She looked out of the window. It was her lift. Time to go.

She'd just got to the bottom of the stairs and shouted out, "I'm off. See you all later," when her phone began to ring. Matt was at the other end.

"Just wondered how you were doing?" he said.

"We're doing very well, thanks. You?"

"Very well indeed. Just wondering if I could take you out to dinner, sometime?"

"That would be nice." Outside, a car tooted. "Matt, could you text me? I've got to interview a witness in London and my lift's here."

Pilot was Eden's London lift. With him at the steering wheel, she checked her phone. Matt's text was there. She replied and dropped her phone into her handbag.

"Arrest sheet's on the back seat," Pilot said.

Eden picked it up to read. *Vanilla Larvey. 43 years old, works as a cleaner. Numerous previous convictions ranging from shoplifting to passing stolen cheques and goods. Following a sting operation, arising from allegations from colleagues, Vanilla was arrested and charged with theft of cash from a colleague's handbag.*

She read on. "A – hah," she said out loud upon learning that Vanilla's employers had the cleaning contract for the office block where the mediation meeting between Tudor O'Connell and Brian Tully had taken place. "Didn't expect to hear their names again," she said.

"Did you ever find that cat of yours?" Pilot asked.

"No," she said. "Someone said they had her, but it was some kid trying to sell his granny's cat. Eric threatened to call the police on him. I don't know how a lump of fur and claws has so wormed her way into our affections, but she has," Eden said with a sigh.

Pilot said something she didn't quite catch but sounded like

Haylee, cat and person. She ran the words over again in her mind. Haylee. Cat. Person. Was he talking about the famous actress or the Haylee whose date with Pilot ended so disastrously that no one on the team was allowed to mention it? The only reply she could manage on the spur was, "Er?"

"You remember Haylee. We went out for that drink."

"The drink where you saw your girlfriend Mace with another man, the girlfriend who Haylee had until then thought was your ex-girlfriend, and you and Mace had a huge fight and then you and Haylee had a huge fight and you ended up getting dumped by both of them?"

"Yeah that drink, that Haylee," Pilot said. "Anyhows, me and her bumped into each other in the corridor. She said my moustache made me look a bit Desperate Dan-ish, which is better than a bit desperate, which is what I thought she was going to say. I was going for hipster, but whatever."

"Glad you've patched things up," Eden said. Pilot obviously wanted to talk about Haylee. "So, Haylee's a cat person, is she? It's important to find stuff out like that about people right from the start. I was always more of a dog person, but I do miss Betty Boop."

"I didn't mean she prefers cats to dogs, that would be too weird," he said. "Cat-person is her avatar."

"You've already exchanged avatars?" Eden teased. "On a second date?"

"It wasn't a second date. For our second date I've invited her to mine for dinner. She said yes, but now I'm worried about what to cook. I was thinking of cow pie, keeping to the Desperate Dan theme."

"Dottie's a brill cook. She'll rustle you up a cow pie and gravy. She won't mind."

"Yeah, well, as it so happens, Haylee's a vegan," he said.

"And it was going so well."

. . .

An hour and a half later saw Pilot and Eden interviewing Vanilla Larvey in a police station in a London suburb. One glance told Eden that Vanilla was not the type of woman to be fazed by a police interview. She was quite blasé about the whole thing. A sparkly headband kept Vanilla's long hair from her face. Her blue eyeshadow sparkled, as did her rouge lip gloss. Vanilla's top revealed nearly as much of her bosom as it concealed. She was bangled and ringed up. On one ear she wore her row of looped earrings, on the other, a row of studs.

"I'm Detective Constable Philpot, and this is Detective Sergeant Hudson," Pilot said. "Just to be clear, Ms Larvey, we're not here to interview you about the charge of theft."

"I know why you're here," she said, peering at herself in a vanity mirror as she spoke. She adjusted her hair and looked up. "You're here 'cause I know something about the man who was killed. Tudor O'Connell. I want something for helping you, all right? I'm not helping for nothing." She folded her arms defiantly.

"The Crown Prosecution Service is prepared to offer you a deal if the information you provide helps us with our inquiries, Ms Larvey," Pilot said.

"What does a deal mean?" she said.

"In a nutshell, a guaranteed non-custodial sentence in return for us learning something we don't already know," Eden replied.

"Well, I can guarantee you don't know this," Vanilla said. She gave a squeal and reached for her mirror, blinking furiously.

"Are you quite all right, Ms Larvey?" Eden asked.

"My eyelash has come loose." Vanilla dived into a bag by her feet from which she produced a make-up bag. A pair of false eyelashes was placed on the desk next to the vanity mirror. Eden and Pilot watched Vanilla remove the offending eyelash, blow on it, then dot a thin layer of glue along its vein before reattaching it. She blinked again a few times. "That's better," she said. She pushed the equipment to one side. "I clean the Whiteroa Building, over on Lion Street," she said. "My manager told me to clean the Gents on the second floor. He hates me. Gives me all the crap jobs — no pun intended. Just so you get the setup and understand how I came to overhear what I did. The whole of those Gents is tiled: walls, floor, the lot. Everyone can hear everything. Also, while it looks like all the cubicles are on one side and the piss holes on the other," she motioned with her hands, "there's actually another cubicle hidden around the corner, out of sight, which is where I was on the morning in question, having a ciggie. I'd just lit up when I heard the door. Typical, I thought. I threw my cigarette down the loo and stayed put. I heard someone doing his business at the urinal, then the door again. Initially I thought it was him leaving, but then I heard two men. Things were heated. One said, *'Your thieving bitch of a wife thinks she can steal my copyright, does she?'* The other got defensive, started saying they hadn't stole nothing. By now, I'm out of the cubicle and getting as close as I can without being seen. They were hissing at each other like Tom cats. I couldn't see a thing from where I was, so I turned my phone on its side and pushed it along the floor as far as I could get and took a photo. They didn't notice. One said, *'You don't frighten me'* and the other says back, *'Oh yeah? Ever heard of death by litigation? No? Well, you're about to.'* I heard footsteps and the door open and shut. When I took a peek around the corner this man was doubled-up, like he'd been punched. I heard the door and darted out of sight. A different man said, *'Are you okay?'* I heard a *'Yes'* and the door open and close. I waited for *Are you okay* to finish and leave before clearing off myself. No one was outside."

The information was certainly very interesting. "Can we please see the photograph you took, Ms Larvey," Eden asked.

Vanilla reached into the bag again and searched through it for her phone. When she finally found it, she scrolled through her photographs, proudly showing one to Pilot and Eden. They looked at it for a few minutes.

"This is a photograph of two pairs of men's shoes," Eden said.

"I know," Vanilla said. "But look how pointy and shiny them shoes on the right are. Like winkle pickers. Not many men got shoes like that." She put her finger above a pair of black patent-leather shoes which ended in sharp points. Eden and Pilot had both seen shoes like this before. In Tudor O'Connell's wardrobe.

"Although the shoes are unusual, Ms Larvey, I'm afraid they alone do not positively identify either of the men in this photograph as Tudor O'Connell," Pilot said.

Vanilla grinned and squealed. "There's more. I went straight from the Gents to Reception to tell my mate about the row. She's the receptionist. I was at the Reception desk when the lift stopped, and a man stepped out. He had on those same pointy shoes," she pointed at the photograph, "and the same striped trousers. He had his phone to ear and was heading towards the door. My mate called out to him for his lanyard. He still had it around his neck. He rolled his eyes, took his lanyard from round his neck," she demonstrated, "and literally hurled it at her with a right arrogant 'Okay?' I jumped in and caught it. My mate was so pissed off with him for chucking it at her like that, she didn't even notice me pocketing it."

"That still doesn't positively identify him as Tudor O'Connell," Eden said.

Vanilla looked very pleased with herself. "The lanyard had his name on it." She reached into her bag, triumphantly producing the lanyard. She removed it from a clear plastic bag, holding it by its green ribbon and dangling it in her hand.

"Soon as I saw his name in the papers, I recognised it. I mean, how many people have a name like Tudor O'Connell. Right?"

Eden reached over and took it from her. The name on the lanyard was Tudor O'Connell.

"We'll need you to look at some photographs, Ms Larvey," Pilot said.

"We had a deal, you and me," Vanilla said. "Something for something."

"We did, Ms Larvey," Pilot said. "And you have been most helpful."

"I have, haven't I?" she giggled. "Death by litigation. That was a new one on me. Had to look it up."

In exchange for a suspended sentence for the offence for which she had been arrested and the other offences she was suspected of left to *lie on the file*, Vanilla agreed to look through a collection of photographs of various random men, one of whom was Tudor O'Connell. She easily identified Tudor O'Connell as the man she'd seen that day.

Once Vanilla Larvey had been shown from the room, Pilot and Eden looked at each other, startled by the development.

"Okay. Tudor threatened a man that day at the hotel. You and me both know it was Brian Tully, but how can we establish beyond all reasonable doubt that the other man in the argument *was* Brian Tully?" Pilot said.

"It was," Eden said. She tapped the other pair of shoes captured in Vanilla's picture — a pair of Navy canvas espadrilles. "He was wearing shoes like that the day the Governor and I called. You ever heard of death by litigation?"

He shook his head. "New one on me."

Eden Googled it.

Death by litigation: (A US saying.) Used to describe a situation whereby a claimant to litigation (and invariably the party with the deeper pockets) relentlessly pursues litigation against a defendant, regardless of merit or likelihood of success, until the other party either dies or goes bankrupt.

Chapter 24

BLACK KNOCKED on the door of Lilah O'Connell's cottage. She wasn't slow to answer.

"Detective Inspector," she said. She wore dungarees over a T-shirt. Her hair was clipped to the top of her head. "What a pleasant surprise. Come on in if you'd like." She left him standing on the doorstep, the door wide open. He followed her inside, closing the door behind him.

"I'm in the kitchen," she called out. He found her filling the kettle. He couldn't help noticing that in the time it had taken her to walk from the front door to her kitchen, one strap of her dungarees had become unfastened and allowed to hang loose. "If I'd known you were coming, I'd've baked a cake," she said. "Tea or coffee?"

"Neither. I'm on duty."

"I should hope so, seeing you're here."

Her cosy kitchen was small and cluttered. There were hand-painted wall tiles. Plants and herbs crowded the windowsills and spider plants hung from the ceiling in macramé plant pots. She dropped a tea bag into a mug.

"Take a seat," she motioned to the round kitchen table in an alcove. He sat at the table and waited for her to finish pouring hot water into the mug. She left the tea bag in the mug and joined him at the table, sitting to face him, mug cupped in her hands. The smell of lemon and ginger from the hot drink mixed with the smell of the herbs coming from the windowsill.

Lilah's eyes flickered to his moustache. He'd waxed it that morning now that the tips were long enough to curl upwards. "Mon Dieu," she said. "It's almost as though I'm talking to the great detective himself. How can I help?"

"We've found a concealed lean-to in a field. The evidence we've retrieved from it suggests someone was using it to put together blackmail letters, opening up the possibility that your letter was one of many similar," he said.

"Oh, yes?" she said, cool as a cucumber, as always.

"We've recovered other material from the site, too."

She took a sip of her hot drink and then another. Black showed her a photograph of a roll-up cigarette. "The cigarette contains cannabis and was found in the vicinity of the lean-to. The cannabis cigarette has tested positive for your DNA."

"Would you like one? Oh no — you're on duty."

"Is this all a big joke to you, Lilah?" Black asked.

"No, Detective Inspector, it isn't," she replied, "and the longer my dad's killer's out there, the less funny it gets, which is why I must ask what you're doing here, getting your knickers in a twist over a spliff. If that's more important than murder, I must request someone else be put in charge of the case." The casual and slightly flippant side of her personality had vanished.

Black gave her the name of the farm on whose land the lean–to and spliff had been found. "Blackmail may lie at the centre of your father's murder and therefore I'm interested to learn what you were doing by the blackmailer's lair."

"Blackmailer's lair," she repeated. "I enjoy a spliff. It's recreational. I'm not always that careful of disposing of them. Hugo's always on at me about it. That farm is down the road from here.

I pretty much go everywhere on foot. I don't drive. Haven't got a licence. I smoked a spliff, I chucked it away, you found it." She took another sip of her drink. This seemed to relax her. She even smiled. "Maybe that's why I got a letter? The blackmailer saw me and decided to chance his or her luck but sexed the demand up a bit. That means it's someone I know."

Brian Tully appeared petrified at the sight of Eden on his doorstep again and yelled, "Tam —Tam." There was panic in his voice. Eden lowered her eyes and saw, on his feet, a pair of the Navy canvas espadrilles, identical to those captured in Vanilla's photograph.

Tam Tully appeared at the kitchen door and immediately took control. She invited Eden inside, apologising for her husband's rudeness in leaving her on the doorstep, and took her through to the living room. The Tullys nervously sat beside each other. Eden faced them. Brian was still visibly shaken. The colour which had drained from his face upon opening the front door still hadn't returned.

"How can we help you, officer?" Tam said. It was clear that she too was nervous but keeping it under wraps. After asking her question, she straightened her skirt a few times, looking down as she did so, before looking up again.

"Mr Tully, a witness has come forward claiming to have overheard an argument between you and the late Tudor O'-Connell in the Gents toilet of the Whiteroa Building on Lion Street, London on the day you and Tudor O'Connell met there for the mediation hearing," Eden said.

Brian Tully gave a little gasp. He then said. "Well he or she is a liar."

"Mr Tully, our witness overheard Mr O'Connell threaten you with *Death by Litigation*," Eden said.

"What does that even mean?" Brian said.

"It roughly translates as the threat of endless litigation until the other party to the action dies or runs out of money," Eden explained. "Do you have anything to say about this, Mr Tully?"

Brian looked to his wife for help as though a helpless child. The fight had left him. "Tudor O'Connell was a bully," he said. "A bully."

"Detective Sergeant..." Tam said, "Can I say something?"

Eden said, "Please do."

"There was an argument. Just as you've been told." Brian leaned forward abruptly but Tam reached an arm out to calm him down. "I didn't know anything about this argument when you were here last. Brian had kept it from me. To protect me."

"She was sick with worry as it was, without that," Brian said.

"It's the way he is," Tam said. "After you left, he broke down in tears. I got it out of him, bit by bit. I didn't know whether to cry or hit the roof. Not only hadn't he told me, more importantly, he hadn't told you. It made us look as if we had something to hide. We talked all night about whether to call you. Brian swore nobody else was around. We couldn't see how anybody else could have heard the argument."

"There wasn't anyone else around," he said. "How...?"

"There's a cubicle around the corner," Eden explained, at which Brian's head slumped forward.

"We should have told you," Tam said. "We were stupid to think we could just ride it out. Sweep it under the carpet. It was a misjudgement, for which we apologise."

"We just wanted it to go away," Brian said.

"Those things he said to Brian could be misconstrued as a motive, we understand that," Tam said. "But we didn't kill Tudor O'Connell. This man," she touched her husband, "hasn't even got points on his licence, for goodness sake. We have an alibi. What your witness heard was Tudor O'Connell the bully."

"He was trying to intimidate us into backing down," Brian said.

"This isn't the States, you can't just keep on and on with litigation," Tam said. "I checked."

"I didn't mean to lie," Brian said. "I just... I just wanted it to be over." He slumped forward again.

"We are guilty of the sin of omission, Detective Sergeant," Tam Tully said. "Nothing more sinister. We are no more murderers than we are plagiarists. We've worked for everything we've got in this life, unlike Mr Tudor O'Connell, who never worked a day in his life." She was getting crosser and crosser. "The man was a congenital liar. I've been on the webpage. Never read so many lies. The studio wasn't kept as a memorial to Gethsemane. They chucked her stuff out after she died. His dad carved the TreeHouse sign for his first wife, not his darling Gethsemane. And she was the garden designer not..."

"Tam," Brian said softly. "I don't think you ranting is helping."

"I'm sorry, Detective Sergeant," Tam said. "I just get so angry. That man continues to haunt us from his grave. And all because I rejected him decades ago."

Eden got to her feet. "I think that will be all for the time being, assuming there is nothing else you have omitted to tell me, Mr and Mrs Tully?"

"No," Tam said.

Brian repeated, "No."

They walked her to the door, where Tam Tully said, "Thank you for being so understanding." Brian nodded his agreement. They remained at the door until Eden had driven away.

She picked Pilot up from outside the shopping complex where she'd dropped him.

"I had another word with the lady who owns the deli," he

said, seat-belting himself in. "I also spoke with the lady who runs the gift shop. They've both known the Tullys for yonks. Both are definite it was her in the shop with him parked outside. Deli lady even knew the time because she had the telly on and her favourite daytime soap had just started when Mrs T turned up." As Eden drove off, he added, "Oh yeah, your local cat charity rang." Eden had left her phone with him. "Someone's just handed in a black cat."

Chapter 25

BLACK WAS on his way back to the station from Lilah's cottage when he got a message that Father Dermot Hanrahan wished to speak to him. He drove to the church where he found Father Hanrahan waiting in the church porch. The priest took Black inside straight to the lectern at the altar end. The lectern's stand, Black noticed, now stood half as high as it had done on the afternoon of Tudor's memorial service. Without another word, Father Hanrahan stepped up onto the hexagonal stand. The arm rest and the reading stand were now at the perfect height for him.

He climbed off and said, "The lectern is designed to be raised and lowered, depending on the height of the user. Allow me to show you." He pressed a disc of in-laid wood at the stand's centre, causing the small disk to flip on its side. Father Hanrahan put a finger in each of the small gaps created, and gave a quick twist followed by a tug. The hexagonal stand rose. The motion repeated, it rose further.

"I haven't needed to adjust the height since the day it arrived. It's bespoke and I'm the only one who uses the lectern. Visitors use the pulpit," he motioned towards the wooden pulpit at the top of winding steps. "The lectern is always kept at the right height for me. I'm not sure if you noticed, but on the day of poor Tudor's memorial service, it was too high. I only noticed it myself less than half an hour before the service was due to start. Now you've seen how easy it is to adjust. Naturally, when I saw how tall it was, I tried to do just that, but I couldn't get the damn disk to budge. It was firmly stuck. I really thought Tudor was playing a trick on us from heaven. There wasn't any time to do anything about it and I carried on with the service. I felt as ridiculous as I'm sure I looked, but I put it out of my mind by concentrating on the matter in hand. When that was finished, I went to the TreeHouse along with half the congregation. It wasn't until the next day that I got a chance to have a better look. I discovered the plughole had been glued into place. No wonder it didn't budge. I ended up having to use a penknife to free it. I dismissed the incident as a bad attempt at humour and decided to ignore it. It hasn't happened since, I'm glad to report. But it's been weighing on my mind ever since and I felt you should know about it."

Black squatted by the lectern and gave it a tap. It was hollow. "Does the stand come apart, Father?" Black asked, "I'm wondering if anything could have been put inside it?"

"I don't believe it does, although I have never tried."

Black got to his feet and said, "Let's turn it on its side."

The priest blanched. "Please be careful. It cost a fortune."

Father Hanrahan had reluctantly taken hold of one side of the lectern as Black took hold of the other, when he suddenly said, "Wait, wait!" He ran off into a side room, returning with a thick blanket which he spread on the ground. "One of my practitioners knitted it for me."

The two men turned the lectern on its side and gently lowered it onto the blanket. Black squatted to push gingerly at the base of the now-sideways lectern. He kept pushing until the piece of plain hexagonal hardwood loosened sufficiently for him to be able to manipulate it onto its side. This allowed him to remove it completely. This left a hollow hexagonal box. He laid the hardwood on the blanket and shone a torch around the empty space.

"Well, will you look at that?" Father Hanrahan said.

Whilst the exterior was highly polished and inlaid with marquetry, its interior was unvarnished and rough to the touch. Tiny pinpricks marked the wood. Black asked the priest what they were. "Something to do with the manufacture, I suppose."

"We'll need to take it for detailed forensic examination," Black announced, getting to his feet. Father Hanrahan looked dismayed by the news.

"We'll be careful not to damage it," Black said. "Maybe you'd like to explain the real reason you've decided to tell me about this now, Father, and not at the time?"

"All right. I knew straight away Ivy was behind it," Father Hanrahan said. "She didn't want Tudor's memorial service held in St. Edmunds, but the family outvoted her. That made her angry and she vandalised the lectern to make me and the service ridiculous. I didn't want to dignify it by making a fuss."

"And you changed your mind because?"

Father Hanrahan bristled. "Bettina rang me. Said Ivy'd been giving interviews again, making out she's the only victim."

"Basically, you wanted to teach her a lesson?" Black said. The priest struggled for a reply.

"Is there any CCTV of this church?" Black asked. The question had been raised at the beginning of the enquiry, but he couldn't remember the answer off the top of his head.

"There was until last month when we were burgled, and the wires cut. We haven't yet replaced it. Time and money being against us."

Chapter 26

EDEN SPENT the journey to the cat's home preparing Dora for the possibility that the handed-in cat might not be theirs.

"I know, Mum," she said bravely.

The show of bravery ended the minute they came to a stop outside the country property containing the cat charity where Dora leapt out of the car and ran towards the entrance.

"Wait up," Eden called out in vain.

Eden found her at the reception, fingers clutching the desk. "We've come about the black cat handed in earlier," Eden explained to the volunteer. Dora's eyes were tightly shut. She pulled her hands from the desk and crossed her fingers, whispering, "Please let it be Boopy. Please."

"The neutered male missing his right ear?" the woman asked.

Eden felt her daughter slump beside her. Before she had a chance to speak, Dora looked up and said, "Yes, that one."

"Dora, unless Betty Boop has had a sex change and lost an ear, it's not her, love," Eden said.

"I know, Mum. But we can still take it."

"That particular cat has already found a new home," the volunteer informed them.

Dora's eyes welled up. "At least the cat has found a loving home," Eden said, struggling to console her daughter. "We'll make a donation, as we're here," she added, taking out her purse.

"We have other cats who still need a good home," the volunteer said. Eden flinched. She didn't want to be saddled with a strange cat. She wanted Boopy or none at all. She had a sinking feeling she could end up re-homing half a dozen cats if she wasn't careful.

"Duchess has been with us for six months," the volunteer continued, turning her computer screen to show them Duchess. "She's an older cat, good with children and completely white."

"We'll take her," Dora said.

"Dora — what if Betty Boop comes back? How will she feel about us replacing her with another cat?" Eden asked.

"Boopy's my best friend, Mum," Dora wailed, "but we need to face facts. Boopy's not coming back. We need to move on with our lives." Tears streamed down the child's face.

"Duchess really is a lovely cat," the volunteer said. Through her tears, Dora looked up at Eden expectantly. The volunteer looked at her expectantly. On the screen, Duchess looked at her expectantly. For heaven's sake, Eden thought. "We'll take her," she said, "but only her."

As Eden loaded the cat basket into the car, Black was at home at an upstairs window, binoculars to his eyes. In the air, a few fields away, the merlin hovered. Focussed. In the fields below her were a group of birdwatchers, drawn to the area by news of a merlin. The breeze gently lifted her and suddenly she made her move, pursuing her prey on the wing. Her prey, a sparrow, was fast, but she was faster, darting after it, intercepting it in the air to applause from her human audience before carrying it in her talons to her perch on the Church spire.

"I feed those sparrows," Black's girlfriend Chloe wailed.

Chapter 27

THE RECONSTRUCTION of the murder of Tudor O'Connell began at exactly the same time as had the fateful tour those present were there to re-enact: 10:30 a.m. The day was chosen because it was forecast to remain dry. Black decided to take the part of the still-missing Nick Pilsworth himself. Pilot was to play the late Tudor O'Connell. Everyone else played themselves. The entire reconstruction was to be recorded from various angles, with police officers posted throughout. Eden remained indoors in the kitchen of the TreeHouse to watch the reconstruction from an array of screens.

The reconstruction began at the front of the TreeHouse. Tudor O'Connell had written his opening words in advance and Pilot repeated them. "Thank you for your interest in the Tree House. As Gethsemane's son, I have made it my life's work to keep her memory alive and I welcome the chance to work with you all."

The introduction over, they set off to and through the gate, letting it swing closed behind them. Black gave the gate one quick tug to make sure it was locked. The group paused in the courtyard for the prescribed period, where, once again, Pilot repeated Tutor's words. Once through the Orangery, they assembled on the lawn. "We'll begin the tour proper in the Event's Room and make our way there via the Winter Garden," Pilot said. This part he was having to wing.

The police officer hiding in the sculpture heard Pilot's words; he also heard the group traipse past him and into the grounds. And then he heard a further set of footsteps — those of Caro May hurrying after the group after tying her shoelaces. Once he was sure it was safe, he slipped through a gap he'd found in the base of the sculpture and lowered himself to the ground. Before the reconstruction had got underway, he'd had a go at climbing through the sculpture's open top, but the tarpaulin made it too difficult. It wouldn't have left him enough time, he realised, and so he abandoned that idea. But the replacement exit was one that worked.

Pilot strode ahead of the group, Hugo kept to the rear with the remainder of the party in between. Black hung back a little. Hugo did likewise to walk alongside him. He could still remember the pained small talk he'd had with Nick Pilsworth. "What brings you to the TreeHouse?" he asked, adding, "and wouldn't we all like to know the answer to that?"

"I'm an Arts teacher," Black said, sticking to the script.

Once out of the sculpture, the officer slipped over to the archway. The group had reached the end of the Herb Room. He waited for them to move into the next garden room then stealthily and quickly skirted along the inside of the Herb Room, and into the slanted cutting in the hedge. Once through it, the race was on to reach the Events Room before the party.

As the group stepped inside the pruned Rose Room, three magpies pecking at the dirt flew off. Hugo patted his stomach, turned to Black and said, "Three for a girl." Then added, "He went back around this point."

Playing his part, Black said, "Going to go, not feeling right." He turned around to head towards the house.

"Are you all right, Sir?" Hugo called.

"What's going on at the back?" Pilot cried out.

Over the heads of the group, Hugo said, "Guest doesn't feel well. He's going back."

"My wife will let you through the gate," Pilot replied, talking over everyone's head.

Hugo waited for Black to disappear from view into the preceding garden room before starting after the group who were now filing out of the Rose Room and into the Winter Garden.

Once across the Winter Room, Pilot crossed the footpath outside it to stand just inside the arched entrance to the Events Room, forcing the group to congregate on the path. He took a few steps backwards, beckoning Hugo to join him. After he did, Pilot pretended to give him instructions. The group continued to wait obediently, as they had on the morning but, unlike then, the group were now staring in horror and disbelief at the scene in front of them — a verdant murder scene framed by a hedge. The atmosphere was sombre. Two of the party spontaneously burst into tears. Another began shaking. Each, though, forced themselves to take in the scene as they had been asked to. They saw a large rectangular lawn and some beaten down winter grasses. They saw two brick walls, one to the rear, the other to their right, broken up by a wooden gate. They saw a tall broad hedge dividing the space from the adjoining Topiary Room. They saw a pond with a bridge over it, and on the other side, a large beech tree. Everyone had been asked to look out for anything that appeared in any way different from how it had been on the day of the murder. But as they stood there, their eyes taking in this scene, no one spoke out.

Pilot pulled them from their thoughts by announcing that something had come up and Hugo was going to take over the tour. Hugo rejoined the group as Pilot started to walk towards the gate.

"No," Caroline May said, "he can't have moved until we were out of sight. I was last to go, and he was still there."

Pilot stopped in his tracks and turned to face the group again. Hugo said, "Dad was behind me. I didn't look." Pilot remained where he was until the last of the group was out of sight, unwrapping and popping a piece of chewing gum into his mouth.

In the alcove, facing the entrance to the Topiary Room, Hugo sat himself down on the stone seat, enclosed by hedge. Before anybody moved, a police officer asked, "Do any of you remember turning around at this point and looking behind you?" The group stopped and looked at each other. Each either shook their head or said no; they hadn't. The first into the Topiary Room was Ren Hoffbrand. The others were close behind.

Inside the Events Room, Pilot had reached the gate where he removed a pair of reading glasses — which he didn't need — from his jacket pocket and put them on. From the corner of his eye, he saw something move. He lowered the glasses to rest on his nose and turned towards the tree to see his colleague moving in his direction clutching a garden stake. Pilot hadn't been sure who was going to step out — sculpture man or the spare murderer hiding behind the tree, just in case. Sculpture man winked, as though to say, "Made it." Pilot stood stock still as his colleague slowly but deliberately advanced towards him, wearing his best murderous look.

Harry Thorne and his son Will started off at the same time as they had on the day of the murder, this time with a police officer in Harry's van. Will, at the wheel of the digger, took up the rear. With the roads blocked off to traffic, there was little risk of separation or delay. They arrived. They parked. They walked to the front door. They rang the bell. When there was no answer, they rang it again. Bettina O'Connell yelled, "I heard you! I'm coming!" There was stomping along the hall and the front door opened. This was the first time since the murder the three had met.

"The boy and I are most sorry for your loss, Mrs O'Connell," Harry Thorne said. His son nodded gravely. "Still can't believe what's happened."

"Thank you, Harry," she said. "We'd better go through the motions, I suppose. Can you remember what we did next?"

"You took us to the cottage garden," Harry said.

She nodded and stepped outside. She hesitated. The front door was still open. "I must've closed it," she said, pulling the door shut behind her. "I can't remember doing it, but I must have."

They took the same route. Bettina and Harry opened the double gate. No one spoke as they crossed to the cottage garden. Young Will glanced across the courtyard. He froze. That, he definitely hadn't seen on the morning of the murder. His dad also looked over his shoulder and gave a double-take before pushing Will onwards to the cottage and its rear garden.

Once there, Bettina and the Thornes stood around awkwardly until young Will cleared his throat and said, "Think this is where you ran back to the house, Mrs O'Connell."

"I still haven't apologised for that," she replied. "I've been wanting to..." She glanced at the supervising police officer. "I don't have to hijack the digger again, do I?"

"Reckon that won't be necessary," was the reply.

"As I was saying, I wanted to apologise, but I was too ashamed of myself. It was unforgivable of me to drag you into a private fight. I hope you received my cheque."

Harry nodded his acknowledgment. "We all do stuff out of character from time to time, Mrs O'Connell. There's no more to be said on the subject. Will — I think you ran into the road about this time to get a signal."

As he disappeared, Ivy appeared from behind the studio, yelling, "You crazy bitch!"

"Well, you've got into your part," Bettina said icily as Ivy reached them. "I presume we don't need to restage the argument, officer?"

"That won't be necessary either," she said.

"Sorry to disappoint you, dearie," Bettina said.

In the Topiary Room, Nico and Zyline Angeles cast only a cursory glance at the ornamental hedging. They did pretend to size the space up and take a few prohibited photographs. At the end of the large space, by a copper mother frog reading a book to the baby frog on her lap, Zyline pointed in the direction of the house. "We were here when we heard the crash. It came from over in that direction. We turned around."

"Did you see anything?" the police officer asked.

As her husband shook his head, she said, "Just the others, wandering around."

"Please do as you did on the day," the officer said.

Aware of what they were going to find upon emerging from the archway in the hedge, they hesitated before stepping through it into the Events Room.

Pilot was uncomfortable. Not even a tarpaulin separated him from the cold, dank earth. He was meant to be keeping as still as possible, but grass had got up his nose and his forehead was sinking in the mud, giving him a chill headache. He wasn't convinced he was even breathing.

Zyline was in first. Upon seeing Pilot, sprawled face down on the grass, she yelled, "Oh my god — Nico! He's had a heart attack. Ring for an ambulance." She started to run towards Pilot.

Nico turned and ran back into the Topiary Room, shouting, "He's had a heart attack! Tudor! I'm going to get help." He left the others running in the direction of the Events Room as he himself ran back through the Topiary Room. As he left it, he nearly collided with Hugo running in. "Your dad's had a heart attack. I'm going to call an ambulance."

Nico turned Hugo around and pushed him along the path until they reached the entrance to the Events Room. Here, Hugo turned left and Nico right.

Pilot allowed Zyline Angeles to turn him on his back. He heard the others thunder across the lawn. They arrived in quick succession: Ren, Alf and Caro from one direction, then Hugo, last, from another.

Pilot heard Caro May say, "Oh my God — blood! He's hurt himself," and felt himself being turned on his side.

He heard Zyline say, "Oh my god? What are those holes in his coat? Has he been stabbed?"

He heard Alf Hoffbrand yell, "I can't get a signal," and Caro May, "Me neither."

He heard Alf ask Hugo for the gate code then Hugo scream he couldn't remember it. Ren told Alf to give her a hand up. This was followed by the sounds of Alf helping his wife look over the wall. Pilot heard her say, "The field's empty. He's got away."

Pilot, now on his back, opened his eyes and sat up. "We had to get back to call the police. We came back together," Caro May said. "We were scared to remain."

Hugo's head slumped forward. "I should've stayed with him. I should've stayed."

. . .

Pilot had calmly waited for his killer to join him at the gate. He'd turned his back and finished inputting the key code when a couple of taps on his back told him his life was over. He'd knelt on the grass, which knocked his glasses off. His colleague had little difficulty in pushing him flat on his face with one hand, whilst using the other end of the garden stake to hold the door open. Pilot heard and felt his killer deftly step over him and slip out of the gate. Pilot wasn't long dead when he heard Zyline Angeles yell, "Oh my god — Nico!"

Outside the gate, Pilot's killer, dressed in dark clothing, face concealed, and still clutching the garden stake, ran across the sheep-less field at full pelt. Less than a minute to kill and escape through the gate. Even less for his strong young legs to take him across the field to the thicket of trees. Twenty, maybe thirty seconds to weave through those trees to the bike on the hardstanding, then he'd be away. Even if the killer hadn't hidden a getaway vehicle in the thicket, there was always the tree-lined track across the road. Concealed by the trees, he paused to allow a car to pass, before emerging and running across the road, seen by no one.

He returned to the roadside where he looked back. Even if the group had opened the gate or looked over the wall earlier, it wouldn't have made any difference, he now realised. There was never any chance of their catching sight of the killer. The time they spent trying to resuscitate Tudor did for that.

Black had reached the Orangery without setting eyes on anyone (apart from carefully positioned colleagues). He couldn't help but notice how well the clipped hedging concealed those behind it. From the Orangery he crossed the courtyard. The closed, locked gate blocked his way, leaving him no choice but to climb it. There weren't any easy footholds and the gate was quite high. He was still on it when Bettina and the Thornes appeared in the courtyard, en route to the front of the cottage. Will glanced to his right, saw Black stuck on the gate and hesitated. Will's dad did likewise and appeared just as surprised. Father and son eventually continued on their way, with Will shooting Black a look over his shoulder.

In that moment, Black realised there wasn't any way anyone got over that gate that morning without being seen. Nick Pilsworth hadn't left the way he came. Black climbed down, catching his coat as he did so and made his way to the kitchen to join Eden. He remained standing while she sat. On the screens, Will dashed off in the direction of the road, Ivy appeared, then Val Simpson, then Nico Angeles. Will then reappeared, only to run off towards the road again, this time followed by Nico, while, in the courtyard, Ivy yelled, "I must go to him."

"I'm his wife, not you," Bettina said.

"Not now, you two," Val Simpson said.

Watched by Black's team, Harry Thorne stayed where he was as the three women disappeared into the Orangery. Nico and Will were the first to return to the courtyard where they were quickly joined by Ivy, Bettina, Val, Hugo and the rest of the tour party. Ivy ran past Harry Thorne and into the cottage. Nico ended up going after her as the rest of the group traipsed into the house, where Bettina and Hugo retreated to one room, and Val took everyone else into the study. This left Harry Thorne by the cottage and Will on the other side of the double gate.

"Okay, we'll take a small break and have another go," Black said, "only this time I'll double back to the tree."

Chapter 28

THE RECONSTRUCTION DEBRIEF took place the following day. "The reconstruction was useful, but hasn't jogged anyone's memory as yet," Black said. "It's getting lots of eyeballs on the webpage and will go out on tonight's news. It has demonstrated that someone hiding in the sculpture could overhear a conversation outside it. More importantly, it proved someone inside the sculpture had enough time to climb out and still reach the beech tree before the group turned up. Me taking the part of Nick Pilsworth was also very helpful. Will and Harry Thorne didn't see a man climbing over the gate, meaning Nick Pilsworth did not escape that way. I too found it easy to slip through the concealed exit in the Herb Room and sprint to the beech tree. I was easily in place before the others arrived. I heard them arrive and heard indistinct voices across the space."

Pilot had an observation to make. "Having calmly stood there as someone advanced on me with a garden stake, I ain't so sure I'd have calmly stood there as someone advanced on me with a garden stake. Even if I knew them. I'm asking myself, did the killer pick the weapon up once he or she reached Tudor? I know we haven't found any incriminating garden stake type holes in the lawn, but it could've been leaning up against the wall. We're talking about a garden stake, here. It's possible no one even noticed it."

Black asked the team member who shadowed Lilah O'Connell if there was anything of note to report.

"Not really, Sir. We set off at roughly the time she said, arriving at the house at about the time she did. We hung around for a bit longer than I'd have done if I'd wanted to know what was going on. Time we got moving, half the county was on its way."

"Does anyone have anything else to report?" Black said.

"Only that forensics have come back on the interior of the church lectern, Sir," Eden said. "They've recovered minute traces of dust and skin particles, but no blood or significant human DNA. No traces were found of the microscopic particles recovered from the crime scene. The pinpricks were made by an unidentified object, likely after the lectern's construction."

Pilot also had something to report. "Sadly, no satellite or drone imaging of the murder scene has come to light. The property has anti-drone devices. That might explain the lack of phone signals."

"Well," Black said, "that would be a bit easy for us."

"The show the lady in the gift shop was watching when Tam Tully arrived was broadcast at its regular time," Pilot said, "supporting Tam and Brian's alibi."

"Let's go over what we still don't know," Black said. "We still don't know what part the mysterious items sent to Ivy play in all of this, if any. We still don't know if our killer sent the note luring Tudor to the windmill or if that was a tragic coincidence. We still don't know who Nick Pilsworth is. We still don't know why he was there that morning, nor how he left. We still don't know who inputted the gate code. We still don't know who sent Tudor the *get out of my grill* text, and we still don't know why. We still don't know if Tudor was the blackmailer. We still don't know if the letter Lilah O'Connell received was part of the same blackmail. We still don't know if blackmail was the motive for Tudor's murder. We still don't know if Lilah even was where she says. In the absence of the dog walker, we still don't know if Valerie Simpson was actually where she says she was either. We still don't know if Hugo was on the phone during the time he was separated from the group. We still don't know why Tudor waited patiently at the gate. We still don't know if the murder was premeditated. We do know that, if it wasn't, our killer is incredibly lucky not to have left us more to go on."

Black reflected for a moment. "Let's take another look at the suspects we know about." He paused to take a drink of water. "Our prime suspect remains fake Nick Pilsworth. It's possible fake Nick Pilsworth might have been there for some reason other than murder but got cold feet and is scared to come forward with everything that's happened. That doesn't explain how he escaped into thin air.

"Let's talk about the other members of the tour party. All were in the Topiary room when Tudor was killed. Logistically, I can't see how any of them could have committed the murder. If it was them, where was the murder weapon, and how did they dispose of it? Also, why was Tudor still at the gate? No incriminating evidence has been found on any of them, nor can we find a motive for any of them."

He took another drink of water. "Neither Val Simpson nor Father Dermot Hanrahan have any motive for murder that we can find, but both are close to the family, particularly Bettina. The family is riven with tension, but enough for murder? Finding oneself a suspect in a murder investigation must be a terrifying experience — nonetheless, the Tully's lied and have a good reason for wanting Tudor dead, but their alibi checks. The dog-walker Val Simpson claims to have spoken to still hasn't come forward despite requests. Was the dog-walker involved somehow? As an accomplice maybe?"

"Could our killer have been a contract killer, do you suppose, Sir?" Pilot suggested.

Black telephoned Judy McDermott to run the idea by her. "You've investigated contract killings," he said. "What's your view on the Tudor O'Connell murder being a professional job?"

"I'm not hung up on the idea, frankly," she said. "I've investigated two professional killer cases. Both victims were successful, wealthy businessmen. I'm certain the wife was behind the first killing and the business partner behind the other. I was never able to prove either, and both remain unsolved. Both victims were shot at close range, one while on holiday, the other on his front doorstep as the family slept upstairs. Significantly, in both cases, the killer struck under cover of night, dressed in dark clothing, and arrived and escaped on a motorbike, and used a silencer. Your killing is a messy stabbing in broad daylight with people a stone's throw away, with your killer escaping on foot across a muddy field in gardening shoes. This is not the hallmark of a contract killer, Guido."

Black relayed this information to Pilot.

"I didn't say they were good at their job," Pilot said.

Chapter 29

AT THE END of another long day, Eden texted she was on her way home. She'd just put her jacket on when the station land-line rang. She ignored it and let one of the night shift pick it up. She'd got as far as the door when a voice called out to her. "I think you'd better take this one, Eden. One of the tour party has remembered something." She returned to her desk and the call was rerouted to her phone.

"It's Caro May," a woman's voice said. It sounded as though she was whispering. Eden called her details up on screen. Caroline May, known as Caro, was in her late forties. She owned a gift shop on the High Street with a profitable online side. She'd been at the TreeHouse to connect with the O'Connell Trust to sell her products through their gift-shop.

"What's on your mind, Mrs May?" Eden asked.

Caro didn't immediately reply. Her breathing sounded heavy. Eden could barely hear her hushed words, nervously spoken, "The reconstruction..."

Eden flicked open a ring binder notepad and reached for a pen. Those in the incident room around her had fallen silent. Other than her laboured breathing, so too had Caro May. It sounded as though she was in a wind-tunnel. Was she jogging?

"I'm having difficulty hearing you, Caro." When she still didn't speak, Eden said, "We can offer you protection, Caro." She was still on the line. Eden could hear her breathing, but she didn't speak. Eden gently prompted her. "Please carry on, Caro." Electrical interference crackled over Caro's next words, and all Eden got was, "...wasn't there."

Eden sat bolt upright. Adrenalin pumped through her veins. Her colleagues had gathered around her. "Who wasn't where, Caro?" Eden said. She heard a noise — was it a gasp? — then the phone went silent. "Caro?" she said. "Caro?" She continued talking to the silent phone until forced to put the receiver down.

With the murderer still on the loose, Eden was extremely concerned. But she had to keep calm. That gasp may have been exasperation at another driver, or a near miss, or any one of a number of plausible and innocent explanations. Nonetheless, around her, her colleagues sprang into action. Caro May had withheld the number she'd called from. An alert was put out on her car. Her landline was called, so too the shop and her mobile phone. None were answered and messages were left. Eden sent a quick change-of-plan text home as she waited for Caro to call back. When this didn't happen, Eden reminded herself that it was early evening. Caro could be stuck in heavy traffic. Every ten minutes, she redialled Caro May's mobile, shop and home landlines, but with no more success than her colleagues. She too left messages. With tension mounting in the incident room, squad cars were sent to both home and shop. Caro May was in neither. Her mobile phone was traced and found in the shop. Had she forgotten it when she left?

Eden tried to put her growing sense of unease to the back of her mind. Caro May had only just called in with vague, unspecified suspicions. Even if she had confided those to someone else, that person was hardly likely to have communicated Caro's suspicions to the subject of them. Your imagination is running away with you, Eden, she told herself. She probably called, realised she was late for something and ran out the door. That was all. Maybe someone turned up at the shop and dragged her out for a drink? But, try as she did, still her concerns mounted. She telephoned Black. He, too, was gravely worried.

"We've got half the force scouring the country for her," he said. "Sadly, there's not much else we can do until she turns up — dead or alive. If there isn't any news by first thing tomorrow morning, let's you and me meet at the TreeHouse. Don't let it prey on your mind. Take yourself home and leave the job at the door."

She half took his advice and went home. "Call me, when you find her. I don't mind what the time is," she instructed her colleagues as she left.

Once through her own front door, Eden called the station. Caro and her car were still unaccounted for. She forced herself to eat, despite having no appetite. She spent the rest of the evening sewing Dora's latest Brownies badges onto her daughter's uniform with Dora sat beside her, regaling her with the latest news from her favourite cartoon, "...she really wants to, but she can't say anything. It's really sad, Mum."

The distraction did some good but, try as she might, she couldn't put her concerns to rest. Caro had called. She'd sounded scared. Had she been running? Why had she gasped? Why hadn't she called back? Where was she? And most importantly — who or what wasn't where?

Chapter 30

EDEN SPENT the night staring between the ceiling, her alarm clock and her phone. At four a.m. she gave up and went downstairs to make herself a pot of tea. She rang the nightshift to learn that, although officers were stationed outside Caro's home and shop, there was no sign of her or her car. "First light, we'll start searching."

"Where are her kids?" Eden asked.

"With their dad. He's not heard from her either."

Eden woke up in the kitchen, slumped across the kitchen table, Dottie looking over her, wondering whether to wake her. It was seven a.m. Eden checked her phone. No messages. She called the station. Still no news. She gave a sigh. Dottie put a cup of tea in front of her. "I have to be at the TreeHouse for eight," Eden said.

"Well, you'll have time for breakfast, then," Dottie said, using a pair of wooden tongs to extract crumpets from the toaster.

"Where's Dora?"

"Playing yo-yo with Duchess. I'll take her breakfast up to her. Give you some space."

Eden ate her hot, buttered crumpets while staring at her phone, willing it to ring. She pushed her plate away and got to her feet. She put her coat on and was taking her car keys from the bowl by the back door when Dottie reappeared. "Aren't you going to get dressed first?" she asked.

Eden looked down. She was still in her nightclothes.

She set off for the TreeHouse, Caroline May's disappearance weighing heavily on her mind. Her route took her cross-country. She was making good time until her journey ended abruptly with a fallen tree blocking her path making further travel along the narrow country road impossible. She looked behind her and saw the entrance to a field, cut into the raised grass bank which edged the road. She reversed up to it and pulled in. She was about to pull out to travel in the opposite direction when a small red Fiat with a woman at the wheel came bombing along the road at some speed. Eden couldn't help noticing the driver wore dark sunglasses despite the earliness and murkiness of the morning.

The small car whizzed past her. Wouldn't waste your petrol, love, Eden thought, just as the sound of a car screeching to a halt punctured the air. She heard the car reversing. To give it space to turn, she started to reverse further down the track. The Fiat ignored the track, reversing along the road at considerable speed, passing her in a flash of red. She caught sight of the back of a blonde bob.

Small red Fiat gone, Eden was free to continue her journey. After checking the route, she set off. At the turn-off, she caught a glimpse of the little red Fiat still reversing down the country road, at speed, the driver's face still turned in the direction of the road she reversed along. Eden wondered if the driver intended reversing all the way home.

Eden parked next to Black's car in front of the TreeHouse, stifling a yawn. Having been unable to sleep, she was now having difficulty staying awake. She got out of the car and turned to face the morning sun, feeling its rays on her face. Black asked her if she was all right.

"Not really, Sir," she said, opening her eyes. "I have a bad feeling about this. Sensible, middle-aged women simply don't disappear into thin air, more especially after calling the police with information about a murder inquiry."

"Well, for her sake, let's hope she isn't sensible," Black said.

"I keep asking myself, has she been attacked because she was about to tell us something? But how did the attacker get to her first? Who would she have told before us? Her family claim not to know anything."

They made their way towards the grounds. "It's a concern she hasn't been in touch and we haven't located her or her car," Black said. "But there could be an innocent explanation. Let's hope it's one of those."

They continued in silence. "I couldn't sleep either," Black admitted after a while. "I've been recording the antics of the little merlin who's taken up roost in a church spire. I spent the early hours watching her acrobatics. Her name's Marlene." He took his phone out to show Eden the bird. "Isn't she a beauty?" he said. The phone's video screen showed Marlene watching the ground from her elevated position, suddenly taking off to dart through the air, fast as a bullet in a downwards trajectory before pulling herself up to fly low and flat after her target, a pigeon. The pigeon desperately tried to escape. It failed. "Chloe's been putting bird seed down in the field outside the church to lure pigeons," he explained. "She didn't approve of Marlene's previous dietary choices."

The video ended with the merlin returning to the spire with her meal to applause from her human fan club below. Black's distraction plan worked. Despite its grisliness, his recording of Marlene drew Eden's mind from the fate of Caro May.

Eden opened her iPad. On it were the photographs taken on the day of the crime. She and Black walked slowly through the garden rooms, stopping frequently to take in the scene and compare it with the photographs. Nothing en route struck them as unusual or stood out as different to the photographs they constantly referred to.

In the Events Room, Black said, "Of course, Caro may not have been referring to a person who wasn't there. She might have been referring to an object which was there on the day of the crime but not for the reconstruction."

"A decorative garden stake leaning against a wall, for example," Eden said. "Not necessarily the kind of thing people register first time round."

They spent some time there. Their eyes moved from the images on the iPad to the space around them. Apart from the removed body, neither could see any major departure from the scene they looked at to the scene captured on the morning of the murder. "If this turns out to be a publicity stunt by Mrs May, I'll throw the book at her, I swear to God," Black said.

Once back at the house, Eden stopped at the French windows leading to the study. She pointed at the *Ark of Life* and said, "I took a couple of sneaky photos to make into a print for Dora for Christmas. You can't see from here, but one of the dodos is pregnant. She'll love that. She studied dodos last term."

"Didn't dodos lay eggs?" Black said.

"They couldn't fly either, but there's three flying in the top right corner," she replied.

Black squinted at the picture hanging across the room. He gave a shake of his head and headed towards the propped-open gate. Eden followed him. "See you at the station, Detective Sergeant," he said at his car.

At her own car, Eden stopped and turned around. Had she just seen movement at an upper-storey window? She took a few steps backwards to look up at the house and saw someone dart out of sight, leaving the curtain swaying. "What the...?" Eden said. She looked over her shoulder. Black's car was turning out of the drive. She returned to look up at the window, shouting, "Police. I know you're in there. Please show yourself."

Denys meekly came to the window and gave a shrug.

"Could you come down, please?" Eden asked. "And bring anybody else up there with you. This is still a sealed site." She waited by the door for Denys to emerge. He was followed by Hugo. She'd thought that was it until Bettina O'Connell traipsed out. The three lined up in front of her, looking like naughty school children.

"What are you doing here?" Eden asked.

"We've been allowed access," Bettina said. This, Eden hadn't realised, but the property might well have been returned to the family before Caro May went missing.

"We've a hell of a lot to do if we're to open up on time. We're massively behind," Hugo said.

"Why were you hiding upstairs?"

"We saw you arrive and..." Denys trailed off.

"We couldn't face answering any more of your questions, all right?" Bettina said wearily.

Eden opened up her iPad. "As you're here, Hugo, I'm going

to show you some photographs taken on the day your dad was killed. Can you look at them and tell me if you see anything different in these pictures from how you remember things immediately before your father's death?"

Hugo nodded, and she began swiping across the screen. He looked at the photos as she swiped, shaking his head. "Not that I can see," he said. She kept going until Hugo suddenly covered his face with his hand and shrunk back. His mother looked over his shoulder and gave a gasp, walking away quickly, her hand over her mouth too. Eden looked at the picture on the iPad and saw Tudor O'Connell's splayed body.

"I'm sorry," Eden said. "I should have warned you." Denys shot her a cross look and hurried over to his mother-in-law to take her in his arms.

"Thank you for your assistance," Eden said. "I am sorry to have delayed you. If I've upset your mother or you with any of these pictures, it wasn't intended."

She returned to the station where, for the rest of the day, those who had taken part in the reconstruction arrived at the station to be shown the photographs taken on the day of the murder (the body of Tudor O'Connell edited out). Nobody could make out anything strikingly different. Each shrugged or apologised or replied, "Can't help," "Sorry, no, nothing," or "Not sure what I'm meant to be looking for?"

Eden wandered into Black's office to update him. He was at his desk, the copy of *Spirit* magazine spread open to the photographs of the study which he was studying through a magnifying glass. "As we're looking for differences, I decided to compare our photograph of the room with the one in the magazine," he explained.

Her eyes fell on Ivy sitting next to Tudor on the mirrored loveseat, Degas in her arms. The sight of baby Degas made

Eden think of something. She turned the magazine towards her, picked up the magnifying glass and held it over the three extinct, flightless birds, wings outstretched, airborne across the canvas of the magazine photograph. None of the three had an obviously bulbous belly, but the three-dimensional nature of the picture necessitated a thick frame. She'd only noticed one of the dodos was heavy with chick when helping to reassemble it.

"Is something on your mind, Detective Sergeant?" Black asked.

"This picture," she pointed to the magazine photograph of the *Arc of Life,* "has an index on its rear listing everything featured. Number three is *Pregnant Dog.*" That the dog had a bulbous belly was evident in the photograph. "But the dodos were just referred to as *Three Flying Dodos,* not *Three Flying Dodos, one pregnant.*"

"That's because they laid eggs." On such matters, Black could be a bit of a purist.

Eden found her photographs of the painting on her phone. She enlarged the one taken at an angle and showed it to Black. "Wouldn't she have mentioned in the index something she'd gone to so much trouble to create?" Eden asked.

In Tudor O'Connell's study, Black reached up to remove *Ark of Life* from the wall. He turned it over. *Three Flying Dodos* was listed at number 57 on the rear index. Eden held onto the frame as Black used a craft knife to cut through the double-sided tape keeping the backing board in place. Eden felt the whole thing come apart. Together they laid the back board, frame and glass on the floor and gently carried the artwork, still on its mounting board, over to Tudor's desk where Black's eyes meticulously scanned it. He ignored the dodos for the time being and concentrated instead on attempting to get another of the three-dimensional pieces on the artwork to move. All stayed put, having been varnished to the piece. He picked the picture up and, looking at it side on, concentrated on the suspect dodo.

"The fat one isn't varnished into place the way the others are," he said, taking out his craft knife once more. "Evidence bag at the ready please, Detective Sergeant." He gently prised the dodo's bulbous belly away from the rest of the bird which remained on the picture, albeit damaged. Good job this is a replica, Eden thought.

Black studied the small, semiprecious stone which had been the dodo's swollen belly. He held it between his fingers. The stone, round on the visible side and flat on its underbelly, was the same colour as the dodo to whom it had been attached.

Black held the stone up to his eye and, closing the other, peered at it, then invited Eden to do the same. She saw a thin line, almost invisible, encircling it. Black used tweezers to prise the small stone open. From this, he extracted a slip of laminated paper. Blank. Black turned it over. "Great snakes," he said.

He let the tiny slip of paper lie in his open hand. On it was a row of emojis.

"Well, I wasn't expecting that," Black said. "I'm not sure what I was expecting, but it definitely wasn't that."

He dropped the piece of paper with the row of emojis into an evidence bag.

Chapter 31

GUIDO BLACK GOT to his feet in the Incident Room to address the team once again.

"Mrs Caroline May took part in the reconstruction and a day or so later rang us here, claiming to have something to report, but the crucial part of the sentence was inaudible and all Eden caught was the words, '*wasn't there.*' What did Caroline May mean? Who or what wasn't where? We don't know because she's gone missing and all attempts to trace her have thus far failed. Her bank account hasn't been touched since she went missing and her phone unused. Even her car has fallen off the radar We have no hospital admissions of anyone matching her description. I don't need to tell you how rare it is for someone to disappear in the manner she has, let alone after calling the police. We must consider the possibility that she staged her disappearance, either for attention or self-publicity. Equally, we must consider that she has been taken against her will and her life is in great danger. Until we know either way, we must presume the worst and continue to do everything in our power to find her."

Pilot said, "We've established that Caro May didn't call us

from her own mobile phone. We're still trying to establish the number and location she called from."

"It sounded like she was moving around outside," Eden said.

"Caro May was in the shit financially," Pilot said. "She'd borrowed heavily to buy her ex out of the family home, her shop was making a loss, she couldn't get out of the lease and the webpage, whilst profitable, basically cannibalised from the shop. Going into business with the O'Connell Trust was her last chance."

"We need to consider the possibility that somehow or other she'd worked something out but approached the killer rather than us, and it all went wrong," Black said.

"She sounded frightened," Eden said.

"Was her call made in fear of her life or to try and save it?" Black said. "I don't need to remind you that of the eight who started off from the front of the TreeHouse that morning, two are missing — Nick Pilsworth and now Caro May — and one is dead. This is not a good attrition rate. On to other matters."

He called up the emojis.

"These were found carefully and deliberately concealed in a picture in Tudor's study in such a way as to make it most unlikely they'd be found accidentally. Ordinarily, I wouldn't consider a row of smilies significant, but someone went to some trouble to hide these. Forensics haven't found any fingerprints or identifying information on the laminated paper they appear on. Any number of people had access to the study. I understand new emojis are released regularly, which will tell us when they were hidden."

Pilot got to his feet and said, "I've been on emojipedia." As he spoke, he highlighted the relevant emoji: "Our emojier opens with a Smirk – a suggestive little emoji, the smirk. Says sly with a hint of sexual innuendo. Next, we have Puke-Up. Nothing suggestive about Puke-Up, 'cept it can also mean disgust or phoney. After a second Smirk we have Grinning Squinting Face, which roughly translates as awesome. Then Drooling Face with Saliva, which either says I'm hungry or I'm gobsmacked with lusty longing. Something to remember when using it. Smiley Face's neighbour is passive aggressive Up Side Down Face and his neighbour is Exploding Head ..."

"My head's exploding with all of this," one of the team called out.

"Interestingly, a pair of zipper mouths , meaning top secret or shut your face, are squeezed between Death and Love of Money."

"Innuendo, disgust, awe, lust, happiness, shock, aggressiveness, loss, desire and zip it," Eden reflected. "That's a lot of emotions."

"It's an emotional family," Black said.

"Maybe it's a concept for a new Mr Man series," Judy joked. "Miss Gobsmacked and Mr Hostility Signalling invite their friends round for tea and cake."

"Let's see if the family can shed any light on what it could all mean," Black said.

In her hotel room, Ivy stared at the row of emojis. "What is this?" she said. "A child's puzzle?"

"They were found very carefully hidden somewhere in the house and can only have been hidden after Degas was born," Eden said.

"How is this linked to Tudor's death?" Ivy said.

"We're trying to establish their significance," Eden said.

"I cannot help you. I cannot see how this can have anything to do with Tudor's murder," Ivy said.

"Tudor owned a pair of emojis pyjamas," Eden said.

"I bought them for him last Christmas. It was something

fun. He liked smileys. So does Degas. If Tudor hid them, he did not tell me. Ask Bettina or the kids."

Eden showed the emojis to Lilah O'Connell. "These were found concealed in the vicinity of the TreeHouse. Do you have any idea what, if anything, they represent?"

She looked at them. "Can't say I've ever seen them before. Dad liked to play odd tricks on us when we were kids. He hid things for us to find; a kind of brain challenge. Maybe this got forgotten?"

"The emojis are too recent for that to be the answer," Eden said. "Of that we are sure."

"Then I give up."

Hugo came out with pretty much the same explanation as his sister. "Maybe he hid them for Degas to find when she was older?"

Eden showed Bettina a copy of the emojis. "Do you know what this is?" she asked Bettina.

"Emojis, I'd say," she said.

"They were hidden in Tudor's study. Do you know why and what, if anything, they represent?" Eden asked.

"Haven't a clue. Maybe they're the number to his safe?" Bettina suggested, with a gentle smile, fingering the emojis.

"Did he have a safe?"

"If he did, he didn't tell me."

Val Simpson gave a double-take and said, "Sorry, my love — can't help you."

"On the morning of Tudor's murder, you, Hugo, the Hoff-brands, Caro May and Zyline Angeles waited in the study for the police to arrive," Black said. She nodded. "Was anybody ever alone there at any time?"

"No one. We stayed put till you showed."

Pilot showed Denys the row of emojis, who picked the piece of paper up and ran his eyes along the row. He identified each in turn.

"You certainly know your emojis, Sir," Pilot said.

"Important to get emojis correct. Fire begins with sparks."

"These were carefully hidden. Do you any idea what they might mean?"

"Did Tudor hide them?"

"We don't know, but it's certainly possible," Pilot said.

Denys folded his arms and leaned back to have a ponder. Suddenly, he leaned forward and clicked his fingers. "I have it," he said. "This one time, just after Ivy have the baby, I come across Tudor on his computer looking at ladies. Not nudy. All dressed. Even so. I'm shocked. '*A tomtit in your hand is better than a crane in the sky, Tudor,*' I told him. '*Relax,*' he said. He explained the pictures were of the ladies he'd dated before Ivy. Picked was how he put it. He said he was only looking through the photos for old time's sake. Believe it or not, he had kept their photographs, and the scores he'd given each of them at the time." Denys emphasised the word *and*. "I said to him, '*If Ivy finds this, she'll think you are out chasing hares again.*' To which he said he'd better make sure she didn't find them then." Denys picked up the row of emojis and said, "What this is, is understandable to a hedgehog."

Just as Pilot was about to say, to a hedgehog possibly, but not to me, Denys continued. "This is only half. Somewhere else is hidden a row of ladies' faces. These emojis, they are their rankings. The score he gave them." He rolled his eyes and discarded the emojis onto the table. "That man was a spoonful of tar in a barrel of honey. May his memory be eternal," he added hastily.

After watching the interviews in his office with Eden, Black said, "These emojis could literally be anything. A child's game, the number of a secret Swiss Bank account, a telephone number, Tudor O'Connell's boastings, the killer's calling card left to taunt us, or a communiqué between two or more people."

"Say Denys is right? Say Tudor hid up photographs of his ex-girlfriends somewhere else?" Eden said. "Say Ivy found them and confronted him?"

"I can see why they might have had a fight — but murder?" Black said.

Chapter 32

THE SEARCH for Caro May was looking more and more like the search for a body. Eden tried not to think about it. She didn't want anything to put a dampener on her evening — dinner with Matthew Pritchard.

He'd booked them a table in a Trattoria. They sat in the corner, their table covered in a crisp red linen tablecloth under a crisp white linen tablecloth. Along with cutlery and glassware was a vase of fresh yellow freesias and blue hyacinths. Eden had dressed in a grey woollen dress with a chunky cobalt necklace; he in pale checked linen. They ordered wine, garlic bread and olives.

Her eyes had just turned to the menu when Matt said, "We need to get one thing straight from the start, Eden."

Here it goes, she thought. I'm not to read too much into anything, get too excited, start plotting our life together. Such arrogance. Such presumptuousness. Shame. He seemed so modest. Just as she was wondering whether to pack the evening in before it began, he carried on. "Doing your job involves knowing as much as possible about the case. Doing my job properly depends on the opposite. I need to know as little as possible and therefore please, no talking about the current case, if you don't mind. The defence will roast us alive us if they find out."

The waiter, who had arrived with their nibbles, must have overheard the end of Matt's comments because he said, "I can recommend the oven roast calves liver. It comes with red wine gravy and butter mash." Matt said it sounded nice and ordered it. Eden chose the risotto. As those on first dates do, they chatted. He'd been divorced for a long time, wasn't currently seeing anyone, and, like her, had one daughter, only one old enough to be at university (psychology and law).

"We were both too young," Eden said of her short-lived marriage to Dora's dad. "People warned me, but I knew best. He was, and still is, gorgeous. Greek. I dreamt of us running something like this, a little taverna on the Greek Coast. But it wasn't to be. I flew out to be with him, madly in love. Less than two years later, I'm on my way home with Dora in her cot. He was a charmer. That was the problem."

"I'm sorry. Does Dora see her dad?" he asked.

"She spends every summer in Greece. She loves it. Tears my heart out when I put her on the plane, but she needs and wants him in her life and I'm not going to stop that. She has half-siblings now and his parents are there. I just hope to God she never decides she wants to move out there permanently." She thought it fair to explain her unusual living arrangements.

"Eric is my stepdad and Dottie's his mum, making her my step-grandmother. Eric was briefly married to my mum, Dixie. Dixie couldn't cope, and Eric took me to live with him. Leah, my half-sister, is his. I'm not. He didn't need to take me in but he did, and I never felt any different. Dottie looked after us while Eric worked really long hours. If it wasn't for them, I'd have ended up in care. They never made me feel uncomfortable or expected gratitude, although they have it in spades. When I came back from Greece I tried to manage by myself, but with Dora and a full-time job it was impossible. Everything

I earned was going on childcare. And the guilt. Eric and Dottie sat me down and invited me back. Dunno how I'd manage without them."

"Why couldn't your mum cope?" he asked.

"Dixie was a drunk — a beautiful drunk who should never have had kids."

"Your real dad?"

"Eric's the only dad I've ever known or want to," she said. "This is where you say shouldn't I try and find him for Dora."

"No, this is where I say: how are you liking working in team Black?"

"Loving it," she said. "The thrill of the chase, sifting fact from fiction, closing in on the killer. Love all of it. What does that say about me?"

"That you're in the right job," he said. "Was the trauma of your early childhood the reason you joined the police? For the order and stability?"

"I'd love to say yes, but I really wanted to be Cagney — or Lacey. I didn't care. I loved the idea of producing a flashing light from the glove compartment and roaring after a car who'd just cut me up. Not that I've ever actually done that." He laughed and asked if she wanted the dessert menu. Caro May's disappearance came into her mind from nowhere. "You've heard about..." she stopped herself from saying Caro May, remembering their earlier conversation about the case, but struggled with a replacement. "Betty Boop," she said.

He looked slightly taken aback. "What about her?"

"She's gone missing."

He hesitated before replying, "I hadn't realised cartoon characters could go missing. Has Road Runner got her?"

She was saved by the arrival of the waiter. "I'll have the Neapolitan ice cream, thank you," she said. "And a coffee."

Chapter 33

THE NEXT MORNING, Eden dropped Dora off at school on the way to work. She'd just got back to her car, parked on the roadside outside the school, when she heard a voice behind her say, "Hey, Eden, how's it going?"

She turned to find Alex Doherty and his son, Jos. "See you're saddled with the school run too," he said, ushering Jos towards the school with a gentle shove in its general direction. "Last time I saw you was in a police interview room."

"Nice to see you, Alex," she said, opening her car door. "Must be on my way." She was inside and about to close the door when a car, travelling in the opposite direction, screeched to a halt in the middle of the road. Sheryl Teal emerged from it and advanced towards them, her face like thunder, apparently oblivious to the furious hooting and yelling coming from the motorists she'd blocked in both directions.

Eden hadn't seen her since their telephone conversation. She wasn't sure if she or Alex was the target of Sheryl's ire but, completely blocked in like the other motorists, she could only wait and see. Sheryl reached them and, somewhat to Eden's relief, completely ignored her to yell, "What the hell is this?" at Alex while waving a phone in the air.

Everyone was agog at the spectacle. Parents told their children to go inside, usually twice. Eden glanced at the school to see if Dora had gone inside. Her eyes fell on little Jos. The poor mite was rooted to the spot. Tears were starting to run down his cheeks. Sheryl seemed unaware of everything around her. She pushed Alex with both hands. "Is she another mum? Is she here?"

Dora appeared to stand next to Jos. The children watched in confusion. The headmistress was hurrying towards them; she did not look happy. Eden knew how she felt. She wound down her window. "You two need to sort your problems out at home," she said, just as the headmistress reached them.

"I can't have you carrying on like this," the head said. "I must insist you take this somewhere else." She was breathless from having run from her office.

"Don't stress yourself," Alex said. "I'm going." He turned on his heels. Eden glanced over at the school. Thankfully, the children had been taken inside. She began winding up her window.

"And what the hell does *Get out of my grill* even mean?" Sheryl yelled after Alex. He ignored her and continued in the direction of his van. "You being stalked? Some loop about to turn up at our doorstep?"

Alex had pulled open his van door when Eden, now out of her car and advancing on him, said, "One minute, please, Alex."

After taking a full statement from Sheryl Teal, Eden and Black next interviewed Alex Doherty. Alex had declined legal representation, stating the wish: *To get on with it*, and *Can't wait all day for a brief to show. I've got a business to run.*

Black held up the phone Eden had taken from Sheryl outside the school. It was in a police evidence bag. Black referenced it as item 884: an unregistered pay-as-you-go Nokia mobile phone.

"Mr Doherty," Black began, "your partner, Sheryl Teal, has informed us that she came across this phone hidden in your sports bag and managed to access it. She declined to tell us how she got the code."

"Never seen it before," he replied.

"How do you explain us finding your finger prints on the phone, Sir?" Black asked.

"Sheryl planted them, 'cos she's got it into her head I've been playing away and she wants to land me in the shit," he replied, his arms folded.

"The fingerprints on item 884 only match yours and are layered, suggesting extensive use of the phone, by one individual only. My forensics team has also found microscopic skin particles which match your DNA, again on item 884. Did Sheryl plant that too?" Black said calmly. "Now, can we start again please? Is this your phone?"

"No comment," he said.

"In the weeks leading up to Tudor O'Connell's death, messages were sent between this phone, item 884, and a phone registered to Tudor O'Connell," Black said. "I will now read the series of messages found on item 884 and Tudor O'Connell's phone. Sent from item 884 to Tudor O'Connell's phone:

Get out of my grill

Sent from Tudor O'Connell's phone to item 884:

I'm not in your grill house and never will be if I ever find out where it is!

Sent from item 884 to Tudor O'Connell's phone:

Don't you play the innocent. I'm warning you! You've got all you're getting

"Why did you send Tudor O'Connell those text messages, Alex?" Eden asked.

"No comment."

"Your partner, Ms Sheryl Teal, believes money has gone missing from her account. Did you send this to Tudor O'Connell after receiving a blackmail demand?" Black said.

Alex looked at his shoes. He hesitated and said, "No comment."

Eden had a go. "Alex, I'm not quite sure if you get the gravity of this situation. Tudor O'Connell has been murdered and at the moment you appear to have a motive for that murder and no proper alibi. You might want to be a bit more forthcoming."

"Okay, okay," Alex said. "Guilty to the messages and to using Sheryl's money to pay him off. But not guilty to murder. I had nothing to do with that." He pointed as he spoke.

"Let's begin with the money, Mr Doherty," Black said.

"Out of the blue, I found this envelope under my van wipers. Inside was this letter, like something from an Agatha Christie. Words made from bits of cut-up newspapers. The letter said I'd been seen with another woman and they could prove it with photographs and the like and if I didn't want my girlfriend and kid to find out, I was to leave cash in the abandoned boat hut by the river at midnight. Thought it was worth it and left the money there, like they said, but after pretending to drive away, I doubled back on myself and saw a car go past. I didn't see the driver, or get all of the registration, but it was the make and the colour of O'Connell's car, and the last three digits were the same as his. He knew Sheryl and me were an item..."

"And based on this, you concluded it was Tudor O'Connell who sent you the demand?" Eden said.

"I did. You don't see many cars down there, even during the day, and this was the middle of the night. I had his mobile number and I sent him the message and got the one you read out back. But I didn't kill him. I ain't gonna go down for life for seven hundred and fifty quid."

"You might have if you believed the blackmail was going to continue," Eden said.

"But it didn't. I never heard from him again. And even if I had," he added, pointing his finger at Eden and Black in turn, "I'd have fessed up to Sheryl, not done him in."

"Who was the woman you were seen with?" Black asked.

"I don't know her name. It's all anonymous. There's this Whatsup App we use. Everything gets set up."

"There isn't a Whatsup App on this phone, Sir," Black said.

"I used another phone. And no, I haven't got it. I got rid of it as soon as I could. Chucked it in the sea if you must know. Should've chucked item 884 after it," he motioned towards the Nokia, "but I forgot I had it."

"How many letters or other demands did you receive in total, Mr Doherty?" Black said.

"I've told you — just the one."

"Where did you go after leaving your doctor's surgery, Alex?" Eden said. "You were there for no more than thirty minutes, including waiting time. We next have your van on the other side of town, two hours later, on route to your next job. Where were you in between times?"

He leaned back in his chair, clasping his hands to his head and looked embarrassed. "I went home to watch some porn and do what men do when they watch porn."

Alex was taken to the cells.

"I want him in an identification parade — he might be Nick Pilsworth," Black said.

Eden returned to speak with Sheryl Teal again. "Sheryl, you don't have much by way of an alibi for the morning of Tudor O'Connell's murder," she said.

"I've told you where I was. I was trailing Alex. Why the hell would I want to kill O'Connell? If I was going to do anyone in, it would be Alex."

"Maybe the idea was for Alex to go down for a murder he didn't commit. You were the one who gave his name up."

"Christ, Eden," Sheryl said. "You have one imagination on you, love. I just wanted to know what he was really doing."

"I need to know your movements that morning, starting when you left the house and ending at the swimming pool."

Sheryl folded her arms. "I left before him and parked up around the corner. Him and Jos left the same time. I hung back a bit, then followed him to the surgery. I made sure there were always a couple of cars in between us."

Chapter 34

THE CALL they had all dreaded had come. The body of a woman matching Caro May's description had been found by the river. Black and Eden arrived together, driving past forensic vehicles, scene-of-crime vans and police officers combing the banks with dogs and poles. They parked on the quayside. This slopped gently towards the river. On the riverbank, wet-suited divers waited for the signal to go in. The two were directed towards a canoe club, its canoes chained to concrete posts.

Matt Pritchard arrived at the scene, sombrely suited up in PPE. The three did no more than nod at each other. This wasn't the time for social niceties. They ducked under a cordon of police tape and crossed to a body tent. A police officer stood guard outside. It was Eden who lifted the tent flap to allow them a look inside. A second officer stood guard over a shape covered by a sheet of tarpaulin on the ground. There was also an upturned canoe in the tent. Once they were all inside, the officer lifted the tarpaulin to reveal a woman's face and shoulders.

"That's Caro May, definitely," Eden said.

"We haven't touched the body, Sir. She was found like this. Covered in tarpaulin then the canoe placed over her," their colleague explained. She pulled the sheet back further to reveal a knife sticking out of Caro May's chest.

Matt leaned forward. "Single stab wound, upward thrust to the heart, straight through the left ventricle, I'd say. Death would have been fairly instantaneous. Blood splatter and particles from a shattered knife handle are the routes to conviction."

Black nodded to the officer to replace the sheet, and Mrs May's face was covered. Eden and Black left Matt Prichard in the tent. "Who found the body?" Black asked a police officer. "Some unfortunate, intent on an early morning canoe ride?"

"One of our officers, believe it or not, Sir. Called to attend a local man who'd reported finding a car in his garage which wasn't his. The officer realised the number plate had been tampered with. When he removed the gaffer tape, it was Caro May's car. That's why she didn't flash up on ANPR. He called for reinforcements but found her himself under the canoe."

"How exactly had the number plate been tampered with?" Black asked.

"Gaffer taped to turn the F and the L into Es."

From the corner of her eye, Eden saw Caro May being stretchered from the tent to the back of a waiting van to be taken to the pathology lab. "I'll get on with the post-mortem today, Guido," Matt Pritchard said from the tent doorway.

Back at the station, Black, standing next to a photograph of Caro May, updated the team on the sad news. "Carolyn May, always known as Caro, was a forty-eight-year-old mother of two teenage children. Matt Pritchard will carry out the post-mortem later today, but it appears she died from a single stab wound to the heart, making her face-to-face with her killer when she was attacked. The attack happened under cover of darkness. She died where she fell. The killer did no more than chuck some tarpaulin over her and place a canoe over that. Her car was left in a nearby garage which the owner admits was unlocked."

Black took a breath. "Caro wasn't in the vicinity of her shop when she called Eden, as we first thought. The burner phone she called from has been retrieved from the river. Did she disguise her own number plates and drive herself to the river for a prearranged meet up, only to end up dead; or was she ambushed and forced to drive to the river? Did someone else drive her car there? Now we have the car we should be able to trace its route and get some images. Eden, you said she sounded scared?"

"I now believe she was trying to keep her voice down, Sir," Eden said. "I think she was hiding from the killer and knew she didn't have much time."

"Why didn't she give a name?" Pilot said in exasperation.

"Maybe she did," Eden said, "only I didn't catch it."

"To my mind, Caroline May's murder definitely rules out a contract killer," Judy said. "If the killer was an anonymous professional, how would Caroline know who to contact?"

"It looks increasingly as though something happened at the reconstruction to make her suspicious. We stopped for more than one break. She was seen going for a wander. I suspect something she saw triggered some memory. Tragically, financial woes may have caused her to offer the killer silence for money. At some stage she realised the killer wasn't going to play ball and she escaped, hid up, called us, but ran out of time. The ten-million-dollar question being: what made her suspicious?"

"If it was the reconstruction that jogged her memory, are we ruling out anyone not there, like Alex Doherty and the Tullys, Sir?" Pilot asked.

"The only people free from suspicion are Tudor O'Connell and Caro May," Black answered. "Caro may have shared her suspicions with someone else, possibly without realising it or given herself away by her behaviour on the day, and the killer approached her, not the other way around."

The meeting broke up, leaving just Black and Judy in the room. "I accused her of staging her disappearance," he said.

"You raised it as a possibility," Judy reminded him. "You wouldn't have been doing your job if you hadn't. Don't beat yourself up. There's enough queueing up to do that to us as it is."

"One thing we now know for certain, Judy. Our killer will stop at nothing."

By the end of the day, they knew more about Caro May's last movements. "Caro's car, plates altered, was captured at the traffic lights on Merdle Street, one hour thirty-eight minutes before she called the station," Pilot said. "Our next image was captured by a traffic cam on the road out of town. Caro's car is the second in line."

He called the image up. It was poor quality but showed a woman at the driving seat who resembled Caro May. "We don't have any more sightings of the car. It seems she drove herself. There are a couple of routes from there to the river, along unlit country lanes. The image shows her alone in the car. Forensics have been all over the car and have eliminated everybody who's been in it. Down by the river there isn't much by way of lighting and no cameras. The blood is by the body. After pushing the car into the garage, our killer escaped by torchlight to wherever their own vehicle was. The river continues to be searched."

"Matt Prichard's post-mortem has confirmed that Mrs May was stabbed through her left ventricle and left to die," Eden said. "There are similarities with the Tudor O'Connell killing in that both victims were stabbed. Differences being, Tudor was stabbed through the back and the weapon removed, Caro May through the heart and the weapon left in. He in daylight, she under cover of darkness. We've spoken to the suspects in the Tudor O'Connell murder. The Angeles were clearing up after a wedding, the Hoffbrands were in Ireland. Mr and Mrs Tully had family around. Alex Doherty was asleep on his friend's couch. Bettina was having dinner with her children, including Denys. Valerie Simpson was helping Father Hanrahan with church matters. Ivy was seen entering the hotel, but not leaving again. This is supported by the receptionist and the cameras in and around the hotel."

"How's Caro's family holding up?" Black asked.

"Not good, Sir," was the reply.

Chapter 35

ALEX DOHERTY'S ID parade was almost identical to Brian Tully's, except that neither Annie Threadneedle nor Hugo participated as they both knew Alex. The parade was completed without Alex Doherty being identified by anyone. At the end of all, it fell to Eden to say, "Everybody's free to go, you included, Alex."

She was at her desk, typing up the notes of the ID parade, when the duty sergeant rang to inform her that various members of the O'Connell family were at the front desk asking for her.

Eden walked into a meeting room to find Hugo, Denys and Lilah furtively whispering. They stopped the instant she appeared. Hugo and Denys looked as guilty as when she'd seen them at the TreeHouse. Lilah was her usual, slightly detached self. Eden took a seat. "How can I help you?" she asked.

Lilah had evidently been appointed spokesperson. "Mum and these two haven't been entirely honest with you. They weren't at the TreeHouse that day to get the house sorted."

"What day are we talking about?" Eden asked.

"The day you saw us at the window," Hugo said.

"They were waiting on a journalist," Lilah said. "Sue Tuncliffe. She mostly writes for the local paper."

"Ivy gave her side of things, we wanted to give ours," Hugo said.

"We were waiting for her when your Detective Inspector arrived," Denys said.

"I saw him from the upstairs window," Hugo added.

"Straight away Mum called to cancel the interview," Lilah said. "When no one picked up, Hugo went to head Sue Tuncliffe off at the top of the drive."

"But she never arrived," Hugo said. "I waited for ages. Long after you drove past."

Eden wasn't sure where the story was headed.

Lilah picked it up. "Sue Tuncliffe initiated everything. She called us — said she'd seen Ivy's recent *wounded bird* interview and reminded us we were just as much victims as Ivy. Said our voices should be heard, and the local paper had bought the story if we were prepared to tell it. We thought — why not tell our side of things?"

"Bettina was the most for it," Denys said.

"I've come in her place," Lilah explained. "She couldn't face coming here. It's been one thing after the other."

"And now the poor dead lady," Denys said.

Eden didn't really have time for this. "There is no law stopping you from giving interviews," she said, "but be careful not to give away anything which might compromise any future trial."

"That's not why we're here," Lilah said. "Sue Tuncliffe wasn't legit. We kept ringing her to rearrange, but she didn't call back and we rang the paper. They knew nothing about any interview with us. The editor checked with her, but she knew nothing about it."

"Before we agreed to the interview, we checked her out,"

Hugo said. "There is a Sue Tuncliffe listed on the newspaper's web page as a freelance journalist."

Eden could well imagine a journalist after photographs of the scene and quotes from the family, but why go to the trouble of using another journalist's name? Wouldn't she want the credit for the story? And why hadn't she called back to rearrange the interview? She thought back to the car she'd seen reversing at speed that morning. "Did any of you actually see this woman in the flesh?" she asked. They all shook their heads. She logged in and searched for *Sue Tuncliffe – freelance journalist*. When she saw Sue Tuncliffe's photograph, a jolt of recognition hit her. Sue Tuncliffe wore her hair in a short blonde bob. The woman at the wheel of the small red car had a blonde bob. Was that why she'd been wearing dark sunglasses at that time in the morning? To disguise her appearance? Did they have another imposter on their hands? She realised Hugo, Denys and Lilah were staring at her.

"Is there a recording of her phone call to you?" she asked, but they just looked blank. "Well, thank you for telling me all this," she said. "I may need to ask you some further questions but leave it with me for the moment. I don't think it's anything to worry about. Probably some jobbing journalist after a story and photos." The three looked rather surprised and relieved, even Lilah.

Eden returned to her desk. What make of car had the blonde bob woman been driving? She called up the scene that morning in her mind and saw a Fiat. What she needed was a registration number but, try as she might, Eden could only remember the last digit. Come on, woman, think. You're a police officer. The problem was — she hadn't looked. She'd been far too preoccupied wondering what would happen to the reversing car if something came the other way. What kind of police officer are you? she asked herself. But the more she thought, the more she racked her brain, the worse it got. Well, at least she had the last digit. She ran a check on red Fiats ending with that digit.

At Eden's house, Dottie was staring at a mysterious text from Dora: *Meet me at the bus stop.* What bus stop, she thought. The one at the end of the road? Dora normally walked the few minutes it took to get home from there. Was she burdened down with something? Dottie went to the window and saw the bus pass by. She'd got to the end of the path when the bus pulled away, leaving an empty bus stop. Dora hadn't disembarked. She must be on the next one, Dottie decided, turning back. She'd reached the door when she discovered another text: *Elmr Hlll.* Elmr Hlll? She must mean Elmer Hill, a stop early on Dora's route. Why had she got off there? She called Dora but didn't get a reply. What on earth was going on? She grabbed a coat and her bag and walked to the bus stop, giving Dora another call, which wasn't answered.

Dottie sat at the front of the bus and spent the journey looking from one side of the road to the other. After fifteen minutes the bus turned into Elmer Hill — a quiet, fairly affluent, residential street lined by large, semi-detached properties set back from a tree-lined verge with large front gardens and sweeping drives. The bus drove past Dora sitting alone, quite calmly, at a bus stop on the other side of the road staring intently at something.

Dora was so engrossed she didn't notice Dottie until she sat next to her. Dottie put her hand on Dora's and said, "All right, love?"

She was greeted with a big grin and the words, "It's Boopy."

Dora pointed to a semi-detached house on the other side of

the street. Dottie's heart sank. She looked over to the house. Its curtains were wide open and the lights off. She could see four windows on two floors with various objects displayed, but she couldn't see a black cat looking out. "I can't see anything."

"She's there," Dora said, her eyes not moving from the property's upper floor. "I saw her in the window."

"There's lots of black cats, love," Dottie said.

"It's Boopy! She looked at me. She recognised me."

Dora squealed and pointed to the window. "There, Granny." Dottie followed the pointing finger. A black cat had appeared in an upper-storey window. The cat curved its back in a stretch, turned around and disappeared to settle itself down on something. Even with her old eyes, Dottie could just make out the tip of a black ear.

"Let's go and get her," Dora announced, getting to her feet and extending her hand to Dottie.

"We can't just knock on the door and ask for their cat, love," she said.

Dora started to get distressed. "She's not their cat."

"There's lots of black cats in the world, Dora," Dottie repeated.

"I know my own cat, Granny. It's Boopy."

"They'll think I'm a mad old lady trying to steal their cat," Dottie said. "Tell you what, why don't we get Mum to give them a call tonight and ask them how long they've had the cat? Look, here's our bus." Dora didn't look convinced. Her eyes went back to the upper-storey window. Dottie firmly took hold of her hand as the bus came to a standstill. She felt Dora resist.

"Let Mum handle it. Mum's a police officer. People don't lie to the police." She felt Dora's resistance lessen. "What about macaroni cheese for dinner?" she suggested. This was always a favourite.

Dora looked at her. "With little sausages?"

Dottie nodded.

Dora cheerily waved the cat goodbye. "Bye bye, Boopy," she said. "Don't worry — we'll be back."

Eden had discovered there were more than four-and-a-half-thousand contenders for the red Fiat. For God's sake, she thought, wondering whether banging her head against the wall would help.

"So, now we have a second imposter?" Black said from behind his desk.

"I've spoken to the family again," Eden said. "They suggested the interview take place indoors, but fake Sue Tuncliffe wanted both in and out. Various locations were best, is what she said."

"If she set the whole thing up to retrieve something, what the hell have we missed?" Black said. "We've been over and over that place."

"The phone she used is unregistered," Eden said, "and we're still trying to trace the car. I'm confident it was a woman at the wheel but couldn't say much more. Every one of the suspects claims to have been somewhere else at the time."

"I can't help thinking it would be easier to jack this job in for something easier. Like String Theory. No one's expected to solve that," Black replied.

The end of another exhausting day saw Eden slumped in an armchair at home, listening to Dottie explain why she had to ring a family on Elmer Hill about a cat. "I know it's not ours, but I promised her you'd call."

"You must be joking?" Eden said. Dottie merely gave a weak shrug. Eden could imagine that conversation. *Haven't the police got anything better to do than look for cats? Like find the person who burgled my mum/mugged my mum/kidnapped my mum at gunpoint/entombed my mum in concrete up to her neck?*

Dora skipped into the room. "Mum, someone has Boopy. We need to go and get her."

Eden shot Dottie a cool look and said, "I called them. It isn't Betty Boop, baby. I'm sorry."

"Now I've had to lie to her," Eden said after a disappointed Dora had stomped upstairs.

"If it makes you feel any better, Maisie the rabbit didn't really retire to a farm for its twilight years," Eric said. "But don't tell your sister."

Chapter 36

"Mr Doherty," Black said, speaking to Alex Doherty back in the interview room. "I'm going to read out a series of deleted text messages my team have recovered from the Nokia phone you have previously admitted is yours and referenced item 884. The wording of the texts is duplicated in the folder in front of you and referenced item 886. Every text was sent or received within a thirty-minute period, on one day, six weeks before the murder of Tudor O'Connell."

Black held the transcript up. "Received on your phone: *I've got another one.* Sent from your phone: *When?* Received on your phone: *Just now.* Sent from your phone: an expletive. Sent: *How much now?* Received: *A grand.* Sent: *Ignore it.* Received: *I can't. I'll be ruined.*

"Mr Doherty, this second exchange of texts establishes that you do, in fact, know the identity of the woman you were seen with by the blackmailer. Please save the taxpayer the expense of tracing that person."

"I want her name kept out of this," Alex said.

"I will do my best to protect the innocent, Mr Doherty, but please remember I am leading a double murder investigation," Black said. "Name and address, please."

"Her name is Shiri Brooks-Dagless. She's married to a client I do a lot of work for. He mustn't find out. For her sake."

"Is Shiri Brooks-Dagless's husband violent?"

"He might be. He has it in him."

Dressed casually in a pair of jeans under an anorak, Eden arrived in an unmarked car at the spacious detached house Mrs Brooks-Dagless shared with her family. With her children at school and Mr Brooks-Dagless at work, Mrs Brooks-Dagless was alone in the front garden, raking leaves from the lawn. She stopped, hand on rake, to watch Eden step out of her car and walk up to her. Upon reaching her, Eden discretely showed her badge.

"My name's Detective Sergeant Hudson. Am I speaking with Mrs Shiri Brooks-Dagless?"

Shiri Brooks-Dagless looked visibly shocked. "What's this about?"

"Am I speaking with Mrs Shiri Brooks-Dagless?" Eden repeated.

"You are."

Shiri Brooks-Dagless was an attractive woman. Alex Doherty was an attractive man, and very flirtatious. They were about the same age. Eden could imagine the sexual chemistry. She wondered how long it had taken them to fall into bed. "Your name has come up as part of an inquiry into a serious crime," Eden said.

"I haven't done anything."

"This is a delicate issue. Can we go inside, please?"

"You can stay out here while I call my husband," Shiri said, clasping the rake with both hands.

Eden took a step closer and lowered her voice. "I need to talk about Alex Doherty, Mrs Brooks-Dagless." Shiri Brooks-Dagless looked shocked. "Why don't we step indoors and I'll tell you what I need to know, and then you can decide whether you want somebody else present or not."

Mrs Brooks-Dagless let the rake fall to the ground and shook her gardening gloves off, letting them fall to the ground, too. She turned and led Eden through the garden and around the side of the house where a door took them into a utility room. Shiri deposited her garden shoes by the door. Eden asked if she should also remove her shoes, but Shiri Brooks-Dagless gave a slight shake of her head. She took Eden into an immense kitchen of marble surfaces and splash backs. A door next to a large window led to an outdoor eating area. Shiri picked up a remote control and pointed it at the window, and blinds descended.

"We'll talk through there," she said, leading Eden into a small room off the main kitchen. White chairs with orange seats and backrests surrounded an octagonal white table. Cushions rested on a window seat, mirrors and pictures hung on the wall. The table was clear, other than condiments and some placemats stacked in the middle. Another remote control closed this room's blinds, too. Shiri announced she was going to get herself a glass of water and asked Eden if she would also like one.

"No, thank you." Shiri Brooks-Dagless returned to the kitchen. Eden heard running water and ice clink. Shiri returned clutching a tall glass of iced water and sat down. Eden sat next to her in an attempt to gain her confidence, sure that she had used the time to come up with a story.

"I'm not sure if I can be of much help," Shiri said. "Alex Doherty is just our handyman. My husband knows him far better than I do. He just does odd job for us. You know. The usual." Eden had learned early in her police career to keep a straight face no matter what. It was a useful trick.

"Mrs Brooks-Dagless, I'm going to show you an exchange of text messages taken from a mobile phone belonging to Mr Do-

herty. Mr Doherty claims the texts were between you and him."
Eden passed across a transcript of the text messages found on
Alex Doherty's Nokia phone. Shiri's hands shook as she read
through them. "I don't know anything about this," she said,
throwing the transcript on the table. Eden picked it up and
returned it to its folder.

"Mrs Brooks-Dagless, please allow me to speak bluntly," she
said. "We are unconcerned about your private life. My
colleagues and I will do everything in our power to protect you,
but we need to eliminate you and Alex Doherty from our
inquiries. If you're not honest with us from the outset, I cannot
guarantee your relationship with Alex Doherty will not come
out."

"I've no idea what you're talking about," she said. "I don't
know what you're trying to insinuate." Shiri pushed her chair
back and stood up. She sounded brave, but Eden sensed she
was close to losing her bottle. Eden reached over and touched
her hand. Shiri pulled it away abruptly. "I've told you there's
nothing to come out. If you don't leave, I will call my husband."

"If you feel you need to do that, then please do," Eden said.
She remained in her seat. A few minutes passed in a tense
stand-off, ending with Shiri Brooks-Dagless collapsing in her
seat. "Mrs Brooks-Dagless, no one is judging you. We know you
and Alex have been the victims of blackmail." A look of panic
crossed Shiri's eyes. "I need you to tell me everything." Shiri
began hyperventilating. "You need to be honest with me, Shiri."
Shiri cradled her body in her arms. "Your husband doesn't
need to know anything, Shiri. Not if I can eliminate you from
our enquiries."

Although she exhaled and seemed to visibly relax, fear and
confusion were still evident in her eyes. "I am just a trophy
wife, sitting alone in a trophy home. Sometimes I get so lonely,
I can't tell you. Alex came here to put a few loose tiles back. I
made him coffee and one thing led to the other. He came back

every week after that. Fix a tap. Replace a fence post. I could always find a reason. My husband even started joking about the number of times he was here. Asked if we were carrying on. For me, it was about companionship as much as anything. I'm such a cliché," she said.

"You're not the first, love," Eden said.

"I don't know who found out about us, but Alex found this note under his window wipers saying someone knew about us and demanding money." She wrapped her arms around her body again, and her head fell forward. "If my husband finds out, he'll divorce me. Under the prenup, I'll lose everything. I have nothing of my own."

"So you paid up?"

"We had no choice. Alex paid the first time, but then I got one. In the post. Thank god I was alone when I opened it. I took the money from my husband's account. He's got so much, he didn't notice. We hoped that would be it over with, but then I got another one. Again, in the post. That time I sold some things to pay the money they wanted." She burst into tears, hands over her face. Eden reached into her bag and produced a packet of paper handkerchiefs, which she handed to her.

"I've been so stupid," Shiri Brooks-Dagless said, wiping her eyes. "He's probably got a bored housewife fuck rota."

"Shiri, do you have the letters?" Eden said.

She shook her head, "I'm not that thick."

Eden asked where she was on the morning of Tudor O'Connell's murder.

"I'll need to check in my diary," she said.

Eden followed a still shaky Shiri Brooks-Dagless into her front room and over to a bureau. An A4 diary was produced. Shiri flicked back through it. Her relief was evident. "I was here." She closed her diary. "That's my cleaner's day. I don't go out when she's here."

"I'll need her to confirm your story," Eden said.

"What will you tell her?" the panicky Shiri returned. "I know," she said, calming down again, "tell her a woman matching her description has been seen passing fake cheques the day in question. That way she'll say it can't be her because she was here with me."

Eden was quite impressed at Shiri's problem solving. She asked Shiri where she was on the evening of Caro May's death.

Shiri re-checked her diary. "I had a bridge evening here. We don't start until seven thirty. We finish between ten thirty and eleven, but the ladies often hang around far longer if we start to chat. That evening, we were up past midnight."

This would put her in the clear. "I'll need names," Eden said.

"What will you tell them?"

"I'll tell them there was an incident nearby, around the time they were leaving, and ask if any of them saw anything suspicious," Eden said.

Shiri Brooks-Dagless visibly relaxed. "Thank you," she said, reaching to the chain she wore around her neck and kissing the gold cross on it. This gave Eden an idea. "Mrs Brooks-Dagless, forgive me for asking but are you a church goer?"

"Yes," she said, hesitantly. "Are you going to accuse me of hypocrisy?"

"I'm not going to accuse you of anything. I just want to know, are you a Catholic?"

"Anglican."

"Does that involve Confession?" Eden said.

"No, we don't do that at our church. I didn't tell anyone about me and Alex and neither did he. We only ever met here. Someone must have seen him leaving here."

．　．　．

With the idea that the blackmail might be linked to Confession now in her head, Eden rang Lilah O'Connell from her car. "Lilah, do you take Confession?" she asked.

Lilah snorted. "You're never suggesting the good Reverend Father is our blackmailer? Wait till I tell Hugo and Denys. And Val. And Mum!" She sounded triumphant. "And no, not any more. I used to go to Confession to get Mum off my back, but when she gave up the habit, so did I."

"Don't you get on with Father Hanrahan?" Eden asked.

"When I was a kid, I confessed to nicking a classmate's bike. Big mistake. Hanrahan made me write *Thou Shalt Not Steal* two hundred times. Mum and Dad inevitably found out and I got it. If you're of a mind that the blackmailer picked on me after overhearing something I said at Confession, think again. Ever since *Thou Shalt Not Steal,* I've not confessed to anything more serious than a bit of blasphemy or fancying one of the gardeners."

Eden hesitated. "Apologies for my directness, Lilah, but have you ever had a sexual relationship with Alex Doherty?"

At the other end of the phone, Lilah laughed out loud. "I wish. He's fit. Sadly not, Detective Sergeant. I don't shit on my own doorstep."

Not to be deterred, Eden rang Hugo and Denys. "Are either of you regular church goers? St. Edmund's Church or another church?" she asked.

She heard them laugh. "Only for weddings and funerals," Hugo said.

"And christenings," Denys yelled in the background.

"Mum goes to church. Uncle Mungo went. Even Dad used to. Didn't do any of them much good," Hugo said.

. . .

Next, Eden rang Valerie Simpson. "Val, I'm trying to establish how easy it would be for someone to overhear a confession in the confessional?"

"Well, anything's possible, love, but I never have, even when immediately outside the room. The doors are deliberately made thick. I've never found any hidden recording devices either, and I've cleaned enough confessionals in my time. Only things I've ever found are umbrellas, hats, or spectacles — I've found enough of those over the years. I don't know what your line of enquiry is but, in truth, most Catholics don't confess to much more than coveting their neighbour's loft conversion or eating a bacon sarnie on a Friday. Learning what goes on at Confession would be a big effort for little return."

Eden drove to the church of St. Edmund. Her arrival coincided with the end of service. She waited for the congregation to drift out. When alone with Father Hanrahan in the empty church, she showed him a copy of Lilah O'Connell's blackmail letter. The priest read it.

"Good Lord!" he said. "I don't know what the world's coming to."

"Has any of your congregation confessed to sending letters such as this one?" she asked.

"The sanctity of the confessional is sacred, Detective Sergeant, but the answer is no, nobody."

"An awful lot of secrets must get spoken in this church." She thought she had chosen her words with care, so as not to sound accusatory, but the Reverend Father disagreed.

"Are you suggesting I'm a blackmailer, Detective Sergeant? I am the Pastor of this Parish. I counsel. I perform the sacraments of the Church, the Eucharist, and take confession..." He was red in the face.

This is going well, Eden thought. "I apologise if I have

offended you, Father, but you've misunderstood me. Is it at all possible that anyone could have overheard a confession?"

He mellowed. "Confession takes place behind those doors," he pointed to a pair of doors to the side of the organ. "The doors are soundproofed. What you're suggesting is impossible."

She wandered over to the doors and opened and shut them a couple of times. They were indeed thick and, she noticed, reached floor level. "And nothing is recorded?" she asked him.

"Good Lord, no." He walked towards the church door, clearly expecting her to follow. She did. At the door, he said, "Now, if you'll excuse me — I have church business to be getting on with."

Eden returned to the station. She began by confirming the alibis Mrs Shiri Brooks-Dagless had given her for the two dates in question. Then she spoke with Black in his office.

"Shiri Brooks-Dagless has admitted to the affair with Alex Doherty. She's terrified of her husband finding out. She paid at least two ransoms, he paid one. Her alibis check out for both murders. Alex Doherty doesn't have much by way of an alibi for the O'Connell killing, and he lied. But a double murder to cover up a bit on the side seems a bit drastic. I had a hunch the blackmail could be to do with stuff overheard at Confession, but it's another dead end I'm afraid, Sir."

The door to Black's office opened and the Chief Constable himself appeared. Eden and Black immediately jumped to their feet. He bid them sit down again and joined them.

"You're looking more and more like Hercule Poirot every day, Detective Inspector," the Chief said, his own moustache also well-established.

"Thank you, Sir."

"How are you getting on with that murder of yours?" the Chief asked.

"We're making slow but steady progress, Sir."

"Interesting thing. Last night my wife reminded me that we've actually visited the vicinity of your murder scene."

"Sir?" Black said.

"In case you didn't know, my wife is a botanist. Her comments made me take a quick look through the evidence again. One of your witnesses is lying to you, Detective Inspector."

Chapter 37

BLACK FACED Lilah O'Connell across a desk of an interviewing room.

"Lilah O'Connell, can you tell me again where you were when your father was killed?" he asked.

"Up at the old oak."

"The centuries-old sessile oak tree?"

Lilah hesitated then nodded.

"For the record, the suspect has nodded her agreement," Black said. "Ms O'Connell, please turn to image twenty-seven in the folder in front of you. I'm calling the same image up on the screen." The image was the pencil sketch of the oak branch with its leaves and acorns, taken from Lilah O'Connell's notepad and signed and dated by her. "Please confirm this is the sketch you claimed to have been making on the morning of your father's murder?"

"That's one of mine. When finished, I always date in the bottom right-hand corner."

"Turn to the next image in your folder please, Ms O'Connell," he said.

She did. It was a photograph of the ancient sessile oak tree. "This, Ms O'Connell, is a photograph of the tree you claimed to be sketching that morning." Black zoomed in on one of its branches from which sprouted leaves and acorns. "Please compare the branch with your sketch." The images appeared alongside each other on the screen. "The picture on the left is the sessile oak you claimed to be sketching. The picture on the right is your sketch, image twenty-seven. Please note the acorns on the sessile oak tree do not hang from stalks as they do in your sketch, but instead grow out from the branches themselves, whereas its leaves grow from stalks, unlike the leaves in your sketch, which grow from the branches. These differences are the main differences between an English oak and a sessile oak. The leaves and acorns in your sketch, Ms O'Connell, are the leaves and acorns of an English oak, not a sessile oak. English oaks are plentiful and widespread and don't offer much by way of an alibi. Yet it was a sessile oak you claimed to be sketching when your father was murdered — the only sessile oak in the region, as it so turns out — conveniently placing you some way from the murder scene. Unfortunately for you, the rarity and age of the sessile oak draws people with an interest in botany to it."

"Can I say something, Detective Inspector?" Lilah asked.

"Yes – you can tell me where you were when your father was murdered."

For the first time in the enquiry, Lilah was on the wrong foot. "I was at the sessile oak, but not to sketch. I was there picking up drugs. There's a nook in the base of the tree where my supplier drops them and I leave cash. An honesty nook."

"Ms O'Connell, why did you not tell me this earlier? You've already admitted to the recreational use of cannabis resin."

"We're not talking cannabis," she said. "We're talking Marching Powder."

"Cocaine?"

"Yes," she said. "I'd just collected it when the sirens spooked me. I ended up chucking it in a pond. I always have my sketch pad on me. When I saw all the police cars, I signed and dated the last sketch I made."

"Your alibi is now that you were at the sessile oak tree when your father was murdered, but picking up Cocaine, not sketching?" he said.

"Yes — Cocaine. But only for my personal use," she said hurriedly. "I don't supply."

"I'll need to know who supplied it to corroborate your story or else it's hardly an alibi."

"I genuinely don't know," Lilah said. Her voice, normally so controlled, was now fast. "I pick up the drugs and leave cash. I've been doing it like that since school. I've never seen the other party. I haven't got a name. You have to believe me. I want to find who killed my dad as much as you."

"I will need to refer this conversation to the Crown Prosecution Service. For the time being, you're free to go," he said.

Lilah O'Connell got to her feet. "I'm sorry for misleading you, Detective Inspector. I want this to end in a conviction, I really do. Dad and I weren't on good terms when he died, which makes it so much worse. I want you to nail his killer, I do. If I'd thought it would help, I'd have told you the truth from the start. But I can't see as it's made any difference."

Eden looked up from her desk to find Pilot skulking. "Er...can I have a word in private?" he stuttered awkwardly.

"Sure."

They decided to use Black's empty office. "What's up?" she asked, wondering if he was after advice on his love life again. He hesitated and looked a bit awkward. Her heart sank.

"You're going to tell me something about Matt I don't want to hear, aren't you?"

He seemed a bit surprised and broke into a grin. "No," he said, "but cute. It's Dottie. She's here."

"In reception?" she asked.

"Not exactly," he said.

Eden stormed into the waiting room to find Dottie seated in a lounge chair, flicking through a magazine, a tray of tea and biscuits on a coffee table to her side. Eden remained standing, Pilot next to her, grinning. "What have you got to say for yourself, old lady?" she demanded.

"At long last. The rugby starts in an hour."

"Well, you should have thought of that before you got yourself arrested," Eden said.

"Technically, she hasn't been arrested. She's helping us with our enquiries," Pilot said.

Dottie gathered her belongings together. "I take it I'm free to leave?"

"Not so fast," Eden said. "Catnapping is a very serious offence."

"I really don't think it is," Dottie replied. "Anyway I wasn't going to catnap her. I just wanted to snip off a bit of fur, but she wouldn't keep still. Kept twisting and turning. That's why I put her in the cat box. I was always going to let her go."

"Why did you want her fur?" Eden asked.

"Dora's still convinced she's Betty Boop. You have to admit, they do look alike."

"That's because they're both black cats," Eden said.

"Did you manage to get any fur?" Pilot said. "'Cos if you did, we could get it tested."

"Not you, too?" Eden said.

Dottie dug around in her pocket and pulled out a plastic bag containing strands of fur. "'Fraid I left the poor thing with a bald patch."

"Yeah, the owners mentioned it," Pilot said. "I'll need some of Betty Boop's fur to compare."

"We've still got her old brush at home," Dottie said, "that'll have her fur on it."

"You get it to us, and I'll get the samples to the lab," Pilot said.

"I don't believe I'm hearing this," Eden said.

"It's a million-to-one shot," Pilot said, "but as I always say — a million to one is a million better than two million to one."

Dottie got to her feet. "Well, if you don't mind, I have to be on my way. Don't want to miss the kick-off."

"You could be charged with a public nuisance offence, you know that, don't you?" Eden said, slightly annoyed that Dottie didn't seem to be taking the situation seriously.

"I don't think that will be necessary," Pilot said. Dottie smiled and offered him the plate of biscuits. He helped himself and she put the plate down again before Eden could do the same. "I'll walk you to the door, Dottie," he said.

"Don't mind me," Eden called after the pair ambling down the corridor.

"Now," she heard Pilot say, "I hear you make a mean steak pie. Thing is, there's this girl I like, but she's into veggies, which I only like made from potatoes and fried."

Eden rolled her eyes but, as she watched them, Dottie's concern about missing the start of the rugby made her ask herself a question. Had Alex Doherty really spent a weekend in London for the rugby, as he had told Sheryl Teal, or had he been there for another reason?

Chapter 38

THE NEXT MORNING saw Eden and Black return to St. Edmund's Church, summoned by Father Dermot Hanrahan. The Father was leaning against the pulpit steps clutching a bunch of leaflets. "I sent her out with a pile of these," he said, waving the leaflets as he spoke. "We often leaflet. Inviting people to the church or to publicise a church social. I deliver on foot, Val cycles. She can cover quite a distance."

"But you haven't seen her since she set off yesterday?" Black said.

The Reverend Father took a step backwards and sat down on the wooden steps, resting his elbows on his legs, his face in his hands. "It was my idea to flush the killer out. If something's happened, I'll never forgive myself."

"Flush the killer out?" Black said.

His head still lowered, Father Hanrahan held the leaflets aloft for Eden to take. She and Black read each in turn:

Numbers 32:23

Be sure your sins will find you out.

Luke 5.31

Jesus answered them: It is not the healthy who need a doctor, but the sick. I have not come to call the righteous, but sinners to repentance.

Acts 3.19

Therefore, repent and return to God so that your sins may be wiped away.

Revelations 3.3

Remember then, what you received and heard. Keep it and repent. If you will not wake up, I will come like a thief, and you will not know at what hour I will come against you.

Romans 2.5-11

But because you are stubborn and refuse to turn from sin, you are storing up terrible punishment for yourself. For a day of anger is coming, when God's righteous judgement will be revealed.

Eden and Black glanced at each other in confusion. "I'm sorry, Father," Black said, "but how were these fliers meant to flush the killer out?"

"Guilt," he said. "Fear of retribution and the need for forgiveness. I may sound like a foolish old man, but I believe most people would gladly confess to their sins and serve a jail sentence than be deprived of the everlasting bliss of heaven."

"I only wish that was our experience, Father," Black said.

"Just to be straight, you asked Valerie Simpson to leaflet for you, as she had many times before?" Eden said.

"Yes. She arrived early yesterday evening," Father Hanrahan said. "She'd spent the day up at the TreeHouse. We had a spot of supper, just some soup and a slice of pie, then she put the leaflets in her basket, and off she went."

"Even though it was getting dark?" Eden said.

"She wanted to make a start. Many of the lanes are lit and she has a light on her bike and another on her helmet. She always takes the same route. Knows it like the back of her hand."

"When did you become concerned?" Black asked.

"I didn't expect her to get everything delivered last night, with the time she set out, but normally she gives me a call to say she's finished for the night — but this time she didn't. I thought maybe she'd just forgotten, but when she still hadn't called this morning...and I've not been able to get hold of her. I called Bettina but they've not seen her since yesterday either. I took the car out and drove around looking for her, but it's like she's disappeared without trace. I even knocked on a few doors on her route. She definitely delivered some of the leaflets. All I can tell you is she's still not home, and no one up at the house or in the village knows where she is. I even called her sister on the coast, but she's not heard from her since last week." He looked pleadingly at both of them in turn. "With everything that's been going on, with what happened to that poor woman, not to mention Tudor, I just hope to God..." He buried his head in his hands again and mumbled, "What if she stumbled across something...?"

"Don't worry, Sir," Eden said, trying to sound more reassured than she felt. "We will find her."

"I'm sure you will," Father Dermot Hanrahan said, looking up. "But will you find her alive?"

They returned to the car engrossed in their thoughts. Eden was worried about Valerie Simpson. Black was, too, but something besides that was niggling at him. He was sure he'd just seen or heard something crucial to the enquiry. But what? After issuing a missing person alert for Valerie Simpson, they drove to the TreeHouse.

Bettina, Hugo and Denys were there. They spoke in the front room. Other than some kitchen chairs, the room was empty. Even the piano had gone.

"Oh, my God!" Hugo said. "Not poor Val too." Denys' hands went to his mouth. Bettina was so shaken by the news her legs gave way. Hugo helped her to a seat as Eden fetched her some water.

She took a few sips. "I've known Val for so long," Bettina said. "She's a friend."

"We don't as yet know that anything has happened to her," Black said. "When was the last time you saw her?"

"Yesterday — here," Hugo said. "She came round to help out. She left about, I dunno — about, what...six wasn't it, Denys?"

"About then," he replied. "Said she had some leafleting to do for Father Hanrahan."

"And none of you have heard from her since?" Black asked.

They all looked at each other and shook their heads and muttered, "No."

"Where were you all last night?" Eden said.

"Hugo and I were at home watching *Zombies V Cockneys*," Denys said.

"We're huge zombie fans," Hugo admitted.

"After dinner with my daughter at her house, I stayed in," Bettina said.

"Was your daughter with you?" Eden said.

"There's no point lying. She went out after we ate. I can't say when she came back. I was asleep."

Black and Eden called next at Lilah's house. She answered the door, but made no attempt to invite them in. She seemed genuinely unsettled. News of the disappearance had reached her. "Makes you wonder who's going to be next?" she said distractedly.

"When was the last time you saw Val?" Eden asked.

"A little after six. I was drawing the curtains and saw her cycle past. We waved to each other."

"What did you do last night?" Black said.

"Mum and I had dinner, then I went out."

"Where did you go?" Black said.

"Out for a spliff. I know it's my house, but Mum's doesn't like it. I called in on my local on the way back for a whiskey. I was back for eleven. I'm going to suggest to the others we all move back into the TreeHouse," she said. "For safety."

They called Ivy from the station.

"The last time I saw Valerie Simpson was the day of the reconstruction. I haven't seen her since, and before you ask, I was here all evening. Ask the hotel desk."

Eden did. Ivy's story checked out. As did Lilah's claim of an evening drink at her local on her way home.

On the way back to the station, Eden said, "Why Val? Was there something she hadn't told us?"

"That, Detective Sergeant, is the ten-million-dollar question," Black said.

"It's not looking good, is it, Sir?"

"I've been more optimistic, Eden," Black said.

Chapter 39

AT HER STATION DESK, Eden studied some newly arrived CCTV surveillance of the Twickenham Stadium taken on the day Alex Doherty told Sheryl Teal he was there for the rugby. Intel had been through the images, harvesting the relevant ones for Eden, highlighting Alex in the crowd where necessary. The images began with Alex Doherty leaving his car at a hotel car park and walking from there to the Stadium. He entered via a turnstile gate, climbed three flights of concrete stairs heaving with other spectators, bought himself a beer and a burger and took them to his seat. Here he ate, drank and chatted with his neighbours until kick-off.

Eden sped through the images of Alex intent on the game. At half-time Alex Doherty, along with more than half the stadium, got to his feet to slowly make his way from the seating bowl to the concourse. Even with an arrow above his head, it was becoming harder to pick him out in the crowd. Eden fast-forwarded to the start of the second half. Alex's seat was still empty and remained so upon resumption of play, and throughout the game. A coat was eventually deposited on it. Well, well, well, Eden thought.

She opened the second zip of CCTV surveillance and

watched Alex Doherty descend the deserted stadium stairs and exit the stadium. Outside the turnstile he made a phone call. He remained on the phone as he returned to the hotel. There, he crossed the lobby to the lifts. So, Sheryl was right all along, Eden thought. He wasn't in London only to watch the rugby.

Alex stepped out of the lift on the fourth floor. At room 116, he gave a single rap on the door. The door opened, but only just. Alex gave it a push and stepped inside, closing the door behind him. Eden fast-forwarded again, but the door remained closed. The time, displayed in the top right-hand corner, flashed by.

Alex Doherty left the room at 9:05 a.m. the following morning, making no attempt to disguise his appearance. Not so his lady friend. She emerged twenty minutes after him. She left as she had arrived, dressed in a trench coat, collar pulled up to her nose, hair disguised by a headscarf, sunglasses on, head lowered, even in the lift. While Alex had brazenly breakfasted in the hotel restaurant, she had slipped from the hotel into a large shopping mall. Here, she disappeared. While Eden didn't recognise the woman, she knew it wasn't Shiri Brooks-Dagless.

"Who is she, Alex?" Eden asked.

Alex groaned and flinched when he saw the images. "You must think me some kind of sex maniac."

"What I think isn't relevant," she said. "I need to know her name, Alex."

"Why? This all happened before O'Connell was done in."

"You've told us you believed Tudor O'Connell was blackmailing you, Alex. He may have been blackmailing her."

"How? How could he have known about Twickenham? He could've seen my van outside Shiri's or overheard me on the phone to her. But to follow me all the way to London and hang around a hotel? Then target her, who he didn't know from Adam. He'd have targeted me, not her."

"I give you my word that we will do our best to protect her, but I need to know who she is, if only to eliminate her from our enquiries. Now please, Alex, her name."

He groaned again. "I don't know it," he said. "We met through an app. First time we set eyes on each other was in that room. She said she was Jane January. I said was Mick Marsh. It was sex without strings, Eden. A bit of fun that's turned into a nightmare. I wish to God I hadn't started it now. Everything's fucked up. My kid's in tears the whole time. Sheryl hates me. But none of it's got anything to do with what happened to O'Connell. Okay?"

"Alex, we believe the blackmailer targeted more than one victim," Eden said. This was something of a bluff on her part. Shiri Brooks-Dagless lived on an avenue, whereas the green edging on the stencil letters S, T and R, suggested a street address had been stencilled at some point. "Is there anyone else we should know about?"

"Contrary to what you clearly believe, I don't actually have a harem, Eden," he said. "Some of my customers like a joke. They pretend to like a bit of rough. You know me. I play along. Maybe Tudor, or whoever the blackmailer was, saw me and them having a laugh, got the wrong end of the stick and sent them a letter? But if me and Shiri weren't his only targets, I don't know who else was. No one's said anything to me."

"Unless you have anything to add, you're free to go for the time being."

"Thanks for nothing, love," he said, getting up and sauntering out of the room.

. . .

Eden made her way to Black's office. Before she had a chance to speak, Black said. "What else did we see at St. Edmund's as well as Father Dermot Hanrahan?"

"Quotes from *The Bible*?"

"Carvings."

"Sir?"

"Get your coat, Detective Sergeant. We're going on a visit."

When aren't we, she thought, returning to her desk for her coat.

Chapter 40

BLACK AND EDEN faced the Tullys in the couple's cosy front room. Even though the fire roared in the inglenook fireplace, nicely warming the room, the couple shivered with cold.

"Mrs Tully, I'm going to read back something you said in your last statement to us," Black said. He picked up a printout and read, "*The man was a congenital liar. I've been on the webpage. Never read so many lies. The studio wasn't kept as a memorial to her. They chucked her stuff out after she died. His dad carved the Tree-House sign for his first wife, not his darling Gethsemane. And she was the garden designer, not...*"

"What of it?" she said attempting to keep calm but there was panic in those words.

"How did you know Tudor told the guests that Emlyn carved the TreeHouse sign for Gethsemane?"

She paused before replying. "I didn't. I was referring to the lies on their webpage. It says Emlyn O'Connell carved the Tree-House sign for his darling Gethsemane, but he didn't. Tudor told me himself that Emlyn carved it before he met Gethsemane."

"The webpage says nothing of the sort. It says very little about the property as a matter of fact, having been set up originally as a merchandise place. It makes mention of the studio and gardens but says nothing about Emlyn carving the Tree-House sign for Gethsemane," Black said. "Tudor's lovingly carved anecdote might well have become a permanent embellishment to the Gethsemane myth, but that morning it seems to have been a spontaneous remark, made in response to interest from the group. Therefore, I must repeat my question. How did you know what Tudor O'Connell said to his guests that morning?"

A connecting door opened, and a man stepped through it. Black got to his feet and said, "Dr Nick Pilsworth, I presume?"

"The name's Roger Stenn. Tam's me sister," the man said.

"How did you know we were here?" Eden asked, also on her feet.

"I live next door. Saw the car arrive. Let myself in. You've no business pointing the finger at Tam or Brian. They didn't kill O'Connell any more than I did."

Tam looked to Black and said, "Roger was there that morning, but he didn't kill Tudor. That was nothing to do with him."

"Maybe we could start at the beginning?" Black said.

Roger Stenn sat down next to his sister and brother-in-law. Eden and Black also resumed their seats.

"I've been married to this man for nearly thirty years," Tam said, "and in that time, I've only seen him cry when his parent's died, and that day he came back from London."

"Tudor O'Connell would stop at nothing to ruin us," Brian said. "He wanted to make an example of us."

"He was always a little shit," Tam said. "He was the only one at art school with any money and boy didn't we know it."

"The whole thing was my idea," Roger said. "Plant a bug and dig up some dirt on him to use back at him. Two can play dirty."

"But first we had to decide where to plant it to produce the best results but not get found," Brian said.

"I bought the magazine to read the interview and hung onto it," Tam said. "I knew there were pictures from his study in it." She got up nervously and crossed to a chest of drawers. She opened the last drawer and, after a search around, pulled out an issue of *Spirit*. She removed it from the plastic folder protecting it to flick through its pages. She handed the magazine to Eden, open on the photographs of Tudor and Ivy in the study. "My relationship with Tudor was a little more than I said. We were together for months. All through the spring and the summer. Once he took me to the TreeHouse to introduce me to his dad. Gethsemane had died by that time, more's the pity. I never liked the Indian mirrored loveseat — bit garish for my taste and very uncomfortable — but when I saw from the magazine photos that they still had it, I had a light-bulb moment. Having sat in the thing, I knew its finials unscrewed," Tam continued. "All we had to do was hide the bug in a copycat finial and swap it with one from the loveseat, and we were away." Tam pointed out a pair of decorative cut-glass ornaments on either corner of the loveseat's ornate headrest.

"I nearly had a heart-attack when you opened the drawer with the cupboard knobs that day in the studio," Brian said, with a bit of a chuckle. "We planted the bug in one of the diamante ones from that drawer."

Eden looked at the picture of the loveseat. Diamante door-knobs? Cut glass finials? Who in all likelihood could tell the difference?

"We still had to figure out how to get into the house. Tam or Brian couldn't set foot in the place, it had to be me," Roger Stenn said.

"Then I saw the advert for the TreeHouse open day," Brian said.

"I found a perfect candidate online. An art lecturer called Dr Nick Pilsworth," Tam said. "I created a fake email address and booked him on a tour."

"Tam did Roger's makeup. She made him look like an old man, because people don't notice old people as much as younger people," Brian said.

They do if they look like ageing werewolves, Eden thought.

"There were prosthetic noses at the back of the drawer of glass eyes you pulled out," Tam said. "That's why I started speaking ten to the dozen. Didn't want you looking any further."

"On the day, I drove to the nearest town, parked up and got a bus for the remainder of the journey," Roger said.

"But how did you get into the study?" Black asked.

"I intended to go through the French window," Roger said.

"Believe it or not, I still have one of their spare keys," Tam said. "Tudor never knew I'd taken it. I'd helped myself to it because of its association with Gethsemane and hung on to it. When I saw the colour spread in *Spirit*, I realised the French doors were the same. It wasn't serendipity. I don't believe in that. The building is listed. They couldn't change the doors if they wanted to, unless they broke beyond repair or something."

"The idea was for me to break away from the group at some point and test if the key still worked," Roger said. "If it did — bingo. If it didn't, I'd rejoin the group and find another way in as the day went on. But, as it happened, some lady in the group used the inside cloakroom and I slipped in after her. I went straight to the study and swapped the finials. Took hardly any time. Tudor had just turned up and they were all fawning over him when I re-emerged. Genuinely don't think anyone noticed me go in or come out. I thought it might look a bit suspicious if I disappeared straight away, so I stuck with the group for a bit then made my excuses and left. No one was in the courtyard, so I let myself through the gate..."

"How did you let yourself through the gate?" Black said. "It was locked."

Roger smiled. "When we arrived, the gate was weighted

open. I expected it would be closed after us and, needing as quick a getaway as possible, I waited for the young man to start shaking hands and introducing himself to slip away over to the gate and put some plastic guards into the mouth of the lock. They're tiny things with an adhesive base. Tam sticks them underneath everything to protect the surfaces. I stuck some together and placed them in the mouth of the lock. They're soft enough to allow the gate to appear closed, but with them there it couldn't completely engage and lock. I just gave the handle a turn and it opened. I took the discs with me.

"The gate had just closed behind me when I heard voices in the courtyard, so I got a move on. There wasn't anyone out front and I legged it — cross country. Ended up getting a bit lost. I could hear all these sirens wailing. I was convinced my bug had been found and they were after me. I was in such a panic. Then I saw the church. I must've gone round in a complete circle. I ran inside. I was alone, thank heavens. I was still wearing my disguise. I took my shoes off and made for the organ, hoping to change behind it, when I saw a couple of doors. I jumped inside one into a confessional. There was a chair and a curtain across a latticed screen. That's where I got changed."

"Where were your change of clothes? There aren't any reports of you having a bag on you," Eden said. "Just a heavy coat."

"My hunchback wasn't just there for the disguise, it was my rucksack containing my change of clothes. My hand was literally on the door handle when I heard a noise outside, like a suitcase being wheeled across the church floor. I froze, praying they weren't going to burst in on me. I just wanted to get the hell out of there. In the end, they went into the next room. I could hear heavy breathing and grating noises through the latticed screen. Whoever it was, was in a bigger panic than me."

Eden was listening to this with a mixture of fascination and annoyance. The information could prove very important, yet they were only just hearing it. She wondered how Black was going to react.

"Grating?" he said.

"Yeah, like a squeaking noise," Roger said. "I don't know how to put it. It was like something was being prised opened. I stood stock-still. Hardly dared breathe. My heart was beating ten to the dozen. I'm surprised next door couldn't hear it."

"Was it a he or a she?" Black said.

"Thought I heard someone swear — reckon whoever it was hurt themselves — but can't say if it was a male or female. After some minutes, I heard the door open and someone wheeling the suitcase out. They must've picked it up after, as I didn't hear any more wheeling, just running and a door open and close. I plucked up the courage to peep out. The church was empty, and I bolted."

"There aren't any reports of a man matching your description emerging from the church," Black said.

"That's because I didn't use the main door," Roger Stenn said. "I followed my neighbour out of the door at the end of the church which he or she kindly left unlocked — told you they was in a bigger panic than me. It took me out to the graveyard. That was the most dangerous bit. I had to clamber over a wall and run bent double alongside a field. I kept going, trying to keep out of sight. When I couldn't run, I walked. I walked and walked and walked, keeping away from the roads. When I was far enough away, I jumped on a bus. Ended up God knows where. Took me hours to get home. Tam and Brian were frantic."

"At any stage, did you catch sight of the person in the next room?" Eden asked.

"I didn't," Roger said.

"After you split from the group, but before you left the Tree-House, did you see or hear anybody you haven't already mentioned?" Black asked.

"I didn't."

"Did you see any open doors or windows or ladders at or around the property?" he asked.

"No, nothing like that. I didn't really see anything at all suspicious."

Black folded his arms. "All three of you have lied to the police during a murder investigation, wasting our time and withholding information useful for the inquiry, and you, Mr Stenn, were at the murder scene and have no alibi for the killing."

"I've told you what happened," Roger Stenn said. "It was the worst luck, him being killed the day I was there, but I didn't do it."

"Your search team clearly haven't found it, and as we'd failed to get it back, our bug must still be in the study," Tam said.

Eden looked at her. What did she mean by *as we'd failed to get it back*? "Mrs Tully, did you pretend to be a journalist in an attempt to gain entry to the TreeHouse to retrieve the bug?" Eden asked.

Tam nodded sadly. "It was a huge risk, but what choice did we have? Brian was on the verge of a breakdown. He was convinced you'd find it and trace it to us. Ivy's interview with *Spirit* was the hook. They bit. I was on my way when the Detective Inspector drove past me. I thought the whole thing was a sting and you'd be lying in wait for me."

"The car you used?" Eden said.

"A red Fiat," Tam said.

"I picked it up at an auction for cash," Roger Stenn said.

"We've spent a lot of time and resources looking for that car," Eden said.

After mumbled apologies, Brian said, "I know this all looks bad for us."

"It doesn't look good," Eden said. She asked Roger Stenn his whereabouts at the time of Caroline May's killing.

"He was here with us," Tam said. "He was the family I told you we had round for dinner."

"The bug still being there proves us innocent," Brian said.

"How so, Mr Tully?" Black said.

"Roger couldn't have been planting the bug and killing him at the same time," Brian said.

"Mr Stenn could've planted the bug at an earlier date and later returned to kill Tudor O'Connell when the bug failed to provide any useful information," Black said.

"What, kill him and leave our bug behind for you to find?" Roger asked. "That would be a bit thick."

"How would Roger have got in?" Tam said.

"By using the key to the French windows you've already admitted to possessing. Maybe you could dig that out for us?" Black said.

As his wife went for the key, Brian said, "Trying to dig up a bit of intelligence to use on a man is one thing. But to take a man's life is altogether another."

"Nonetheless," Black said, "you have both wasted police time on a murder enquiry; committed trespass, which is a civil offence; and have bugged someone's house, which is a breach of the Human Rights Act 1998, specifically Article 8. You will be hearing further from us, Mr and Mrs Tully, and Mr Stenn."

Once in the car, Black said, "A good day's work, Detective Sergeant. We've killed two intruders with one stone."

"We've viewed the Tullys differently for a while now, and now have her brother at the scene," Eden said.

"If Roger Stenn is lying, he's our killer. But if he's telling the truth, who did he hear in the confessional and what were they up to?" Black said.

"That Valerie Simpson was a church key-holder may be significant," Eden said.

They drove straight to the TreeHouse. At the French windows, they tried the key. It worked and the door opened. There wasn't even a security bolt. They both slipped on a pair of shoe covers and stepped inside. The loveseat stood to one side of the French windows. Its intricate mirroring glistened under the last of the day's sun. The pair of cut-glass finials, mounted on small wooden bases, stood on either corner of the chair's ornate headrest. Gloves on, Black ran his hands over each. Both unscrewed as easily as Tam had said they would. But in which was the bug? Eden shone her torch at each finial in turn.

"That one," she said, training the beam on the left of the two. Black leaned closer. The light had picked out a tiny line dividing one of the finials in the middle. Black quickly unscrewed the whole piece, holding it up to his eye. "Best let the lab loose on it," he said, dropping it into an evidence bag. They took the other one as well.

As she put the key in her front door, Eden stopped to mull over events. They had jewellery inside globes, killers inside sculptures or behind trees, blackmailers inside lean-tos, emojis inside pieces of art, and now recording devices inside furniture. What an odd case this was turning out to be.

Chapter 41

EDEN DIDN'T THINK she'd been asleep for very long when the phone rang. It was the station. She was to go to the river bank. The desk sergeant at the station couldn't tell her any more.

Her mind immediately went to the missing Valerie Simpson. This can't be good, she thought, climbing out of bed. She threw on some clothes, slipped downstairs, scrawled a hurried note, grabbed a coat and scarf, and slipped out the back door.

The drive to the small tarmacked lane she'd been called to took only fifteen minutes. She parked as close as she could get and walked the rest of the way. The lane was reserved for cyclists and pedestrians. It was sandwiched between a tall fence, behind which was a factory unit and a grass bank tumbling down to the river. The sun still hadn't risen, and visibility was limited.

Black was already there, as were the dog team and police divers. "A member of the public has informed us that her daughter came home last night with a skipping rope, which she claimed to have found tied between two trees along this lane," he explained. "The mum didn't think anything of it until she was driving to work an hour ago — she's a nurse — and heard a news item about Val Simpson's disappearance which mentioned this lane as part of the route Val took."

"Why didn't we find the rope, Sir?" Eden asked. "We searched the lane."

"The child has now admitted to finding the rope earlier than she originally said," he replied. "The morning after Val's disappearance."

"Oh," Eden replied. "Oh."

"The family are coming here when it's light to see if the child can identify the trees she found the rope tied between."

Eden checked her watch. It would be light within the hour.

"I suggest we hang around in the meantime and see if anything turns up," Black continued.

Eden looked around. If Val had cycled into the rope, she'd have come off her bike, likely at speed. Even landing on the grass would have left her bleeding and injured. The attacker would have had the advantage. She wandered over to a shivering, wet-suited police diver on the riverbank and joined him in gazing into the dark water. How long could anyone survive in there at this time of year? she thought.

She heard Black say, "Let's concentrate our search in this area, a few hundred metres to either side and down there to the river." Why, she wondered, if this was really where Val came off, had no trace of her been found before now? "Haven't the blood dogs already searched the lane?" she asked the diver.

"They were down to search this stage later today," was the reply.

From along the lane, somebody called out, "Sir!" Black and Eden looked over at a colleague squatting by a birch tree. They hurried over to him.

"Look at this, Sir," he said, shining a torch on the tree,

revealing a horizontal wound in its scaly bark. "It's all the way around, like something's been tied around it."

The three crossed to the birch tree on the other side of the lane and found almost identical marks around its trunk. "I'd say this is where the rope was, wouldn't you?" the officer said. "I'll get some samples taken from the bark."

Although still fairly dark, it was growing lighter, aiding the search. Police officers used sticks to beat away the grass in the search for clues and scanned the ground with torches while the dogs searched with their noses. There was a yell and a raised hand. It was blood. On the grass. A member of the team carefully snipped at the tiny green blades by the river's edge, dropping them into a small evidence bag as the dog responsible for finding the microscopic drops of blood sat nearby, attached to his trainer.

"With the tides around here," one of the divers said, "she could be halfway out to sea by now."

"If her body was weighted, it might still be at the bottom of the river," Eden said.

"We mustn't get ahead of ourselves," Black said. "We don't know that anything bad has happened to Val. All we have is evidence of a scuffle. The blood and skipping rope might turn out to have nothing to do with her." It was an attempt to convince himself as much as the team. He wandered over to the bank. If Val had played a part in Tudor's murder, and fearing the net was closing in or in fear for her own life, she might have staged her own disappearance, he told himself, only to remind himself that he'd suggested the same of Caro May. Let's hope for Valerie's sake this time you're right, Guido, he thought.

Eden had caught up with him and was now standing beside him.

"Val has a family on the coast, doesn't she?" he asked.

"A sister, yes. She's aware Val's missing."

"Best arrange for someone to go around and stay with her."

"Someone's already there, Sir."

The morning passed slowly and sombrely, with no real news until, just before lunch, the discovery of Val Simpson's bike at the bottom of the river. "Damn, damn, damn," Black said. He and Eden were in his office.

"We've only found the bike, let's not forget, Sir," she said.

"Bodies wash out to sea, bikes sink," he said. "What on earth did Caro May and Val Simpson know that we can't see?"

They both jumped when the phone on his desk rang.

Eden stepped into an interview room. Shiri Brooks-Dagless was sitting beside a fresh-faced trainee sent by his legal firm to take notes. He grinned sheepishly and immediately opened his notepad. Shiri was very nervous, making only brief and awkward eye contact.

"How can I help you, Mrs Brooks-Dagless?" Eden asked.

"After we spoke, I took legal advice." Shiri paused and cast her eyes down. "I've been advised to clarify something with you. By not doing so, it could look bad for me if it came out." Eden did not interrupt. She didn't want to turn the tap off in mid-flow. "When you came to my home, you showed me some texts referring to a demand, which, if you recall, at the time, I said I knew nothing about. Do you remember?"

Eden nodded. She'd taken Shiri's words as part of her general denial of things and hadn't pressed the point. "When I said I had never seen those texts before, I genuinely hadn't. But you would not listen."

Eden stared at her. Oh god, she thought. "Mrs Brooks-Dagless, I'm going to have to restart this interview and record it.

You'll need to excuse me. Please make yourself comfortable. I'll have some tea sent in."

When she returned, the young legal trainee was on his feet, pouring milk into a mug of tea.

"I'm being mother," he joked.

Eden informed Shiri Brooks-Dagless that the interview was now being recorded as the trainee scribbled furiously. "Mrs Shiri Brooks-Dagless, I'm going to show you a transcript of an exchange of text messages taken from the mobile phone of Alex Doherty, with whom you admit to having been intimate. The transcript is in the folder in front of you and will also appear on the screen."

The text messages appeared on the screen:

I've got another one

When?

Just now

Expletive. How much now?

A grand

Expletive. Ignore it

I can't. I'll be ruined

"Mrs Brooks-Dagless, could you confirm that the first time you saw the text messages currently displayed on the screen, was the day I visited you at your home?"

"Yes, that's true," Shiri said. "I'd never seen them before that day. I said so at the time, but you misunderstood, and things moved on so quickly."

"For the avoidance of doubt, could you please confirm that you neither sent nor received any of the text messages currently displayed on the screen in front of you?"

"I confirm. We got letters, not texts. Photocopied letters. Threatening to tell my husband what was going on." She rested her head in her hands. The trainee reached over and squeezed her hand to comfort her. Eden warmed to him. He was probably in his first few weeks in the department, but he was doing his best. Shiri looked up. "Your visit told me what I'd secretly suspected all along. I was just a name on Alex Doherty's list. Stupid. Stupid." She thumped her forehead with her fist a couple of times. "Stupid."

Eden was none too pleased when she faced Alex Doherty across the desk of the same interview room. He'd been escorted from his work to the station.

"You've lied to me, Alex."

He looked taken aback and said, "What're you talking about, love?"

"My name is Detective Sergeant Eden Hudson," she said. Alex visibly stiffened. "You told me that the exchange of text messages we found on your phone was between yourself and Mrs Shiri Brooks-Dagless." She called them up on the screen. "Mrs Brooks-Dagless has informed us that she did not send nor receive any of these messages."

Alex's eyes glanced up to the text messages. Eden waited for him to say glibly – *Oh yeah, now I remember* — but he didn't. He looked her straight in the eyes and said, "No comment."

"Who is the other party to the text messages, Alex?"

"No comment."

"Was it the same lady you spent the night with in a Twickenham hotel?"

"No comment."

"Why will they be ruined? Bit extreme."

"No comment."

"Mrs Shiri Brooks-Dagless claims both you and she received letters containing threats to tell her husband of your affair if the demand wasn't met. She said the letters looked like they were photocopies rather than originals. Were you behind the letters all along, Alex?"

He looked taken aback. After a pause, he said, "No comment."

"Were the blackmail letters an attempt on your behalf to obtain money from Mrs Brooks-Dagless?" He rolled his eyes. "I will ask you one more time. Are you the blackmailer, Alex?"

"No comment."

"Alex, did you send the texts we found on your phone to yourself to throw us off the trail?"

"No comment."

"Had Tudor O'Connell discovered you were behind the blackmail?"

"No comment."

"Was Tudor O'Connell about to unmask you as the blackmailer?"

"I want a lawyer. And no comment."

"Alex Doherty, I am remanding you in custody on suspicion of blackmail and murder," Eden said.

"Yeah, well, cell bed can't be any lumpier than me mate's sofa," he said. He folded his arms across the desk and leaned as close to Eden as the desk would allow. "I want a lawyer."

Yeah, you need one, son, she thought.

Eden went straight from the interview room to Black's office. "If Alex Doherty is our blackmailer and Tudor O'Connell found out somehow or other, then Alex has a much bigger motive for murder then we thought. He knows the property inside out and the gate code. He knew all about Ivy's mysterious gifts, and if he suddenly stepped out from behind a tree, Tudor might have been intrigued enough to have waited. Alex has had plenty of opportunity to dispose of the evidence and he hasn't got an alibi. I don't like to say it, I like him, but it's not looking good for him. It's poor little Jos I feel for," she said.

Black leaned back in his chair and put his hands behind his

head. "Screwing rich married women, then making out a blackmail demand has turned up, which they pay in cash? Ingenious in its simplicity," he said. "But why send Tudor O'Connell those texts?"

"To throw us off the trail?" she suggested.

"But they didn't. They led us straight to him. And why kill him in the TreeHouse grounds? Why not a hundred other places? Why take the risk?"

Pilot put his head around the door. He was out of breath. "We've found Valerie Simpson."

Chapter 42

VALERIE SIMPSON WAS in a private room on the third floor of the local hospital. A police officer stood guard outside the door. Despite being badly bruised, with cuts to her face and a drip in her arm, Val appeared to be in good spirits. She was sitting up in bed, reading a cosy murder. Cards, chocolates and bottled soft drinks were arrayed on a bedside table. The curtains were wide open and the window slightly ajar.

"How are things, Val?" Black asked from the end of the bed.

"Been better, been worse," she said with a partly raised hand.

"Glad to hear it," Black said. "You had us worried there."

"Are you able to tell us what happened, Val?" Eden asked.

"I can. Quite clearly."

"In your own time, Val," Black said as, beside him, Eden took out a hand-held recording device and, after identifying the date, place, and parties to the discussion, placed the device on the bedside table.

"I'd gone out leafleting for Father Hanrahan. He had this notion we could guilt out the murderer. Didn't believe it myself but couldn't see as it could do much harm. I took my bike, like I always do. I'd nearly done, but as it was getting dark, I decided to leave the rest till morning and make for home. I was cycling down the lane, near its end, when suddenly my bike hit something, and I'm chucked up in the air. I came down on the grass. I really scraped myself landing." She held up two bandaged arms. "I cannot think what I hit."

"Someone tied a skipping rope across the path," Eden said.

"Was that what it was?" Val asked. "Coming off my bike wasn't the half of it. I was still on the ground wondering what the hell had happened when I was jumped on."

"Did you see who it was?" Eden said.

"Wish I had. I'd have given 'em what for. They were kitted out in black from head to toe, with a ski mask, everything. I just saw a dark shape. I raised my hands to protect myself, but they started kicking me. I curled into a ball — that just made them worse. I thought if I could get into the river, I could escape. I didn't even mind drowning. I just wanted it to end. I started to roll myself down the bank and got a bit of help in the form of another few kicks. I remember going under the water. It was so cold."

"How many attackers were there?"

"Can't say."

"Could you tell if your attacker was male or female?" Black asked.

"I don't know," she said wearily. "It was so fast. It was all I could do to survive."

"Do you remember anything after falling in the river?" Black said.

"Not till I woke up in the squat, in a onesie, inside a wheelie bin turned on its side. Fosset or Foskett, I was never sure, said it was his bed, but no matter. He was the one who fished me out. I owe him. Any longer in the water and I'd have expired from cold. There was three of 'em. Fosset or Foskett, JonJon and Mary. Mary'd put me in the onesie. Promised me it was clean as she'd only shoplifted it that morning. They poured as much cider down me as I could drink, on a kill-or-cure basis." She laughed and then groaned in pain. "I kept saying I needed to let people know where I was, but no phone ever appeared. They dried my cash out and used it to buy more cider and bacon sarnies. I told them there weren't no point hanging onto me, they weren't going to get much of a ransom for me. Eventually, one of their mates came round and recognised me from the news. Said there was a reward and they took me to the hospital. I don't think they meant to keep me prisoner, they just have short-term memory issues and competing priorities."

"Can you think why anyone would want to attack you, Val?" Eden said.

"I reckon someone thinks I know more than I'm saying, but I don't. I've told you all I know."

Bettina and Lilah O'Connell appeared at the door. Bettina nodded indifferently in their direction. Lilah was more cheerful and smiled. She clutched a bag. "Can we come in?"

"We're just leaving," Black said.

Bettina gave Val a kiss while Lilah produced a Jack O'Lantern from the bag. Along with eyes and a mouth, Lilah had given the Jack O'Lantern a moustache for *Movember*. "I carved it myself," she announced, putting it down near the window. She then produced a bottle of home-made wine.

Black and Eden paused in the doorway. "We'll be on our way, Val," Black said. "If you remember anything, anything at all, call the station."

Val nodded as Lilah continued, "It's one of the batch I made last year from nettles. It's matured with age. You can drink it without hurling now."

"She had a lucky escape," Black said in the car on the way back to the station.

"Her injuries support her story of being catapulted into the air and rapidly kicked. Would be difficult to stage-manage that many cuts and bruises," Eden said.

"I don't doubt her story. Someone meant to kill her, but why? What does our killer think she knows? We've got suspects and motives coming out of our ears but only one person in custody, and the evidence against him is highly circumstantial. Without more, we'll have to let him go."

Chapter 43

A FEW MORNINGS on saw Eden and Pilot closeted in a room with a local A-to-Z on the table. The blackmailer's most-used letters, identified by the thickness of the green edging around individual letters on the stencil, were displayed on a screen. Eden tipped the same letters from a box of Scrabble onto the table. Her eye fell on the Y. She picked up the tiny Scrabble square and waved it in Pilot's face, "Why would the blackmailer use a Y in his or her demands, nearly as much as E?"

"Pay up, snappy-snappy?" Pilot suggested. He curled the edge of his moustache tightly around his finger, releasing it with a snap.

"It has to be part of a street name," Eden said.

Noticing that Eden had begun to look down the Y section of the A-to-Z's index, he said, "The address needn't start with a Y. Our victim might live on Strychnine Street or Cyanide Close or ..."

"Yaggy Lane," Eden said, holding the page out for him to see.

Pilot inputted Yaggy Lane into the Police Computer. The number or name of every property on it appeared. It was a long lane. Some houses would undoubtedly be let. There was nothing for it but to trace and ring each property owner in turn.

"This is going to take forever," Pilot said.

Eden decided to go to the vending machine for two coffees. On the way, she saw Black by her desk. He was staring into the bunch of long-stemmed roses he clutched. The bouquet was wrapped in cellophane. She wandered over to him.

"These arrived for you," he said, not lifting his eyes from the flowers in his hand, nor making any attempt to pass them to her, so deep in thought was he. She stared at him, continuing to stare at the bouquet. When he finally looked up from the flowers, it was to say: "The pursuit of revenge is rarely a good idea."

Father Hanrahan came to the front door of the priest house himself.

"Are you alone, Father?" Black asked.

"I surely am. Please come in. I'll be glad of the company," Father Hanrahan replied, stepping to one side to let them in. "Do please go through to the parlour. You know where it is." He followed them into the room and moved three high-backed chairs around until they faced each other. "I'll make us a pot of tea," he said.

"That won't be necessary, Father," Black said. "Let's just sit down and talk."

They waited for him to take a seat before doing so themselves. "Father, you said you believed the elevation of the church lectern was a malicious joke played on you by Ivy Lee-O'Connell," Black said.

"I don't want to make an issue of it, Detective Inspector. Ivy's suffered enough."

"Ivy doesn't come into it, Father," Black said. "You raised the lectern to that height yourself."

"And why would I do that?" he replied, bristling.

"Because you'd earlier concealed something inside its base and couldn't lower it again until able to safely discard the object still inside it," Black said.

"I have no idea what you're talking about," Father Hanrahan said.

"At first, I couldn't imagine what made the small, regular indents we found on the base's interior, nor make a connection between them and the death of Tudor O'Connell. A colleague receiving a bouquet of flowers from her boyfriend brought me to the solution."

The two men looked each other squarely in the eye, gauging the other's thoughts. Father Hanrahan drew his gaze away first. Black continued. "The bouquet drew my mind back to an old TV drama. I'm sure you remember it — *A Bouquet of Barbed Wire*."

"Did your colleague's bouquet of flowers come wrapped in barbed wire?" the priest asked.

"No, but the poor little lapwing left on Ivy's back door was," Black said, "after being killed by you, Father."

"I did no such thing."

"You were behind all of Ivy's strange gifts," Black said. "You explained away your delay in responding to Bettina's call by saying you were in the shower, but you weren't. You were listening to Bettina's message as she left it on your machine. And as you listened, the first thing which came into your head was the barbed wire. You still had the roll, and fearing the bird be unearthed as part of the investigation and the roll identified as yours, you disposed of it in the only way you could in the time you had. You hid it in the base of the lectern."

"I did no such thing."

"Someone was on the other side of the confessional screen,

Father, who heard everything," Black said. "I should have remembered earlier that lecterns are on wheels."

"Our witness even heard an ouch. Prick yourself on the barbed wire, did you?" Eden asked. Father Hanrahan looked away. "Bit unnecessary to kill a little bird over some resentments."

"The bird died of natural causes," Father Hanrahan said. "She was dead when I found her."

"And you decided to wrap some barbed wire around her and leave her on Ivy's doorstep," Eden said. "What if her kid had found it?"

"Things got out of hand, all right?"

"So, you admit to being behind the campaign all the while?" Black said.

"I will not lie anymore," the Father replied.

"Why don't we start at the beginning?" Black instructed.

Dermot Hanrahan rocked himself in his chair, both angry and embarrassed at the situation he found himself in. "The first two items weren't for Ivy. They were meant for Tudor. I'd come across the old Hamlet programme when having a clear out. As I looked at it, all I could see was Bettina in tears, telling me Tudor had left her. The Brotherhood of Man album I had in my own collection. I really believed that when Tudor saw them, he'd be carried back to the early days with Bettina, when the children were born, and remember all the happiness they'd felt then and put Ivy aside. I only ever intended to bring him to his senses. To reunite him and Bettina. Instead, he and Ivy just laughed at Bettina and called her ridiculous."

"And the ripped-up leaves of ivy scattered on the doorstep?" Eden asked.

"That was for Bettina. Just before they split up, Bettina had found a bit of ivy in Tudor's pocket. She hadn't thought anything of it at the time, but when he left her for Ivy, she understood. Ivy? Do you see? He carried the sprig of ivy around with him to remember her name. How romantic. Ivy still doesn't know about that. The leaves were a gift for Bettina, to cheer her up. A shared joke," Father Hanrahan said. "I should've stopped at that point — and would have done, had someone not gifted a box set of *The Tudors* to the church jumble sale. I couldn't resist it. I pulled out the episodes about Catherine Howard and put them through their letterbox."

"For what reason?" Black asked.

"That woman corrupted Tudor. She made him stray — not only from his wife, but from the face of God. In my mind, that makes her a loose woman."

"And the torn jeans in the car engine?" Black asked.

He snorted. "Ivy came here to inform me that Degas wouldn't be attending St. Edmund's, nor raised a Catholic. The discussion turned into an argument, which the young lady decided to end by throwing my car keys into a hedgerow. I never did find them and ended up having a new key cut." He was clearly still angry about the episode. "I couldn't let that pass. I sneaked in past midnight, opened the boot of Ivy's car, and tied a strip of denim from an old pair of gardening jeans around the carburettor. I am not proud of myself. My behaviour has been petty and immature. I'll have to make my peace with my maker, but I can honestly say my only regrets are Bettina continuing to get the blame. Even the children sat her down to tell her they knew she was hurting, but she had to move on."

"And the bird?" Black said.

"You were right, Detective Inspector. It was inspired by a *Bouquet of Barbed Wire*. I wanted Tudor to realise what a mess he'd made of family life. Once again it backfired and Tudor and Ivy united against poor Bettina."

"Is Bettina O'Connell aware of this?" Eden asked.

"Innocent in every way. As bewildered as everyone else.

Asked me who I thought was behind it. She suspected Denys or Lilah."

"Had Tudor O'Connell twigged you were behind the campaign?" Eden asked. "I can just imagine his reaction, if he had."

"I wouldn't still have this job if he had. If you're suggesting I killed Tudor to avoid being unmasked, I can assure you, you're way off. Tudor had no idea I was behind those things. He went to his grave convinced it was Bettina."

He got to his feet, as did Black and Eden. "I'll get my coat," Father Hanrahan said. "I presume you wish me to accompany you to the station?"

"Not for the time being," Black said. "Please keep everything we have discussed today to yourself. No confessions or apologies at this stage."

When they returned to the station, Pilot was still phoning property owners. "Yeah, we own a house on Yaggy Lane," the other party to the call said. "We let it out, do everything ourselves. Don't bother with agents."

"Could I take the name of the tenant from you?" Pilot said.

Pilot gave a double-take when he heard the name. "Thank you very much for your time," he said.

He noticed Eden walking towards him and hurriedly scrawled something down on his notepad. This he held to his chest. "Guess who lives on Yaggy Lane?" he asked, turning the notepad to show Eden the name written on it.

"No shit," she said.

Chapter 44

IN HIS OFFICE, Black was hungry. He couldn't remember when he'd last eaten. He opened his lunch box and helped himself to a marmite and marmalade sandwich he'd made for himself hours earlier. He took a bite and settled back to watch Hugo and Denys' wedding reception.

In a hotel ballroom, guests took their places at tables covered with crisp white linen and festooned with posies of flowers, white candles, crystal glasses, silver cutlery and fine porcelain. Gold Greco pillars dotted the space. A five-tiered, iced wedding cake stood on one, vases brimming with fresh flowers on the others. Chandeliers hung from the ceiling. Cherry blossom was draped across a wall, a flock of paper butterflies fluttered across another. A makeshift stage elevated the high table where Denys and Hugo took centre stage, surveying those below. Both wore white morning suits with cheerful waistcoats. Hugo's top hat was white, while Denys' was the colours of the flag of Ukraine: yellow and blue.

Lilah sat next to her brother, her braided hair the same lilac as her dress. She'd painted half a rainbow on each hand, which she held together to the camera to show solidarity with her brother and brother-in-law. A young woman sat between

Denys and a middle-aged couple — Denys' sister and parents, Black decided. Tudor's brother Mungo sat between Denys' mum and Bettina. Tudor and Ivy were positioned at the far end of the table from Bettina. Tudor was dressed in a morning suit, Ivy in dark green silk. A matching jacket hung on the back of her chair. She was wearing the pearl earrings, Black noticed.

While Ivy was laughing and smiling, Tudor looked sullen. Unopened wedding gifts were piled up on a separate table to the side of the high table. In addition to the video, a photographer moved among the guests, snapping smiling subjects through a long lens, many instinctively edging closer together and toasting the happy couple. Waiters appeared and began serving from large silver platters. Black couldn't make out what it was the guests were being dished up, but it couldn't have been any nicer than his own sweet and sour sandwich. He took another mouthful. He fast forwarded. The four-course meal, cake cutting, and speeches passed in a blur. He picked things up again at Hugo and Denys, clutching microphones, belting out *Nice Day for a White Wedding*. He thought he'd noticed something and replayed the last few scenes again. It was as he'd thought. Time to make a house-call.

In a police interview room, Dr Marie Pilcher glowered sullenly at Eden. Marie was accompanied by her solicitor, Sheila Calvert. After confirming for the record that Marie Pilcher was a doctor at the local health surgery, Eden said, "Alex Doherty is registered as a patient at the practice."

"My client does not deny this," Sheila Calvert said.

"Dr Pilcher, Alex Doherty was being blackmailed. A series of text messages, recovered from Alex Doherty's phone, are shortly going to appear on the screen. You can also find text messages replicated in the folder in front of you, referenced LE920."

The messages recovered from Alex Doherty's phone appeared:

I've got another one

When?

Just now

Expletive. How much now?

A grand

Expletive. Ignore it

I can't. I'll be ruined

Marie Pilcher remained impervious. Eden continued, "We have information to suggest that you, Dr Pilcher, are the other party to these messages."

Sheila Calvert spoke, "My client wishes to say no comment."

"Our information suggests that written correspondence was sent to 27 Yaggy Lane, a property you currently rent. This written correspondence was a demand for payment in return for keeping compromising information concerning a relationship between yourself and Alex Doherty private," Eden said.

"My client wishes only to confirm that she rents 27 Yaggy Lane," Sheila said. "One of the many properties on that lane."

"I'm going to show Dr Pilcher an image taken by a camera in the lobby of a hotel chain in Twickenham, London, on the..." The image showed a woman, head bowed, crossing a hotel lobby, wrapped up in a raincoat, collar turned up, hair in a scarf, and wearing knee-length boots and dark glasses. She pulled only a small holdall and strenuously avoided looking up. She was about the same height and build as Marie Pilcher and bore other resemblances to her. The next image was the same woman emerging from the lift, then opening and stepping inside the door to room 116. "Can I ask if this woman is you, Dr Pilcher?"

"My client does not wish to answer that question."

"Dr Pilcher, I'm going to show you images of Alex Doherty

taken in the same hotel an hour later." The image showed Alex entering and walking across the hotel lobby, stepping into and travelling up in the lift to emerge on the fourth floor where he knocked on door 116 and disappeared inside. "Were you inside that room, Dr Pilcher?"

"My client does not wish to answer that question, Detective Sergeant," said Sheila Calvert.

"The next set of images were taken the following morning," Eden said. The images which followed were of Alex Doherty leaving the room undisguised, followed some twenty minutes later by the heavily disguised woman pulling the same holdall. In the next lot of images, the same woman disappeared into a shopping mall. "This next image was taken by a camera just outside the shopping centre and is timed thirty minutes after the image just shown. Details of the camera and its position are in the folder." The camera had captured a woman, unmistakably Marie Pilcher, dressed in jeans and a jumper, leaving the shopping centre, stopping only to discard a holdall, identical to the one in the earlier images, in the bin.

Sheila Calvert's right eye twitched involuntarily. It was a twitch which said, *I do wish my clients wouldn't lie to me.*

"You really didn't want anybody to recognise you at the hotel, did you, Dr Pilcher?" Eden said.

"Detective Sergeant, we have not yet established that the woman in the hotel and Dr Pilcher are one and the same," the solicitor reminded her. "All we have established is that my client was in a shopping centre in London at the same time as a woman in a raincoat."

"Dr Pilcher, four items of clothing have been recovered from your property under a search warrant. The items of clothing are a coat, a scarf, knee-length boots and a pair of dark glasses." All four appeared on the screen. All were identical to that worn by the woman who'd spent the night in a hotel room with Alex Doherty. Sheila Calvert's eye twitched again. "It is possible for two women to own similar outfits," she said.

"Identical outfits, Ms Calvert," Eden said. She turned to look at Marie Pilcher. "Even in the modern age, Dr Pilcher, there would be penalties for a doctor discovered to be having an affair with a patient. Those penalties range from a fine to being struck off, not to mention the damage to your personal reputation. Two young, attractive people — one a doctor, the other her patient — involved in a sexual liaison? We all know how that will play out in the media. Is that what you meant by the words – *I'll be ruined?*"

"Now you're just speculating, Detective Sergeant," the solicitor said.

"Alex Doherty had an appointment with you at the clinic on the morning of Tudor O'Connell's death," Eden said.

"That is a matter of fact," Sheila Calvert said. "My client also had appointments with other patients before and after she saw Alex Doherty and indeed was at the surgery for the rest of the working day."

"Dr Pilcher, Alex Doherty has already admitted that he believed Tudor O'Connell was behind his blackmail. Dr Pilcher, did you and Alex Doherty conspire to murder Tudor O'Connell to put an end to the blackmail campaign?" Eden asked.

"My client will not be answering that question, Detective Sergeant."

"Was the intention behind Alex Doherty's appointment that morning to run through things one more time?"

"My client will not be answering that question either."

"Or was the idea to give Alex an alibi?" Eden asked.

"Again, Detective Sergeant, we make no comment," Sheila Calvert said.

· · ·

The door to Val Simpson's small terrace house stood open when Black arrived. The boot of her car was also open and inside lay a pair of suitcases. Black knocked on the front door and took a hesitant step inside. Val was at the top of the stairs, about to lug a heavy suitcase down it. Both hands gripped its handles. "I'm going to my sister's place," she said.

"Allow me to help you with that," Black said, moving towards the stairs. Val waited where she was as Black climbed them, took the suitcase from her and carried it downstairs. She followed him down.

"I'll put it in the car for you," he said.

She waited at the front door as he did just that. "Anything else or shall I shut the boot?" he asked from the car.

"'Less you can fit the kitchen sink in, reckon that'll be it, thanks," she said.

He slammed the boot closed and returned to the front door. "Can I come in? I've a few more questions."

She took him through to her kitchen/diner, at one end of which was a small alcove taken up with a table and chairs. This is where they sat.

"Val, I've been watching Hugo and Denys' wedding video. Interesting thing. You disappear after the speeches and don't reappear for quite a while. Can you tell me where you were?"

"What's it matter after all this time?" she asked.

"It might be relevant to the murder investigation."

"Come off it. There's close to two years in between."

"I appreciate that, Val. Nonetheless, you need to tell me where you were."

"I didn't want her name dragged into this. I love her." Alex spoke earnestly. His and Eden's eyes were locked. "I was going to leave Sheryl. Get meself another doctor. That way her being my girlfriend wouldn't matter. But before I got my act together,

Marie started getting these letters. They were just like the ones Shiri and I got. I couldn't believe it. Marie doesn't need to know about Shiri. That's over. Like with the letters me and Shiri got, we paid up. We didn't know what else to do. Then we got another. It was Shiri revisited."

"Is that when you double-backed and saw his car?" Eden said.

He rolled his eyes. "It was after the first letter Marie got. But we still got another. I saw Marie that morning to collect her share of the demand." He grinned wryly. "We went Dutch. I left the van at home so as not to be identified if I was seen. The note said to leave the money at some letter box right out in the sticks. I cycled there, left the cash, then cycled home for my van. I was halfway between when Tudor was done in. I still think he was behind the blackmail, but that doesn't mean Marie and I did it. We didn't have any reason to kill him. We're going to pack up and leave the UK. She's a doctor — she can get work anywhere. So can I."

"All right, I'll tell you," Val said, "but it mustn't go any further. My cousin is one of the junior chefs at the hotel where they held the reception. I went to say hello. He bunked off and we went outside to have a cigarette. We ended up emptying a couple of bottles of the hotel's best wine. Next morning, he packed me off with a couple of steaks. If it gets out, he'll lose his job and not likely to get another one. Not in catering."

"If you'd decided to emigrate, why pay the last blackmail demand?" Eden asked Alex Doherty.

"Marie's a very private person. She couldn't've coped with it getting out she was carrying on with a patient. You know what those trolls do to women. We decided to pay up and clear off, and that would be the end of it. If I was going to murder someone, I'd run them over, at night, and bury them under someone else's patio. I wouldn't kill them in broad daylight, with no alibi to fall back on." He leaned forward and, again, locked eyes with Eden. "I lied because I love Marie — not because I'm a killer."

If only you'd told us this to begin with, Alex, Eden thought.

Black, back at his office, addressed Tudor O'Connell's image. "Who hated you so much, Tudor, that they were prepared to kill you?" He pressed play, freezing the recording on a frame of Hugo. "Your own son maybe? A kindly boy you did nothing but undermine. Did he snap?" He moved to a still of Denys. "Or was it the son-in-law who blamed you for driving a wedge between him and the man he loved?" He moved to a still of Lilah O'Connell. "Or was it the contemptuous daughter?" He pressed fast forward to a still of Bettina. "Or was it the wronged wife, who did for you?" At a still of Ivy, he said, "Was there trouble in paradise?" At a still of Father Hanrahan he said, "Had you discovered what the good father was up to, Tudor? Did he kill you to shut you up?" At a still of Val Simpson, "Did loyal Val do it? With you out of the way, Tudor, Ivy'd quickly clear off, and it would be back to the old regime." He moved to a still of wedding guest, Alex Doherty. "Alex had reasons to want you dead, as did the woman he lied to protect," he said, moving to a still of Marie Pilcher, also at the reception as a family friend. "Was it your own doctor, Tudor? Did she kill you to avoid a naming and shaming?" On a second screen he called up images of Tam Tully, Brian Tully and Roger Stenn. "You were hell bent on destroying these people, Tudor, but did they destroy you first?"

He returned to the wedding reception and pressed play. Lilah had joined her brother and brother-in-law onstage to sing:

We're the three best friends
That anyone could have,
We're the three best friends
That anyone could have...

Black's eyes wandered from them to the display of the now-opened wedding gifts. He froze the image and enlarged it, looking along the row of gifts. He moved forward and zoomed in on a pair of identical porcelain figurines.

Chapter 45

MATT PRITCHARD WAS WAITING in the car park to give Eden a lift home. She climbed into the car and gave him a kiss and said, "Hello, and thanks for the lovely flowers."

"Hello to you, and I'm glad you like them." He returned her kiss. "Turns out you're not the only brilliant detective in the family, my dear."

"Oh, yes?" she said, putting on her seatbelt.

"Oh, yes." He turned out of the car park. "The results are back on the DNA test on the cat Dora saw in the window. Believe it not, it's Betty Boop."

Had she not been sitting down, she'd have fallen over. "No shit!" she said.

"Ten billion to one it's another cat. People have got life for less convincing odds."

As Eden closed the front door behind her, Dottie appeared at the kitchen door. Her eyes moved from Eden to Matt then to the little face staring out from the cat basket in Eden's hand and back to Eden again. "Dottie, this is Matt, Matt this is Dottie," Eden said.

"Glad to finally meet you," Dottie said, crossing the hallway to join the pair. Now it was Eric's turn to appear in a doorway. His eyes went from Matt to the cat. A *not-another-one?* look crossed his face. Eden introduced Matt to Eric.

"Where's Dora?" she asked.

"In her room," Dottie said.

"Dora!" Eden called from the foot of the stairs. "Come down, please — I've got a surprise for you. No running." She put the basket down by the side of the stairs, out of sight. From overhead, a disembodied voice yelled, "Coming."

A door opened and shut, some footsteps could be heard, and young Dora appeared at the top of the stairs, a look of expectation on her face. She hurried downstairs, slowing the pace at the last three steps to jump.

"Dora, this is Matt. Say hello," Eden said, pushing her daughter's hair behind her ears.

"Hello," Dora said, politely but indifferently. "What's the surprise, Mum?" Dora's eyes followed her mum's to the cat basket around the corner. Her face lit up.

"Boopy!" Dora squealed. "Oh, Boopy, it's you." She ran to the cat, kneeling down and rattling the metal basket as she tried to open it. Eric eventually unfastened it, allowing Dora to reach in for the cat who came purring into her arms. She hugged and kissed her. "I missed you so much," she said.

"Why don't you introduce Boopy to Duchess, love," Eden said.

Dora pushed past Eric into the living room, the cat in her arms, to whom she explained the new living arrangements. "While you were away, we got another cat. Her name's Duchess, but I love you the most, Boopy."

"Come through," Eric said to Matt. "Don't stand on ceremony."

Matt followed him into the living room where, in a corner, the two cats eyed each other suspiciously with Dora invigilating. "Park yourself wherever," Eric said. "You a home brew man?"

"I'm driving, so maybe a coffee, thanks."

Still standing in the hallway, Dottie said to Eden, "He seems nice."

"I think so."

"I have to ask. Is it really Boopy?"

Eden nodded. "Good job you went back with your scissors. Don't ask me how, but the cat she saw on Elmer Hill was her."

"Ye of little faith," Dottie said. "What on earth was she doing in a house on Elmer Hill?"

"They'd driven past here, and their kid had commented how much Betty Boop looked like their black cat. When theirs went walkabouts, the kid was so upset they catnapped Boopy in a smash 'n' grab operation — but without the smash. They just grabbed her and made out she was theirs. The kid bought it."

"And you win mother-of-the-most-perceptive-child award."

"My kid's a chip off the old block," Eden replied.

"What about the catnappers?" Dottie said. "You going to throw the book at them?"

She shook her head. "They've got enough on their hands having to tell their ten-year-old that the cat's gone missing again."

"I'll set an extra place for dinner," Dottie said, returning to the kitchen.

Chapter 46

"MORNING, TEAM," Black said to those assembled. He pointed an image of Gethsemane's *Ark of Life* displayed on the screen behind him. "Let me return to the emojis concealed within this picture. Fun as it's been learning a new language, I no longer believe the meaning of the emojis significant. What matters is their position on the keyboard," he said.

"Intel considered but discounted that idea, Sir," Eden ventured. "Smirk, for example, is the twentieth emoji on the keyboard used, and cat is animal twenty on the painting. Therefore, we have either twenty or three for the number of letters in cat, or twenty-three, or twenty-four if we add twenty, three, and one for smirk coming first, or twenty-five if we add its position to the number of letters – or forty if we add them together. The possible combinations are endless and always produced some huge incomprehensible number."

"Respect to Intel for trying, but that's both under- and over-complicating it," Black said. "The answer was staring us in the face the whole time. The relevance of the emojis' position on the emoji keyboard does not correlate to anything in the picture. That was a red herring. The emojis' position on the keyboard correlates to an animal on the same keyboard. *Smiley*

Face is the first emoji. The first animal emoji on the keyboard is a dog, also a Chinese zodiac animal. To what do the Chinese zodiac animals correspond? Lunar years. We are after a number after all. We need to find that number to establish who hid the emojis and why. The Chinese zodiac is infinite. Our emojier must have kept things simple. I suggest using the last digit of the animal's last lunar year to see what that produces."

"Who do you want on this, Sir?" Pilot asked.

"Well volunteered, that man," Black said.

After working through numerous coffees and takeaways, Pilot and Eden, closeted in a small room, had managed to turn the row of emojis into a row of twelve Chinese zodiac animals displayed on one screen with their years displayed on a second. The numbers seemed to stretch forever.

"So, where do we go from here?" Eden asked.

Pilot deleted everything, bar the last five years, for the first animal in the sequence. He then deleted the current year. This still left an awful lot of years. "The Governor said start with the last digit, so let's start with the last digit," he said.

The last digit — the last year the animal reigned — was a nine. Eden wrote that down. The last digit of the next animal in the sequence, was a one. Pilot searched on his computer for any matches to the two-digit combination. "Ninety-one is the dialling code for India, and the Trafalgar Square bus," he announced.

They carried on. When they had finished, they'd produced a twelve-digit number. "Let's give it a call, see if it's a telephone number," Pilot said, dialling the number. He put the call on loudspeaker. To their surprise the call was answered. "*This is the New Delhi office of private investigator Dr Vihaan Ahuja. We are now closed, please leave a message.*"

Pilot was so surprised he replaced the receiver without

leaving a message. The two stared at each other. "A private detective?" Eden said.

"A New Delhi private detective," Pilot said. "The killer's first mistake?"

Eden quickly Googled Dr Vihaan Ahuja. "Vihaan Ahuja. Private Investigation Services. Discreet and efficient. No job too big or too small. 24-hour worldwide service," she read out loud. She turned to Pilot and said, "No shit."

He rang the number of the private investigator again, this time asking Dr Vihaan Ahuja to ring him at the Vale of Tye police as soon as he got the message.

In his office, and after taking in the new information, Black said, "Ask our colleagues in the New Delhi police to kindly send over anything they have on our private detective. Then go home. It's getting late."

At his desk, Pilot checked the time. The day had vanished. The last thing he did before setting off for home was to email the New Delhi police. He'd got as far as his car when the night shift were on the phone. "Delhi police on the line for you, Pilot." He looked up and saw a team member at the window, mobile pressed to an ear, Pilot's landline receiver in the other hand, which gave a quick wave. A dash across the car park and a short lift ride brought Pilot pantingly back to his desk.

"Detective Philip Philpott here," he said, trying to catch his breath. "Thank you for holding." He took a slug of stale water from a bottle on his desk.

"Detective Protima Khatri of the New Delhi police here," a female voice replied. "How are you doing? I have been assigned to your case and have your email in front of me."

"I'm well, thank you, and well impressed by your efficiency. I didn't expect such a fast response," he said.

"I'm here on a ten-hour night shift and am very bored," came the reply. "The New Delhi police are always willing to help our colleagues from across the world. Your email requests background information on Dr Vihaan Ahuja. Can I please ask what your interest in our Dr Ahuja is, Detective Philpott?"

"Dr Vihaan Ahuja's name has come up in connection with a serious matter and we need to get hold of him."

"I know the gentleman very well."

"You do?"

"Oh yes," she said. "Dr Ahuja is a very helpful man. If you need to find somebody, he'll find them for you. Daughter seeing an unsuitable boy, he'll find what it takes for the boy to go back to his Mama and Papa. Husband or wife working too many late nights, he'll find out what's really keeping them in the office. He's a very helpful man."

"Does this extend to involvement with crimes of violence?"

She squealed. "No way! Not his style."

"Does he have any criminal convictions?"

"He soon might," Protima said. "He helped procure some sperm for a lady failing to get pregnant. She was married to a man almost two metres tall — over six-foot — and her only requirement was that the donor be as tall as her husband to avoid difficult questions. Our helpful Dr procured her the sperm, problem being it was his own and he is nothing near six-foot tall. The truth has come out, the couple are divorcing and an official complaint has been filed with us."

"Might you know where he currently is?"

"Yes — asleep in one of our cells," she replied.

After recovering from the surprise that this hadn't been mentioned from the outset, Pilot said, "Over the sperm thing?"

"No. For falling asleep at the wheel of his car and crashing into the Chief's Mercedes."

"How long are you intending on holding him? We need to speak with him." It was late. Black had already left the station and Pilot was loath to summon him back.

"Oh, he's going nowhere. The Chief loved his Mercedes more than his wife and children."

It was the following morning when Dr Vihaan Ahuja was put on the line to Detective Inspector Guido Black. Detectives Pilot and Protima listened in on the call. The conversation was disappointing. Dr Ahuja had many clients from all over the world, including the United Kingdom. He did his best for all his clientele. He had never heard of the Vale of Tye nor knew anyone with the last name O'Connell. And as for how the good Detective Inspector had decoded his telephone number from a row of smiley faces concealed in a painting by a dead artist was not something he could comprehend. Maybe the good Detective Inspector had not actually found a hidden code as he believed? Maybe the good Detective Inspector was a bit too clever for his own good? Maybe what the good Detective Inspector had actually found was a row of smiley faces?

When the call was over, Protima came back on the phone. "Sometimes he's more helpful than at other times. Leave it with me. If he's holding something back, I will find it for you."

Chapter 47

AT HOME THE EVENING BEFORE, Black had been disappointed to find no more sightings of the merlin, only an annoying number of pigeons. At the crack of first light, he made his way to the church. He wasn't alone there.

"If you're here for the merlin," a solitary bird-spotter told him, "there's no sight of her anywhere."

"She's gone?"

"To perches and pastures new."

While Black was sorry the merlin had decided to fly off as unexpectedly as she had arrived, looking around the open countryside gave him an idea; and therefore, after he came off the phone to India, he went to the Incident Room to hang a fresh Ordnance Survey map of the area up alongside an aerial picture of the TreeHouse. He'd decided to plot the movements of each of the suspects on the morning of the murder of Tudor O'Connell again in case he'd missed anything.

He initialled yellow stickers to indicate the actors: NP/RS for Roger Stenn as Nick Pilsworth; HOC for Hugo O'Connell, etc. He stuck the tour party, HOC and TOC on a round piece of paper, and, on the aerial photograph, placed it at the front of the property. IL-OC was stuck on the wall side of the garage. He stuck a sticker marked *?Killer?* behind the Orangery on the spot of the statue. The paper circle he then moved en bloc to and through the Orangery and onto the garden rooms, leaving them temporarily in the Rose Room.

?Killer? dashed quickly from the Orangery through the Herb Room to the Buttercup Meadows and from there to the Topiary Room and on to the Events Room. In the Rose Room, NP/RS was carefully peeled off the circle of stickies. With one hand, Black moved the paper circle to the Events Room, using his other hand to move NP/RS to the side of the property where he left it. TOC he left in the Events Room to meet his end, while placing the paper circle in the Topiary Room after slapping HOC in the middle of a yew hedge. He then placed three more yellow stickers, initialled HT, WT and BOC on a triangular piece of paper. This began at the front of the house and ended up behind the cottage. NP/RS now moved to some fields at the front of the house and was left there. He put LOC by the old sessile oak, AD on the road out of town, VS in the orchard, and DH in the Priest's House. This just left Valerie Simpson's dog walker. Black made up a yellow sticker and stuck it just outside the orchard. He stood back to survey the plan. The main actors where now in place.

He moved BOC to the front of the house (for the digger) then back to the cottage. WT he moved from the cottage to the road and back again. He moved IL-OC from the skip to the cottage and VS from the orchard to the cottage via the road. Tudor O'Connell was now well and truly dead. Black moved various people around. Ten stickers ended up in the courtyard, RS and DH in the church. By now, Lilah O'Connell must be on the move. Her sticker followed the route she claimed to have taken. AD was placed at the drop off point. DH left the church, followed by RS. DH travelled to the house along the road, while RS was deposited in the surrounding countryside.

Black took his time studying the maps. He put some stickers back in their original places, for a second go. This time, *?Killer?* was played by RS, doubling back through the Buttercup Meadows and Topiary Room to the Events Room. He had yet another go. In this re-enactment, HOC was the killer, starting off from the alcove. Then he had LOC, VS, IL-OC, and finally DH, play the killer. Each started off behind the beech tree.

"I thought I had persuaded Dr Ahuja to provide details of his international clientele," Detective Protima informed Pilot. "But all he has given me is a list of his clients' initials, their nationality, and the date of their instructions. I said we needed more, we needed his clients' full names and the nature of their instructions. He has thus far refused, pleading client confidentiality. Do not fear, I'll lean on him. Not literally. There are laws. One more thing," she added. "I have heard on the grapevine that Dr and Mrs Ahuja visited your country last year for a wedding of an English school friend of their son. All I know is that their son's friend goes by the nickname Colonel Mustard."

Last year? Pilot thought. That was when the emojis were hidden.

Black faced Lilah O'Connell across the table of the interview room.

"Lilah O'Connell," he said, "you have provided us with the route you say you took from the sessile oak to the TreeHouse on the morning of your father's death. That route takes you past the churchyard at the rear of St. Edmund's Church. That morning, had you done as you said, you would have been passing the churchyard at around the same time that it was crossed by two people in quick succession. It defies belief that neither saw you, nor you them. Frankly, all three of you are in need of a witness for your alibis, yet you haven't mentioned seeing anyone in the churchyard, nor they anyone on the lane. This makes me think you weren't at the old sessile oak tree when your father was killed, after all. Perhaps you'd like to tell me, Ms O'Connell, where you actually were?"

He waited for her to speak, but the cat had got her tongue. He continued. "Twice now, you have provided a false alibi for the murder of your own father with whom you enjoyed a fractious relationship..."

"I was at the lean-to. I'm the blackmailer. I can prove it."

Pilot pulled to a halt outside Lilah's cottage where he, Black and Lilah piled out of the car to walk in single file to her back garden. There, she pointed out the large tub she'd bought in the garden centre. "It's in there. If you'd come back and searched it a second time, you'd have found it." She kicked the tub over on its side, causing the plants and dirt to tumble out. She squatted by it and used her cupped hands to claw out the pot's remains. Gravel and compost spilled out. When she could dig no further, her filthy hands grasped and pulled at something until eventually a large self-sealing polystyrene mailing bag, about 600mm x 900mm, emerged, ingrained with dirt. The bag held some largish item. Black snatched it from her. It was heavier than he thought.

"Inside," he said. She wiped her hands on her jeans and led the way to her back door, which she opened for them.

Black placed the mailing bag on a kitchen counter and Pilot slit it open with a penknife. Inside was a printer. Lilah took a step back to lean against one of the kitchen cabinets, her arms crossed across her chest, her ankles crossed, too: her only sign of discomfort.

"Explain?" Black said.

"Words made from stuck-on letters look amateur and child-ish, and they fall off. I made the letters at the lean-to and took them home to photocopy. Photocopies look better and are harder to trace. I burnt the originals. I couldn't do it for the envelopes and used a stencil instead. You took my computer straight away, but never came for my printer."

"Why bury it in the garden?" Black asked.

"In case you came back for it. Photocopying leaves a digital record."

"Ophelia O'Connell, you are under arrest for blackmail and for obstructing the police in the course of their enquiries," Black said.

The journey back to the police station passed in silence.

"I was exceptionally careful," Lilah explained, once back in the interview room. "I always wore a jumpsuit, gloves and a hairnet to avoid contamination, like in a factory. I'm not going all poor little rich girl when I say my lifestyle is expensive, but it is. Dad kept us all on a pretty tight leash. One day I happened to see Alex Doherty turning up the drive of some big house. I looked through the hedge. There was something about the way the lady let him inside — it was furtive. He was there for a long time and went back a couple of days later – I kept an eye on the place. It was so obvious he was having it off with a married woman. She was clearly loaded. I couldn't resist it. It was a punt as much as anything. I made up some blackmaily wording, stuck it on a piece of paper and copied it. I left the letter under his wipers. The drop-off point was in the middle of nowhere. I swept in on a motorbike with no number plates and used a hook to grab the parcel. I half-expected to be arrested. The money was all there."

"You have a motorbike? I thought you didn't have a driving licence?" Black said.

She gave a sigh and a shrug. "I keep it in a lock-up. I only meant to do it the once, but it was so easy. She could obviously afford it. Thought it a bit risky to leave another letter on the van, so I posted the next one to her address."

"What address did you send the letter to?" Black said.

She gave Shiri Brooks-Dagless' address in full.

"But you didn't stop there did you, Lilah?" Black said.

"Things got a bit out of hand," she admitted. "One afternoon I followed him from the TreeHouse on my motorbike. I kept my distance. He doesn't know I can drive, and I had the helmet on, of course. Anyway, he didn't see me. I couldn't work out where he was headed. He kept turning back on himself. Eventually he ended up at Marie Pilcher's place. Oh yes, I thought. I parked up and snuck across her garden to look in the window. They were in her front room, at it hammer and tongs. I rang Sheryl and innocently asked what doctor she and Alex went to, said I was thinking of changing mine, and she said Marie Pilcher was their doctor. Naughty lady. She got three letters in the end."

"Alex Doherty believed your dad was the blackmailer," Black said.

"The motorbike got a flat, so I took Dad's car to the drop-off point. It was night, but the moon was bright. Alex must've spotted the car, but not seen the driver. He could never prove it was Dad and, besides, what could he do? Marie's his doctor. She'd be in big trouble if it got out. Poor Dad, he hadn't a clue what that text was about."

"Can we move to the day of the murder, Lilah?" Black said.

"I was up at the lean-to, finishing off a letter to some London second-homer I'd seen stealing from Annie's shop, when I heard sirens. I got out of there as soon as I could. The jumpsuit and hairnet were paper and the gloves corn starch.

Very Eco. I quickly ripped everything up and threw it in the river. But I still had the next letter and didn't know what to do with it. I hadn't had time to address it and my stencil was still in the lean-to. In the end, I put my own address on it using my artistic skills to make out the address had been stencilled."

"How many people have you blackmailed, Lilah?" Pilot asked.

"I don't make a habit of it," she said. "I'm no angel, but neither are they. Alex and Sheryl have a kid together, Marie is his doctor, his other fancy woman is married, and as for the Londoner..." she rolled her eyes. "She could afford to buy Annie's store, yet there she was, pocketing pens."

"Lilah, nothing you've said excludes you as the murderer," Black said. "We only have your word that you were at the lean-to, and since you've already lied to us — several times — your word is not reliable."

"I had no reason to kill Dad."

"Ophelia, you may still be as young as your namesake, but you have little of her naïveté. You are more than aware of life's harsh realities. However, you chose to justify your offences. Blackmail-funded drug use is a serious crime for which people go to jail. At the very least, you risked having a criminal record for life. You poured scorn on your dad and his new partner, making clear your disapproval of the relationship which you thought ridiculous. I suggest your dad found out what you were up to and was about to teach you a lesson by involving the police."

"He didn't know."

"Well, he isn't here to say so," Black pointed out.

"Dad and I argued over Ivy, yes, but we were still speaking. No way would he have done that to me."

"To repeat — he isn't here to say so," Black repeated.

Chapter 48

AT HER DESK, Eden sat back in her chair. She'd been able to establish a lot but still needed to make a call. An information request preceded it and records were to hand.

"The wedding reception was held here, and the vast majority of guests stayed over at the hotel, including Dr and Mrs Ahuja," the hotel manager said.

"Do you have the name of the wedding couple?" she asked.

"Kirsty Smith and Thomas Colman."

"How is Colman spelt?" Eden repeated.

"C-O-L-M-A-N – like the mustard," the hotel manager said. "The groom's moniker is Colonel Mustard."

When she came off the phone to the hotel, Eden went on to Mrs Kirsty Colman's Facebook page. Under a photo of Kirsty and Thomas leaving their local church arm in arm, showered with confetti, Kirsty's status read: *Married – to Col. Mustard.* Kirsty Colman's settings didn't give Eden access to her photographs, but a featured post gave Eden the wedding photographer's name. On his webpage, Eden found a sample of the Smith/Colman wedding photographs with a blog from the photographer:

Colonel Mustard and his future Mrs Mustard, alternatively known as Thomas and Kirsty, couldn't have chosen a better day for their wedding. The weather was as glorious as the day itself. The blog went into some detail on Kirsty's outfits for the day (traditional white silk and lace for the wedding, something more risqué for the evening) the flowers, (brides, church and centrepieces) and the beautiful grounds where the reception took place on that warm, dry summer's day.

An array of photos followed. Eden skimmed through them. She hadn't time for close-ups of rings or bespoke ivory wedding mules (with satin ankle straps) or glasses of sparkling champagne supplied by whoever; nor for photographs of the groom and his best man loosening their ties, or the bride's parents dabbing away tears, however touching. She had little interest in the couple themselves. She was after the guests. Taken outdoors, on the lawn, the sun high in the clear sky, the final photograph of the gallery proved successful. It featured the young couple surrounded by family and friends, a smiling Vihaan Ahuja and his wife in the second row. Eden made the photograph as large as she could. She studied every face in it but didn't recognise one. Hmm. She gave Kirsty Colman a call.

Despite the no-expense-spared ostentation of her wedding, young Kirsty came across as sensible and grounded. Eden sent a car to collect her and she was at the station, with her guest list, within the hour. "Work had to let me go with it being a police matter," she explained in the visitor room. Eden sensed Kirsty's excitement at finding herself in the centre of some important event. "Why do you need my wedding guests?" she asked, her eyes wide and questioning.

"We're investigating a serious matter," Eden said. "The

name of a guest at your wedding has come up in our enquiries. Can I ask how you and Thomas know Dr Vihaan Ahuja?"

Kirsty's eyes widened further on hearing the name. "I don't. Their son, Aarush, was Tommy's best friend at school. He's responsible for the Colonel Mustard nickname. It was an all-boys school," she explained. "Tommy once spent a whole summer at their house in India. He knows the family really well. Aarush should've been at the wedding as well, but his wife went into labour early."

"Can I have a look at the guest list, please?" Eden said. Kirsty handed over a printout. Eden read it through a couple of times, but, as with the faces on the wedding photograph, she didn't recognise any names on it. "I'll need a copy of this."

"It is a copy. You can keep it," Kirsty replied.

Eden got to her feet. "Thank you for your help. If you've been put to any expense, you can get a Claims Form from reception."

Kirsty looked quite disappointed. "Is that all?"

"For the time being, Mrs Colman. Please keep everything we've discussed to yourself."

Kirsty perked up at the thought of a part two and left quite happy.

Eden read through the list again. This time one name stood out: Tanya Lee. Lee was Ivy's last name. She called up the list of Vihaan Ahuja's customer's initials and saw, in the UK section of the list, the initials: T.L. She called Kirsty's driver and asked him to turn back.

Kirsty reappeared quite quickly, only too happy to be of further help. Eden asked her to identify Tanya Lee from the wedding photograph. Kirsty hesitated before pointing to a woman standing alone at the end of the back row, next to Vihaan Ahuja. "How do you know this woman?" Eden asked.

Upon hearing the question, the previously chatty Kirsty became uncharacteristically bashful. She squirmed and, after a pause, said, "You won't let on what I say, will you?"

"Not unless it's directly relevant to the case," Eden said.

"Thing is, I can't afford all the designer stuff you have to have nowadays. You have a designer dress, you have to have designer shoes, handbag, jewellery to go with it and the same again for the going away. It costs a fortune. We haven't got that type of money. Tanya," she pointed at the woman in the photograph, "got me all of it for a tenth of what it would cost. I don't know how she did it. I didn't ask. A friend of a friend got me her name. Tanya asked if she could come to the reception and take photos for marketing purposes. Said I didn't mind so long as she didn't use my real name in her marketing."

After showing Kirsty out, Eden called Val Simpson. "Val, do you know the name of Ivy Lee's mum?"

"Now, let me think. I've met her a few times. Didn't get on with Tudor. But who did? It begins with T. Trinnie? Tracy? No, that's not it. Tanya. Her name is Tanya. Tanya Lee."

Eden felt her heart speed up at the name. They had another suspect. Someone mentioned more than once during the enquiry, but who, until now, had remained invisible: Ivy's mum. She rang the number Tanya had given Kirsty but got only dead noise.

Chapter 49

In a police interview room, Black peered at Ivy Lee-O'Connell across his horn-rimmed spectacles. Eden, watching from an adjacent room, couldn't help noticing that Ivy was in yet another outfit – Yves Saint Laurent, if she wasn't mistaken. Had she ever seen Ivy in the same outfit twice, she mused?

"Ms Lee-O'Connell, do you recall, at an earlier stage of the investigation, we showed you this row of emojis?"

Ivy didn't bother to glance at the display, and Black continued. "Our investigations have now established that, far from being an innocent-looking bit of fun, these emojis are a coded telephone number."

"Tudor was involved with someone else?" she asked sadly. "Please, don't break my heart." She half turned away and briefly touched her heart with her fingertips.

"The telephone number is of a New Delhi private detective, Dr Vihaan Ahuja."

"I've never heard that name. I have no need of a detective. Maybe Tudor had me checked out before he married me?"

"We've established a possible connection between your mother and this detective. Dr Ahuja was a guest at a wedding in

Britain, at which your mother was also a guest. Can I ask where your Mum is right now?" Black asked.

"I haven't a clue where she is. Or what number she's on."

"You're telling me you've lost contact with your mother? Even though she is taking care of your daughter?"

"Mum does what the hell she wants. She's a power unto herself. You can't imagine what it was like growing up."

"Aren't you concerned for Degas?" Black asked.

"She'd never do anything to Degas. She adores her. Just sometimes she forgets other people worry. If and when she gets in touch, I'll make sure she speaks to you," Ivy said.

"Do you have any idea why your mother might need the services of an overseas private detective?" Black said.

"Have we established that she did?"

"She has access to the TreeHouse where we found the emojis. The emojis lead to him. They've met."

"Could be for any one of a dozen reasons. She likes her side hustles, Mum. Probably something to do with that."

"Someone went to a lot of trouble to disguise Dr Ahuja's number."

"If Tudor found a number written down he didn't know, he'd have rung it and asked questions. I don't poke my nose in Mum's business, but Tudor felt differently. He liked to know what Mum was up to — to protect Degas, he said."

"But why leave the number at the TreeHouse?" Black said. "She doesn't live there."

"She does visit," Ivy said. "If she was the person who hid the number, I can only imagine she did so in case she ever needed it again and disguised it to prevent Tudor finding out her business."

"She never mentioned a Dr Vihaan Ahuja or having employed a private detective?"

"Never." Her tone was growing impatient.

A knock at the door was followed by Black being handed a

message. He stopped to read it and then looked up to say, "Your mother and daughter landed in Hong Kong the day before Tudor's murder." Ivy flinched at the word murder. "She checked out of her room a few days back and there the trail goes cold."

"Oh my god," Ivy said. Her hand reached for her mouth. She quickly removed it and raised her hands. "No, no. Mum would never do anything stupid when she has Degas. Everything's all right, Ivy."

"Does your mother have more than one passport?" Black asked.

"How would I know? Don't start suggesting Mum killed Tudor because you can't find his killer. It's a preposterous suggestion. Why would she kill Tudor? She wasn't even in the country. You need to stop chasing dragons, Detective Inspector, and find Tudor's killer." She got to her feet. "And as for where my mum is, I'd like to know myself."

When Black returned to the incident room, he found Eden standing by Pilot's desk, listening to a recording. "Hugo O'Connell's phone network just sent this over, Sir," he said, replaying the recording. A voice, unmistakably Hugo's own, begged: *Please, Denys, pickup. Please. If it's you, pickup. Denys, I'm sorry. I can't say it any more. Are you there listening? Denys? Denys? Please.*

Pilot ended the call. "It continues like that for nearly three minutes," he said. "The timing of the call overlaps Tudor O'-Connell's killing. If Hugo killed his dad, he did so while on the phone to Denys."

"Phone in one hand, garden stake in the other," Eden said, mimicking her description.

"It pushes him further down the list of suspects," Black said. "Are we any closer to establishing Alex Doherty's movements after leaving the surgery?"

"We're ploughing through traffic cams along the route he says he took, but he ain't the only man in Lycra and a helmet out cycling that morning. Separating him from all the others is proving tricky," Eden said. "Why do so many people cycle with their heads down?"

"Ivy claims not to have heard of Dr Vihaan Ahuja," Black said.

"Hong Kong police suspect Tanya Lee of leaving the country with Degas under false passports. An international arrest warrant has been issued," Eden said.

"Did Tanya Lee ask Dr Vihaan Ahuja to rustle up a couple of false passports for her and the kid?" Pilot speculated.

"Tanya could've returned to the UK under a false passport, killed Tudor, and flown back without us even knowing that she'd been in the country," Eden said.

"But why?" Black asked. "What reason did she have to kill Tudor O'Connell?"

Chapter 50

"Good afternoon, Detective Pilot and Detective Sergeant Eden," Protima said from the screen on Pilot's desk. "I've got more out of the suspect. I went to see him in his cell, where I told him: '*My friend, you are in above your head. Your name has come up in a murder investigation. Murder most foul. I know you to be no murderer, but will a jury?*' I waved the extradition treaty between your fine country and mine under his nose. I reminded him of a recent plot of a very popular daytime show here in India. The one where a character lied to the police to protect an individual he'd seen running from the crime scene. I said: '*Like poor Anas – you too will go down for a long time for failing to cooperate with the police, but unlike Anas, you are not a character whose actor merely wishes to leave the series.*'"

Pilot imagined her alone in a cell with Dr Vihaan Ahuja, lecturing him whilst simultaneously waving the extradition treaty in his face and wagging a finger. "He sang like a canary," she said. "He remembers Tanya. She took him to one side after the wedding. Said she needed discretion. Said she needed..." Protima proceeded to tell them why Tanya had hired Dr Ahuja.

"No shit," Eden said.

.   .   .

Eden surveyed the scene. In each room, curtains and rails had gone from the windows, thrown out or sent for storage with the ornaments, bric-a-brac and most of the furniture. In the centre of the room, sheets draped what little furniture was left. Clean squares stood out against otherwise discoloured walls where framed paintings had once hung. In the upstairs bedrooms, not even the beds remained.

"They got rid of the lot before Tudor died," Val said. "Soft furnishings, bedding, carpets, curtains, the lot. All ripped out and dumped. House and cottage. It was showing its age. Most of it dated from when Bettina and Tudor got married. Ivy didn't want to be reminded of that, as you can imagine. She used the renovation as an opportunity to have a clear out."

Degas' bedroom was completely empty. "Where's her stuff?" Eden asked. "Clothes and toys and stuff?"

"Ivy sent her off with everything she thought she'd need, including her favourite toys. The rest she got rid of. Went to a jumble sale. They grow out of stuff so quickly, Ivy didn't think there was much point keeping it."

Eden looked around the near-empty room. In a corner stood a toy chest. She opened it. Only a few overlooked wooden toys remained.

"Wardrobe? Chest of drawers?" Eden said.

"Second-hand. Passed down from when Lilah was a kid. Ivy really hated that. Wanted everything to be brand-new when they moved into the house."

Eden wandered into the bathroom. There was no cabinet or drawers to open. Everything had gone. Even the bathroom suite. "What happened to Degas' toothbrush and hairbrush?" Eden asked.

"Chucked the old ones. Sent her away with new."

. . .

At his desk, Black read through the print-off of Protima's emailed report:

He remembers Tanya. She took him to one side after the wedding. Said she needed discretion. Said she needed a test done. Who's the daddy? One of two. He read on. *Tanya Lee didn't say who the test was for. She provided Dr Ahuja with a sample of hair and asked for the result to be posted to a care/of address. Tanya Lee paid Dr Ahuja cash in advance. He swears he hasn't seen or spoken to her since.*

He still had the report on his screen when Matt Prichard telephoned. "You're after Degas O'Connell's paternal DNA, I hear," Matt said. "I've looked through our DNA case samples. We haven't anything catalogued for the child as she wasn't considered a suspect. We've got DNA from Tudor and Ivy. If we can find a strand of hair which matches Ivy's maternal DNA, but isn't from Ivy, that leaves Degas or Tanya. We haven't any DNA for Tanya that I'm aware of. I've asked the medical geneticist we subcontract to give you a call."

Alone in his office, Black's thoughts swirled. Even if the paternity test established Degas' paternity and it wasn't Tudor, what was to be gained by killing Tudor? Plenty of men had raised other men's children over the centuries, many knowingly. Black didn't want to telephone Robert Standley. He was too close to the family. He took out his little black book.

Chapter 51

Ivy Lee-O'Connell was accompanied by her lawyer, Mrs Averil Hughes. Despite her youth, Averil Hughes' reputation was growing. She was famously bright, multilingual, and reputedly fearless. Although Black had heard her described as a performance addict, at this precise moment she sat quietly beside her client, observing the proceedings.

"Where is my child? Have you found her?" Ivy said.

"We still haven't been able to locate either your mum or Degas," Eden said.

"Oh, my God!" Ivy jumped to her feet, took a couple of deep breaths and sat down again. "I mustn't panic. Mum adores Degas. She'll see her all right."

"Ivy, we now know for sure that your mother instructed a private detective," Black said.

"Oh, God," Ivy said, half-burying her face in her hand. "What's she done this time?"

"She needed to establish paternity — one of two men."

Ivy burst out laughing. "I told you she has lots of side hustles."

"Who was the paternity test for, Ivy?" Eden asked.

"How should I know? For someone who needed one, I'd

say. A little paternity testing business on the side would suit Mum right down to the ground. She might have been enquiring for a friend. She wouldn't judge." She giggled. "Could even have been for herself. Nothing would surprise me."

"Wouldn't you have known if your mum was pregnant?" Eden asked.

"I only see her a few times a year. She and Tudor never got on. Unless she had it with her, I wouldn't necessarily know if she'd had a baby, let alone if she was pregnant. Her business is her business."

"Ivy, your mum requested the test after Degas was born. Is there some doubt over her paternity?" Black said.

Ivy gasped. "How dare you! How very dare you!" she said. "Tudor is Degas's daddy." She became overcome with emotion and was unable to talk.

Averil Hughes' eyes narrowed as she readied to pounce. Her eyes bored into Eden and then into Black. It was him she addressed. "Is this a murder investigation, Detective Inspector, or slut-shaming?"

"The former, Mrs Hughes," he said.

"Well, it doesn't sound like it to me. You are throwing unsubstantiated allegations at my client. Ivy came here to help the investigation, and this is how you treat her? Tudor O'Connell is the only man Ivy has ever loved. She expected to grow old with him. And now you suggest he is not the father of her child on the basis of a test which could have been for anyone? I am almost speechless."

Ivy got to her feet. Mascara and make-up streaked down her face. She wiped her eyes, making it worse, and blew her nose. Averil remained seated as Ivy let rip, almost hyperventilating in her fury. "You have really screwed up, Detective Inspector. My Tudor was killed in broad daylight and because you haven't got a clue who did it, you blame me. Poison Ivy. The marriage breaker. Do you think I don't know what you think of me? The ruthless gold-digger."

"Ms Lee-O'Connell," Eden said. "Please try and calm down."

"Don't you patronise me," Ivy replied.

"Ivy is correct. Your old-fashioned views have tainted your judgement, officers," Averil Hughes said.

"My mum did someone a favour and now I'm a killer. And don't accuse her. I spoke to her after Tudor was taken from me. She was in Hong Kong." She picked up her handbag from the floor. "I'm beyond anger, Detective Inspector Black. I'm so disappointed, so bitterly disappointed." She walked to the door and left the room, leaving the door ajar. Averil, who had remained silent and motionless throughout, her eyes not once leaving Eden or Black, slowly rose to her feet. She peeled her eyes away from the detectives and crossed the room to close the door, remaining inside to slowly return to the desk where she placed both her hands flat. She leaned in towards Black, her face as close to his as it could go, her bobbed hair masking her profile from Eden. "Degas is Tudor O'Connell's daughter unless proven otherwise. Your allegations are entirely unsubstantiated. Ivy has implored her mother to return with the child. Look somewhere else for your killer, Detective Inspector. My client and her mother have alibis, in case you have forgotten."

She re-crossed the room and opened the door, holding it open long enough to allow Black and Eden the sight of Ivy sobbing outside it before she stepped through it. The door gently closed on Averil leading her distraught client away.

"That was one of our more successful interviews, Sir," Eden said.

Black returned to his office to speak with medical geneticist, Hassana Oni. "The problem," she explained, "is simple.

Murder in the Garden of Gethsemane

Without either the child or a sample from her, we need at least six to ten strands of hair, each with the hair follicles intact, before we can conduct a hair-strand DNA test. Matt tells me we'll be lucky to find as many as six, let alone with follicles."

"We're looking for a needle in a haystack," Black replied.

"We really need the child herself," Hassana said. "But even with her, it's not open and shut."

"It seldom is," he replied.

"Shall I take you through paternity tests for dummies?" she asked.

"Please do."

"Paternity tests do no more than calculate the probability of a man being the child's biological father. They do this by comparing a child's genes with that of the alleged father and calculating how much DNA they share. No two people get 100 percent. Whole-blood siblings can share a surprisingly low amount of DNA, whereas half siblings can share a surprisingly high amount, as can some unrelated strangers. It depends on the genetic inheritance. We classify the results of paternity tests on a paternity index: 99 percent proves the child's biological father, although many jurisdictions accept 90 percent. Any result giving 85 percent or over and the man might still be the father, but equally might not. This is where it gets tricky. A paternity index of 86 percent doesn't disprove paternity nor does it prove it. Much less than 85 percent and it's likely he isn't, but not certain. It depends whose dominant genes get carried over and whose aren't. Two brown-eyed parents can produce a blue-eyed baby. A sample of the other contender would help accuracy enormously."

"We don't have a name, Black said.

"One thing which might help us is Tudor's age. I understand he was an older dad. Older fathers pass on more genetic mutations to their kids than younger fathers, simply because older people carry more genetic mutations than young people.

Given Tudor O'Connell's paternal age, there's a good chance we might find the same genetic mutation occurring in both the child and the father. Enough to swing it."

"But we'd still need a sample from the child?"

"Oh, yes."

Black stared at the white board on which he'd written the names of the principle suspects. Annie Threadneedle wasn't on the list, she hadn't left her shop, nor was Sheryl Teal. Her car's registration number put her elsewhere. Ren and Alf Hoffbrand weren't on the list either. They were never alone and nowhere near.

The remaining suspects therefore were:

Tanya Lee- Ivy's mother

Tam Tully - legal defendant

Brian Tully - legal defendant

Roger Stenn - brother of Tam Tully

Lilah O'Connell - daughter

Hugo O'Connell - son

Denys Koral - son-in-law

Bettina O'Connell - wife

Father Dermot Hanrahan - family priest

Alex Doherty - local handy man

Dr Marie Pilcher - family doctor

Valerie Simpson - employee

Ivy Lee-O'Connell - partner

Nico Angeles - visitor

Zyline Angeles - visitor

Of course, some were more suspect than others.

Black's thoughts were interrupted by Eden appearing at his door. He said, "We're beginning to amass a surprising number

Murder in the Garden of Gethsemane

of suspects." He stared at the board. "But what we have in suspects, we lack in proof. We have nothing tying any of them to the murder of Tudor O'Connell or Caro May or the attempted murder of Val Simpson."

"Malaysia police have taken Tanya Lee into custody, Sir," Eden said. "She was staying with friends."

He dragged his eyes from the whiteboard to turn in her direction. "And the little girl?"

"In the care of Malaysia social services. A saliva sample is on route to us. It'll be couriered straight to the lab for testing." She opened her iPad. "There's also this. It's just come across from Hong Kong airport." She started to play a recording. It opened on a queue of people at a departure lounge gate, waiting to board. She froze it on a woman holding a little girl's hand. Both pulled hand luggage (the child's designed as an elephant). In the same hand as pulled her on-board luggage, the woman clutched travel documents. "The woman has been positively identified as Tanya Lee, and the child with her, Degas O'Connell," Eden explained. "On the screen, Tanya and Degas are minutes from boarding a flight from Hong Kong for Kuala Lumpur. Both boarded and were on board for the entire flight. The images were recorded just a couple of hours before Tudor O'Connell met his death."

"Tanya Lee was over the South China Sea when O'Connell was killed?" Black said.

"Basically," Eden said.

Black interviewed Tanya Lee from his office. Tanya was in an interview room in a police station in Kuala Lumpur. "Mrs Lee, we have information that you attended the wedding of Kirsty and Tom Colman in Salisbury in Britain," he said. She said nothing. "At that wedding you asked a third party to arrange a paternity test on your behalf. The father being one of two men."

"What of it?" Tanya Lee asked.

"Was this paternity test on behalf of your own daughter, Ivy?"

"It was not."

"Was the hair sample you provided, a sample taken from your granddaughter, Degas O'Connell?"

"No, it wasn't. If you must know, the test was for a good friend who does not trust her daughter-in-law."

"Can I press you for more information? I'll need your friend's name to corroborate your story."

"I will not provide that. The issue was very confidential to my friend and it must remain between us. I will be answering no further questions."

Tanya Lee leaned forward and closed the laptop. By the time the Malaysia police had re-established the connection, Tanya Lee had turned her chair around, leaving Black staring into the face of a Malaysian police officer and the back of Tanya Lee's head.

Chapter 52

EDEN ACCOMPANIED Black to an interview room, explaining that the twenty-five-year-old man he was about to meet, Omer Germain, had driven down from Scotland. "Where he lives," Eden added.

"I'm an offshore support engineer," Omer told Black, taking a sip of black coffee. Omer was casually dressed in jeans and a zip fleece over a long-sleeved polo. He had a thick mane of dark brown hair. "I've been in the middle of the North Sea for the last two months. I had no idea. I'd week-ended here with Humphrey — he's my rescue mongrel — before returning to the rigs. I had no idea," he repeated. As he spoke, his brown eyes darted between Eden and Black. "My girlfriend couldn't make it that time, but because I liked it so much, I wanted to come back with her. I've got some leave due. I'd started looking for guesthouses and all this stuff about a murder in the area came up. When I checked the date, I realised it was when I was here. I went straight on to the police webpage. I couldn't believe my eyes. I said to my girlfriend — *'You don't think I'm the missing dog walker, do you? Me and Humphrey match the description. Come to think of it, I did hear police cars.'* She told me to get myself down here straight away."

Black unfolded an Ordnance Survey map of the area and indicated on it the position of the TreeHouse. "This is where the murder took place." He gave the date and time of the killing. "On this map, kindly indicate the route you took on that day."

Omer quickly looked over the map. "I was staying over here. It's not on the map." He tapped the table a couple of times outside the edge of the map. "I parked about here." He touched the map to show the spot. "I walked Humphrey for a couple of miles. We took in a circular route, ending up back at the car." He traced a circle on the map with his finger.

"Did you see or speak to anybody on your walk, Omer?" Eden asked. "Anyone at all."

"I bumped into a lady leaving an orchard..." he found and indicated the place on the map. "I'd just come down the foot-path here..." he drew his finger along the map, "and was about to cross the road to pick this path up..." he pointed to a path skirting the edge of the field, accessed from the road. "She had this big bag of apples on her," he said. "We had a bit of a chin-wag. She told Humphrey he was handsome, said I wasn't bad either, and gave me an apple."

"Did you see anyone else?" Eden asked.

"As a matter of fact, I did. When I was up here," he tapped the map, "I saw a flash of blue, which I thought might be a kingfisher. Or a scarecrow. I took my binoculars out to have a look around and saw this girl on the horizon. She had long blue hair and was running across a pumpkin field. I only saw her from the back. She had on an army flak jacket and clutched something, like a large envelope. She looked a bit furtive. Set Humphrey off."

"Did you see anyone else?" Eden asked.

"No," he said, "no one."

Black and Eden got to their feet. Omer did the same, only for Black to say, "Please stay where you are, Mr Germain, if you don't mind. I'll send someone to take a written statement from you."

"I'll get you some more coffee," Eden promised.

In his office, Black spoke to Eden. "Omer's story supports Val and Lilah's alibis. The Angeles and the Hoffbrands support each other's alibis, as do Father Hanrahan and Roger Stenn. The phone recording supports Hugo O'Connell's alibi. The local deli owner supports the Tullys' alibis. Will and Harry Thorne support Bettina and Ivy's alibis. Marie Pilcher was with a patient, Denys Koval was in the Ukraine, and Tanya Lee was crossing the South China Sea. Have I missed out anyone?"

"Alex Doherty?" Eden said. "We can't prove his alibi."

Pilot knocked at the door and entered. He held an iPad. "A traffic-cam caught this," he said. "We believe it's Alex Doherty. The bike's identical to his and he has cycling gear same as that." The image he called up showed two Lycra-clad, male cyclists, waiting at traffic lights in the box at the head of the traffic. One wore a cycling helmet, reflective sunglasses and a vented face mask. The other didn't. That cyclist wasn't Alex Doherty. Both men stared up at the lights, willing them to change. Suddenly the sunglasses were lowered. Pilot froze the image. "You know him best, Eden. Is it Doherty?" he asked.

Eden stared at the frozen image. The cyclist's eyes squinted. "I'd say so," she said.

"Not only does it put him in the right place to be dropping the demand off when and where he said," Pilot said, "it puts him at the other side of town when O'Connell was done in."

"They've all got alibis?" Eden said. "Every single one of them? None of 'em did it?"

Chapter 53

BLACK, Eden and Pilot, along with most of the rest of the station, filed upstairs and into the conference room where the Chief Constable was about to make a very important announcement.

The conference room was wider than it was long. Its tables and chairs had been removed to allow everyone to fit in. The Chief Constable presided over the gathering from the giddy heights of a small podium. Matt Pritchard was one of the last to enter, having driven from the pathology lab. Upon seeing him arrive, Eden nodded hello and moved to stand next to him at the back of the room. The Chief tapped the glass in his hand to get the room's attention.

"Ladies and gentlemen, fellow officers, fighters of crime, righters of wrongs," the Chief Constable began, "a big thanks to everyone who took part in this month's *Movember*, either by participating or sponsoring. I'm delighted to announce that, as a force, we've raised an extra £600 on top of last year's £1,800, making a massive £2,400 for Men's Health."

The room broke into applause. "Almost as important are this year's winners," he continued. "Before I announce them, can you give a big round of applause for those who bravely beat the itch to nurture and tend and trim their tashes." Those gathered in the room clapped. The Chief was passed a large silver envelope. He slowly opened it and pulled out the card it contained. "The winner of this year's *Best Moustache goes to...*" he hesitated a few seconds for suspense, "... Matt Pritchard – for the classically 1930s, but high-maintenance, Clarke Gable."

"My hero," said Eden as Matt walked up to the podium to accept the prize: a bottle of wine. The Chief Constable waited for Matt to return to his place, before continuing. "This year we've decided to also award a prize for *Best Mocktache.*" He was handed a second envelope and opened that, too. After removing the card, he said, "The winner is none other than our own Superintendent Judy McDermott and Maxi the terrier, for their Dick Dastardly and Muttley impersonations." On the screen beside him a picture appeared of Judy as Dick Dastardly and her little dog Maxi, who Pilot had turned into a Muttley GIF, complete with paw over mouth and snickering shoulders rising and falling. "I understand the final version took a bit of work, not least because our own Detective Inspector Guido Black's left shoulder, arm and leg somehow managed to end up in the photograph." After the appropriate laughter, the Chief continued. "Unfortunately, neither Maxi nor Judy can attend in person, but have joined us by Zoom."

Judy's photo was replaced by the real thing, sat at her kitchen table, clutching her terrier Maxi. Maxi, his head to one side, ears twitching, was looking straight into the laptop, transfixed by the people on it. "Maxi and I would like to thank the Academy, our families and the Force for giving us this opportunity," Judy said. Her young son, Oliver, appeared at her side.

"Hi, Ollie," the Chief Constable said, waving at him. "Great photo-bomb." Ollie waved back, then decided to climb up onto the table. Judy tried to stop him, Maxi tried to follow, the butter dish was knocked on the floor with a loud crash, forcing Maxi to change tack and dive for the butter. "Maxi, don't eat that, you'll be sick," Judy could be heard calling as the connection died, and she disappeared from screen.

"Always end with a laugh," the Chief Constable said, "or is it never work with animals and children?"

Eden said goodbye to Matt and returned with Pilot to the Incident Room. "Think Judy was thanking the police force for her win, or the metaphysical energy force that binds the Galaxy together?" Pilot speculated.

"Would explain why Dick Dastardly beat Ming the Merciless," Eden said. She stopped. Black wasn't following them. She returned to the conference room and found him in the same place, consumed by his thoughts as all around him people were returning tables and chairs.

"Everything all right, Sir?" she asked.

"Please get our suspects back in, Detective Sergeant," Black said.

Chapter 54

EACH OF THE SUSPECTS, some accompanied by lawyers, others not, stared at Black. Their faces filled his screen in a chequerboard. He was in his office, they in police interview rooms in the Vale of Tye police station; or, in the case of Tanya Lee, in the Malaysian equivalent. Black was the *In-Meeting Controller*. He saw and heard everyone and got to choose who they saw and heard.

He began by addressing all of them. "The question we continually returned to in this murder investigation was a conundrum. Why murder someone in broad daylight with more than half a dozen people milling around? Either our killer was a very lucky maniac, or he or she took a huge risk for a big gain. There could only be one answer. Our killer needed an unimpeachable alibi to defeat a strong motive. Each of you has a motive — some stronger than others — and each an apparently unimpeachable alibi. But which of you is our killer?"

His next words were directed to only one person: Tanya Lee, sitting in a Malaysian police interview room. Muting everyone else, Black said, "Mrs Lee, did you pay Dr Vihaan Ahuja to arrange a contract killing of your son-in-law, giving you and your daughter an alibi?"

She didn't reply.

"When you were choosing an in-flight film for your grand-daughter to watch, Tanya, were you wondering how your paid assassin had got on?"

Tanya locked eyes with him. "I reply only as I do not wish my silence to be used against me or my daughter. We are innocent."

Black then muted everyone except Tam Tully. "As a young woman, you had walked through those grounds, Tam. Did you tell your brother Roger about the secret passage in the hedge, allowing him to beat Tudor O'Connell to the Events Room, and there murder him?"

"I did not," Tam said.

Black enabled Brian Tully and Roger Stenn to join the conversation.

"Mr Stenn, your sister and brother-in-law had every reason in the world for wanting Tudor O'Connell dead. You were in the immediate vicinity. Your alibi for the murder rests on having overheard someone else enter a church confessional, but your alibi falls apart if you arrived at the church to see that person leave the confessional rather than hear them enter."

"Everything happened the way I told you," Roger Stenn said.

"We didn't have anything to do with his death. None of us," Tam said. On either side of her, her brother and husband shook their heads, agreeing with her.

Black next addressed Denys Koral. "Denys, were you really trying to explain the offside rule to uninterested teenagers when your father-in-law was killed, or was it you who killed him?"

"From the Ukraine?" Denys said.

"You were substituting for the normal referee. Who'd have known if someone else took your place?"

"The team pick me from photograph you show them."

"Your substitute could have made sure he looked enough like you to pass muster," Black said.

"I did not kill my father-in-law," Denys said.

Black entered the siblings, Hugo and Lilah O'Connell. "Lilah, our eyewitness places you by the lean-to at the time of your father's killing," Lilah gave him a told-you-so look, "but the witness only saw you briefly from the back. Our witness could have been mistaken. Lilah, were you at the lean-to? Or were you at the murder scene, plunging a pair of blades into your father's back?"

"I was at the lean-to," Lilah said.

"Denys, did you disguise yourself as your sister-in-law and hang around the lean-to, to provide her with an alibi?" Black said.

"No — I was on a football pitch. In Ukraine," Denys said.

"What about you, Hugo?" Black said. "Did you pretend to chat into your phone, when in fact you were really keeping lookout? Or was it you who did the killing? Passing the weapon to your sister to pass on to Denys to dispose of? Denys, Lilah and Hugo — three best friends — did you do this together?"

"You hang noodles on our ears, man," Denys said.

Black paused the three from the conference call and entered Marie Pilcher, accompanied by her lawyer, and Alex Doherty, who was unrepresented.

"Dr Pilcher was with a patient at the time of Tudor O'Connell's murder, but the only evidence supporting your alibi, Alex, is an image of a man whose eyes, in the brief glimpse we have of them, appear similar to your own, upon a bike the same make and colour as yours. It was days before we discovered a connection between you and Tudor O'Connell and even longer before you, Dr Pilcher, came onto our radar. Between you, there was plenty of time to dispose of evidence."

"That *was* me," Alex said, emphasising the *was*. "I disguised my appearance, okay? It seemed a good idea at the time."

Black next addressed Nico and Zyline Angeles. "We only have your word for it that Tudor O'Connell was splayed on the ground when you appeared on the other side of the pond."

They both looked genuinely astonished. It was Nico who said, "We couldn't have done it. He'd have been out of the door and away by the time we got through the Topiary Room."

"Not if he'd been distracted by whoever involved you in this crime. The same person who disposed of the evidence as you raised the alarm."

"Why would we have been involved?" Zyline asked.

"Money?" Black said. "Nico, you followed Ivy into the cottage. Did you do this to destroy evidence?"

"No — to sit with her, out of compassion. Before that morning, I had never seen the woman before. On my life."

Black paused the Angeles from the conference call and entered Valerie Simpson. "Val, you say you picked some apples for lunch, chatted briefly with a young dog walker, and strolled to the TreeHouse to find a demolition derby in progress?"

"I don't say, I *did*," she said.

"I don't believe for one moment that you killed Tudor O'Connell yourself, Val, but did you feel so sorry for Bettina or the children that you became a party to a terrible thing?" Black asked.

"I don't understand what happened that day," Val said. "I only wish I did."

Black next selected Bettina O'Connell to address. Her solicitor, Robert Standley, sat next to her.

"Bettina, Tudor was the love of your life. You bonded over the Brotherhood of Man, but he broke your heart in pieces just like you broke that first album he bought you."

Before she could reply, Black ended her participation, and selected Ivy. She, too, was accompanied by her lawyer, Averil Hughes, who was in turn accompanied by her shy young assistant, there to take notes.

"Out of the blue," Black said, "a series of odd items — gifts, shall we call them — arrived at your home, Ivy. No note, nothing. One even contained a few episodes of *The Tudors*. Do you remember which episodes, Ivy?"

"I couldn't have cared less. They went straight in the bin," Ivy said.

"Someone took them out again," Black said. "The selected episodes covered the marriage of Henry VIII to Catherine Howard."

"I'm disappointed, but unsurprised, to learn that the campaign against Ivy was steeped in misogyny," Averil Hughes said.

Here, Black ended his questioning of Ivy and recommenced his questioning of Bettina. "The DVDs sent to Ivy obviously hinted at infidelity. Less obviously, so did the *Hamlet* theatre programme."

"Did it? How?" Robert Standley asked.

"Hamlet is tortured by the possibility of his mother's historic infidelity, is he not?" Black replied.

"This isn't an English lit lesson, for God's sake," Bettina said. "Besides, Ivy got sent that stuff, not me."

"Ivy wasn't the intended recipient," Black said. "That was a red herring."

"Are you suggesting I was unfaithful to Tudor?" Bettina said. "How dare you? I don't have to put up with any more of this." She got to her feet. Robert Standley also stood up but only to put his hands on her shoulders. "Please, Bettina. Sit down. We'll get through this. We will."

Bettina reluctantly sat down. "Tudor was Lilah and Hugo's dad," she said. "Is it my fault they take after me?"

Black ended Bettina's participation and re-addressed Ivy. "I watched *The Tudors* for the first time, Ivy. Not the entire series, only those episodes pushed through your letterbox — the Catherine Howard years. As I watched the episodes, I realised why the sender selected those episodes, and it had nothing to do with Catherine Howard's sorry tale. The episodes were selected for another reason entirely, one which became apparent to you, Ivy, after you retrieved them from the bin to watch them," Black continued.

"I did no such thing," she said. "That would be to dignify it."

Next came Dermot Hanrahan. "You were behind the album, the theatre programme, the DVDs, the shredded foliage, the vandalised car engine, and the barbed wire around the dead bird, Father," Black said.

"Shame on me. Foolish, spiteful old man that I am," he replied. "I am deeply ashamed of myself. When able to, I will apologise to Ivy in person. Just so you are aware, Detective Inspector, I have triggered the formal laicisation process. I intend to retire to a religious retreat. As part of this process, I have fully confessed my sins and received absolution."

"I very much doubt you have fully confessed all your sins, good father," Black said.

"I can assure you I have."

"Father Hanrahan, you clashed with Ivy and sympathised with Bettina."

"I did."

"To the extent of murdering Bettina's husband?"

"Detective Inspector, putting the immorality of murder to one side, I could not possibly have got from my home to the TreeHouse then back to the church in time."

"You didn't arrive at the TreeHouse until just before we did. If you fled the murder scene on a pushbike, such as the one we found under your stairs, there was time."

"I was at home when Bettina called me on my landline."

"Bettina called both your landline and mobile, Father. You could've picked the message up cycling back from the Tree-House after the murder."

"I was overheard in the confessional."

"After the murder. You had just enough time to dispose of the barbed wire and drive back to the TreeHouse."

"I respect and admire Bettina. Possibly, I am in love with her. But to suggest I would risk eternal damnation to avenge Bettina O'Connell — the suggestion is absurd."

"But did you kill to protect yourself?"

Black added Bettina O'Connell, Ivy Lee-O'Connell, and their legal representatives into the conversation. "After the theatre programme, the DVDs and the shredded ivy leaves came the jeans in the engine, and lastly the little lapwing found dead and wrapped in barbed wire on the doorstep."

Ivy turned away, while Bettina sat stony-faced.

"Taken at face value," Black continued, "a little bird was cruelly killed by someone who disliked its owner. On a slightly deeper level, it could have been taken as an attack on the messed-up O'Connell family. However, I don't believe that was the message. The subliminal messaging in this gift was much deeper than that, as it was in every item sent." He paused before addressing Father Hanrahan. "Father, you have admitted sending the items I have just mentioned."

"So, it was you?" Ivy said.

"Dermot — you stood back and watched me get the blame?" Bettina said.

"Explain the reason behind the Levi jeans in the car engine, Father?" Black asked.

"Simply an act of petty vandalism," Father Hanrahan said.

"I don't believe that, Father," Black said, "any more than I believe the shredded ivy leaves were an in-joke between you and Bettina, or that the whole thing was a crazy idea to reunite Bettina and Tudor. It is the absolute duty of a confessor not to betray any sin confessed by a penitent during the sacrament of penance. Am I right, Father Confessor?"

Father Hanrahan appeared surprised by the change of direction. "You are, Detective Inspector."

"And the penalty for doing so?"

"Who would do so?"

"The penalty, Father?" Black repeated.

The priest hesitated before he said, haltingly, "Excommunication from the church."

"No prospect of retirement to a religious commune in such circumstances?" Black said.

"I'm not sure I follow," Father Hanrahan said.

"A man arrived at your door, Father, in the dead of night, waking you from your slumber, needing to pour his heart out. He came to you because he trusted you completely. He came to you to unburden himself. You took him through to your little parlour room and there, in the strictest of confidence, he opened up to you, sharing his feelings of wretchedness and guilt at his betrayal of another, and his pain and guilt on watching his child being raised by another man, a man the child believed its father. That man needed forgiveness and he came to you for it — certain his confession would go no further, for a confession given to a priest is sacrosanct. It was a confidence you betrayed, Father."

"I didn't, I wouldn't. Detective Inspector, please."

"But you did, Father. That is exactly what you did. I daresay you have heard many confessions over the years, but that day you heard something which so horrified and dismayed you that you were unable to keep it to yourself. As a priest you couldn't share it, but as a human being you couldn't just sit back and do nothing, and thus began your little campaign."

"Preposterous, absolutely preposterous," Father Hanrahan said.

Black paused the screen on Father Hanrahan. This just left Bettina and Ivy.

"Bettina," Black said, "the theatre programme had nothing to do with your daughter's name, any more than the album had to do with your first date with your late husband. These were red herrings, as was the bird being delivered dead and wrapped in barbed wire. In that case, the message was in the species of bird. The bird was a female lapwing and the female lapwing is polyandrous. The paternity of her progeny uncertain."

Robert Standley looked up from his note-taking to say, "Well, it's a fact-a-minute here, isn't it?"

"Allow me to share a few facts of my own," Bettina said. "The female lapwing may be polyandrous and the paternity of her progeny uncertain, but I'm not a lapwing." She got to her feet again. "I've just about had enough of this."

"Bettina, I'm afraid you need to sit down," Robert Standley said. "Detective Inspector Black is investigating not one, but two murders and an attempted murder. His line of questioning is allowable if intended to establish motive." Bettina fell silent and resumed her seat, her fury simmering under the surface.

"Detective Inspector," Robert Standley continued. "My client and her husband were already divorcing. Infidelity by either party isn't taken into account on reaching financial settlement. Even if Bettina had been unfaithful," he turned to her, "which I know you weren't, Bettina," he turned back to Black, "that alone would not affect the settlement reached with Tudor, and therefore I cannot see how it gives my client a motive for murder."

"The Trust is for the descendants of Gethsemane O'Connell," Black said. "Gethsemane had only one child, a son — Tudor. Making his kids, and only his kids, the next generation of beneficiaries."

"Not this again," Bettina said. "If my kids aren't Tudor's then they must be the Angel Gabriel's."

"We have the result of the paternity tests. There is a very good chance that Tudor O'Connell fathered Hugo and Lilah. The result of the paternity test on Degas..." Black hesitated, "... was inconclusive. It gave only an 89.8 percent chance that Tudor O'Connell was Degas' dad."

"That does not sound inconclusive to me," Averil Hughes said. "You traduce my client's reputation, Detective Inspector, yet provide no evidence."

"Tudor might well have accepted the odds, were it not for the identity of the other contender."

"There is no other contender," Ivy said.

On his square of the screen, Dermot Hanrahan was in a miserable huddle. He looked up on hearing Black's words. These were directed only at him: "It was Tudor O'Connell's half-brother, Mungo, who called on you that evening, wasn't it, Father?"

Father Hanrahan nodded sadly.

Black continued. "Your campaign was never directed at Ivy. The whole thing was for Tudor's benefit. The Theatre programme was only chosen because Hamlet suspected his mother of infidelity with her brother-in-law. The message in the album was the word *brother*. Even the shredded ivy leaves were just another part of your information campaign. The name Ivy means faithful."

Black paused and took a breath. "The flaw in the plan would be Tudor's response once he got the subliminal message. Once he got there, he'd inevitably understand who was behind everything and, more importantly, how he may have come by the information. You hadn't thought it through, Father. I can just imagine Tudor's reaction. Tudor, who had once trusted his darkest secrets to. A man who can betray one man's confidence can betray another's — and you had gone further. You had betrayed a sin confessed by a penitent during the sacrament of confession. In his fury, did Tudor threaten to denounce you?"

"Tudor was an idiot. No matter how hard I pressed the message home, the penny never dropped," Dermot Hanrahan said.

"Even if what you say is true, the longer Tudor remained alive, the likelier it was that the penny would drop and, when it did, Tudor's revenge may not have been limited to Ivy. At some stage, that penny dropped with you."

"It wasn't like that. It wasn't a confession. Mungo turned up in the dead of night and I took him through to my little parlour room where we talked. Yes, he told me everything, but at no time did he ask me to take his confession."

"So you say, Father, but in the end Mungo came to you as his priest and you shared his secret — albeit subtly — without his permission or knowledge. If Tudor informed the church of this, you'd have ended your days excluded from the church, which is your whole life. An ignominious and lonely end."

The priest slumped forward again. "Detective Inspector, I am innocent of the mortal sin of murder."

"The evidence is against you, Father."

Black's next comment was addressed to both Bettina and Ivy. "Let's take another look at the material used to vandalise Ivy's car. Only the belt from the denim jeans was found in the car engine, with the label still attached. A pair of Levi jeans. And here is our message: Levi. A message sent to a man who knew his *Bible*. A man who knew Leviticus 18:16."

"Leviticus 18:16?" Robert Standley said. "*You shall not uncover the nakedness of your brother's wife? If a man takes his brother's wife, it is impurity...*"

"The subliminal message contained in every item was *brother*," Black said.

Bettina burst out laughing. "You think I had an affair with Mungo and Mungo fathered one of my kids and someone found out more than twenty years later, and I killed Tudor to stop him disinheriting them?" She shook her head. "I'm glad I hung around now."

Robert Standley put the lid on his fountain pen and laid it down on his notes. "Detective Inspector, I am the wrong side of sixty-five. I attended my first police interview at the age of sixteen as a clerk's clerk. Since when I have attended almost as many police interviews as you, but never in my career have I heard such a ludicrous police case."

Black addressed Ivy. "A lot happened in the Catherine Howard season of *The Tudors*, Ivy," he said, "including a fascinating subplot about Anne Stanhope, the Duchess of Somerset, and her affair with her real-life brother-in-law, who fathered her children. Degas was conceived near to or on the night of Hugo and Denys's wedding. Mungo left the wedding early, supposedly to drive home, but I don't think he got very far. I put it to you, Ivy, that you didn't slip away from the Reception to wash wine from your dress, but to engage in a sexual relationship with Tudor's half-brother, Mungo, with whom I suspect you were having an ongoing relationship."

"Lies," Ivy hissed.

"Mungo was parked nearby waiting for you. That is how you lost the earrings you accused Bettina of stealing. The earrings weren't in a jacket pocket, they were in the glove compartment of your lover's car, Ivy — with him already on his way home," Black said. "You had to think quickly when you realised you'd lost them and where."

Averil frowned and cast a glance at Ivy. She didn't so much as move. "Detective Inspector. Ivy had too much to drink, misplaced her earrings, and jumped to the wrong conclusion. There was bad blood. It happens."

"Ivy — you may still not have got it when the smashed Brotherhood of Man album turned up," he emphasised the word *brother*, "but on top of a theatre programme for a play where someone has a relationship with her husband's brother, you grew worried. The gifts continued. The same subliminal meaning in each. The same message repeated over and over. Someone knew your secret and, to make matters worse, there was no sign of the campaign ending. Eventually, even Tudor would twig. You couldn't allow that to happen. The DNA test your mum arranged was inconclusive. The Trust is for the descendants of Gethsemane O'Connell. If Degas wasn't one of those, where would that leave you, Ivy? Back to pedalling your sculptures?" Ivy slumped back in her seat and shielded her face.

Averil leaned forward. "You make serious slurs against my client when she is at her lowest point, Detective Inspector. I have warned you already about this line of questioning. If it continues, I will make a formal complaint and insist you are replaced."

"Mungo refused to return the earrings, didn't he, Ivy? He hung onto them instead," Black said.

"Supposition," Averil Hughes said.

Black continued. "Terrified he would use them against you, you went to Mungo's flat to recover those earrings, expecting him to be out drinking with Hugo. You let yourself into the flat with the key he'd given you. Only, Mungo and Hugo had returned to the flat. You found them insensible from drink. Out cold. Hugo swears he turned his uncle on his side, yet he was found on his back. This could have happened naturally, but I don't think it did. I believe you deliberately put Mungo in that position in the hope that he would choke to death on his own vomit, which he did. This done, you recovered the earrings and left."

"Detective Inspector, please provide proof of these outrageous allegations," Averil Hughes said. When Black did not reply, she added, "I thought as much."

Black now allowed Bettina O'Connell and Robert Standley to listen in, too.

"Despite his own transgressions, Tudor would no more forgive yours, Ivy, than become a Trappist Monk," Black said. "Tudor had to die before he deciphered the meaning behind the gifts. Discovering the identity of the person behind the campaign would have to wait."

"Charge my client with murder, or desist from calling her one," Averil said.

"An 89.8 percent chance of paternity isn't sufficient when

the other contender is a paternal half-brother. If Tudor ever learned about you and Mungo, he'd have tracked down every living male relative and exhumed Mungo if he had to, to prove it one way or the other. Either way, you were out on your ear, with Degas too if she turned out not to be his. That Trust was your meal ticket for life."

"Fascinating though this is, none of it relates to my client. She had no reason to kill her husband and has an unbreakable alibi," Robert Standley said. "I take it Bettina is free to go?"

"She isn't, Mr Standley," Black said.

"I was on the other side of the grounds," Bettina said.

"And there we have it," Black said. He called up the Tree-House map. "Bettina, Tudor was seen crossing the Events Room by the same people who found him minutes later, spreadeagled on the grass, stabbed through both lungs by a killer who escaped through a gate to the field outside where we found footprints running from the scene, the victim's blood, and micro-particles from the murder weapon.

"After taking part in a reconstruction of the killing, Caroline May telephoned this station in a state of some distress. She left a garbled message, with only two words audible: *'wasn't there.'* The line then went dead. Tragically, Mrs May was killed, taking her crucial piece of information to her grave. What *wasn't there*? A person or an object? And where was *there*?"

"Detective Inspector," Robert Standley said, "Bettina was eating dinner with her son and son-in-law when Caroline May was killed."

"My client also has an alibi for the night Caroline May was killed," Averil Hughes pointed out.

"Your client claims to have been in her hotel room all night. She wasn't seen leaving by the staff nor caught on camera," Black said. "But there is a way. Your client's room is next door to the staff stairs. Ivy, I believe you changed into a maid's uniform, put on a wig, slipped down the service stairs, and slipped out of the busy 24-hour hotel by the rear staff exit without anybody being any the wiser. Who notices hotel staff?"

"More supposition," Averil said.

Black produced a suitcase and gave it a reference. "This was taken from your client's hotel room, Mrs Hughes. It contains a false bottom." He demonstrated. "The suitcases tested positive for clothing fibres and human hair which isn't from your client. A matching strand was recovered from Mrs May's body."

"My client is not the only woman to wear a wig occasionally," Averil Hughes said.

"She's the only one I know with a motive for both murders—"

"You have nothing better than some old clothes and wig fibres?" Averil Hughes interrupted.

"Some old clothes and wig fibres from which forensics have recovered microscopic particles of blood from Caro May, no doubt transferred to your client from the clothes worn during the attack and from her to the items found in the suitcase." Black's next comments were directed at Ivy: "You used the same *modus operandi* to attack Val Simpson, Ivy. Traces of her blood were also found on the items in the suitcase. The attack on her was the key to solving this case. To explain why, we need to return to the mysterious gifts. Although Tudor was dead, someone out there still knew your secret. It could only be a matter of time until they played their hand. When I realised Val Simpson was also missing for part of the wedding reception, I began to wonder if that absence played a part in her attack. Had the killer also noticed her absence, I asked myself.

"That was the real reason you watched Denys and Hugo's wedding video so many times, Ivy. Not to remember happier times, but to establish who else wasn't there. You realised Val Simpson was also absent during the same period of time. It was obvious. Val had seen you and Mungo together. She knew your secret. You thought she was behind the campaign of gifts. She too had to die. Only this time you bodged it, thank God."

"Mungo and Ivy are guests at a family wedding, therefore Mungo and Ivy were having an affair," Averil said. "Mungo died, therefore Ivy murdered him. Ivy was the victim of a hate campaign, therefore Ivy murdered the only man she's ever loved. Ivy stayed in a hotel. She had a suitcase, therefore Ivy murdered Caroline May. Two years earlier Ivy was at a wedding. Two years later, a guest at that wedding was attacked, therefore Ivy was also behind that attack. Speak to evidence, Detective Inspector. So far, you have presented no evidence."

As Averil spoke, she leaned in, whereas Ivy did the opposite. She leaned back in her seat, her hands gripping the armrests. This was her only sign of emotion, but her eyes did not leave Black's face.

"Ivy, you claimed Tudor cut his finger when Degas burst a balloon. But the wound was fresh. Made when Degas was already with your mum. I don't know how he got that wound, I can only conjecture you staged an accident, but the wound gave you enough blood to drip microscopic particles of it along the field the night before the killing, when you also laid the footprint trail and threw around some paint particles. All as Tudor lay in a deep sleep, knocked out from the sleeping tablet you gave him."

"You try and trick my client into admitting a thing she cannot have done, Detective Inspector," Averil Hughes said. "For shame."

"An essential element of the plan was witnesses, and what could be more perfect than a tour party? The last people to see Tudor alive would be the first to see him dead. There couldn't be too many people milling around, though — our killer still had to get away. That day, the only member of staff due in was Val Simpson and she never got in before mid-morning. Lilah rarely called in anymore and Hugo, of course, was leading the party. Perfect. This couldn't be a rehearsal. This was the real thing."

Ivy was containing her emotions but Averil Hughes looked more and more interested in how this was going to play out, and Robert Standley appeared baffled.

"Detective Inspector," he said, "we do appear to be going round and round in circles. We've been here for over an hour now, and I'm no further forward in understanding how my client fits into any of this?"

"By pushing the note luring Tudor to the windmill through the letterbox, for one," Black said.

"You'd better be able to prove that, Detective Inspector," Robert Standley said.

"Tudor found and read the note, possibly out loud, allowing Ivy to say — '*You must go. It won't take more than an hour. Hugo can manage, for God's sake. We won't get a second chance*'."

"Detective Inspector," Averil Hughes said. "My client could not have killed Tudor. Your people could not make it work. My client has an unbreakable alibi. Speak to the evidence. I beseech you."

"Let's take a break," Black said.

Chapter 55

"The weapon has been recovered," Black said, the interview now reconvened. He addressed only Bettina O'Connell, Ivy Lee-O'Connell and their legal representatives. "This is a replica of it." He held aloft a long metal shaft, crossed at its end by a much shorter horizontal bar. A prong protruded from each end of the bar. He gave the exhibit a reference and said, "A photograph of the item, with its dimensions, can be found in your folders."

After Averil Hughes and Robert Standley turned to the page, Black continued. "The blades are concealed in each of the prongs." He gave the long shaft a twist at its head. A stiletto knife jutted out of each prong.

"How ingenious, the old sword-in-the-walking-stick trick," Robert Standley said gleefully, quickly falling silent upon a glare from Bettina.

Black continued. "A retractable pitchfork would be a better analogy, Mr Standley. Placed gently on the back, prior to releasing, it takes no strength. Those razor-sharp knives go straight through the body, rupturing and deflating both lungs. A quick movement with the weapon still in place alters the shape of the wounds, and another quick twist of the head in the opposite direction retracts the blades." He did this, and the knives instantly retreated into their prongs. "The distance of the attacker from the victim, and the amount of clothing worn by Tudor, meant little or no blood splatter ended up on the attacker. Tudor's habitual gum habit served as an aide by causing him to choke."

"Where has this weapon been hiding the whole time, may I ask?" Robert Standley said.

"The weapon was recovered from the metalwork sculpture outside the Orangery," Black replied. "The weapon was made to be reinserted in place in seconds. A twist lock had been incorporated into the sculpture, making it nearly impossible to remove this piece once it had been slotted into place and locked in." Black looked at Ivy. "You made the sculpture, Ivy, in Gethsemane's studio. An ingenious idea, fashioning your own sculpture in such away. We've recovered Tudor's blood and DNA particles from the concealed knives and fibres which match the coat he was wearing. Interestingly, we also found linseed oil, whose only purpose can have been to throw the blood dogs off the trail. We are confident this is the murder weapon," Black said. "Caroline May, the poor woman, must have taken a sneaky look under the tarpaulin when she claimed to have been tying her shoelaces. When she returned for the reconstruction, she wandered off and had another look, but this time saw a metal bar, where previously there had been space. How had it got there? The area was locked down after the killing. The significance slowly dawned on her, but instead of telling us, she saw a way of clearing her debts. She'd ask the sculptress."

"Yes, yes, but where does my client fit into all of this?" Roberts Standley said.

Black was not about to be hurried. "Having disposed of the murder weapon," he said, "Ivy's only escape route was through the cottage window. The group confirmed the window was shut and the shutter drawn, and we found it locked from the inside with a bar drawn across the shutter. Ivy couldn't risk leaving the window ajar and the shutter unbarred, herself. The wind might have blown the shutter open, or someone in the party might have noticed the window ajar, or Tudor might have discovered it and closed and locked it. Disaster! That was the second part you played, Bettina. You waited for the group to move off before unlocking the window, removing the bar from the shutters, and leaving enough of a gap for Ivy to get her fingers in, before running back to the main house where the Thornes had arrived at the front door. You didn't reckon on a man breaking away from the group. Luckily for you, he was in such a panic he passed the window without noticing anything amiss.

"The window left in this way enabled Ivy to open it and, shoes off, climb inside and lock up behind her before making her way downstairs. She now must leave the cottage without being seen." Black turned to address Bettina. "The Thornes had worked for you before. You knew that digger of theirs needed a key to get started and that young Will had a tendency to leave it in the lock. But in case he didn't, you'd taken the precaution of having a substitute cut. We found it in the pot on the cottage windowsill. That part of the plan was yours, Bettina. It was a very clever one, because it ensured Harry and Will Thorne were running towards you, up on their digger, when Ivy legged it from the cottage to run behind the studio and from there to the skip, from where she re-emerged a few minutes later. From up on that digger, Bettina, you could not have failed to see Ivy sprinting past. You had to be involved. That's why the skip was there, not to keep it hidden from visiting groups as claimed."

"The back door of the cottage was locked from the inside," Averil Hughes pointed out. "How did Ivy lock the back door from the inside when she was outside?"

"Ivy was first out of the Orangery. She ran straight past the Thornes and into the cottage. She was inside before anyone else. She ran to the back door, turned the key in the lock, then dropped it in the pot, en route to the cloakroom, where she made herself sick. This is where she was when Nico followed her inside."

"Why would I help that woman kill Tudor?" Bettina blurted out.

"Because Ivy reminded you that Tudor had joined a dating site while still married to you, Bettina, and left you for someone he met there. I have no doubt Ivy told you in no uncertain terms that even if Tudor ended his relationship with her, he'd quickly find yet someone else; leaving you, Bettina, rejected for the second time. But I don't believe you were only driven by trying to avoid this double humiliation. It was the prospect of a loss of face even more humiliating than the first, combined with the loss of your way of life, which drove you. That you've never been less than immaculate throughout, Bettina, shows the importance you place on keeping up appearances. Your best friend Val summed this up when she said, 'Bettina was every bit the Lady of the Manor – she loved the part.' Your contract with the Trust was unlikely to last for long and when it ended, you'd inevitably be excluded from the TreeHouse and everything that went with it and left with a pittance to live on. But as Tudor's widow you'd still be the Lady of the Manor, with the accompanying lifestyle — a lifestyle to which you've grown accustomed. A lifestyle you weren't going to get elsewhere."

Robert Standley interrupted. "If I may say something, Detective Inspector, this is absurd. Bettina, with your permission, I need to share a confidence with D.I. Black."

"Be my guest," she said.

"When Bettina came to see me to tell me that Tudor had found someone else, she understood the marriage was legally over, but, as she put it, her faith doesn't recognise divorce. Tudor could get all the pieces of paper he wanted, she said, but to her marriage is a holy sacrament for life and, as far as she was concerned, they would still be husband and wife in the eyes of God. Bettina asked me if there were any legal grounds for their having the marriage annulled, allowing her to start again. For example, to remarry. As I saw it, she might have two possible reasons to apply to annul the marriage. Either she hadn't consented to the marriage, or the marriage was never consummated. As Bettina is mum to Hugo and Lilah, to claim the latter would be an admission of adultery. Bettina said neither ground was true, and to claim so would be a lie before God. With annulment off the table, I advised her to appoint her own divorce lawyer. I could not act for her. What I'm trying to articulate, Detective Inspector, is this. If my client's faith compels her to continue her post-divorce life as though still the wife of a man shacked up with someone else, possibly even remarried, do you not think it might compel her away from the murder of another human being?"

"Robert's right," Bettina said. "I'm a Christian. A practising Catholic. I could never commit murder. Murder is a mortal sin."

Black looked at her. "You lost your faith some time ago, Bettina. You'd followed the tenets of your faith without question — then, one day, your husband announced he no longer loved you. While he turned his back on God without a consequence that you could see, your life came crashing down around your ears. You did everything right, and this was how God repaid you. He didn't punish Tudor, he punished you. God had abandoned you, and therefore you abandoned him."

"But I found him again."

"Your rediscovered faith, Bettina, was no such thing. Your eloquent plea — that *'it wasn't me, m'lud. I'm a devout Christian'* — was all part of the plan. It was another red herring."

"Who says?" Robert Standley demanded.

"Your client maintained it was the interview Tudor and Ivy gave to *Spirit!* which helped restore her faith when Father

Hanrahan had already told us that Bettina returned to church only after the lapwing was killed, sometime later. Lilah also let slip that Bettina no longer attended confession, once such an important part of her faith."

"We are uninterested in your case against Mrs O'Connell," Averil Hughes said. "My client has an unbreakable alibi."

"Your client couldn't have emerged from behind the tree, crossed the pond, killed Tudor O'Connell and escaped through the gardens in the established timeline. Yet the weapon was concealed in the sculpture by the Orangery. How is that possible?" Black asked. "There is only one solution. The killing happened earlier than we thought. Allow me to show you a recording made at first light this morning."

He called up a picture of the Events Room. The space was still and empty. Pilot, in the part of Tudor, stepped through the double archway and walked towards the gate. Ivy looked deflated. Bettina looked as though she was a rabbit trapped in headlights. Robert Standley simply look bemused as he glanced between his notepad, where he scribbled furiously, and the screen. Averil Hughes, on the other hand, put her elbows on the table and rested her chin on her folded hands. This was a big case for her, irrespective of how it went for Ivy.

When Pilot reached the gate, he stopped to take a pair of glasses from his jacket pocket. Suddenly, from nowhere, Eden, visible from the waist up, was behind him, clutching the replica murder weapon (with corks on its spiky ends). Only the transparent bed of grasses was between her and him.

"Where did she come from?" Averil said.

Oblivious to Eden behind him, Pilot tapped in the code as Eden lunged in his direction, pressing the corks against his back. "Was my client camouflaged as a grasshopper, Detective Inspector?" Averil said.

"Showing the suspect item 07339," Black said. On the screen appeared a pair of oblong, unframed mirrors of equal length, hinged in the middle to form a > shape and broad enough for a man or woman to hide behind. Against Ivy, they would have stood waist-high. "Your client was squatting behind, or rather inside, these mirrors, Ms Hughes, when she rose to kill Tudor O'Connell."

Robert Standley blinked a few times, taking in what he'd just witnessed. "He'd have seen her," he said.

"Did you see her?" Black countered. "An essential element of the plan was the weather. The night before, when the footprint trail was laid, had to be dry and frost free. The day itself couldn't be too sunny — reflection. Nor could it be raining — raindrops. Never has a murder so hung on the weather. Any change to the outlook would have meant rescheduling. As it turned out, the weather was perfect. Heavy and overcast, but with no immediate threat of rain or drizzle.

"To return to your question, Mr Standley, mirrors placed at such an acute angle would reflect only the grass on either side, effectively merging into the green of the lawns. The wispy grasses further aided the camouflage by lessening the brightness of the glass against the natural background. They were also a handy place to conceal the weapon. The placement of the mirrors was paramount. They had to be far enough away from the boundaries to make the space appear complete to any onlooker, yet close enough for the kill. The area was large enough for that. It wouldn't have been possible anywhere smaller. Tudor and the group's presence would scare away any remaining birds not already driven away by Ivy."

"Tudor would have seen his own reflection in the mirrors when passing," Averil Hughes said. Her statement was less assured than usual. A slight tilt at the end suggested it was a question.

"Not in a pair of mirrors set up in the shape of a greater-than sign, he wouldn't." Black held up a piece of paper with a > drawn on to it. "The mirrors in such a position would only reflect what was on either side of them. Showing the suspect item 340," he said.

Robert Standley furiously sketched the mirrors on his notepad as the scene was replayed. This time the police camera, positioned at head height, faced the grasses. Pilot walked again from the hedge archway to the gate. Eden, squatting inside the long mirrors, was invisible. Pilot's reflection wasn't caught as he walked by. To any onlooker, only Pilot was in this space. Eden again stood up. She counted to five and disappeared again.

"Had Tudor looked carefully, or for long enough, or been close enough to peer over the top," Black said, "he might very well have seen something. But he was marching determinedly towards the gate, focussed only on learning the identity of the phantom gift sender and getting back to the tour party before Hugo caused too much damage. I want to show you one more thing."

In the next recording, Pilot walked right up to the mirrors. It wasn't until he was nearly on top of them that the outsides of his legs were reflected in the pinnacle of the >.

"In their hurry to get to the body," Black said, "the tour party trampled underfoot any evidence of Ivy or the mirrors having been there. That's why Ivy made sure they were corralled into the Topiary Room by telling Tudor earlier that it was essential they didn't see the gate code."

Here, Black paused. After a drink of water, he went on. "The hinged mirrors folded together were quite light and portable. You ran with them, Ivy, climbed through the window with them and threw them in the skip, as Bettina drove the digger into the wall, drowning out the sound of breaking glass. Bettina, you saw Ivy running towards the skip, so it was relatively easy for you to time the crash to coincide with that. We erroneously believed the broken mirrors in the skip belonged to the bathroom cabinet. I tip my hat to the pair of you for the genius and sheer audacity of this plan. Risky, but worth it, given the stakes. Excuse the pun."

Black paused again, then added, "You may well argue, Bettina, that you had no idea why Ivy needed the window in the cottage opening, or that you weren't the person who opened it. But you cannot claim not to have seen Ivy emerge from the cottage and sprint towards the skip. You could not have failed to see her. You saw her, and you saw the mirrors she carried — yet you did not mention this. Not once."

Averil Hughes' young assistant shyly looked up from her notes to glance at the screen and the mirrors depicted there. She pulled a face, gave her right hand a shake, and returned to her copious note taking. Averil simply stared at the screen with a look of amazement on her face. Ivy looked sullen and petulant, arms and legs crossed. Bettina looked as though she couldn't decide whether to laugh or cry.

"Are you intending to charge my client with the murder of Caroline May and the attempted murder of Valerie Simpson, as well as the murder of her husband?" Robert Standley asked in his usual direct manner.

"Bettina was shell-shocked at the news of Caroline May's death, and even more devastated when Val Simpson went missing," Black said. "Her evident relief when Val Simpson was found alive suggests you, Ivy Lee-O'Connell, acted alone in these endeavours. "And one more thing," Black added, as Ivy and Averil Hughes both opened their mouths to say something, "in case there is still any doubt. More important than finding the forensic evidence in Ivy's suitcase linking her to Caroline May's murder and the attack on Val or finding the murder weapon and the forensic evidence attached to that, we also found a fingerprint on the weapon, Ivy. You had on the gardening gloves you claimed you wore to load the skip. But you couldn't conceal the weapon wearing them, so you took them off. Despite your attempts to erase them, you left one fingerprint behind."

Black charged Ivy Lee-O'Connell with two counts of murder and one count of attempted murder and Bettina O'Connell with one count of being an accessory to murder and conspiracy to commit murder.

Chapter 56

JUDY JOINED Eden and Pilot in Black's office, along with other members of the team. They all gathered around Black's desk. "How did you work it out, Guido?" Judy asked.

He began with a Christie quote, "*For somewhere there is in the hay a needle and among the sleeping dogs there is one on whom I shall put my foot and by shooting the arrows into the air, one will come down and hit a glass house.*"

He continued. "Both Bettina and Ivy lied early on in the investigation. Bettina by claiming to have rediscovered her faith much earlier than the evidence suggested, and Ivy by claiming Tudor cut his finger when Degas burst a balloon after Degas had already left with Tanya. But what reason did either have to lie, when they had alibis and little by way of motive? There was also Bettina's slight delay in coming to the door, and her behaviour that morning. What an extraordinary thing for a middle-aged woman to do! There was so much we didn't understand. The note promising to reveal all at the windmill. Caroline May's words — what wasn't where? The attack on Valerie Simpson. That was even more confusing than the attack on Caro May. Why was she attacked? Val had no reason to kill

Tudor O'Connell. And why so late on in the sequence of events? She had no idea herself.

"Then there were the strange items. These were always loose threads in our enquiry. Ivy was the target there. She also went missing from Hugo and Denys's wedding reception. Everything kept going back to Ivy. Even the emojis led to her in the end. She also had an old unused phone to hand, Tudor's old phone. She kept it in a drawer. This gave her access to an unchanged emoji keyboard, avoiding the problem of new emojis throwing her code into disarray.

"In fact, the more we learned, the more Ivy came under the spotlight. But she still had an uncrackable alibi. This brought me back to the question we'd been asking from the beginning. Why plan a murder so meticulously, yet take so many risks? The answer could only be to create an alibi. An uncrackable alibi. By now, every suspect had an alibi, but only Ivy's rested so completely on timings. I applied the scientific method and became quite certain that there could only be one way this crime could have been committed, and that was by moving the timescale forward a little. That meant moving our killer's starting position. But if not behind the tree, where was the killer?

"By now, I'd taken to watching the little merlin who'd taken up residence in the church spire, from where she was almost completely camouflaged, appearing from nowhere for the kill. Was our killer hiding behind some kind of fake background, I wondered. Why had we not found it? Had our killer escaped across the field after all, scenery in one hand, weapon in the other? This would have ruled Ivy out." He paused to refresh himself with coffee. "I wondered if the killer had photoshopped him or herself out of the murder scene? But how? Judy's slap-stick moment, highlighted Bettina's diversion. But this raised another question. Why did Ivy need to get to the skip at all? To dispose of evidence, of course. And that gave me the answer.

Well, that, and the merlin again. I'd needed the help of a mirror to identify her. And it was when I remembered that, that it all fell into place.

"Eden nearly got there when she thought the blackmail might be linked to the confessional. But we didn't quite get there that time. In the end, though, we must thank the little merlin. A beautiful assassin, the merlin, and the only bird of prey who sometimes hunts in pairs."

There was a knock on the door, and the Chief Constable stepped in. "Are our suspects cooperating, Detective Inspector?" he asked.

"If by cooperating you mean throwing each other under a bus, Sir, then yes, they are cooperating," Black said.

Another knock came at the door and a junior member of the team appeared, holding an envelope. This was passed to Black. He opened it and read the contents. "The results of the second paternal DNA test are back. Degas has a rare genetic mutation, also identified in the DNA of Tudor O'Connell. The mutation was not seen in Mungo's DNA. Looks like Tudor's the daddy after all and Ivy needn't have bothered herself."

Chapter 57

EDEN TOOK her place in the public gallery of the Crown Court, alongside Hugo and Val Simpson. From there they watched Lilah O'Connell, in the court below, receive a two-and-a half-year jail sentence, suspended for two years, in exchange for pleading guilty to blackmail and recreational drug use. They watched Lilah being led from the courtroom.

Denys was waiting for them in a small room, normally used by Court officials. He had Degas with him.

"I'm sorry we had to drop one of the murder charges against Ivy," Eden said. "We just didn't have enough evidence to put before a jury to prove she killed Mungo. But you weren't responsible for your uncle's death Hugo, any more than your dad's. Ivy came into your lives and destroyed your family as you knew it."

"She tried to destroy it," Hugo said, "but we won't let her." He reached out to take the child in his arms. Degas happily gurgled, oblivious to the carnage she had been born into.

"We've applied to adopt her," Denys said.

"We want a brood," Hugo said.

"I can't think of anyone better to raise her than you two. I wish you all the happiness in the world," Eden said. She walked with them into the corridor. She left them waiting for Lilah, while she made for the entrance. But before she got there, Lilah herself appeared at a door. Eden nodded to her and continued on her way.

"Thank you for finding Dad's killer," Lilah called after her. "However painful."

Eden stopped and turned. "Just doing our jobs, Miss," she said. "Just doing our jobs."

THE END

"THE 12:57 KILLER"

A wealthy man is discovered battered to death at home. His community are quick to blame burglars. Called to investigate DI Guido Black and team widen their search, uncovering feuds, envy and betrayals going a long way back. Events take a dramatic turn when a second body turns up.

A complex crime story, where the clues pile up, suspects abound, and the identity of the killer is key.

————

Available exclusively at Amazon.

Visit **mybook.to/1257killer** today.

Printed in Great Britain
by Amazon

17614450R00210